aíseal mór was born into a rich tradition of irish storytelling and music. as a child he learned to play the brass-strung harp carrying on a long family tradition. he spent several years collecting stories, songs and music of the celtic lands during many visits to ireland, scotland and brittany. he has a degree in performing arts from the university of western sydney and has worked as an actor, a teacher and as a musician.

BOOK TWO OF
THE WANDERERS

THE SONG
OF THE
EARTH

CAISEAL MÓR

EARTHLIGHT

LONDON · SYDNEY · NEW YORK · TOKYO · SINGAPORE · TORONTO

You can visit Caiseal Mór's website at www.caiseal.net
or email him at harp@caiseal.net

First published in Great Britain by Earthlight, 2000
An imprint of Simon & Schuster UK Ltd
A Viacom Company

Simon & Schuster UK Ltd
Africa House
64–78 Kingsway
London WC2B 6AH

Simon & Schuster Australia
Sydney

A CIP catalogue record for this book is available
from the British Library

1 3 5 7 9 10 8 6 4 2

ISBN 0-671-03729-3

Printed and bound in the UK by
Omnia Books Ltd, Glasgow

DEDICATED
TO THE
POETS
AND
THEIR
HARPS

ACKNOWLEDGMENTS

his novel and *the circle and the cross* which preceeded it only exist because several people other than myself had enough confidence in me and my writing to lend their full support to the project. Foremost among them is Selwa Anthony, my literary agent, whose warmth and vast experience have been an inspiration and guide to me.

I cannot thank Julia Stiles, who edited the manuscript, enough for her help and suggestions. Without her friendly and very positive criticism this novel would not have been all that I hoped for.

Nancy was an invaluable help in finishing the work. I thank her for putting up with me while I was writing this novel.

To all those friends who read the novel in its early stages go my thanks also but particularly to Orlagh and Mahesh who gave me some perspective and reminded me to answer some important questions left over from *the circle and the cross*.

WESTERN OCEAN

GIANT'S BRIDGE

SLANÉ

TEAMHAIR

RATH
OWEN

BALLY CAHOR

CASHEL

ARDMÓR

BALLINSKELLIGS

EIRINN

ISLES OF ALBA

CRUITNE

DAL ARAIDHE

EIRINN

CANDIDA CASA

INIS MANNAN

BARD'S ISLE

CYMRU

GAUL
AND
BRITAIN

CYMRU

+ EBORACUM

MARE
HIBERNICUM

SAXON
SHORE

CUNOMORI

BRETONS

KINGDOM
OF THE
FRANKS

+ NANTES

PROLOGUE

ill your lungs with the cool untainted air that is only found amid soaring white-capped mountains. Ease your traveller's thirst with a deep draught snatched from a roaring highland waterfall. Watch awe-struck as a wall of fog rolls down from the tree-topped ridge to absorb you entirely in a great misty avalanche.

When purple lightning strikes the apex of the ancient standing stone, listen with all your being for the magnificent voice that follows after the fireball. The words of the thunderclap hold the world enthralled, warning all creatures of the fate that befalls those who dare defy the fury of nature.

The breeze in the hills, the murmur of the swollen stream, the clumsy rumbling of the wailing storm may fill the soul with wonder or with dread. The sonnets of nature may inspire the spirit to contemplate greater unknown patterns which bind it to this world but too often they remain impenetrable and mysterious. Untranslated, these songs pose more questions than they answer. And they do not calm the tremors of a restless questing heart.

To understand the utterances that emanate from the world's secret internal sanctuaries takes a lifetime of dedication, study and patience. There are those who would say that it takes more than one lifetime to acquire such skills. After all, anyone can hear the Raven calling on a grey day in the fields,

1

but how many will ever learn the skill of listening to what the bird has said?

That was the first great truth I was taught when, as a boy of nine summers, I took to the life of a traveller. Until the day I first met my teacher I did not realise that the inner voices of the Earth go too often unnoticed, too seldom recognised. He often pointed out to me that few folk have the patience to sit and listen to what the world around is telling them. Some are too frightened of what they might hear. Most are too busy planting, reaping and collecting firewood for the winter to have the opportunity for such pursuits.

I was very fortunate. My teacher decided to share his wisdom with me. Often in the first seasons that I was with him he would seek a still clearing in the core of the forest that was bathed in the bright morning light. When he had found a comfortable spot he would sit down upon the springy carpet of pine needles, face raised toward the treetops, hands at rest. He would calm his thoughts, focusing all his being on the task. By example I learned to do the same; to hear with the ears of my soul, filtering out the other countless noises, sights and distractions that snatch at the senses demanding attention. In time I discovered how to open my soul to the music of the Earth as it was played out beneath me.

The melody begins as a gentle pulsing hum reaching out from deep below the topsoil, growling as it rumbles along the ground, faintly reaching through the soles of resting feet. The first time you recognise this murmuring under the Earth you will ask yourself, as I did, how you could have lived so long and never noticed this mighty voice before. Then it will be possible for you to behold the deepening tone sending forth its revitalising energy to every part of your body.

Nine winter seasons passed while I learned how to use all my senses to develop the skill of listening to the world about me and to comprehend the subtle ways of music. Nine summers flitted by to the daily droning of the war pipes, the call of the wooden whistle and the rhythmic pounding of the goatskin drum. For nine cycles of the sun I studied the voice of the harp and the ways of harpers, striving always to mimic precisely the lilt of the songmakers with my fingers.

The old people, the Danaans, who were in this land before the tribes of the Feni and the Desi and all the other Gaelic folk, had a special name for the harp. They called it the loom of music. Only someone who has never heard the instrument played could fail to understand why. On the honey-coloured brass wires of the harp is woven the fabric of melody and the cloak cloth of storytelling.

I had to learn to listen properly before I was allowed to even so much as touch an instrument. When my teacher was satisfied that I could use my ears with sufficient attentiveness he made me crouch over the harp for days on end setting sharp-ened fingernails to repeating old tunes. In the first few seasons I played until the tips of my fingers blistered and bled. And that was only the very beginning of my training.

My guardian, who was one of the most learned tutors in the five kingdoms of Eirinn, primed me to be a student of the old ways. Gobann was the greatest harper of his time. He possessed an instrument of rare craftsmanship that some said had been enchanted by the Faery folk. The poet knew ancient airs and merry dances that no other living soul remembered. Sometimes he allowed me to

3

listen when he rehearsed a composition of his own, distilling the elements of each melody until he brought the tune gradually to life. And when he was happy with the result of his labour he might allow me to attempt to learn the piece.

My fellow student Sianan and I often drifted into sleep wrapped in the countless textures of sound that hummed from Gobann's harp, full of dreams, visions and echoes of the past and future mingled together.

Sianan had gifts that I could only imagine. I was a much slower pupil than her. She possessed a much greater gift for touching the harp than anyone I have ever met apart from Gobann himself. By the end of the second winter that we were with our teacher she had already progressed further with the instrument than I would in the whole of six winters.

Often she would whisper tales to me of the Great Road as the poet played. Occasionally she would chant an air under her breath insisting that I close my eyes in order to share the experience of the music with her. Her singing always made me think that perhaps long ago the Earth lulled its offspring to sleep each night. Through Sianan I came to understand that the tones dwelling within each one of us are mirrored throughout the whole of creation. Nevertheless I could not grasp the deeper truths that she had mastered until I was much older.

At first I could not even perceive that the noises within my own body blended at all with the tinkling of the harp-call. For a long time I could not distinguish exactly what it was that she wanted me to behold.

Sianan had discovered that when she could close all else out to feel only the steady rhythm of her own heartbeat something remarkable happened. In that state she could clearly discern that all the many rattles, all the many threatening rumbles, all the great cacophony of voices that wake a dreamer from sleep, all the soothing lullabies, all the merry jigs, all the bird calls, they can all be heard within the labyrinth of one's own self. She knew of the miracles that resound in each of us.

Gobann taught me to listen to the Road as it stretched out before me at the start of a journey and to take my direction from it. As we traverse the path of life, Gobann often reminded me, we must strive to perform our duties well, toiling to fulfil our dreams as best we can.

The Road that he spoke of led me once to Teamhair, and afterwards to many other places that I had no idea existed until I stumbled upon them. I walked the Great Road to the lands beyond life and I returned only because I had some inkling how to interpret the map I was given. As surely as it once led me away from my own village the Road led me here to these foreign shores, where no-one knows my name nor where I come from as I seek some trace of Sianan.

Gobann left me long ago, making his solitary journey to the halls of waiting. Sianan departed to go on her own pilgrimage some time after that, leaving no word as to where I might find her. I have not given up the search for her. Her wisdom was always more profound than mine, her insights purer. I always knew that she was the truly gifted one and that I was only a poor reflection of an endangered tradition.

The melodies and airs that I heard Sianan humming when we were children linger in my heart, coming back to haunt me now, inspiring me to put the harp upon my knee. But the only tune I long to hear is the call of the Great Road and the drifting gentle lullaby of the song of the Earth.

ONE

ear the rocky coast of Armorica, in what had been known for centuries as the Roman province of Gaul, four horsemen clad in long grey woollen cloaks spurred their steeds at a furious pace along a straight cobbled road. The bodies of the animals steamed with sweat and their iron-shod hooves clattered loudly on the stony surface as the riders made their way westward with all speed.

The force of the wind blew the men's hoods away from their heads. Each rider was shaved across the forehead from ear to ear but with their hair left long at the back. Their haggard faces wore expressions of intense anxiety coupled with symptoms of crippling exhaustion.

The leader of the fugitives recklessly shifted forward in his saddle to lean against the neck of his mount, then he dared a quick glance behind him. His heart filled with dread at what he saw.

Less than a bow shot away to his rear he could discern a patrol column of thirteen battle-hardened warriors who wore the dark green livery of the city of Nantes. These determined soldiers had relentlessly tracked his men throughout the morning, slowly but surely gaining ground. Indeed, the gap between hunter and hunted was closing with alarming speed even though the four escapees knew the roads better than any of the soldiers and had once or twice almost thrown the warriors off the scent.

The veteran commander of the patrol smiled to himself under the cheekplates of his cavalry helm, confident in the knowledge that his soldiers' ponies were still relatively fresh and were used to being driven hard. There was nothing more certain to him than the inevitable demise of these four heretics. They could not run forever from the justice of the Bishop of Nantes.

Unexpectedly the four rebels packed their weary beasts tightly together and turned off the highway onto the grass at a point where the gentle downs led toward the sea. Each of the terrified men gripped his wooden saddle desperately with his knees and clung on to it for very life as he hit the uneven ground. Taking to the fields was a last audacious attempt to escape certain death at the hands of the ecclesiastical authorities.

Within moments of leaving the road they passed through a patch of tall thick grass and their leader caught up his riding cloak under his arm so he could lean forward heavily in his saddle. With quick fingers he unsheathed a small knife from the top of his boot. His cloak was caught in the wind and blew open, revealing the dark brown cloth of a monk's habit underneath. His long dark hair flew free, immediately marking him as a target for the soldiers, but Cieran the heretic did not trouble to conceal his identity any longer.

He had a plan that might give himself and his comrades just a little more time to make it to the nearby beach. Their one hope of survival lay in reaching the small boat that waited to ferry them over the waves and out of reach of the bishop's troopers. As the leader of the monks he was determined that they would all reach that boat alive.

Wielding his little blade in a flash of blue steel, Cieran severed the straps that secured his saddlebags. The fully laden packs dropped away and tumbled along the grass gradually rolling to a stop. His companions' horses following close behind stumbled and kicked the neatly packed parcels so that the cloths and vestments inside were scattered. As soon as it was free of the extra load his horse seemed to gain new strength and it picked up a little more speed, spurting far ahead of the others.

'Cieran! What are you doing?' one of his fellow monks called out, but Cieran was already three lengths of a horse ahead of his companions and the cry was lost in the breeze. It did not take long for the other three fugitives to realise that their leader had shown them a way to gain some more ground on the warriors. And none of them believed that their lives were less important than their possessions.

Within moments all of the monks had cut at the leather straps which secured their bundles, tossing away their backpacks as if the precious contents meant nothing. One man discarded a heavy parcel wrapped in soft deerskin which split open as it struck the ground releasing a hundred pages of a finely worked manuscript to the mercy of the wind. Another sack slid along the grass for a few paces before a large gilt altar cross tore through the thin material that wrapped it.

The glint of gold caught the officer of the guard's eye as his pony reached the point where the quarry had turned off into the fields. Without hesitating he raised his voice to the dozen mounted warriors under his command ordering them to leave the object where it lay. His troop of horse-soldiers had tailed the monks half the morning and he was not about to let his men be distracted from their goal for some trifle that could easily be retrieved later.

His warriors responded to their lord's commands as if they were privy to his thoughts. In moments they were fiercely lashing their ponies and calling curses and taunts at their quarry. It was obvious to all of them that the chase would soon be at an end.

'Form a line of charge!' the officer bellowed, drawing the words out carefully so that every warrior in the troop would hear him and emphasising the last syllable of the order in the manner of all Roman military commands.

Cieran looked back briefly over his shoulder to see the soldiers turn off the road and begin crossing the meadows. With disciplined precision the warriors spread out abreast in a long file, kicking up the clods of earth beneath them.

One war-pony at the far end of the line stumbled on the uneven ground and the rider fell hard, but having lived all his life in the saddle he never let go of the reins. Moments after striking the ground he swung himself back into the saddle hardly losing the pace. These were some of the best horsemen in Gaul. The nobleman in charge noticed the warrior falter but did not turn to acknowledge the trooper's clumsiness. He would chastise the man later, for now he had other things to think about. This was the part of the hunt that he enjoyed the most: the lead-up to the kill.

By the time the fugitives had reached the foot of a steep hill some five hundred paces from the road, the warriors had closed the gap even further and now Cieran regretted his hasty decision to leave the even pavement of the Roman cobbles. The enemy's mounts seemed able to gallop as well over the rough grassy clods as they had on the stones.

His own horse, however, more used to drawing carts, now found the going very hard. Cieran rode up to where the ground began to steepen just below the hill and paused to rein in his mount. He took a moment to appraise the situation.

Before he had a chance to clear his thoughts his comrades caught up with him and brought their wild-eyed horses to a halt. They were all certain what would befall them if they should submit to the soldiers but it seemed now that there was little alternative. In those few seconds as their horses tried to catch their breaths each man looked to the other and said a silent farewell to his companions. One way or another, they all knew, this was the end of the chase. The only sound that any of them heard was the hard breathing of the animals as they cleared the foam from their nostrils and the shouts of the warriors as they closed in.

Cieran hardened his resolve. He refused to submit to the force of the bishop's men. Come what may he would not allow himself to be caught without putting up a fight.

Hauling on the reins he faced his mount toward the summit of the hill. 'If they're going to hang me they can bloody well earn the privilege!' he cried. Then he raised his left hand in the air and with the wooden heels of his boots he gave the horse under him a great kick to spur it on. The other three horses reared, neighing in confusion, but their masters took up Cieran's cry and laughed as if this were a children's game of chase that they were playing.

'We'll give their ponies a run they won't forget!' cried one monk. By this time Cieran was a good distance up the hill and the others had brought their horses to rein, steering them off on separate paths in a final attempt to split their pursuers. At least this way perhaps they would not all be captured.

The troop of warriors reached the foot of the hill only twenty breaths later but none of the soldiers had expected the enemy to use this tactic. They pulled up their ponies in confusion and looked to their commander. The nobleman in charge quickly sectioned the warriors off and the twelve men-at-arms drew their swords for the final confrontation. Then they broke off into four groups of three, taking up the pursuit once more.

The sudden fire that had filled Cieran gained precious time for all the monks. One of the brothers made directly for the cover of a wooded grove and his horse disappeared from the view of the soldiers in a matter of moments. Another made his winding way to the left of the hill toward open ground beyond which lay a marsh and then the seashore. The third brown-clothed monk doubled back to head down the road in the direction from which they had just come for his horse was so weary that he feared it would soon drop dead of exhaustion if he pushed it further on the grassy meadows.

Cieran urged his horse toward the very top of the rounded hill hoping to outpace the soldiers. He thought that if he made directly for the safety of the woods on the other side he might somehow make it to the beach.

'God, let the boat be waiting!' he prayed aloud.

He reached the summit of the rise quickly and safely and turned round to check that his brothers were clear of the enemy. The warriors had hesitated far too long and were now a good distance behind him and to his relief he could see that they had little chance of overtaking him, for a dray horse, even when weary, takes longer strides than a war pony, especially on a steep path. Now it would be easy for him to outpace the soldiers. Cieran laughed aloud in triumph and turned his horse down the other side of the hill making for the edge of the forest at breakneck speed.

But in his haste to make the cover of the woods he had not reckoned on the treacherous clods of turf that were scattered on this side of the hill, churned up by a herd of sheep. The slippery soil that had washed down the slope during the recent rains made his ride doubly dangerous but he did not see the peril until it was too late. Cieran was within twenty paces of the trees when his horse caught one hoof in a hole and stumbled, sliding forward through the mud. The animal careered down toward the woods and swung her body completely around as her rump scraped along the earth. Then Cieran heard a loud and sickening crack. The sound of his horse's foreleg splintering as it twisted and snapped. The mount screamed in agony and thrashed about in panic, baring her teeth.

In the next instant the startled monk was lurching sideways, hurled from his saddle to land heavily face-first in the grass at the edge of the trees. With the wind knocked out of him he could not even lift himself to make for the safety of the woods. The sweet aroma of freshly turned earth came to his nostrils mixed with the smell of horse manure and for a moment Cieran experienced an inexplicable feeling of peace. He managed to turn his head to look back up the hill but hardly had time to curse his misfortune before he was surrounded by three mounted warriors whose sharp sword points were levelled at him.

The soldiers dismounted and worked swiftly to tie his hands and feet with strong ropes while he was still too stunned to resist them. Though he knew this would be his last chance to try to escape, Cieran's senses were numbed from the shock of the fall and he could not raise the strength to fight off his captors. Certain that he could not escape the bindings, the warriors dragged him unresisting to the summit of the hill behind one of their war-ponies and there they waited until their officer and all the other soldiers returned after their long and fruitless search for the remaining fugitives.

The officer was the last to return, unwilling to admit that three of the four men had escaped when their capture had seemed so certain. He climbed the hill on foot shielding his eyes with a leather-gloved hand as he walked. Methodically he scoured around, seeking for any sign of the other monks. The countryside was deserted but for a few cows. There was no trace of the heretics.

At the summit of the hill the officer removed his helm and threw it violently at one of his warriors who caught it and fell in behind his master leaving a discreet distance of several paces. The other soldiers stepped aside to avoid their commander's anger.

Finding no-one else within striking distance the nobleman walked directly to the restrained monk, intending to give vent to his frustration. Despite the fact that Cieran sported a newly broken nose and other bad facial cuts the officer recognised him immediately. He spat at the prisoner and thanked his God that luck had delivered this prize above all the others into his hands. At the foot of the hill the monk's horse was still neighing in great pain near where it fell. The officer motioned to one of his men to go and silence the beast, then he knelt down next to Cieran.

'Your brothers may have slipped through the net for the time being but at least I have managed to catch the biggest fish of the four, the leader of the heretics,' the officer jibed.

'There are finer fish still swimming in the sea than have ever been caught,' Cieran replied.

'But what sort of a fool would exchange a king salmon for three herrings?'

'A salmon may live long out of water.'

'He will not live longer than it takes to light the cooking fire,' the officer sneered. Then he leaned in close to the monk and whispered, 'There is nothing I like more than the smell of roasting salmon.'

Cieran turned his head enough so that he could face his captor then spat a wad of blood-soaked phlegm at the man. The officer stood up, wiped his face with the sleeve of his green tunic and sunk his leather boot into the prisoner's stomach. 'You stupid Hibernian bastard! What made you think you could get away from us? Eh, Cieran?'

The monk did not acknowledge the taunt so the officer knelt down to strike him hard on the cheek with the back of his hand. 'The Holy Council will carve you into little pieces for certain this time. The Bishop of Nantes doesn't appreciate having his summons ignored.'

Cieran still offered no reply. His captor saw this silence as a gesture of defiance.

'We'll have to beat that out of you before you're brought before the bishop.' And then he landed a great kick to the monk's ribs which doubled Cieran over in agony but still he did not utter a cry of pain. He did not even flinch. He simply rolled over on the grass to pray silently, offering his soul up to God and preparing himself for his own martyr-dom.

Having relieved his frustration a little the officer ordered his soldiers to tie Cieran to the back of a war pony. 'The man who is responsible for his escape this time will burn as a traitor among the heresy flames in his stead,' he promised them.

Then he mounted his own pony and led the way back toward Nantes muttering curses under his breath on all foreign heretics.

TWO

wenty-four foot soldiers of the Imperial Legion, an old style eagle standard held aloft at their rear, broke ranks within a spear-cast of the finely decorated villa that belonged to Tullius Piscis. Their segmented armour clattered loudly as the centurion in charge dismissed his men. Within moments red cloaks and shiny helmets were thrown off beneath the trees at the side of the road.

The bright colours of the soldiers' uniforms, the polish of their weapons and the exotic manner of their speech brought men in from the fields to satisfy their curiosity. Women braved the light rain, gathering in little groups at a discreet distance to get a look at the strong warriors in all their finery. None could remember having seen legionnaires attired in this grand manner for many a year. The footmen looked as though they had stepped out of the ranks of a Roman army from some bygone age.

Their commander, a middle-aged centurion of the guard proudly mounted on a white horse, was completely satisfied that his legionnaires were too exhausted from their march to do anything but behave themselves so he left them to their rest. Ignoring the gathering crowd he rode on behind the main wagon toward the place where the name Tullius was painted in large garish red letters above the gate of the villa.

This was the home of the rich Gallo-Roman land-lord who owned all the fertile ground in the district. Tullius Piscis was the descendant of an august family who had clung resolutely to the vestiges of the old establishment though Rome had ceased to be an empire in all but name long ago. His ancestors' bloodline had supplied high officials to the Roman administration of Gaul before the great city itself had fallen to the barbarians but Tullius had never been as public-minded as his forefathers.

Not long before this Roman gentleman had been due to come into his inheritance, news came to Gaul that Rome had been sacked by wild German tribes. That was the moment when Tullius lost all hope of ever serving in the eternal city or of making his fortune as a senator. From that day on he had concentrated on the business of buying and selling. He would forever after prefer the life of a merchant to that of the endless duty and obligation that was the lot of a petty official who aspired to high office. Now he was bald, wealthy, rather over-weight and grateful that fate had been so generous to him.

The villa that he had inhabited was typical of the kind with which expatriate citizens of Rome tended to endow their descendants. It was a gaudy and somewhat exaggerated copy of a design that was really only practical in the southern parts of the empire. In northern climes such as here in Armorican Gaul, the villas proved drafty and difficult to heat so that the inhabitants were often forced to wear their cloaks indoors.

The grand central garden courtyard had seen innumerable feasts and clandestine meetings. It had been host to chieftains and princesses and victorious military officers, as well as a haven for spies, thieves and turncoats. There had been a time when Tullius' home had been the social hub of the whole district of Nantes. Now, however, in these troublesome times, the abundant well and the white-washed villa were merely a stopping place on the road to Lyon, and few sensible Roman citizens trod this path since the barbarian incursions had begun. So when the enterprising Tullius caught the glint of a polished silver cuirass and then spied the yellow canvas cover drawn over a wagon that sported a Christian banner, he nearly leapt for joy at the opportunity of providing shelter and provisions for a large party of strangers.

'Travellers always want food and lodgings,' he reminded himself and quickly calculated that supplying this party could bring in enough hard cash to help with the reckoning of his several substantial and embarrassing gambling debts. The canny merchant turned over in his mind what would be needed for the kitchens and storehouse. He was not quite sure where he would get hold of a barrel of Breton ale and enough fresh bread this late in the day and he knew that could be quite a problem. Soldiers always like to drink fresh ale. An answer had still not presented itself to him when the wagon drawn by two stout ponies came to a halt at the entrance to the villa. He decided to solve the problem of the alcohol later.

By the time he had reached the gate dragging his unwilling daughter, Tullia, behind him, he could see that the party had travelled long and that they were all very weary. He was overjoyed.

'Welcome to my house!' Tullius called out to all in greeting, waving his arms wide in an exaggerated manner to emphasise the warmth of his salutation. While his lips were moving his deft mind was still working on the problem of where to obtain sufficient supplies.

'My family and I are pleased to have your company,' he continued, indicating that Tullia represented his only blood relative.

The daughter was taller than the father but she shared his dark features and his keen eye for an opportunity, but in every other way she was like her late mother. Tullius knew that the presence of a beautiful woman when lodgings were being arranged was an attraction that many men found impossible to ignore and so he had ordered her to dress in her best long white robe of fine linen, the one edged in blue. That morning one of the servants had washed her black hair so it was curled and oiled in the latest fashion. As it happened Tullia was also intelligent and well educated. Her father had primed her well for her role in the family business as a gracious and entertaining hostess.

Not leaving anything to chance Tullius decided immediately to dispatch a trustworthy servant to his neighbour requesting two barrels of beer and whatever food could be spared, though he knew that the man would demand an extortionate price. However, Tullius had not managed to attract his chamberlain's attention when a dour-faced man with chestnut hair sticking out from under his travelling hood edged a leather-booted foot out of the wagon and stepped down. The man, obviously a cleric of some authority by the air of confidence that he exuded, carefully gathered his flowing brown travelling robe under his left arm to prevent it touching the wet ground.

The churchman turned around to search for his walking staff from the place where he had been sitting and as he did so his hood dropped away from his head. This bared to the gaze of all present a circle of pink scalp shaved clean at the crown of his head. Everyone knew that the tonsure of Saint Peter was the badge of a pious man devoted to the ascetic life and to the service of the Holy Mother Church. The servants began to buzz with excitement about their visitor. Many of them were Christians themselves.

Tullius saw immediately that this fellow was not a Roman, despite his commanding stature and the noble profile of his nose and chin. He was a Celt and very likely a Breton as well. His bright blue eyes spoke of that heritage. Yet there was an echo of Rome in the way his hair was trimmed to outline his face and a pale shadow of the old empire in his haughty stance.

'A half-breed,' Tullius decided. 'Are there no pure-blooded Romans left in the world?' he mourned to himself.

As the cleric reached for his staff another much younger fellow with yellow blond hair dressed in almost identical fashion to his master jumped from the wagon and grabbed the wooden stave.

'Here it is, Father,' the younger man said, glowing at having the honour to serve the other cleric. From under his hood the older man let a smile dance across otherwise harsh features and reached out to take the staff.

'Go back to your place now, Secondinus,' he cautioned softly. 'This is none of your affair.'

'Yes, Father,' came the reply and the young man pulled his tattered cloak up around his knees revealing that all the edges were mud-stained and wet. He climbed back to where he had been sitting.

Almost as soon as Secondinus had spoken Tullia's gaze was drawn to him in fascination. She did not notice his grubby clothes, nor his unwashed face and scraggly hair. These things meant nothing to her. She looked directly into his eyes and thought that she had never seen one so beautiful, so full of grace, so at peace with himself and the world. She wanted to be just like him. So lost was she in her thoughts that she did not notice the older cleric approaching her. With his bland greeting he caught her completely off guard.

'A blessed greeting to you, child.'

Tullia bowed her head but found herself feeling a little silly dressed so finely to greet a holy man so she said nothing in return. She had learned something of the Christian ways from the cook and his family and was painfully aware that material comforts did not impress ascetics. Indeed, such men and women tended to spurn all but the most essential of possessions. She allowed herself to smile a little when she realised that it would be difficult to find someone more different from her father than this cleric.

'I am Patricius Sucatus,' the man said in near perfect but rather clipped Latin. 'I am a Christian delegate to the people of the Isles of Britannia and Papal embassy to the Kingdom of Hibernia.'

'A Christian priest?' Tullius ascertained. Though it was obvious that the party was travelling on church business, it did not necessarily mean that they rated a military escort of their own. 'You're well looked after by the Senate for a man who is merely an ecclesiastical,' he added, indicating the centurion who had now dismounted.

'We have come from Ravenna, on the Emperor's and the Pope's business,' replied Patricius, in a strained but polite tone that did not disguise his impatience. Then, without waiting to learn anything at all about Tullius, the priest brushed past the merchant to enter the gates of the villa.

The sharp blue eyes of Patricius scanned the garden courtyard falling almost immediately upon a shrine to an old Roman deity set into the wall of the house and bedecked with fresh flowers.

The priest turned on his heel to face his host and Tullius could plainly see that the man's knuckles were clenched white with rage. Patricius was striving to control his breathing, clearly upset about something. When the priest finally spoke there was a disgust in his voice that was barely contained by the careful manner in which he expressed himself.

'Do you and your family not serve Christ?' he asked his host directly.

Though in truth Tullius couldn't give a dried fig about who worshipped what or where, the merchant knew enough about Christians to realise that most of them were highly intolerant of the old Roman gods. Even acknowledgment of some of the relatively insignificant Gaulish nature spirits would send some priests into a rage. Tullius could see his opportunity to make a small fortune from this band of travellers slipping quickly through his fingers unless he could quickly reassure the priest.

'I am a follower of the Cross,' the merchant lied. 'It is my worthless servants who venerate that shrine.'

Patricius turned to look at the idol once more. 'Then you will remove that pagan abomination immediately,' he ordered, not taking his eyes off the offending statue for a second.

'What?' returned Tullius, unsure whether he had heard correctly.

'If you are as good a Christian as you say,' continued the priest, 'have it removed and promptly bring all your people to the bosom of Christ. It is your duty as their overlord.'

23

Tullius' jaw dropped and as he began to understand what had been asked of him, he had a frightening vision of all his glorious ancestors gathered about him in utter shock. A familiar voice reverberated from deep within his memory. 'That statue has stood more than three hundred years in the niche,' it warned him. 'The wrath of the Gods will descend on you, Tullius Piscis, if you move that stone.' It was his grandfather's stern displeasure come to rebuke him from beyond the grave.

Patricius quickly tired of waiting for an answer and abruptly turned to leave the courtyard, indicating clearly that the merchant had hesitated too long. In that instant Tullius noticed a purse hanging by a cord from the priest's waist. It dragged on the cleric's belt and it was obviously very heavy with gold. The sight of all that ready wealth walking off toward the gate was what finally silenced his grandsire's ghost and untied the tongue of Tullius Piscis.

'I will have one of my worthless servants remove the stone this very afternoon,' the merchant offered, trying to disguise the desperation in his voice, 'if it offends you so much.'

'You need not trouble your servants with the task,' answered Patricius quietly but forcefully. 'I will do the job for you now and I will do it gladly.' With that the priest turned again to face the idol, addressing it as though it were merely a sinner that needed a stern rebuke to bring it back to righteousness.

'Thou art simply a lowly and insignificant servant of Satan,' he informed the stone, pointing his staff directly between the statue's cold and lifeless eyes, 'and so you are not as evil as some others of your kind. But your time has passed.' Patricius waited quietly for a moment but to the everlasting

24

relief of Tullius Piscis the god did not respond. It only sat as it always had, staring off into the distance seemingly unconcerned about the world that bustled around about it.

For a brief moment, while the priest stared the idol down, Tullius could not be sure if Patricius was entirely serious about what he was doing or whether he playing some sort of a prank. It was not every day that the merchant heard anyone addressing an old stone. It was Patricius' next move that convinced Tullius that this cleric was in earnest and so probably not entirely mad.

Having received no objection from the motionless idol, the Christian walked directly up to the stone and, with a horrified Tullius looking on, grabbed the silent deity by the back of the head and jerked it forward away from the wall.

'Be gone to the realms of Hell!' Patricius screamed in a voice that chilled the blood of all the onlookers.

The statue was already loose on its pedestal from several centuries of exposure to the elements and so it rocked without the need for too much encouragement toward the priest who nimbly stepped out of its way as it tumbled off its perch. It struck the ground face first with a loud crack that brought all the household running to see what was the din.

Tullia grabbed the sleeve of her father's tunic to restrain him and while he was distracted the courtyard quickly filled with servants and guests who had been watching from the house. Then, as though they had come out the air itself, a throng of neighbours and farmers appeared at the gate just in time to witness the old god roll off its front and onto its side. Tullius let out an anguished cry and his knees buckled beneath him. His daughter supported him as best she could. Fortunately for her it was not long before he regained his composure and was able to stand without her help. Once he had recovered he pushed her away roughly.

Tullius forced a passage through the spectators to stand as close as he could to the ruined statue. Just as the ancient stone settled on the tiled courtyard a great crack spread down the middle of its body rending the idol into two. When the advancing fracture reached the middle of the torso it widened the weakened stone even more causing the shoulders and head to topple off.

Tullia watched the head as it rolled a short distance on the tiles and she was surprised at how gruesome the beheading seemed. She had never really given much thought to the statue but now she realised that she had long taken its presence for granted. Perhaps it did house some sort of spirit or maybe a god. The stone certainly seemed to have a presence about it now.

It had been a long while since Tullia had witnessed her father's fiery temper but she fully expected that he would fly into a fury at the cleric for the shameful desecration of a household divinity.

Tullia knew that the priest had acted rashly and without respect for his host but she could not help but admire the Christian for having faith that he would not be punished for his behaviour. Papal delegate or not, there were few living who would dare test the goodwill of Tullius Piscis in such a way.

To her surprise, however, her father was so angry at the Papal legate that he could not stir himself to express his outrage and, by the time the merchant seemed ready to really let his blood boil over, something remarkable happened that made him forget the cleric's breach of good manners.

Just as it seemed that the pieces of the idol had settled on the tiled courtyard another wide gap appeared in the neck of the god and a mass of shiny golden beads each about the size of a goat's eye poured from a cavity within the sculpture scattering like grain on the ground. When the merchant realised that the same worldly-wise ancestor who had erected this shrine in homage to a long forgotten state god had packed the hollowed-out stone full of small gold coins, he felt his knees go weak again.

The servants gawped at the fortune that was revealed to them, pushing forward as each person struggled desperately to get a closer look. Tullia rubbed her eyes in disbelief but before she had opened them again she was pushed over by the crush of spectators.

Somehow she managed to roll out of the way of the throng and make it to her feet again. She pushed her way, threatening and cursing, through the excited throng until she stood beside her father. Tullius was looking faint as she reached him so she placed her arm through his to lend him support.

With perfect calm the cleric turned to Tullius and, as if this sort of thing happened all the time, casually inquired, 'Is there enough gold here to cover the board and lodging of thirty men?'

All of those present fell silent expecting the landlord to burst a blood vessel with this last indignation. But Tullius merely looked from the gold to the priest and back to the gold again. 'Aye there is,' he answered, his eyes still wide with disbelief. 'There is enough gold there to cover the lodging of fifty men for a month.'

'Then the Devil will be paying for our sleeping places tonight, landlord.'

At the back of the crowd the young man who was called Secondinus climbed up on his master's wagon and cried out at the top of his lungs, 'A miracle! Father Sucatus has tricked the Devil out of his fortune! Even Satan rushes to aid Patricius in his holy works.'

Suddenly the courtyard was filled with a hundred voices. Every domestic servant and onlooker seemed to have some opinion regarding what they had just seen. Some merely sank to their knees and made the sign of the Cross, for even in this house there were many who were Christian by faith. Some people rushed forward to touch the cloak of Patricius Sucatus in awe and to beg his blessing. Among those who tried to approach the priest was Tullia, swept up by the emotions of the moment.

Tullius, meanwhile, wasted no time ordering his chamberlain to break up the crowd. He was determined to keep peasant hands off his fortune and he knew the best way to do that was to disperse the gathering as quickly as possible.

Naturally he had recognised almost immediately that he had been duped into providing free lodging for Patricius but he was too stunned by what had taken place to argue. And, after all, the Christian had done him a unique service in smashing the idol. That gold could have lain hidden for another three hundred years if the priest had not taken a dislike to the old deity. Tullius quickly resolved to make the best of the situation. All his anger was forgotten, now he just wanted to get the fortune within the privacy of his own room and set to counting it.

'If there is anything I can do for your eminence,' he stuttered, his eyes always drifting back to the gold, 'please do not hesitate to summon me.' Then he ordered his chamberlain to gather the treasure and he took his leave to prepare a secure place for it.

It was some time before Tullius returned to see to Patricius but it was immediately apparent that he had regained some of his composure while he was indoors. 'I will show you to your lodging,' the landlord offered and reached out toward the priest to take his arm. Patricius stared coldly back at his host, silently warning Tullius not to attempt to repeat that gesture.

'I will sleep outside in the courtyard tonight,' Patricius announced. 'My soldiers and fellow priests will be occupying your house.'

'Soldiers!' cried Tullius in disbelief. 'You don't mean to billet legionnaires in my villa, do you?'

Patricius looked down his noble nose at the merchant and raised his voice slightly, speaking slowly. 'Would you prefer that I take all the gold that I recovered in the name of God and billet my people elsewhere?'

'Very well,' answered Tullius backing down. The merchant wasn't sure whether the Christian had the power to repossess a fortune he had so recently bestowed. Nevertheless, he was very mindful that Patricius had two dozen imperial soldiers in his employ who could more or less do as they wished. 'Any breakages must be paid for,' Tullius added.

'There will be no breakages, landlord. My soldiers are Christian and they know their place.'

Tullius did not believe that line for a second. He had met enough Christians in his time to know that almost all of them had some weakness that they indulged in and it was usually something strictly forbidden by their own holy writ. As that thought struck him the merchant saw an opportunity to get his hands on the bulging purse full of gold that dangled from the priest's waist. He moved himself closer to Patricius mumbling under his breath, 'Is there anything else that you might require?'

The priest stared blankly back.

'. . . For your comfort through the lonely night hours,' Tullius explained in a tone that reeked of conspiracy. Still there was no sign of recognition from Patricius. 'Nantes is a town well known for the voluptuous young women who live within its walls and as chance would have it I know of two young things who have long been seeking the solace of the spirit.'

'What?' inquired Patricius, genuinely confused.

'For a moderate fee I could arrange for them to visit you here tonight and to bare their sinful souls to your holy gaze. Lay your hands upon them in blessing, I urge you,' Tullius added before he noticed that the priest's face was growing redder by the moment. The merchant realised he had made a dreadful mistake and skilfully changed tack. 'Or if you are not seeking for female company, perhaps you would prefer to minister to one of the lads from the village . . .'

'You may send a messenger to the Bishop of Nantes telling him that I will arrive at his stronghold tomorrow,' Patricius commanded. 'Tonight I will be engaged in prayer and fasting and I invite you and your household to join me.'

The offer was so sincere that Tullius stopped short, considering whether he should accept the suggestion. The skeptical part of him, and that was the greater part, was not quite sure if the priest was interested in anything more than prayer and so he quickly and politely declined. Then Tullius went straight inside to arrange for a messenger as Patricius had requested.

'Every man has his vice,' the merchant landlord reminded himself under his breath. He knew from personal experience that all too often those who lived behind the veil of piety had something worth concealing. It never crossed his scheming mind, not even for a minute, that Patricius genuinely wished to spend the night in prayer. Tullius had met precious few folk in his life who took pleasure in such simple diversions.

That evening Patricius Sucatus led the Christians of the household in their devotions and offered the sacrament to any and all who would convert willingly to the Cross. Tullia was amongst those who were anointed with the holy oil and water blessed by the spirit of the Christian God. Later she stood in line to take the tasteless bread from Patricius and arranged it so that she was in the company of those believers who received the holy wine from Secondinus rather than from one of the other deacons.

Tullia lingered a few moments after she had sipped the holy drink and wished that she could soak up the light that seemed to surround Secondinus. Rising from her knees she caught his eye and in that moment she made a decision that would change the rest of her life.

It was well past midnight when the assembly finally broke up and all of the travellers except Patricius went to bed. Tullia hid behind an arch for a long time watching as he knelt at prayer before she too eventually retired to her bedroom.

But Tullia did not go to her chamber to sleep. When she was sure that she was not going to be disturbed by anyone she took a travelling bag and in it packed some of her belongings and her writing utensils, carefully sealing the jars of ink and wrapping the Egyptian papyrus and fine parchment so that it would not suffer from any water damage on the journey. She wanted to take all of her scrolls but in the end settled on only three rolled parchments and one bound book for the whole collection weighed far too much for her to lift. Then she went down to the kitchen and wrapped some food in linen cloths, tying the parcel tightly with a string of gut.

When she got back to her room she reprimanded herself for not having included some candles and a cloak of thick wool in her bag. She realised that she would have to leave the book behind and that broke her heart for it was a collection of classical poetry from the time of Claudius and it was her favourite. But it was necessary to carry as little as possible, she decided, if she was going to get away from her father's house without arousing too much suspicion. After she had trimmed her luggage she sat at the end of her bed and listed in her mind everything that she had packed. Then she thought through the rest of her plan carefully. Tullia suspected that many dangers awaited her beyond the walls of her father's villa but any hardship was preferable, she was convinced, to life as a pretty jewel in the crown of Tullius. These holy men were learned and earnest and they led a pure life of devotion, scorning wealth. In her heart of hearts this life was exactly what Tullia had yearned for since she had first learned to read. It was a worthy way to live giving oneself over to scholarship.

Just before dawn when the air was still very damp, grey light filtered through the sparse clouds giving an indication that the sun was about to rise. Before the sunlight burst into gold Tullia slipped out through the servant's door to the kitchen narrowly missing the cook as he stumbled about looking for a lamp. Then, with her heart pounding with fear, she headed across the fields to where the road to Nantes wound around her father's estate to the north. There among the branches of a low bush she concealed herself and waited for Patricius and his party and for her new life to begin.

THREE

s the winter passed into spring in Gaul any road from the coast of Armorica to the lands of the Belgae leading inland was sure to be in appalling condition. Many years of neglect, coupled with months of persistent heavy weather blowing in from the northern seas, had done terrible damage to the lines of communication in this part of the old Empire. Four long months of freezing rain-soaked days turned the highways into swirling masses of mud, difficult to traverse in parts and impassable wherever the paths forded a stream.

Not even a good strong Iberian horse was guarantee of safe and swift passage from the countryside to any of the old Roman towns. Since the retreat of the legions from this part of the world and the invasion of the barbarian Frankish tribes, the military roads had neither been maintained nor patrolled to counter highway robbery. Journeymen had become extremely rare. Those who braved the many dangers were few and considered very likely foolish.

Nevertheless, not far from Nantes on the north-western coast three men led their horses through the swirling muck that was churned up in the aftermath of the latest thunderstorm. One of the travellers wore a patched Roman legionnaire's cloak wrapped close about him to keep out the cold air. He was not very tall and so his cloak dragged in the ankle-deep mud and as Roman military cloaks did not usually have hoods, his black greasy hair was exposed to the drizzle.

The only clue that this man was not a simple craftsman plying his trade from village to village was that he was followed by two servants dressed in poor wet-weather clothing consisting mostly of old blankets artlessly stitched together. Few people could afford to own slaves in these times and their presence indicated that he was, or at least had been in the past, a man of some wealth. Their poor clothing was a sure sign that he could no longer draw on any store of gold.

The three men had already spent most of the day travelling from their landing place at the river mouth. The servants were flagging. In good weather and on a sealed road they might have reached Nantes in much better time. If the sun had been shining and God had eased their way a little they might have been resting in comfortable quarters by now. As it was they all knew that it was very unlikely they would reach the town by nightfall.

Pulling his scarlet cloak around his head to keep out the unceasing rain, the Roman struggled on ahead of his servants with determined steps, dragging his feet through the mud. He wore tightly laced warrior's boots that ensured his feet were kept dry, despite the deluge, so the sludge did not bother him greatly. His mount followed him reluctantly but obediently, slipping her foothold occasionally and blowing the air loudly through her mouth to show her distaste at having to be out and about on such a day.

His two bondsmen, already dallying far behind their master, slowed their pace almost to a halt when they saw him reach a bend in the road not far ahead. Impatiently he stopped to call back to them.

'Get a move on, you lags! We must reach the town today if we are to have any chance of catching the Papal legation.'

The servants offered a range of their best rehearsed assurances and excuses but when they were sure the man had turned away from them again they both cursed him under their breaths.

'Devil take Seginus Gallus,' said the blond one. 'And the bloody Papal legation.'

'All in good time, my dear Darach,' quipped his brown-haired bearded companion. 'There's nothing more certain than that for the likes of him.'

'Pick up your feet, you lazy buggers!' bellowed Seginus back at them. 'Mog, if you don't move your lazy arse I'll give it a damn good kicking. I swear that if we miss this meeting I'll have both your fat hides stripped to be made into covers for my saddle furniture!' Then their Roman master trudged off, disappearing around the corner ahead of them.

'Aye, lord,' called the servant named Mog, his green eyes twinkling with contrition, 'just coming.' But he leaned over to his companion and whispered, 'This won't do. I need a rest and a bite to eat. We've been on a boat two days from Britain and we journeyed ten days on foot before that from the north. I can't keep up with him any more. He treats us worse than those ponies that the painted people of the north keep deep down in the tin mines. At least those poor creatures get fed and watered once a day.'

'What are you going to do?' sniggered the other servant, sensing some cunning plot in the wind.

'Just you watch and learn, gentle Darach, my old friend. Just you watch and learn.'

With that Mog gave his horse a good kick in the foreleg which made it cry out in surprise and try to bolt away from the servant. But Mog had a good hold of the reins in anticipation of the horse's distress and the mount did not break free.

'What is going on?' Seginus called back from around the corner.

'I think my horse has taken lame, my lord,' returned Mog. 'I warned you that it was a bad omen to buy from a farmer who only had one good eye.'

'Damn you, you idle piece of donkey turd!' came the master's reply, but before Mog could protest his innocence, the tone of Seginus' voice suddenly changed. 'Jesus Christ and all the saints in heaven! What in the name of Hell's fallen angel is going on?'

Darach and Mog could only look at each other questioningly for their master was out of their direct line of sight. Before either man could call out to Seginus, they heard several other strange voices raised in urgent demand and there was a threat in the tone of the words that made both servants shiver with fear. They strained to hear what was being said but as chance would have it just at that moment the rain began to pelt down again and with such intensity that all other sound was stifled. It was impossible for them to make out what was being discussed.

As if the unexpected downpour were not enough of an omen of evil carried on the wings of devils, the sky was suddenly filled with a mighty flash of lightning that stained the green fields all about with an eerie purple tinge. Mog counted four heartbeats before the deafening roar of a great thunderclap shook the ground where they stood and put the horses into a near panic. Then the wind began to rise, howling through the trees and shaking the branches violently.

'You hold the beasts,' cried Mog, struggling to be heard over the clamour of the violent squall. 'The storm will be upon us in a short while. I'll go and see if I can find out what trouble Seginus has got himself into.'

Darach nodded his agreement. The rain was now falling so heavily that each drop churned up a little of the mud where it landed, raising a steady brown knee-high haze that seemed to boil all over the road. This made it almost impossible to see where the deepest puddles or the widest wheel ruts might be. After slipping repeatedly and making little progress through the quagmire, Mog changed direction deciding that he had a better chance of catching up to his master if he climbed the bank at the roadside.

'With luck,' he reasoned calmly to himself, 'the height of the ditch will help me get a glimpse of Seginus. Perhaps once I can see what's the matter I will be able to make my way over to him.'

What met his gaze when he finally clambered puffing and panting to the top of the embankment confirmed his worst fears. He only managed to keep his balance at the summit for a few seconds, however, before losing his footing on the treacherous surface and sliding back down the muddy slope.

Distraught, Mog sat wide-eyed where he landed at the bottom of the ditch trying to decide what to do. The glimpse he had of his master was all too brief but there was no mistaking what he had seen. Around Seginus were gathered four mounted warriors dressed in distinctive dark green tunics. They

had long menacing swords pointed at the defenceless Roman's chest. Mog's master was searching
through the belongings in his satchel looking for
something and nervously glancing behind him
looking out for his servants.

Finally Mog stirred himself and rushed over to
Darach, who realised immediately that something
was terribly wrong for his companion's face was
drawn and pale. Without pausing to explain himself, Mog reached up at his saddle to grab the hilt
of his short sword, slowly withdrawing it from its
scabbard.

'What is it?' Darach called above the din of the
downpour.

'Robbers,' Mog replied simply.

Darach did not wait for any further descriptions
of the scene. He grabbed his own sword then tied
the horses together at the reins so that at least they
would not be able to get too far if they decided to
head back to the one-eyed farmer who had so
recently parted with them.

Seginus may have pushed his servants to their
limits at times, but both bondsmen knew he was a
better master than most. They were fiercely loyal
to him and would have laid down their lives for
his safety if the need arose; that is to say they
probably wouldn't stand by and watch him murdered. After all, if Seginus was dead who would
feed and clothe them?

Once the horses were strapped together at the
bit, Mog led the way through the shifting mud
towards the bend in the road. It was a distance of
only twenty paces or so but the rain seemed to
pour down more and more heavily as they
advanced, seeming to defy their efforts, the wind
pushing hard at their chests and slowing them
down.

By the time the two men had come to where they could peer around the stand of bushes that grew at the corner, there was no trace of their master where only moments before Mog had seen him held at bay by the green-clad warriors.

The two men struggled on for a few more wearying steps which brought them to a point where they could look down the long lane ahead of them. The first thing that they both noticed was that the road was cobbled and paved from here on and that the quality of the surface was distinctly better than the old track they had travelled since leaving the coast.

It was Darach who spotted a group of armoured soldiers with green tunics in the distance galloping off at a reckless pace. The strangers were already a long way down the narrow perfectly straight Roman-built road and way beyond hailing distance. In the midst of the strange troop Mog thought he caught a glimpse of a scarlet Roman centurion's cloak, but with the heavy rain and the bright flashes of lightning he could not be sure.

'Maybe it was the Devil that took him,' he muttered, regretting that they had mockingly cursed their master earlier.

Darach, superstitious by nature, crossed himself and recited the 'Ave Maria' under his breath.

As if God were listening to his remorseful prayer the rain ceased in that instant. When the muddy haze had lifted from the road there was no longer any trace of mysterious warriors or of Seginus Gallus, not even a mark in the soaking ground where his horse had trod.

The two faithful servants could only retrieve their horses to set out once more in the direction they had been travelling. They forgot their weariness and their hunger; their one thought now was to make their way quickly to Nantes. Once safe within the city walls their plan was to ask the bishop of that town for help.

They had not journeyed more than four Roman miles before they caught up with a large group of ragged travellers headed with their wares for the market day at Nantes. Wary of all of strangers, they did not greet any of the itinerants but quietly and unobtrusively joined the company.

'We must be very careful now,' Mog advised.

'I can think of no more perfect place to stay hidden than among these country folk. No highway robber would think to attack these poor people,' Darach added. 'And as long as you keep your mouth shut we will not attract any attention.'

'It will not be long before we reach the town. I am sure I can control my urge to speak until then.'

'There is no bone in that tongue of yours but how many times has it broken your head?' Darach replied.

If the truth were to be known the two servants were by now more scared for their own hides than they were for their master's. Years ago they had been separated from Seginus in an emergency. It had cost their master dearly but he had forgiven them, for that incident had taken place in the midst of a war. Such things are bound to happen during combat. This time, however, they had severely prejudiced his safety through their sheer laziness.

'Lord God, do not let those devils harm my master,' Darach prayed earnestly. 'I never meant to curse him, just to slow him down a bit so we could get some rest.'

'Lord God,' prayed Mog with all his might, 'let the master think that this was all Darach's fault.'

With their wagon keeping a tedious pace the travellers moved much more slowly than the servants were now willing to travel. By midafternoon it was obvious that the party would not reach Nantes by nightfall and neither Mog nor Darach were keen on camping in the open when there were brigands about.

'I think we had better try to press on to Nantes and seek help for our master,' Darach advised when it looked like the company might be seeking a good campsite. 'We should not waste valuable time staying with these folk tonight. We should not rest until we have reached the gates of the bishop's palace.'

Not long afterwards they slipped into the forest, continuing to walk with the road on their right and keeping the itinerants just in sight. Long after the large band of travellers had found a camping place Mog and Darach marched on leading their horses. It was exhaustion that finally convinced them to stop for the night while there was still light. They would have to make for Nantes in the morning.

FOUR

n the other side of the sea that was called the Mare Hibernicum by the Romans, not far from the royal enclosure of Teamhair, Leoghaire, High-King of Eirinn and chieftain of all the royal families of the five kingdoms, stood alone on the hill of Uisnech. With an unseeing and despairing gaze he looked out over the fields and woods that marked this spot as the geographical and spiritual centre of Eirinn. He dragged his long fingers through his grey-streaked beard, tugging on the hairs and pulling at the flesh of his cheeks as he did whenever some affair of state upset him.

At the foot of the hill, he could just hear the spirited argument among his nine Druid counsellors though they were far enough away that their words were muffled and dim to his ears. He did not have to hear every syllable to know what was causing them so much dissent. Fifteen summers he had ruled as undisputed overlord of Eirinn and never in all that time had the members of the Druid Council requested that he leave them to their deliberations. He sighed and looked skyward knowing that the time was fast approaching when he must step down in favour of a younger man for the good of the kingdom.

He was growing old. He had worn the five-coloured cloak of high-kingship longer than any man or woman in living memory. He had retained his seat at Teamhair in the High-King's hall throughout the turmoil of the bitterest war to have been visited upon the land in five generations. He had driven the foreign mercenaries and priests out of Eirinn to end that conflict and he had fended off death many times since then. One old saying kept coming back to him: 'Death lurks around behind the backs of the young, but it stares the old in the face.'

When he and Eoghan, the old king of Munster, had defeated Dichu the King of Laigin at the battle of Rathowen nine seasons before, Eirinn had undergone a series of dramatic changes. The man that Leoghaire had appointed to be interim king of Laigin in Dichu's place, a warrior called Enda Censelach, had gone on to wage war with the King of Connachta almost as soon as he had secured himself the throne.

What started as a little dispute turned into a bloody slaughter that was costly to both sides. When he imprisoned the chief bard of Connachta, Enda made sure that only his version of the conflict was made public. In this way the canny King of Laigin had grown in popularity throughout Eirinn by claiming to be a champion of the oppressed. When the ballot was held for the kingship in Laigin, Enda won the election without any opposition.

'If he seeks the high-kingship at the next election I will not be able to challenge him,' Leoghaire admitted to himself. 'Then the great plans of the Druid Council will come to nothing. Enda Censelach will not lift a finger to help our cause. He cares for no-one but himself and the continued prosperity of his clan. He would just as soon sell the whole land of Eirinn to the Saxons as to the

Roman Christians as long as he saw a good return on the transaction.'

One of his counsellor's voices was suddenly raised in anger but the man responsible almost instantly dropped the volume of his speech to a whisper, obviously conscious that Leoghaire might overhear. The thread of the High-King's thoughts was lost as he struggled to discern what the fellow might have been saying that could have caused him to be so passionate in pleading his case. To his disappointment, though, he heard nothing more of the conversation.

'If Enda calls for an election and does not win it then he will certainly wage war on me and the kingdom of Midhe to prove that he is the better man for the job. Everything comes down to war, always war,' he muttered to himself through clenched teeth.

Though Leoghaire surely felt that the clash of arms was now an all-too-common sound in Eirinn, warfare had not always been the way that disputes between kings had been settled. Before the coming of the Roman Christians, battles had rarely been fought with any significant losses to any of the opposing armies. Long and polite negotiations governed by protocol and watched over by Druid Brehon judges usually preceded any actual conflict. Only when neither side could compromise any further and a fight was unavoidable would warriors gather at a place appointed by their chieftains for the battle.

If the last attempts of the Brehons to bring the two parties together failed, the two rival chieftains would each send out the champion of his kingdom to meet his opponent on open ground where everyone could witness the outcome. The two challengers would fight in single combat until one fell. Sometimes the duel would last all day, if the champions were skilled enough. No matter how long it took for one of the champions to triumph, no other warrior would intervene. The army whose champion was eventually vanquished withdrew from the field accepting defeat.

'There was more skill in fighting in those days,' mused Leoghaire. 'There was honour in the contest of one trained warrior clashing with another before all his comrades. Songs were written for the heroes of those days. The bards don't compose poems about these days. There have been no deeds of honour worth recording since Niall of the Nine Hostages was high-king.'

Nine summers had come and gone since Bishop Palladius had come to Eirinn and stirred up King Dichu of Laigin into believing that with the backing of a Christian minority he could rule the whole land as sole monarch. Under the influence of Palladius the old way of fighting was discarded in favour of a new and devastating method. This bishop from the Roman lands brought with him Imperial customs of warfare and Dichu eagerly adopted the foreign tactics. Leoghaire could still remember how he had listened in disbelief to the first reports of the destruction that the army of Laigin had caused as they passed over the land.

The Roman strategies were simple. Sweep down on a column of enemy warriors and attack them without warning, slaughtering or scattering the whole contingent. Such a manoeuvre was so unexpected to the conventional Munster men and the honourable warriors of Midhe that they were often roundly and easily beaten, though they were as brave and as well-skilled as any warriors in Eirinn. Whenever Dichu ordered that no quarter be given even the most valorous of the enemy fled the field fearing for their lives.

Using tactics based on brutality and butchery, Dichu and Palladius gained a lot of ground. Very quickly. Together they marched their army to and fro laying waste to everything in their path until Leoghaire managed to rally the forces of Munster and Midhe and finally defeated the renegades at an ancient hill-fort in the north of Munster. The Battle of Rathowen had lasted through two days of terrible carnage that even now the High-King preferred not to bring to mind. He pushed the memories of those days out of his thoughts as much as possible.

'Rathowen created a precedent,' he said aloud to himself. 'After that wild brawl every petty chieftain from the Skelligs to Fionn's Bridge thought that he could get away with the murder of innocents by force of numbers and all in the name of a just war. Nine seasons of the snows have passed since that fight and we are still suffering the great loss of lives on that field. For a long time the kingdoms were untilled and the crops went unplanted for the lack of sowers and it will be many more harvest times before there are enough strong arms to bring in all the oats and barley in Eirinn. If I allow Enda to bring war upon the land again our people might never recover from the consequences.'

Suddenly Leoghaire's train of thought was interrupted again, but this time it was not a raised voice that distracted him. What stirred him from his reflections was a cold silence where only a short while before there had been many voices engaged in debate. The counsellors were quiet.

But it was more than the quiet that made the High-King uneasy. His keen battle instincts alerted him to the presence of someone standing close behind him not more than a sword's length away. His whole body tensed with apprehension. Silently preparing a defence in case this was an assassin who had approached without any sound, he consciously relaxed himself. Without acknowledging the stranger's presence he kept his eyes on the horizon and moved his hand slowly toward his sword.

Just as his fingers gently touched the ornate hilt of his war-blade a hand came to rest on Leoghaire's shoulder. Like the warrior he was, he spun around in response, taking two steps away from the stranger and drawing his sword swiftly from its leather scabbard in a long graceful sweep. He levelled the point at his opponent's chest pressing down slightly on it to give the message that he was ready to push it further. In that instant the High-King recognised the long blue robes and the face of Cathach his Druid advisor.

The old man was unmoved at this display, calmly lifting the blade away from his body with one hand, smiling all the while. Leoghaire breathed out heavily and immediately sheathed the sword making no attempt to conceal his deep-felt relief. When he noticed that Cathach was still smiling at him, he turned abruptly away and stared out over the fields again. Cathach said nothing for the moment. Finally it was Leoghaire who broke the silence, grunting in resentment at being disturbed in this manner.

The old Druid threw his arms out wide to show the palms of his hands and protested, 'It is only me! You have nothing to fear from a slow feeble poet whose youth is long gone.'

'When a king reigns for as many seasons as I have, he begins to fear that everyone will challenge his right to rule,' countered Leoghaire grimly.

'Come now! Even an old fox must give his cunning a rest,' Cathach laughed, trying to lighten the High-King's mood.

'But in spite of the fox's cunning, he may still find his skin hanging in the marketplace with a small price on the fur,' Leoghaire answered sharply.

'Have I not told you that you will be king another five seasons at the very least?'

'Don't talk rubbish!' Leoghaire spat. 'I am finished with unless I can find some way to pacify that scheming Enda.'

'My fellow counsellors and I have been discussing this very subject,' the Druid cut in, ignoring the king's pessimism. 'We believe that we have come up with a solution to the problem that you should consider. If you are willing to hear me out.'

'You and I, dear counsellor, have chattered about this dilemma until our tongues are numb with talking. Still there seems to be no answer. Was there a simple solution staring us in the face all along?' Leoghaire retorted sarcastically.

'Not an obvious key to fit into the lock. No. A possible pathway that leads around the obstacle, certainly.'

Cathach stroked his long grey beard breathing out slowly to allow some of his own exhaustion to show. Then the old Druid gathered his blue cloak about his shoulders and sat on one of the many large flat stones that littered the summit of the hill. He leaned his staff against the stone and spread his cloak across his knees.

The king followed the Druid's lead, sitting down on a nearby rocky outcrop to wait for Cathach's suggestion. Leoghaire fully expected to be asked to renounce his royal titles so that his honour would not be diminished by the loss of an election. All afternoon this thought had been returning to him again and again. He was sure that it was only a matter of time before someone offered it to him as a way out of the difficulties he now faced.

Cathach sighed deeply. Leoghaire turned his face away from the old man, not wishing his advisor to see the pain on his face when the subject was finally broached.

'Enda Censelach does not really want the high-kingship for himself,' Cathach began. 'Though I am sure that he would willingly take the position if elected. No, it is not the title nor the office that he wants. I believe that he merely desires some of the power that comes with the rank and certainly none of the obligations.' The Druid waited until he was sure that Leoghaire had taken this in and then he shifted in his seat so that he could look out over the fields as he continued.

When he began to speak again his voice took on some of the formality of a storyteller. 'Censelach fought a long and bloody war against Connachta but he is not renowned for enjoying the responsi-bilities of his realm. If he were to attain the office of high-king he would very likely not take his duties at all seriously. Within a full turning of the seasons you would find yourself re-elected simply because of his mismanagement. But the damage that he could do between one summer and the next to all that we have worked for is not to be under-estimated. Our delicate relations with the Church of Rome could be irrevocably undermined.'

'I have never met anyone so full of hatred for the Roman Christians as is Enda,' remarked Leoghaire. He put his hand up to his chin to stroke his beard nervously.

'Palladius had Censelach's three sons brutally murdered because they would not join the rest of

Laigin in the revolt. Enda has never forgiven the Christians for that.' Cathach reminded him.

'That hatred could do more than undermine the relationship, it could put an end to our hopes of an alliance with Rome once and forever.'

'You are right,' Cathach agreed. 'If we show too much hostility to their doctrines they will not believe that our conversion to the Cross is very likely or that we are sincere in our wish to attain their ways when our people finally do begin to take conversion. They must believe that we are earnest in our desire for a peaceful adoption of their beliefs if our own traditions are going to have a chance of survival behind the veil of the Christian rituals.'

'All that you foretold to me after the Battle of Rathowen has come to pass,' Leoghaire muttered with a trace of despair in his voice, 'but tell me truthfully, will Enda Censelach be the ruin of our plans?'

'Enda has a part to play in the great design but I doubt that even he knows what that is yet. Neither myself nor the whole Druid Council can predict exactly what may come of the future. Not even if all the revered sages of the west and east were to confer on the matter would they be able to say with confidence what will happen in the next few generations. The balance between our success and failure is too fine and precarious to be read clearly,' stated Cathach.

'Then how can we know for certain what action to take? Would it not be better to live our lives as we always have and then to face the challenges to our sovereignty as they arise?'

'There will always be the danger that someone like Enda will come along and undo what many generations of tradition have preserved. For example, if Dichu had refused to follow the urging of Palladius then there would have been no slaughter on the fields of Rathowen. Many lives would have been saved if the rebels had respected the traditions of championship. As it turned out a precedent was created on the battlefield that day and it has haunted our land ever since. Cattle raids no longer involve simple pilfering of breed-stock. In these times resistance is met sword for sword and blow for blow. There have been too many murders committed since Rathowen that can be traced back to Dichu's weakness in taking on the Roman methods of war.'

'If I had acted quicker the whole revolt might never have happened,' Leoghaire admitted.

'You had no idea that Dichu would be willing to send hundreds to their deaths in the hope that his wild claim on the high-kingship would succeed. It was the Druid Council who failed to act in time. We should have prevented the spread of the war. Nor did any of us even guess what sort of man Palladius really was.' The old counsellor paused for a moment. He knew that it was useless going over and over this same ground and so he took a deep breath and moved on. 'That is all nine summers past now and there is nothing we can do about it. We can only learn from our mistakes. If we could have known beforehand that Palladius intended to bring this Roman style of war to our lands, perhaps we would have dealt with him sooner, but for the moment there is another moth in the butter who must be scraped out cleanly. Enda of the Laigin folk.'

'What do we do?' Leoghaire sighed. 'I cannot censure him. Going to war with him is out of the question. I could not entice enough warriors away

from the planting of their crops. I wish I could exile
him but I have no excuse.'

'But you could send him away,' Cathach interrupted.

'What do you mean?'

'All Enda really seeks is a way to increase his
fortune. He will do that here in Éirinn unless you
send him to do it elsewhere. After Rathowen and
the war he waged with Connachta, Censelach went
raiding on the east coast of the Briton lands even
as far as the kingdom of Dal Araidhe. He brought
back a great many prisoners. With the ransom that
he extorted from their kinfolk he more than paid
for the adventure. He knows there is plunder to be
had in plenty in those lands.'

'What are you suggesting?' Leoghaire snapped,
horrified. 'That I should send him off to spread his
style of war again to our neighbours in Britain? As
if they haven't got enough trouble with the Saxon
invaders. Or have you forgotten that my clan have
renounced the taking of hostages since my grandfather's time? What sort of a king would I be if I
went back on a policy that has been in force for
three generations?'

Cathach shifted in his seat, dragging his heels up
to touch the base of the stone. 'Commission Censelach to go to the Saxon lands and thence to Dal
Araidhe seeking information on the situation with
regard to the foreign invaders who are settling
there. Put ships at his disposal. Allow him to raise
warriors for his own protection. Make sure that he
knows he has your permission to use force at his
discretion to obtain information. A man such as he
is will take that to mean that he has your blessing
to raid in those lands.'

'That is the Druid Council's advice,' Leoghaire
grunted, striving to keep his voice low, 'that I

should allow him to raise an army! And what will he do when his private soldiers are tired of looting foreign villages? Will he not come back here and sweep through the four kingdoms like the cold north wind and will he not have a trained and well-seasoned force to do it with?'

'By that time Eirinn will have more urgent concerns and Enda will surely be caught in the net of another man,' Cathach insisted. 'For the time being he will be gone long enough to ensure that you and I can concentrate all our efforts on the next great challenge.'

'Censelach will return here soon enough. Too soon I fear. And he will bring war with him.'

'The Council has considered that he may have great ambitions on his return and we have come up with a way of dealing with his designs on the high-kingship.'

'Only the axe of some wild Saxon savage could deal with Censelach better than anyone in Eirinn could,' Leoghaire jibed.

'We cannot rely on the chance that he will fall in battle. There is another way.'

The High-King turned to look at his old advisor. Cathach leaned forward in his seat, gripping his staff tightly. Leoghaire felt his stomach tighten. He sensed that the Druid was about to suggest something that was not very pleasant.

'Enda has a daughter,' Cathach breathed. 'Her name is Mona and she is twenty-two seasons on the Earth. I have not met her but I am told that she is not an unattractive woman. If you were to marry her it would not be unseemly for you to send your father-in-law as an ambassador to the king of the Dal Araidhe. While travelling on the High-King's business he would be your personal representative. That should give him the status he seeks for the time being. And I have checked his genealogy. The girl is related to your clan within nine generations. A son or daughter by her would be eligible to stand for high office by birthright. That alone will make Censelach feel that his clan has a claim to the thrones of Laigin and Eirinn.'

Leoghaire listened carefully to all that the Druid said but he did not turn his head toward Cathach to acknowledge him. 'I swore that I would never marry again after my first wife died,' he protested. 'I have had no time to do anything but to concentrate on keeping the peace. And I have very little patience remaining to expend on a wife and a household.'

Cathach laughed, kicking his heels against the stone like a boy and lifting his staff as he did so to stab it playfully back into the grass. Though the Druid did not use so many words, Leoghaire knew that Cathach was mocking him for being timid about remarrying. Before the Druid had a chance to say anything that might infer that the High-King of Eirinn was shy of a beautiful woman, Leoghaire muttered, 'I am not sure that the girl would be willing to be tied to such an aged relic as myself but I can see that I have few alternatives than to take your advice. We always knew, you and I, that there would be a challenge to my position one day. I expected it much sooner.'

'So did I,' Cathach admitted, still shuffling his feet back and forth like a little boy. 'We have been fortunate that you are so skilled a ruler. It is essential to the Druid Council that you remain in the seat of kingship for some time yet so that our plans may move smoothly through the next difficult stage. The Romans must believe without question that the High-King of Eirinn has taken the Christian faith if we are to rely upon them as allies.'

'Will Enda consent to this marriage?'

'I am sure that he will. She is not his favourite child, indeed she has proven quite an embarrassment to the ruling family of Laigin. Some time ago when she was travelling and studying in the Dal Araidhe she took wholeheartedly to the Christian faith.'

'What?' exclaimed Leoghaire in surprise. 'Then it is certain that Enda will not miss her.' Then he stared at the grass at his feet for a long while considering all that Cathach had said. The Druid eventually put out his hand and touched Leoghaire on the shoulder with the tips of his fingers and the gesture brought the High-King out of his trance.

'She is a Christian!' Leoghaire restated in awe, shaking his head. 'So everything that you predicted is coming to bear fruit. The old ways are passing and a new faith has come to supplant them.'

'Now we must strive to preserve the old traditions within the new faith. That will require that we influence the Christian doctrines, reshaping them if necessary to our own design before they take root.'

'And what about Mona? What if the girl is unwilling to wed with me? Have you thought of that?'

'I have considered that possibility of course,' answered Cathach. 'I am certain however, that when the time comes she will wed you with all her heart.'

'How can you possibly know something like that? She and I have never even set eyes upon each other. Don't you think that it is just a little optimistic to expect that a young woman would want to marry someone of my age?'

'If you are willing to take this road for the good

I can promise you that you will have her devotion until the day she dies.'

'Druid tricks,' sneered Leoghaire with obvious distaste.

'Not at all. There will be no need for deception, I can assure you. If you intend to build a fortress it is better to chose solid ground on which to construct it. That is all we are doing. We are selecting seedlings that show the promise of one day bearing fruit and then caring for them until they do.'

'You must give me your word that there will be no magic used to coerce Mona into marrying me,' Leoghaire pressed.

'But, lord,' protested Cathach gently, 'there is no such thing as magic, only the planting of seeds and the tending of the bough.'

Leoghaire knew that Cathach had avoided his concerns expertly but he was also painfully aware that there were few options open to them if the greater plans of the Druid Council were to have any chance of success.

'Look into it then,' he sighed. 'We will approach Enda with the offer of a marriage but let me be the one to ask his daughter. I want her to see me for who I am. I do not want her head filled with heroic stories concocted in advance by your sweet singing bards.'

'Very well, lord, as you wish but may I suggest that you spend some time studying the ways of the Christians. It will help you if you are to gain the girl's confidence,' added Cathach satisfied.

Then, using his staff to lever himself onto his feet, the old man stood and shook out his robes. In seconds he was off with renewed strength down the hill to inform the rest of the Druid Council of the High-King's decision and to start preparations for a wedding between two of the royal houses of Eirinn.

FIVE

he stone-lined room was utterly dark. Through an ingenious system of double doorways and angled air channels not even the faintest glimmer of light ever entered that place. A cold draft blew constant though feeble down through the empty terracotta pipes that had been laid into the foundations of the great stronghold of Nantes. The walls of the chamber were soaked by an untraceable source of underground water that seeped steadily through gaps in the masonry. The resulting dampness bred moulds that caught in the back of a prisoner's throat, drying it out. After only an hour or two within the cell the unfortunate inhabitant found that it had become painful to swallow or to breathe.

More than a few days locked in the bishop's gaol-room invariably left the unlucky captive with an incessant, nagging, fluid-filled cough and constant sneezing from inhaling the pungent spores of mould.

A longer period of incarceration would almost certainly bring on a permanent weakness of the lungs. But then a longer period locked in this dungeon rarely ended in the prisoner's release. It indicated the singular displeasure of the lord of this place, under whose fortress this strongroom was constructed, and it certainly guaranteed an indefinite sentence. This chamber not only housed dissidents and criminals, it also held the mortal remains of almost every man or woman who had ever been a long-term prisoner of the Bishop of Nantes.

For a long while after the soldiers had dumped Seginus in this cell he sat leaning against one of the walls waiting for his eyes to adjust to the dark. He counted the beats of his heart to gauge the passing seconds but even after five hundred pulses he still could not see his hand, not even when he placed it against the tip of his nose. He began to despair for the success of his mission and for his own survival.

'What is this place?' he moaned half to himself.

From out of the dark a mocking voice answered him and Seginus jumped. 'You are in the care of the Bishop of Nantes, also known hereabouts as Julius the Butcher.'

The presence of another person in the chamber was the last thing that the Roman expected. Having recovered from the initial shock he sucked his breath in through clenched teeth and moved to stand, hoping to put a safe distance between himself and the owner of this voice from the darkness, but he slipped his footing in the slimy muck that covered the floor. His elbow scuffed against the masonry behind him as he fell backwards, tearing the sleeve of his shirt. He heard the other man quietly laughing, obviously amused at the panic he had caused. An irrational fear took hold of Seginus as he sank back down to the damp ground, covering his face with his arms to protect himself from imagined blows.

'Who is there?' he stuttered. His words bounced around the cell to echo in the blackness.

The other man did not answer. Seginus only heard a cold breathy cough and a chortle of wicked amusement.

'Are you one of the guards?' Seginus ventured, fearing that the voice was that of an executioner sent to murder him.

The other man laughed aloud. 'No. Do not fear. I am merely a guest like yourself.' Seginus noticed that the man replied in Latin but with a slight accent that he could not quite identify. There was something very familiar about the way the other prisoner spoke, even something about his laugh that Seginus recognised, but he could not put his finger on what it was.

The thought suddenly struck him that this might be an old acquaintance from the monastery of Saint Eli where he had first worn the robes of a holy brother. The more he thought about it the more Seginus felt as though he knew the man very well. He was almost overcome by a foolhardy urge to tell this fellow sufferer everything that had happened to him in the last three weeks but common sense held his tongue still. Seginus rebuked himself for his witlessness, making a solemn and silent covenant not to say too much too soon.

'It is a long time since I heard a friendly voice such as yours,' the Roman finally offered in a tone that was cautious but not too cold.

'A long while indeed, Seginus Gallus,' came the gravelly reply. 'Nine full measures of a Roman year since you heard this voice or since your words reached my ears but still I would know your speech if a hundred years had passed.'

Seginus was surprised and extremely uncomfortable that this man knew his name. 'Who are you?' he spluttered. 'I cannot imagine how you came to recognise me in the darkness of this place but I swear by all that is Holy that I do not know you.'

'You know me well enough, Roman,' the man laughed again. 'It was I who helped you escape from Eirinn with your two servants when the High-King of that land would have had you put in chains. Surely the time has not been so long that you have forgotten me entirely?'

Seginus frantically searched his mind. He could almost recall the face that fitted this voice but many of the Hibernians had this manner of speech when they used the Latin tongue. His sojourn in the land of the barbarians was too long ago for him to clearly remember all their strange sounding names.

'I will answer the riddle for you,' the other man said half-mocking, as if he understood the difficulty that the Roman was having. 'I was a Druid in those days.' A face presented itself dimly to the searching mind of Seginus but he still could not recall the Hibernian's name and so he did not respond.

The other prisoner waited only a few seconds more before he introduced himself. 'I am called Cieran of Ardmór.'

'Cieran!' Seginus spoke the name in disbelief, immediately recalling the Druid and the circumstances of their meeting at Ardmór on the south coast of Hibernia. 'How in God's name did you come to be here?'

'In God's name indeed. That is a long tale . . .' The Hibernian coughed violently and spat something at the floor. Seginus could not see his companion but he could hear the wheezing breath that followed the cough and he could bring to mind the man's features clearly now from his memory. He recalled that Cieran was dark-haired and tall and that he had been greatly respected by his people. The Hibernian coughed again and then groaned in pain.

62

'Have you been beaten badly?' Seginus asked in fear of what might be in store for him more than from any real concern for Cieran.

'No. I have not been beaten at all, thank God. The good Julius, our gaoler, is a much subtler fellow than that. This chamber is the place where he sends those who he wishes to put out of his thoughts forever. He is very good at forgetting those who cause him any trouble.'

'What kind of trouble brought you here?'

'In some ways it is in part your fault,' Cieran declared coldly, realising fully the irony of his own circumstances.

Seginus felt a sudden wave of fear pass through him. Now he was almost certain that his mission had failed and that he was possibly in grave danger as a consequence of the letters that he had been carrying.

'I long ago took the vows of a Christian priest,' continued the Hibernian. 'I have yourself and your brother in Christ, Declan, to thank for showing me the way to the Cross.' He coughed again and once more spat out a ball of phlegm that had caught in his throat.

'But I did not find the Orthodox Roman way of worship entirely to my taste and so in time I became a follower of the priest called Silvanus.'

'Silvanus the heretic?' gasped Seginus, crossing himself silently.

'There are many who would argue convincingly that it is Pope Celestine and his fat bishops who are the only heretics,' answered Cieran.

'Do not speak so! Not in this place!' Seginus hissed, desperately trying to silence the other man.

'I no longer have anything to fear from the Bishop of Nantes. This dreary black cavern is the worst that he can do to me, short of outright murder, and I am sure that he will not give me the opportunity to die as a martyr nor the chance to quickly alleviate any of my suffering.'

'How did you come to be in Gaul?' Seginus cut in so he would not have to hear any more talk of heresy and the possibility of martyrdom.

'Shortly after the war between the High-King and Palladius had ended, and less than a month after your escape from Ardmór, I was summoned to the fortress of Cashel by the King of Munster. Leoghaire and Murrough had decreed that all those who had aided Palladius and Dichu the King of Laigin were judged to be oath breakers. Breaking loyalty to one's clan and kingdom is considered a most serious crime in the lands of Eirinn.'

Cieran breathed in loudly and then continued, his voice beginning to strain. 'King Murrough was especially angry that you had escaped. He was appalled that someone such as yourself who was so close to Palladius had managed to elude capture. But I believe that you also held Murrough captive for some time. Of course he was only a prince of the kingdom then but that does not lessen the charge. Is it true that it was you who ordered the cutting of the Quicken Tree?'

Seginus put his hand to his throat to wipe away the gathering sweat. 'Murrough is a king now?' he asked.

'Yes,' Cieran replied. 'He was elected soon after the war. That reminds me, did you not thieve a royal seal from Murrough at some stage? I do not know many men who are foolish enough to steal the symbol of a king's clan.'

'Murrough gave the seal to me as a surety that he would keep his word,' Seginus declared and his fingers touched the ring where it still hung about his neck on a strip of leather. He was glad that the other man could not see it. 'In all the confusion of my escape I did not have the chance to return it to him but I assure you that I fully intended to.'

'You used the seal ring to pass through the kingdom safely and so escape as far as Ardmór. It was common knowledge at the time. But that is not what most upset Murrough. He was just as furious that it had been one of his own subjects, myself, who had arranged for your safe departure beyond the reach of his justice. So he decided to make an example of me. I was exiled from Eirinn forever and the Christian community at Ardmór was dispersed and the chapel closed.'

'Is that when you took to the Cross?'

Cieran laughed at the suggestion and the sound echoed in the room. 'No. I did not resort to the Gospels in times of trouble as so many have. I travelled to the land of the Britons under the safe conduct and protection of Abbot Declan. He vouched for me and offered me a sanctuary among his monks. I accepted his protection and it was Declan who, in time, convinced me to take on the mantle of Christianity.'

Seginus pushed his shoulders against the wall behind him straightening his spine and stretching the muscles of his back. He let the air out loudly through his teeth. This confirmed what he had always suspected of Declan, that the abbot was a heretic who only presented a thin pretence of Roman orthodoxy, favouring the ways of the heathen over those of the True Church. Now he had living proof. Here was a heretic who admitted that it had been Declan who set him on the path to Hell.

Another thought struck Seginus in that moment and a bitter memory welled in him. 'When the monastery at Ardmór was closed down what became of the tomb of my brother, the blessed martyr Linus?'

'The tomb still stands. Or at least it did when last I had any word from Eirinn. I am told that many people come to seek healing and favours from Saint Linus the Holy One. Not even the High-King would dare to interfere with the beliefs of the ordinary folk. Indeed, Declan each year sends a party of monks on a pilgrimage to that place to pray at the chapel and to minister to the tribes-people. The monks are tolerated so long as they depart within one changing of the moon.'

'You still have not told me how you came to be here in Gaul,' insisted Seginus.

'I was a Druid before I was a priest. Declan sent me here to the great Druid college of Armorica in the hope that I would be better able to spread the word of the Gospel to my former colleagues. But before I had converted any of the old ones I met with Silvanus. He opened my eyes to the deeper mysteries of the Christian faith and to the true nature of Christ. Eventually I decided to abandon the Orthodox teachings and to join the righteous mission of the Arians.'

'The Arians are the servants of Hell. They have perverted the teachings of our Lord. They even have women amongst them who act as priests, so I have heard.'

'Yes, there are women who are bishops and priests. In fact a widow-woman called Theodora from the land of the Hellenes is their spiritual leader since Silvanus fled to Africa.'

Seginus made a gurgling sound in the back of his throat to register his disgust. 'I am sure you had no trouble falling in with their evil customs. All of your folk are the same.'

'I am nothing more than a savage to you, am I?' replied Cieran, his voice swelling with intensity as he spoke. 'Even if I were to be elected Bishop of Rome I would still be an uncivilised wretch with no hope of redemption in your eyes.'

Seginus said nothing. The room was blacker than the frozen depths of a lake in winter but the Roman could feel the piercing resentful gaze of the Hibernian cutting through the darkness like a shaft of white light.

'Have you forgotten that I saved your life?' Cieran eventually asked when he had grown tired of waiting for Seginus to say something. 'Do you not understand that when I chose to help you I forfeited my own liberty. Does that mean nothing to you? Or is the simple fact of my birth to a barbarian mother in the land of the five kingdoms enough to condemn me to an eternity in Hell?'

'My brother was brutally murdered by one of your evil folk,' Seginus barked, 'on the very day we landed upon your shores. I never met any Hibernian since who was completely Christian in his ways no matter how they might profess otherwise. You are a race susceptible to heresy and the wiles of the Devil.'

'If my folk have a failing,' Cieran strained to call back, 'it is that we ask too many questions and when the answers do not satisfy us we look elsewhere for explanations. I was never convinced that Linus had been murdered by anyone in the village at Ardmór and so I asked many questions.'

The Hibernian stopped short and Seginus held his breath listening intently for what the man was about to say. When he continued Cieran was suddenly calm. 'I believe from what I heard and saw that it was one of your own monks who stabbed Linus to death, 'the Hibernian asserted, 'not one of my people and certainly not a demon come from Hell as Bishop Palladius would have had you all believe.'

'I have heard enough of your venomous babble,' spurted Seginus. 'How dare you soil the memory of a saint? Truly the heresy of the Arians is like a creeping disease, as the sainted Augustine has written, that eats at the very flesh of all that is holy.'

Cieran laughed derisively at the Roman making light of what he said and then the room fell silent again but after a few moments the Hibernian coughed violently as he had earlier, this time spitting out some of the liquid that had settled on his lungs. His breathing steadied but he found that he no longer had the energy to speak further. Across the room Seginus waited for Cieran to continue his tale but it wasn't long before he realised that the Hibernian had drifted off to sleep.

So Seginus sat alone trying not to think of the awful scenario that Cieran had described, that Linus may have met his end at the hands of a Christian monk. He began listening intently to all the sounds around about him to take his mind off what had been said and eventually he discerned that the prison room was quite large but that he and Cieran were probably the only inhabitants apart from a few rodents. He soon lost track of the passing time in the dank blackness. The only way he could judge that any time had passed was that it was not long before his nasal passages were blocked by the fungal spores that floated in the air. Soon after his throat began to dry out making it uncomfortable to breathe through his mouth.

Eventually Seginus managed to drop off to sleep lulled by the sound of Cieran's slow breathing but just as he began to relax he woke with a jolt.

Something large, about the size of a cat, had scurried by brushing close to his leg.

The Roman monk moved to sit up not quite sure what kind of animal it could have been and as he did so one of his hands brushed against a stick. Just at that moment he felt a sharp pain on his thigh. Whatever the creature was, it was sinking its teeth deeply into his flesh and trying to tear a piece from his leg.

Without thinking Seginus lifted the stick that he held in his right hand and swiftly brought it down where he guessed the attacker might be for he still could not see anything in the lightless cell. The weapon connected with its target and the animal squealed loudly, rushing off to a safe corner. He knew of no flesh-eating creature of that size that would dare come so close to a living man.

'You will soon get used to our brothers the rats,' Cieran said, stirring. 'When you are too tired to stay on guard against them you will not even feel their little teeth pinching you and sucking out the blood.'

Seginus realised that he had just beaten off a rodent that was twice the size of anything he had ever seen in his life before. Not even in Rome or Ravenna did the rats grow so large. The monk brought his knees up to his chest and rubbed the spot where he had been bitten. Then he held the stick firmly around his legs with both his hands ready to fend off another attack. It was only at the moment that he caught the strong odour of decaying flesh. An awful possibility crept into his mind. Hesitantly he traced his fingers along the length of the improvised club that he had used to beat off the rat. Its surface was sticky and soft. Immediately he touched the tips of his fingers to his nose and then instantly he recoiled in disgust.

The club that he held was certainly the source of a foul and rotten stench. It did not take a Greek philosopher to realise how improbable it was that any kind of weapon would have been left in a place like this and the grisly truth about the nature of the stick hit him. It was not a wooden club at all; it was more than likely a human thighbone. Seginus wildly cast the hideous object across the room and it landed far away with a dull thud followed soon after by a splash of water.

Though the bone made a lot of noise as it landed Cieran made no acknowledgment that he had heard anything. Seginus realised that the man was probably sleeping again and so he settled down to wait for the Hibernian to wake up.

The hours passed slowly by. Seginus lost track of time once more. For long periods he half slept but he was always on the alert for the return of the giant rat. Sometimes he thought he could see the creature's eyes glowing in the dark. At other times he swore he could hear it shuffling by, testing his defences.

Throughout the endless night of the prison cell Seginus consciously tried to sharpen his senses so that he might hear every creak of Cieran's chest as it heaved to take in breath, or any indication that the guards might return to rescue him. The sounds that reached his ears, however, were mostly unrecognisable. Some seemed so loud to him that eventually he found it hard to gauge exactly whereabouts in the room the Hibernian lay.

His senses were playing tricks on him. He was hungry to the point of experiencing extreme pain in his stomach. Even so he swore that he could smell meat roasting slowly on a spit. All of his clothes were soaking and his hair had become stiff with dirt. Seginus put up with every new discomfort and agony as they arose, not allowing himself to submit to the torture that his senses were heaping upon him.

It was only when Cieran had still not stirred and Seginus had begun to lose the feeling in his legs that he decided he could not stand the agony of the dark prison cell any longer. His head felt like it was going to burst with frustration. In desperation he tried speaking to Cieran but there was no reply or if there was it was little more than a groan.

Seginus yelled. Then he screamed. When there was no answer he began yelping like a dog and thrashing his arms about in the water. Still no reply; no relief from his suffering. With one last effort he raised a strange low call from the back of his throat that grated the already parched recesses of his mouth. Like a bull in the last throes of death at the hands of a gladiator, Seginus began to moan.

The only reply that he got was the dull echo of his own cry flying around the large chamber. The monk soon gave up. He was so weakened from the stifling air in the prison that his voice would no longer obey him.

Then he had an idea and began to seek Cieran by groping about on the floor, but he had not gone far from his place by the wall when he thought better of that plan. He was loathe to find any more rat-chewed human remains. And so Seginus resigned himself to his fate. He leaned back against the wall, drew his knees up to his chest once more and waited and waited.

Though he was finding it difficult to think clearly by now, Seginus began to wonder if this was what Hell might be like. An eternity of lingering in a state neither alive nor dead, tarrying, waiting for who knows what to come to the rescue. A friendly guard? The Angel of Death? The Lord of Light?

Light. That was what he told himself that he missed most. He heard Palladius in his mind reading a passage from the Gospels. 'I am the Light,' the old man intoned and then Seginus swung his body around so that he could kneel to pray.

'I will plead with God to release me,' he wheezed as loud as his strained voice would allow. 'I will beg His forgiveness and recite His litany until I am delivered from this prison.'

But it was not long before Seginus found himself distracted from his task. He always found prayer tedious and difficult but when there was some worry on his mind it became next to impossible for him to form thoughts into respectful pleading. Seginus held his palms together before him for a little while after his petition had lost impetus but it seemed that God was in no rush to answer his servant. As the silence dragged on he began to get an uncomfortable feeling that his God had forsaken him and an overwhelming sense of loneliness welled up inside him. This was despite the fact that a sleeping heretic foreigner was also curled up in this dull purgatory not ten paces away.

The Roman began to wonder at the strange chance that brought him to be incarcerated here with an unbeliever, a heathen who had once saved his life. It had been almost ten years since Seginus had been forced to make a hasty and undignified departure from Eirinn.

He thought back now on how he had hated every day that he had been forced to abide in that country. He had despised the Hibernians, he reviled their unchristian customs. Moreover he still burned with anger at the cruel way in which one of those folk had murdered his brother. He could still see clearly the corpse of Linus lying face down in the embers of a fire on the beach at Ardmór.

Even after all these years he could still remember the smell of singed hair and flesh that had hung in the air afterwards. As he thought on it the foul stench returned to his nostrils and tainted the air once more.

As if the killing of his kinsman had not been bad enough, the barbarians had also taken his teacher Palladius the Elder, the anointed Bishop of Eirinn, and set him adrift unclothed and without oars on the open sea. The old man had drifted for many days eventually finding landfall near the monastery of Saint Ninian on the coast of Britain. After that dreadful treatment Palladius never really recovered his health or fighting spirit. After a long voyage Seginus also came to Saint Ninian's, known in those days as Candida Casa. By that time Declan, who had once been a loyal follower of Palladius, had been consecrated as the abbot of the community there.

A bitter feud immediately erupted between the followers of the bishop and those of Abbot Declan which ended in Palladius taking to the woods with only a few of his most zealous supporters. The old man spent the ensuing years petitioning Rome to have Declan punished and to receive special dispensation for himself to raise an army that could invade Eirinn and win the land over to the Cross.

But Rome had more serious worries than to launch a conquest at the end of the earth. The barbarian hordes were once more perched on the Imperial doorstep and the Church was more than a little preoccupied with preserving peace. The Pope only ever sent one reply to Britain. The charter stripped Palladius of all his former authority as Bishop of Eirinn and further ordered the old man never to leave the bounds of his own monastic community on pain of instant excommunication.

After reading the orders from Rome, Palladius sank into a deep despair, rarely ever leaving the confines of the chapel at his own settlement. It was thereafter left to his followers, chief among them Seginus, to continue to plead on the old man's behalf.

To that end the monk had travelled to Armorican Gaul to speak with the Bishop of Nantes who still held an ancient claim on the Diocese of the British lands. Seginus bore letters from his old teacher that maintained that Palladius had acted justly in his dealings with the Hibernian people.

On the very day that Seginus was due to depart from Britain a rumour reached Palladius that a new man had been appointed by the Pope to be Bishop of Eirinn. This usurper was due to pass through Nantes within the month. Seginus had set off with great speed, desperate to reach the Bishop of Nantes before the Papal legate had a chance to present a case against Palladius and be accepted as his replacement. It was a mission that held little hope of success but even with the odds stacked against him, Seginus had remained unwilling to admit that Rome had acted so swiftly to rebuke someone considered by many to be a great teacher and theologian.

The monk sighed in frustration, struggling to concentrate on his present predicament once more. It was obvious that, for the time being at least, any hope that Seginus had held of being able to help Palladius was beyond his power to realise. All his letters had been taken from him by the soldiers who had arrested him and they had probably fallen into the hands of Julius the Bishop of Nantes. It now seemed more than likely that the newly appointed Bishop of Eirinn had reached Nantes before Seginus, which would explain why the monk was locked in a gaol room with an avowed heretic.

As though the Hibernian knew that Seginus was thinking about him, he rolled over and woke straining to speak. 'Pray for me, brother,' he gasped.

The Roman held his tongue, determined for the moment to make no reply. He found his heart filled with contempt for this man who dared to claim that Linus had not really given his life for Christ as Palladius had claimed. Nevertheless there was a small part of him that was fascinated by the story that the heretic had to tell.

'I beg you, brother, hear me speak,' the man pleaded.

Seginus curled his lip and willed himself not to answer. He reminded himself that this man would be damned to eternal hellfire for his atheistic beliefs. But a nagging doubt gnawed at the Roman's resolve. Though he preferred to believe that Cieran was a worthless liar, it had to be admitted that this man had once put his life at risk to save Seginus. The monk felt he should at least show some small gesture of gratitude. After all, if he were to remain confined in this cell it might not be long before Seginus himself was seated before his maker ready to be judged. It was an act of charity, he reasoned with himself, to feel pity for a misguided soul. By that logic it was not a sin to hear what the Hibernian had to say.

'I must tell someone all that I have learned,' wheezed Cieran. 'My conscience will not allow me to keep the secret any longer.'

But Seginus could not yet bring himself to acknowledge the heretic's plea.

'I will speak even if you refuse to hear my confession. I must put my mind at ease. This may be the last opportunity that I have to do so. You above all others must know the truth. A great wrong has been done and now it must be righted. I could have put a stop to the veneration of Linus as a saint years ago. You see, I have known for a long time the true circumstances of his death. Shortly before I left the monastery to travel here to Gaul, Abbot Declan admitted to me that he personally knew the man who murdered your brother.'

Seginus sat up. 'Who among your filthy kindred committed that foul crime? Name the man and I will think better of you.'

'In the wilds of Britain the clergy have not yet fully adopted the new ecclesiastical fashion of keeping confessions private,' Cieran explained. 'The Abbot of Ardmór absolved countless folk of their sins but he never thought that their crimes should be for his ears alone. The man who murdered your brother was one among many who told the abbot of his misdeeds and then sought absolution. Declan assured me that the killing was done in self-defence and so it could not be accounted as a mortal sin.'

'Who did it?' Seginus snarled, losing patience again.

'The murderer was one of the monks who had arrived in Eirinn with Palladius.'

'Don't talk rubbish!'

'I was told that Linus had made unseemly advances to the brother in question and that in defending himself the young monk inadvertently struck a death blow. Palladius knew the full truth almost from the morning of the murder but he contrived to use the death to further the conversion of my tribespeople. A martyr's shrine is a good focus for an evangelical mission. The bishop was aware that Declan knew the circumstances of the murder and so he shrewdly elevated him to the rank of abbot. Palladius thought that he needed to buy Declan's silence when in fact my friend the abbot kept the matter to himself through loyalty to the murderer. That is of course until he told me about it.' Cieran was struggling to breathe now and Seginus heard him move about again trying to get comfortable.

'I must rest,' the Hibernian mumbled.

'If this tale is true you have broken the sacred bond of confession by telling me about it,' Seginus hissed. 'Your crimes will take you to the very gates of Hell.'

'I will face the justice of my God ere this day is ended, Roman.' Cieran coughed again hoarsely. 'And soon enough we may both meet again before the throne of the Almighty. There is nothing in my heart that would cause me to fear that time but I am not so certain that you have as clear a conscience so look to your own sins before you judge me.'

Seginus quickly sneered back at the Hibernian, 'Do you really expect me to believe a far-fetched story about a holy monk killing my brother and then escaping discovery with the full knowledge and complicity of Palladius?'

'It is too late now for me to argue with you.' Cieran paused as his body was wracked by violent coughs. 'I have a favour to ask of you,' he managed finally. 'I want you to take something for me.' A moment later a metal object attached to a fine chain landed on the floor near Seginus. 'It is my cross,' the Hibernian explained.

Seginus fumbled about until he found it. When the Roman held it tightly in his hand clasping it, he found that it was still warm from being worn so close to the skin. He suddenly felt very strange to have been talking with Cieran for so long yet not to have seen or touched his companion.

'If you are ever in Eirinn again take the cross to Ardmór and place it on the tomb of your brother. If you pray for me then I will perhaps one day find peace.'

Seginus considered refusing the request but he was angry and confused. Why should he do anything for this lying heretic? A voice within reminded him that he owed his life to this Hibernian and he could not bring himself to decline Cieran's entreaty. 'I will do as you ask,' he said.

The heretic breathed loudly out through his mouth and then there was no further sound from him. Either he had decided that he had said all that he was going to or he had slipped into a state of merciful oblivion.

Seginus Gallus had no choice but to sit back against the wall once more and wait for his companion to stir. While he waited he clutched the heretic's cross and he thought long and hard about all that Cieran had told him. Seginus was finding it difficult to admit that he could have been so wrong about Palladius for so many years. He did not want to believe that the bishop had taken advantage of the situation simply to provide his cause with a martyr. Would Palladius have lied to him? He did not want to face that possibility and he did not want to believe that his brother Linus had never really been a saint enthroned with all the others in heaven.

After going over all that he had been told many times, Seginus came to the conclusion that if the heretic's story were true it would be only too easy to prove. There were six monks in the party that landed at Ardmór. There was Linus and himself who were half-brothers through their common father. Palladius the bishop and Declan or Declinu as he was known in those days. Naturally the bishop was above suspicion but Seginus also had a strong feeling that Declan had nothing to do with the murder, for though he was misguided he was very gentle. Then there was Donatus the old scribe who had died at Teamhair. He had been a very godly fellow but he would never have confessed to Declan even if the abbot were the last cleric in Christendom. The two men had no time for each other.

However, there was one other monk in the group that had landed at Ardmór. His name was Isernus. He had been a novice when they arrived in Hibernia, quickly rising under Declan's tutoring to become a fully ordained priest. Seginus recalled that Cieran had mentioned that the killer was a younger monk. Then the Roman suddenly remembered something that he had not thought about for many years.

Linus and Isernus had been good friends, spending all their spare time together night and day. Donatus had often joked that Isernus was closer to Linus than his own flesh and blood. Indeed, now that Seginus thought hard about it, he had to admit that his brother's early preference for the close company of males over that of womenfolk had always been an embarrassment to the family. And the main reason that Seginus and Linus came to be with the mission to Hibernia was that a minor scandal had erupted in the monastery of Saint Eli. Linus had become close to the chief scribe of the community and this proved his undoing for there were others who noticed the attention that the older man heaped on his pupil. As a result Linus was given into the care of his brother and the two of them effectively banished from the monastery.

The Abbot of Eli did not actually order them to leave his community but he made it clear that it would have been very undesirable for them to remain there.

'Is it possible that Linus made advances to Isernus,' Seginus mumbled to himself, 'and that the novice killed him in self-defence?' The implications were immediately apparent to Seginus. If this were the case then not only was the claim to his brother's sainthood false but it was also certain that Palladius knew who had really committed the crime. The old bishop never missed anything that happened anywhere in the monastic community. It was just possible, Seginus reasoned, that Palladius had made a conscious decision to present Linus as a martyr in order to build up a following among the Hibernian people.

The bishop had often played little tricks on the Hibernians to win them to the Cross. There was the time when he had put a mild poison into the daily milk of the chieftain's son. Each morning Palladius increased the dose until the poor little wretch was weakened and very near to death. Then finally the bishop had convinced the chieftain to lay his son on the tombstone of Saint Linus offering up earnest prayers for a cure. After that Palladius simply neglected to add the regular dose of poison. Within a few days the lad had recovered completely, much to the chieftain's joy and to the everlasting wonderment of his tribespeople. That little show of the power of saintliness had persuaded many of the Hibernians to be baptised into the faith.

'If the old man could find it in his heart to so mislead the Hibernians and not suffer any pangs of conscience, could he also have contrived to misrepresent the death of my brother, even to me?' Seginus wondered aloud.

Somewhere in the far corner Cieran gave an exhausted cough and rolled around on the floor getting as comfortable as he could.

'What are you thinking?' Seginus rebuked himself under his breath. 'Would you believe the words of a heretic over those of your venerable teacher?'

He pulled his knees up to his chest and resolved to try to sleep to pass away the time. Seginus could not sleep though. He spent many hours turning this way and that, exhausted but unable to find rest while his mind remained uneasy about the past. Lying on the hard floor was beginning to take a toll of his muscles and joints. His legs and arms were aching from the damp. His breathing was becoming steadily more painful and strained.

In the end he was so tired that he began to doze fitfully and in the half-conscious state that took hold before dreaming Seginus recalled many incidents that he had not thought about since the first days in Ardmór.

His conscience told him that he had used his brother's death as an excuse for a merciless attitude toward the Hibernians. Seginus had been personally responsible for the crucifixion of one heathen warrior whose only crime was that he had insulted the Roman.

At the time Seginus had regarded the death penalty as the only appropriate punishment for any of the uncivilised folk of Hibernia who refused to take to the ways of Rome. He had conveniently laid the blame for all the ills that had befallen him since Ardmór at the feet of that warrior.

Seginus concentrated and discovered that he could still clearly visualise his victim's savage painted face contorting in agony as the long iron nails were driven into his wrists. He could still hear the stifled breathing of the warrior as the captive slowly suffocated under his own weight high on the cross. Or was that the laboured breathing of Cieran that he heard in the darkness? The perpetual night in this cell distorted his senses, allowing the pictures in his head to come to life with sound, scent and texture to accompany them. The foul odour of death stung his nostrils and he tasted the coppery flavour of blood in his mouth though he was certain that he was not bleeding.

In his mind he looked again at the crucified savage of his memories. The fellow looked down at him as he had never done on the day of his execution. The warrior's swollen face was cut, smashed where the soldiers had beaten him mercilessly, but nevertheless Seginus was able to recognise him. Suddenly the warrior's face changed dramatically and the features became shockingly familiar.

Like the painting over the altar of the monastery at Saint Eli, the eyes were full of compassion and a crown of sharp thorns adorned the head.

'This is only my mind playing tricks on me because I have been deprived of food and sleep and light,' Seginus said aloud to reassure himself, but he could not banish the scene from his mind. The Roman tried to look away from the warrior and was drawn to another cross standing behind the first upon which a boy was hanging. Then he remembered that there had been one other Hibernian executed that same day.

The dying warrior on the nearer cross opened his mouth to speak as Seginus struggled harder to block him out of his thoughts. 'Last night a stranger came to my door,' said the heathen. 'I gave him food and drink and played fine music for him.

Then I gave him a sleeping place by the fire and a well-woven wool cover. In the morning he blest me and my kinfolk and outside I heard the birds singing, "Often goes the Christ in the guise of a stranger".'

Seginus felt his guts churn painfully. He sat bolt upright again, stretching his legs out. The monk had an unnerving sensation that the room was spinning slowly around as if by some cunning in its construction it was free to roll independent of the rest of the building's foundations.

His whole body tensed and he strove desperately to drive the images of the two crucified heathens out of his head. 'It is only the result of too little food and sleep,' he kept repeating to himself, and after a little while the spinning stopped but Seginus felt his stomach heave and he dropped his head forward onto his chest to still the persistent dizziness in his skull. He drove the heels of his hands into the sockets of his eyes and pressed until he thought they would crush the front of his skull. Then he gently rocked his body back and forth to soothe the pain.

SIX

Long after, just as Seginus was beginning to feel a little better and to think more clearly, he heard a noise on the other side of the room and lifted his eyes, though he knew full well he would not be able to see anything. For a moment all was still and dark as it had been since the moment he had been imprisoned in the chamber. Suddenly a voice coldly cut through the eternal night.

'Are you all right, brother?' it whispered.

Seginus knew immediately that the speaker was not Cieran for the accent was distinctly different from that of an Hibernian.

'Are you well?' the voice insisted lowly.

'I will be fine in a little while,' Seginus answered, hoping that this was not another trick that his senses were playing. 'Who are you? And where did you come from?'

'Don't you recognise me?' came the injured reply, half mocking and breathy.

'No, I cannot see your face.' The Roman was by this time shaking with fear once again. The observer part of him was sure that something was not right but the monk could not put a finger on exactly what it was that was upsetting him. 'It is too dark for me to see you,' Seginus added.

'That is easily fixed.'

Suddenly the room was full of light, bright orange and painful to look upon. The figure of a

84

man stood behind the source of the illumination so that Seginus could only vaguely discern his outline. The figure was dressed in the long robes of a monk and was leaning on a long staff like a shepherd's crook.

'Who are you?' Seginus repeated, trying to contain his fright.

The only answer he received was laughter. In the next instant the light went out again so that Seginus gasped in surprise at being plunged so totally into a void of blackness once more.

Less than a heartbeat later the Roman felt someone's breath on his face. Such was his surprise that his body jerked around on the floor for a few seconds. It took him a few moments before he could bring himself to put a hand up gingerly in front of him to discover the source of the breath. His fingers found a cold clammy surface that felt as though it was covered in a thick coating of beeswax. His fingertips traced their way up toward what he thought was the nose. The breath seemed to be coming from here.

'But there is no life in this flesh,' he told himself detachedly.

The thought had no sooner crossed his mind than the powerful light reappeared, this time illuminating a foul misshapen face before him. It was some moments before the monk's eyes adjusted to the fierce brightness. But when he could clearly see the face, Seginus was dumbstruck. He gulped the air into his body trying to gather the force to make a sound but the breath refused to leave his lungs again. His hands shook. His mouth dried up. He was so overcome with terror that his whole upper torso began to retch and heave with profound shock. He stared forward wide-eyed at his unexpected guest. There was no doubt in his mind now that this was no human visitation.

Solemnly the monster formed its bony face into an evil and twisted sneer as it raised a hand to its lips touching the fingers gently with a kiss. Awed, Seginus watched the demon softly drop the hand forward and blow the kiss toward him as a young girl might playfully tease her beloved. The gesture passed between them along an invisible route but it struck Seginus like a cold winter gale. His head jolted sharply back against the wall and at the very moment that it touched the skin on his cheek the power to breathe returned to him.

It was as if some invisible bond had been lifted and discarded. Suddenly he found that he had been granted the ability to speak once more and the words burst out of him in a flood of fear.

'By sweet Christ and all the armies of heaven,' he wailed, 'get away from me, you demon!'

The creature grinned wide and stared Seginus in the face with unblinking eyes that were surrounded by countless folds of wrinkled flesh. Then a low evil laugh welled up in the being and it began to heave in amusement.

Terrified, Seginus put his hand up before him so that he would not have to see the monster looking at him and as he did so he heard a loud shuffle moving across the room. The monk instinctively dropped his hand from his face so that he could see exactly what the demon was up to. For no apparent reason it had crossed the room and was now sitting on an altar-like stone at the other side of the cell. The monster dangled its feet back and forth playfully.

'Hello, brother, don't you know your own flesh and blood when you see it?'

Careful not to move any closer than was absolutely necessary, Seginus began to study this evil-looking monster that had addressed him as brother. The creature returned the monk's show of interest by giggling grotesquely at him and baring its blackened teeth. The air became chill all of a sudden so that the Roman thought his blood would freeze. The cold set his teeth to chattering wildly and rendered him utterly speechless.

When he was younger Seginus had read a treatise by Saint Augustine warning the unwary about the power of wicked spirits to beguile their chosen victims. To his frustration he could not now remember any of the powerful prayers that the great saint had recommended for the banishment of such servants of the Devil. The harder he tried to remember the charms the louder the monster laughed, blocking out all his thoughts. Eventually he convinced himself that none of what he heard or saw was real. He told himself that Satan had sent this apparition to try him and to tempt him to the ways of evil.

He tried to think what Palladius would do if he were in this same situation. In a flash he knew what he must do. Seginus rose up off the floor even though his legs were weak and he felt very dizzy. He was determined to make a stand against this creature of darkness.

As he gained his feet he saw an expression on the spirit's face that had the unmistakable stamp of his half-brother. There was a cheeky taint to the ghastly sniggers that could only be inherited from their common father. The eyes though grey and dead were the eyes of the boy's mother, the servant woman their father had often bedded. His resolve melted away and he leaned against the wall, slipping down to the floor again to sit with his knees buckled in front of him.

'Linus,' he stammered after a long pause, 'I know that it is you.' The spirit laughed raucously at the monk's obvious discomfort. Seginus could feel the earth beneath him thudding in time with his brother's laughter as though the drums of Hell were accompanying his merriment.

'If you are my brother,' Seginus called out over the din, 'or I am in the clutches of the Devil, I beg you to tell me what is happening.'

The walls shook in a deep rumble as the drumming ceased and a chorus of laughter broke out all around where Seginus sat. 'Am I going mad? Where am I?' the Roman screamed over the tumult. 'Am I dead? Am I in Hell?'

The phantom burst out into renewed guffaws unable to contain its amusement until finally it lapsed into a fit of coughing and gulping. The stones of the prison cell rang with the icy sound of devilish chortles. There were definitely other spirits joining in now; Seginus could distinguish several voices clearly and he realised that he was surrounded.

When it had calmed itself down a little the spirit levelled its gaze at Seginus and the other creatures seemed to follow its lead so that all became quiet. Then the ghost of Linus spoke again. 'You are not dead yet, big brother. Nor are you in Hell. Not yet.'

The apparition moved with frightening speed to stand so close before Seginus again that the Roman could clearly discern the pores of its skin glistening with a foul-smelling sweat.

'But I will let you in on a little secret,' the spectre whispered.

A bony finger motioned for Seginus to come closer and the monk gritted his teeth knowing that he had no choice but to do as it commanded. He could smell its putrid breath as it spoke.

'One of us is very dead indeed!' The spirit cackled, throwing its head back and screaming with amusement at its little joke. As its hideous sniggers died away the ghost drifted back across the room toward its seat on the altar. There it settled down to observe its victim and the room fell deathly quiet again. The creature's stare was hostile and accusing, full of disgust for the mortal who sat opposite it.

Seginus was still clutching Cieran's cross. The brass arms of it cut into his hand from squeezing it so tightly. He quickly scanned the room looking for the Hibernian but the man was nowhere to be seen. The stillness was beginning to have a very calming affect on Seginus. He relaxed a little, telling himself that this was just a dream.

Gathering his wits the monk shut his eyes in order to banish the vision before him and he softly recited a prayer from the writings of Saint Gregory. 'O Christ, give me strength. Your servant is not what he was.'

He stopped at the end of that line and listened to his own words reverberating around the chamber. There was no other sound. 'The tongue that once praised you has been idle. How can you forgive me?' Once more he waited for a moment to hear his words echoing in the room but this time he was not sure if he had heard another voice joining him, almost in a whisper.

'Give your servant strength. Do not cast me aside.' Now he was certain that someone was following his prayer word for word. 'O to be healed of my hurts.' The other voice gained intensity at this phrase but Seginus decided to ignore it. 'To preach once more of the salvation that you offer and to wash the people clean.' The monk was determined not to open his eyes to look on the creature that he knew was praying with him. He refused to give the spirit any more power over him. 'Do not forsake me, I beseech you. When the storm gathered around me, I betrayed you but let me return to you now!'

The ghost wailed mournfully at the last line of the prayer but Seginus was stronger now. He knew that it had a weakness. The monk made the sign of the cross and kissed Cieran's crucifix that he still held in his right hand. When that was done he opened his eyes at last. The ghost was kneeling at the altar now with its back to him. It seemed to be sobbing.

'What do you want with me?' Seginus demanded.

The phantom stood and turned to face the seated monk. There were tears flowing down its cheeks and its eyes were a bright unearthly red. 'I have come to beg your indulgence, big brother.' Twisted facial muscles distorted the ghostly lips into a pathetic smile.

'How can I help you?' Seginus pressed, determined to remain unafraid.

'My troubled soul seeks for eternal peace.'

'I will pray for you.'

'I need more than empty prayers. All the adoration that is heaped upon my tomb has not saved me from the torments that wait beyond life. You made a promise to me when they found my body. Now is the time to keep that pledge. Only in this way can I find peace.'

'What promise did I make to you?' Seginus ventured reluctantly. 'I do not remember any promise.'

'You vowed to seek revenge for my death,' the ghost hissed.

'If you really are the spirit of my brother Linus then you must know that I avenged your death nine years ago,' the Roman snapped.

'Revenge! You call that revenge! Surely you don't mean the poor Hibernian warrior that you had crucified. Or are you referring to the farm boy that you hung beside him?' There was a bitterness in the creature's voice that lingered in the air long after the words were spoken. 'True revenge involves tracking down the person actually responsible for a misdeed and then dealing with them satisfactorily. Executing some scapegoat isn't good enough. Our father was right. You are stupid and useless.'

'Be quiet, you devil, or I will banish you back to the realms of Hell where you belong.'

'Careful you do not prepare your own welcome in Satan's city, big brother.' With lightning swiftness the ghost rushed at Seginus. As soon as it was very close to him once more it hissed urgently, 'Promise to help release me from my bonds and I will help you to escape this prison.'

'What are you talking about?'

'Until I am avenged I can find no peace!' the creature shrieked. 'You hanged a man and a boy on crosses at Rathowen but it was not they nor any of their people who murdered me. You acted unjustly in my name and now I am answering for your misconduct. If you have pity enough to want to help alleviate my pain then you must seek the man who sent me to this place of suffering. Dispatch him to me so that I can confront him as an equal. Only then will I have a chance of freedom from the sins I committed in life and from those perpetrated after my death in my name.'

'If it was not one of the Hibernians who murdered you, then who was it?' Seginus blurted.

The creature stifled another laugh. 'Can you be so stupid? Have you not been told plainly who the man was?' Suddenly the hideous face contorted further in its rage and the ghost moved closer, forcing Seginus to press himself up against the wall behind him. 'Are you truly so pig-headed that you refuse to accept the truth?' it spat. 'Seek out my killer and send him to me or by all that is holy to you I swear that you will join me here in this undead world where I dwell and we will wait out the rest of eternity in torture together.'

Despite his earlier resolution not to be afraid Seginus found himself shaking uncontrollably. He tried to convince himself that this conversation was too bizarre to be anything but a wild dream.

As if it had read his thoughts the ghost immediately whispered, 'This is no product of your imagination. I am as real as the wall you are sheltering against.'

Seginus knew only that he wanted rid of the spirit and so he decided it would be best to placate it if possible. 'Very well. I will do as you ask,' he mumbled.

Almost before the words were out of his mouth a cold hand caught at his throat and squeezed. 'Promise me,' the creature demanded.

'I promise,' Seginus grunted, his eyes wide with fear. The cold waxy fingers tightened a little more about the Roman's windpipe, gradually throttling him, turning his face purple with their uncanny strength. The ghostly eyes became balls of fire set in black stone sockets, the unearthly mouth curled its lips into a grimacing snarl. Then just as suddenly as it had begun its stranglehold, it let go its grip and the eerie lights in the chamber went out, plunging the cell into infinite darkness once more.

Though the lights were gone Seginus could still make out the blue-grey outline of his tormentor as it squatted like an animal in the corner. As he watched it became a wisp of smoke. It dispersed and scattered but it had no sooner disappeared than it was reforming itself again into a more pleasing human shape. The room filled with a blue tinged light that was gentle and soothing. Seginus could see Linus clearly and he seemed to be wearing a hint of compassion on his face where only hatred had burned just moments before.

'*You* may leave this cell whenever you wish,' the demon announced, emphasising its own bitterness at remaining imprisoned. When it seemed certain that Seginus had got the point of his last remark, Linus drifted back to the far side of the chamber.

Abruptly the Roman felt at ease, as though he had been bound fast by strong ropes for many weeks but had just been set free. He could sense that this creature would not harm him now for he had made a solemn covenant with it. But no matter how he looked at the spirit he could not bring himself to think of it as his brother or even as the disembodied spirit of his brother. This thing was too hideous to be his own flesh and blood.

Suddenly there was a loud clanging of metal outside the cell. The rattling of heavy iron chains against the inner doors of the prison filled the chamber with noise. Some instinct led Seginus to find the little pouch that held Murrough's seal ring and to place Cieran's cross carefully inside where it would be safe.

Just as he finished concealing the cross a shaft of lantern light poured into the little room, dispersing the gentle blue glow. Seginus had to close his eyes and cover them with his cloak for they could not adjust immediately to the lamp's yellow brightness.

'That's him,' a gruff and disinterested voice confirmed. A few breaths later strong hands came down on Seginus, lifting him under the arms and dragging him to his feet.

'Take him to the audience chambers,' the voice commanded.

The bright beams of the lantern caused the Roman to squint whenever he tried to look about him. Even so, he managed quickly to examine the room in the light. He was relieved to find that the ghost of his brother was gone. In the corner where the spirit had hovered over a stone tomb a body lay curled and motionless. The man's legs were drawn up close to his chest in the same way that Seginus had been sitting just before he had the strange visitation.

For a horrible moment the monk speculated that he might be looking on his own corpse and that perhaps these hands that lifted him now belonged to the Devil's brood come to take him to the places of punishment. He did not have time to panic before the figure in the corner moved, slowly raising himself on his elbows.

In the lantern light the monk saw clearly that the figure was Cieran. Even after all these years he recognised the man who had sheltered him in his last days in Eirinn. It was plain, however, that the Hibernian could not see Seginus for where his eyes should have been there were only empty blood-clotted holes. Streams of dark red had run down Cieran's cheeks to spatter across his neck and bare chest. The man coughed then spoke a few words in the Gaelic language. Seginus was surprised that he could understand well enough what was said.

'Farewell, brother,' Cieran sighed. 'Pray for my soul and may God bless you.'

Then the Hibernian curled up again and rolled over on to his side. It was a few seconds before Seginus could think of a reply in the strange Gaelic tongue and by the time he had come up with something he was being dragged out of the cell by the guards. He struggled for a moment and called back over his shoulder, 'An Ainm Athar, An Ainm Mhic, An Ainm Spiórad.'

He tried to fight off the strong hands that held him. There was one thought now in his mind: to return and save Cieran from his prison cell. The warriors who held him, however, were too powerful and Seginus was too weak from his stay in the dungeon. His protests were ignored and the guards easily hauled him up a long flight of stairs with his feet catching on every stone step as if they were sacks filled with wheat.

They had not gone far when Seginus realised that the first Gaelic phrase that had come into his head had been a blessing which was popular with the Hibernian Christians. The words invoked the names of the Father, the Son and the Spirit and was commonly used to summon God into the presence of the dying.

SEVEN

fter climbing twenty steep steps the escort came to a large wooden door reinforced with wide strips of iron. It swung open before them as they approached, giving access to the corridor above. The guards extinguished their lanterns as they passed through into the natural light of the passage. Seginus was still having difficulty on his feet so a warrior was positioned on either side of him. From here on he was carried on their shoulders through the bishop's palace.

They passed a window at ground level on their way to the more secure parts of the fortress and Seginus was struck by the beauty of the world outside. The daylight was more vibrant and colourful than he could ever recall. They quickly passed the window marching on into the heart of the building. Seginus could see that although the palace was primarily a fortification it was nevertheless sumptuously decorated. In fact, as they climbed the stairs to the upper levels, Seginus noted that the passageways were conspicuously strewn with gold and silver ornaments.

Fine embroideries hung behind brightly painted statues in a fashion that had been popular in Rome before the barbarians sacked the city. There were water jugs and bowls everywhere for guests to wash their faces and hands in, and the stone floor had been scrubbed so smooth that it was shiny in places. A scent of flowers filled the air indicating the bishop's passion for rich oils from the Holy Lands. Seginus had not seen interiors like these since he had been to the Papal palace in Ravenna. He found it hard to believe that such luxury could exist in such dangerous times.

Suddenly they rounded a corner in the corridor and came to a pair of large doors. Seginus felt the guards lower him carelessly onto the floor and there he lay for a few minutes while their officer banged his fist on the timbers to summon the door-keep.

The cold flagstones made his hands tingle as he flattened his palms out on them. He revelled in the feeling of being alive. Now that he was seeing the light of day, breathing in fresh scented oils, feeling once again all the sensations of his body, he found it easier to believe that he had been suffering some delusion when he had seemed to be talking with his brother's ghost. This moment was real, he told himself, and there was no doubt that he was no longer dreaming. The dull pain in his legs and arms and the dryness in his throat from thirst told him that he was wide awake.

'It was only an hallucination brought on by the darkness and a lack of food,' Seginus said aloud.

The guard who had supported the monk's right shoulder heard him speak and so he leaned down and whispered, 'Not many live to tell the tale of their stay in the bishop's guesthouse. You would be best advised to treat the whole experience as if it never happened. Mark my words, speak of it to no-one or the bishop will have you back there again.'

'But the ghost knew my name and all about me,' Seginus insisted, still disoriented.

'Aye, well, there's bound to be a few spirits walking round down there,' the soldier replied, 'considering how many heretics have disappeared in the last few years. Just be thankful that you aren't among them.'

At last the doors squeaked open painfully slowly. Behind them two warriors stood sentry in full Imperial cavalry armour before another two great doors. Over their shoulders the horse-warriors wore bright scarlet cloaks made of fine woven wool. Seginus clutched at his own cloak. It had once been as magnificent as theirs. Now it was stitched and patched and the colour was faded. There were dark stains across it and the edges, once hemmed with tiny gold threads, were frayed and disintegrating.

The officer hauled the doors shut behind them and one of the sentries called the escort to halt. A veteran of the guard appeared from a niche to the left of the doorway. 'The bishop's not ready to see you yet,' he hissed. 'He has other guests.' Then the old soldier took hold of the prisoner's chin roughly, forcing Seginus to look him in the eye. 'It must be your lucky day, traveller. But don't get too excited—it will likely be your last.' The other soldiers laughed at the joke, careful not to be so loud that the bishop might hear them.

'Put him in the corner,' the veteran commanded the guardsmen, 'and get yourselves out of the way of the alcove doors. You never know when His Holiness will be coming out of chambers.'

Seginus caught the title 'His Holiness' and was startled by the casual use of the term. This was an expression of respect reserved for the Bishop of Rome alone as head of the mother Church. No-one in the Empire dared assume it for himself but the Pope. Seginus was confused. He knew that Celestine was an old man who rarely ventured beyond the confines of his own fortress in Ravenna. 'Is it possible that Celestine is here in Nantes?' he asked himself. 'If so, then I have a chance of meeting him.'

The prospect of successfully completing his mission once more took up all his thoughts. 'They must have realised that my letters were addressed to Celestine,' he told himself. 'My imprisonment was a mistake.'

Long after he had fully prepared and silently rehearsed his speech to the Pope, Seginus was still waiting in the alcove. No word came from within the bishop's chamber to summon him and eventually he noticed that his mind was beginning to wander. To keep himself alert he decided to study the uniforms of the warriors on guard to find out which legion they belonged to.

They were not all native Gauls, of that he was certain, for two of them spoke an Iberian dialect. Their armour was not all of the same pattern either as one might expect of soldiers who were signed on to the same military garrison. Their helms were more like the type that the Britons adopted for their mounted troops, with intricate decorations along the seams and cheekplates, not really Roman at all except for the general shape. Each trooper wore a pair of deep green cavalry trousers made of rawhide and long black riding boots. Only the two sentries at the door wore scarlet cloaks, the remainder sported cloaks the same colour as their trousers.

The trooper's swords were all of similar make. The leather scabbards were emblazoned with the Holy Cross and the name of Christ in Greek incorporated into the design, the same sign that the great Emperor Constantine had used on his banners a hundred years before. Seginus did not understand much Greek nor could he read books in that language but he recognised the letters *Chi Rho* immediately.

The monk was just beginning to speculate that these men might be mercenaries when one door to the bishop's chamber finally began to open. The gap was not wide enough to walk through when a chamberlain's head poked out. 'Bring the prisoner,' he snapped and then he slammed the door shut again.

'On yer feet, scum!' bawled the veteran, kicking Seginus in the back of the leg.

The two guards grabbed him once more and manhandled him to the doorway. When they were ready to enter, the veteran turned an iron handle and pushed against one of the doors with his shoulder. It gave way to him, rolling back to reveal a chamber about fifty paces wide completely lined with embroidered hangings.

Just by the entrance there were two golden censers set on stone pillars and it was here that the guardsmen waited. The thick smoke of an unfamiliar incense poured from these vessels and wafted about the warriors and their prisoner. Seginus could not see any further than about twenty paces into the centre of the room because of the smoke but he noticed that from the entrance there extended a long carpet of wool wide enough for three men to walk abreast. Scattered throughout the chamber he could make out the shapes of tables which seemed to be piled with scrolls, folded books and maps.

'Let him approach the Episcopal seat,' the chamberlain ordered.

The two warriors pushed Seginus forward through the smoke until he could see an impressive golden chair facing the door and set on a pedestal at the far end of the room. Upon this throne sat a small aging man dressed in long white robes. These vestments were edged with a wide purple band exactly the same as those of a Roman senator.

The man, whom Seginus guessed must be none other than the Bishop of Nantes, wore a strange hat the like of which he had never seen before. The head piece was high and had two points at the very top and it was richly decorated with gold and green thread. From beneath the strange hat, black locks of freshly oiled hair, obviously dyed to cover encroaching grey, flowed out like water from a fountain to fall across the bishop's shoulders. Some of the curled strands were arranged to edge the man's thin wrinkled face. Seginus was not taken in by the dyed hair. By the fellow's face he judged him to be about the same age as Palladius, who was sixty years old or thereabouts.

Around the gold throne there were four small stools all but one of which were occupied by other guests. The spare seat was set apart from the others. The guests all faced the bishop's chair and for that reason Seginus could not see the other faces.

'Kneel to His Holiness, Julius, by the grace of God, Bishop of Nantes,' the chamberlain intoned.

Seginus was stunned by the use of the term 'His Holiness' with regard to a mere bishop of a former Roman province, but he knelt and waited for the expected summons to rise. It was apparent that the Pope was not here in Nantes after all, for Celestine loved protocol. He would not have tolerated another man using his title.

There were whispers in the chamber but Seginus kept his eyes on the carpet in front of him and did not let his disappointment show. Though he could not hear what was being said he was sure that the discussion centred around his appearance. After a short while there was some laughter and a high-pitched voice almost jolly in tone said, 'You soldiers may leave us. Chamberlain, go and see to the preparations for supper.' The warriors immediately withdrew and the door slammed shut again, leaving Seginus still kneeling on the woollen carpet and feeling rather ridiculous.

'So this is Seginus Gallus the servant of Palladius,' the same voice purred. 'You may rise, Gallus, and take a seat with my other visitors.'

Seginus struggled to his feet. He still felt very weak and he realised that he must have been locked in the cell with Cieran much longer than he had assumed. He stood still for a moment trying to hold his balance, his head spinning a little from hunger and from rising too quickly. Cramps had slowed his muscles and his throat was so dry it felt like it was lined with sawdust. As he moved to the spare seat he heard someone pouring watered wine into a cup and he stopped in his tracks to watch the guest, drawn by the sweet sound of falling liquid. He was once again acutely aware of the dryness in his throat.

The guest with the wine jug immediately offered a silver cup to Seginus. The monk snatched it and gulped the refreshment down. Such was the urgency of his thirst that he spilled most of it on the carpet but did not care that he might offend his host with his eagerness. Everyone in the chamber politely ignored him and when he was finished Seginus handed the cup directly back to the man who had poured him the drink. As the stranger took the cup the monk looked at his face for the first time and he nearly fell over in shock.

'Palladius!' Seginus stammered, rubbing his eyes.

'No, no,' a woman's voice interrupted. 'This is Patricius Sucatus, the emissary of the Pope Celestine.'

Seginus examined the man before him a little more closely. The resemblance to his teacher was remarkable but surely this Patricius was much much younger than Palladius. He wore robes of dark brown, not of black as the old teacher did, and his hair was a chestnut brown. The monk had only known Palladius to have quite dark or greying hair. The other thing that Seginus noticed almost immediately about the Pope's emissary was a gentleness in the eyes that Palladius never had.

'I beg your pardon, Patricius, I have not been well of late and my eyes are playing tricks on me,' Seginus apologised.

'Sit down now, Gallus,' Julius urged in his firm but not completely unfriendly manner. 'We have much to discuss.'

Still dazed, Seginus found the one empty stool and sank onto it, relieved that he could rest his legs. He looked around at the others who were seated before Julius. A young noblewoman dressed finely in undyed linen, her head veiled with some expensive-looking fabric, sat beside Patricius. On the other side of her a fair-headed monk attired in identical fashion to Patricius thumbed through his psalter as if there was no-one else in the room.

'When my troopers brought you in,' Julius stated, 'you were, shall we say, too ill to speak with me. It was my duty as the chief representative of the Holy Mother Church in the land of the Gauls to investigate you and your mission. You understand that I had to make sure that you were not an Arian evangeliser or a Frankish spy. As a consequence

I found it necessary to examine the letters that you were bearing to Rome and I have come to know much else about you from inquiries with some of your former colleagues in the Monastery of Eli. So take care that you answer all the questions that are put to you honestly and to the best of your knowledge. If you fail to do so or if you attempt to deceive me in any way you will be returned immediately to the chamber where I had you so recently lodged. I do not need to tell you that if that happens neither I nor anyone else will be sending for you ever again.'

'Yes, lord.'

'Now first of all,' Julius went on, satisfied with the prisoner's compliance, 'you were once a soldier I am told.'

Seginus nodded.

'Is it true that you were stationed in the Saxon lands and so speak the language of that people?'

'Yes, lord.'

'Good,' the bishop smiled, obviously pleased. 'Do you understand the Frankish speech?'

'I understand what is said but I cannot always respond quickly. Their language is merely one dialect of the great family of Allemani tongues, one of which is the native speech of the Saxons.'

'Very good. I can see that a man of your talent would be a great asset to the Church in these times of war with the heathen German tribes. You travelled through the Saxon lands of Britain on your journey here, did you not?'

'Yes, lord. My servants and myself posed as wine merchants who had been robbed in the north by Gaelic brigands. Obviously possessing nothing worth stealing we passed unmolested through the lands that are controlled by the heathen.'

'If you could find your way successfully from the edge of the old empire to Gaul, I imagine that it would not be difficult for you to arrange the safe passage of my guests through seas that are the haunt of the Saxon longships,' Julius stated.

'That depends on what their final destination might be, lord. There are many German tribes besides the Saxons in Britain and some of them will raid even each other if they think it worthwhile.'

'Patricius Sucatus and his mission are sailing for Hibernia,' the bishop announced matter-of-factly, but keeping a sharp eye on the monk's response.

Seginus felt the colour immediately drain from his face. The bishop smiled almost imperceptibly, very satisfied with the answers that he was getting. 'I have heard that you were with Palladius during his disastrous episcopal appointment to Hibernia,' said Julius, feigning disinterest.

Once again Seginus nodded in assent. He had a terrible feeling about where this line of questioning was leading.

'Then you speak the Hibernian language also.' The bishop did not give Seginus the opportunity to confirm or deny his statement but turned directly to the Pope's emissary. 'There you are then, my dear Patricius, we have managed to find you a guide without too much trouble. Gallus can safely lead you through the Saxon seas and then on to the court of the Hibernian emperor. Now there remains the question of the troops under your command. Obviously you won't be needing them all for the journey now that you are travelling with a guide who will keep you from harm. At the same time I would ask you to remember that the lands under my protection are constantly harried by Frankish raiders. It is my prayer that you will be able to see your way clear to assign your entire escort to me.'

'I will give you half my legionnaires, Julius, no more,' Patricius replied. 'For I do not know what dangers the road holds for us.'

'Twelve men!' Julius mocked. 'You would leave me twelve men? What use are a dozen soldiers without another dozen to back them up?' Julius did not raise his voice but it was plain that he was very displeased.

Patricius smiled back at his host. 'You may take the offer or leave it,' he stated. 'I am making it out of charity for your need and prudence for the future.'

There was a brief silence as Julius considered the legate's words. 'Since you have only twelve men to give I will accept your offer graciously,' he answered sweetly, smiling and waving his hand in the air in an ambiguously flowery gesture.

Seginus listened with interest to all that passed between these two men. On the surface the exchange between the Bishop of Nantes and Patricius Sucatus was polite and respectful, but it was obvious that Julius was only making a thin show of courtesy which certainly did not reflect his true feelings on the matter.

Patricius half-turned in his seat to face Seginus. 'Why did Palladius send you with letters to Gaul?'

'Have you not read my master's correspondence also?'

'No,' replied Patricius. 'I have not had the opportunity as yet.'

'Unfortunately,' Julius interrupted apologetically, 'all the parchments that Gallus was carrying with him were destroyed by one of my thoughtless guards who did not realise the full value of the documents. The letters are now beyond interpretation, I am afraid.'

'That is a great pity,' Patricius remarked, not at all surprised at this development. 'Pope Celestine will be most upset at the loss of those papers. The Church is currently trying to judge the case of the so-called martyr Linus of Hibernia, and those documents could have revealed something about the character of the man who is supposed to have witnessed and consecrated the martyrdom.'

'Please express my sincere regrets to His Holiness, won't you,' Julius sighed insincerely.

Patricius turned back to Seginus. 'Did you know of the alleged saint called Linus?'

'He was my half-brother,' the monk blurted and instantly regretted the admission.

The legate's eyes opened wide. 'Then I have been most fortunate in finding you. Your brother's cult has a large following in the southern kingdom of Munster, I believe. But the people there have never really taken on the mantle of the Cross, have they? It is said that they have Arian heretics in their midst, even devilish Pelagians and abominable Coptic monks from Africa.'

'There have been Egyptians who have lived the monastic life in Hibernia since before the father of Saint Ambrose was Praetorian Prefect of Gaul,' Seginus confirmed. 'I know of one who lives in the High-King's household. There may be some Arians in the kingdoms but it is the native priests who present the most danger to Christian folk. These priests are called Druids as they were in Gaul before the coming of Rome. I myself once saw a woman of the Druids weave a spell over the soldiers of Palladius that caused the strength of our mighty army to melt away and so lose a great battle. Shortly afterwards Palladius was imprisoned by the Hibernian Emperor.'

Patricius raised his eyebrows and began to speak as if he were addressing the Senate of old Rome rather than talking as a guest in the bishop's palace. 'If he was so easily defeated by the servants of Satan, then perhaps he was not favoured by God as rightful Bishop of Eirinn. Is it true that Palladius himself was once a follower of the Persian sorcerer who is called Mani?'

Seginus coughed loudly, choking at the suggestion. The charge of being a Manichee was much worse than that of being a simple heretic. Heretics were merely Christians gone wrong. It was well known that the Manichees openly worshipped the Devil, often swaying Christians to their ways by the use of black magic. Saint Ambrose had written four books condemning this evil and powerful sect.

Seginus realised then and there that Palladius would probably never be repatriated by the Roman Orthodox Church. The old man had failed in his embassy and endangered the apostolic mission in Eirinn. Palladius was an embarrassment to Rome. Now his peers would do all in their power to discredit him by rumour, innuendo and the spreading of outright lies so that the former bishop would never have the chance to make the same mistake again.

'I cannot say with certainty,' Seginus offered diplomatically after a long pause, 'anything about the life of Palladius before he came to the Faith for he never spoke about his own experiences.'

'Never mind,' shrugged Patricius, 'I will find out sooner or later. I am building quite a case against Palladius and his false martyr. I must confess that I am quite surprised that he managed to convince the Pope to send him to Hibernia in the first place or that he persuaded an intelligent man such as yourself to accompany him.'

Seginus heard the legate's words and quickly understood his own predicament. He instantly knew that if he did not do exactly as he was ordered by these men he would surely be charged as an accomplice to heresy and heathenism. A charge such as that would surely lead to his execution. On the other hand, if he did as they wished he could end up being instrumental in his own master's death or excommunication.

'I cannot help the cause of Palladius if I am hanging from the fortress walls on a rope,' he decided quietly. 'I must stay alive so that I may serve him in the future.'

'We will sit down soon for a long talk together,' Patricius remarked. 'You are one of the few men in Gaul who can speak with any authority on the matters of Hibernia and the customs of its people. I will value what you have to tell me of the land over which my bishopric has been extended.'

Suddenly Seginus remembered Cieran. 'There is another dwelling within this palace who knows much more than I do.'

'Really!' Patricius exclaimed and then turning to Julius he said, 'Is the good Bishop of Nantes aware of this man?'

'He is,' Seginus replied. 'The man is known as Cieran and he was born in the lands of Hibernia. He speaks Latin, Greek and Gaelic and he is a fully ordained Christian priest.'

'Why did you not tell me about this man, brother Julius?' Patricius chided, pretending to be surprised. 'He is just the sort of fellow I have been looking for.'

'There are two main reasons,' Julius answered immediately, 'why I did not think to trouble you with the man called Cieran. First of all he spent some years as a follower of Silvanus who is yet another of the many heretics that plague the orthodoxy of Rome. From that point of view alone I thought him unsuitable for your mission but there is another factor that precludes him from helping you, brother.'

'And what is that, brother Julius?' asked Patricius full of suspicion.

The Bishop of Nantes drew his lips back over his teeth in a strained smile, rolled his eyes and threw his hands in the air to signal his powerlessness. 'He is dead.'

'That would make his advice difficult to interpret,' Patricius quipped as if he had expected the man's demise. 'I think it is time I attended chapel.' The legate rose from his seat and his two companions followed suit. 'With your leave, brother Julius, I will take Gallus with me.'

'I place him under your protection,' Julius replied.

'Will you be attending the late Mass yourself, brother?'

The bishop stared at his guest in amusement as if the answer were obvious. 'No. Unfortunately I have many other tasks to attend to this evening. But I will see you at noon tomorrow for the blessing of the fields.'

'Alas, we must be gone before first light.'

Julius flashed a determined glare at Patricius. 'I don't think you will be leaving before tomorrow. It is a feast day. There will be no-one available from my staff to tend to your horses. And it would offend my congregation if you left so soon after your arrival. It is not every day that we receive the honour of a visit from a Papal legation. Take your leisure while you may before setting out again. You may peruse my library if you wish. I will order the chamberlain to open it to you.'

Patricius met his host's gaze for a second and then dropped his eyes to the ground. 'Thank you for your advice and your hospitality, brother Julius. As always you are right. We will of course remain here under your protection as long as we are welcome.'

Julius smiled once more in his sickly-sweet manner. 'It really would be wise of you to stay here for a few more weeks, brother, and rest well before your long journey.' That said, the bishop rose and a chamberlain entered the room from behind long curtains that backed the golden episcopal chair. 'Sleep well tonight and peace be with you all,' Julius intoned, making the sign of the Cross. Then he departed through a door behind his throne before his guests had finished the traditional reply.

The very moment that the chamberlain had scuttled after his master, Patricius turned to his companions. 'Secondinus, go to the officer of our guard and tell him to prepare to leave tonight. But for God's sake tell him to keep his men quiet. I do not want to raise the suspicions of Julius unnecessarily.'

'Excuse me, Father,' asked Secondinus, 'will I tell him to select twelve men to remain here with the bishop's garrison?'

'Of course not! That is one of the reasons we are leaving tonight. We cannot afford to leave any of our escort behind.' Secondinus bowed quickly, obviously embarrassed at his own lack of perception, and departed through the main door to the chamber.

'Now, Tullia, what did your inquiries reveal?'

'I have found a boatman who will take us to North Britain. He is a trader called Lupus and he is returning there with less cargo than he expected. Apparently he did not obtain the prices he wanted for the British tin that he usually carries. His vessel is large enough to easily accommodate us all but I am afraid that there will be no room for any of the horses.'

'Very well,' replied Patricius. 'That is a great disappointment but if we were to wait for a ship owner who had room for all the mounts it could be months before we leave. Where do we meet this Lupus and when?'

'After dawn on the coast close to the old light tower,' Tullia answered.

'Well done! I am beginning to regret my initial anger at you for running off from your father. You are proving to be a great help to me. But if we are to be at the coast after dawn and have any hope of escaping the bishop's patrols we will need to leave in a few short hours. Will you go and see to the baggage and the horses, Tullia?'

'Yes, Father,' she answered and she headed to the door, departing on her errand immediately.

Patricius now turned his attention back to Seginus. 'I am sorry if I seemed a little harsh with you in front of the bishop. Are you hungry?'

The Roman nodded.

'Then come to the kitchens with me. I would rather explain everything to you in a place where there is little likelihood that we will be overheard.'

Patricius led the way out of the chamber and down the stairs to a section of the palace that was peopled only by servants who rushed about on their master's business.

'Julius keeps court like a senator,' Seginus noted.

'And he expects the rights and privileges that go with a senatorial appointment,' Patricius added. 'Though the Imperial Senate has no real power any more there are still families that covet the age-old role they played within the empire. Julius comes from just such a lineage. It is to the Church that the old bloodlines of Rome are turning since the fall of Rome, not to the senate or the army.'

They reached the kitchens just as two of the bishop's guards were departing munching loudly on legs of roast chicken and baked turnip. Patricius and Seginus approached the door and the legate lowered his voice. 'As you can see, our good Julius is as close to a military commander as Rome has any more. He organises the defence of Armorican Gaul in alliance with the Bishop of Lyon and he has the right to levy taxes and raise legions in the name of the people and senate of Rome. Power is passing into the hands of these bishops and they are using the church to fill their own grain stores.'

'Very little news of the empire reaches our community in the land of the painted folk,' Seginus admitted. 'I had no idea that the Frankish tribes had advanced this far or that Rome was no longer sending troops to the provinces.'

Patricius pushed open the door to the kitchens and ushered Seginus through. They each took a canvas bag from a stack that were meant to be used by dispatch riders, filling them with bread, apples, roast chicken and pork. Then they both took a small amphora of wine stopped with wax: a full day's ration for a soldier. The kitchen was so busy that nobody stopped to challenge them or even to ask their business. Once they had their sacks of food they left the kitchen by an outside door that led into the adjoining courtyard.

Beneath an oak tree that was encircled by a series of stone benches the two men, monk and legate, sat down to eat. The afternoon sun filtered down through the leaves, scattering patches of light across their laps like little gold coins falling from heaven. Seginus devoured the food quickly as if it had been weeks since his last meal rather than days. Patricius ate only a little then patiently waited for the monk to finish so that he would have his full attention.

When Seginus had sucked the chicken bones dry and had finished picking up the crumbs that were scattered over his tunic he broke the wax seal on his amphora. With great care he took a mouthful of red wine allowing it to enter his throat only after he had swilled it around into every corner of his mouth. In the days when he had been a soldier he would have carried three of these long pointed bottles slung from belts over his chest. His appetite for alcohol had been much greater in those days. For nearly ten years now he had barely touched a drop of good wine. His abstinence had nothing to do with the new monastic rulings that proclaimed that clerics should not indulge in strong drink. It was simply because wine was not a common beverage in North Britain.

'I have forgotten how good the vintner's red treasure can taste,' Seginus commented, using the Gaulish slang for the juice of the grape.

'Wine is also virtually unknown in Eirinn,' Patricius stated. Seginus realised almost immediately that the legate had used the Gaelic word for Hibernia. Before he could question this Patricius answered the riddle.

'I also lived in Eirinn once,' he explained. 'I dwelt there during the time of the high-king who was called Niall of the Nine Hostages. He was well known for his raids on the British coast in search of captives that he could ransom back to their families. When I was barely sixteen years old I was captured by one of Niall's raiding parties and sent to tend sheep in the wild country of the northern kingdom of Ulaid. In my three years of captivity I learned much of the language and something of the customs of Eirinn. I also grew closer to my God during that hard time and discovered that there were already many Christians among the uncivilised folk of that island. When I finally managed to escape in a little leather boat, by God's will I was landed in Gaul and there I took Holy Orders. I never really left Eirinn though. They say that if once you visit that place there is ever after something about it that burns in your heart and draws you to return. So it was that one day many years after I had left that green shore I went to Rome and gained the confidence of the Pope in my plan to bring all the Hibernians to the Cross.'

'But Julius said that you needed someone to translate for you,' Seginus remarked, a little confused.

'The Bishop of Nantes has an inflated view of his own importance in the world,' Patricius went on, lowering his voice. 'By some ancient senatorial privilege he asserts that he has the sole right to ordain bishops and priests for the islands of Britain and beyond. When I first arrived here he demanded that I hand my soldiers over into his service. When I declined he arrested two of them on some petty charge. I have only just been able to secure their release. Now Julius is insisting that he and only he has authority to ordain me as Bishop of Hibernia. I was warned far in advance about this man and so I thought it best not to reveal how much I know about Eirinn. Indeed, the more I plead ignorance the more convinced he is that I am having second thoughts about ever going there.'

'Why would he not want you to go to Hibernia and spread the word of the Cross?'

'He wants that honour for himself. You see, Pope Celestine is old and ailing. He will most certainly not live more than two or three years. Julius has his sights set on the Papacy. If he were to bring Hibernia and North Britain to the Cross it would certainly sway the college of church fathers to elect him to the bishopric of Rome.'

'Surely it would take much more than two or three years to convert all those heathen!' Seginus exclaimed.

'You do not understand,' Patricius laughed. 'If I were to fail to arrive in Eirinn that would leave Julius free to fabricate his own reports to Rome concerning the conversion of the population. Undoubtedly he would present the account with a heavy bias toward his own good works, real or not. In fact I believe that he would do anything to make himself look like a great evangelist. And he can do the whole job without ever having to leave home.'

'He is a bishop!' Seginus exclaimed. 'How can you make such accusations about a man who holds holy office?'

'You have been sheltered from politics in the land of the painted people, haven't you?' Patricius commented, not sure whether it was possible that Seginus could be so unworldly. 'I know that this is his plan because he offered me a share in it. He told me that if I were to stay here and compose my reports claiming that upon my arrival I found that the Bishop of Nantes had already turned the whole of Hibernia to Christ, I would receive which-ever bishopric I desired when he was elected Pope.'

When Patricius noticed Seginus' shock he tried to stifle a smile. 'I will never forget the look on Julius' face when I politely refused his suggestion.

He must have thought that I was greedy because he went on to offer me more than one bishopric!'

The legate's expression changed suddenly. 'Then I realised my mistake. I should have agreed to go along with his plan and then later slipped away unnoticed for I have been stuck here with all my retinue for over two weeks now. Every time a boat is organised for us something happens to postpone our departure. I fear that Julius will soon tire of this game and that I may end up in the same cell that you were unfortunate to have found yourself occupying. That is why we are going to try and get away tonight. Tullia, bless her ingenuity, has arranged for a boat to be ready for us and the warriors are going to create a disturbance that will distract our host for a short time. Seginus Gallus, you are welcome to join us if you wish.'

Seginus stared uncomfortably at his feet. 'Is it true that you are investigating Palladius?'

'It is true, that is one of the tasks that has been set for me. There are many charges that have been laid upon him.'

'And my brother Linus?'

'One of my tasks is to gather information that will confirm his sainthood.'

'I have been placed under banishment by the High-King of Eirinn,' Seginus admitted. 'It is dangerous for me to return to Hibernia.'

'If you stay here you will end up back in the cell under the palace, that is certain, for my escape will send Julius into a rage.'

'Then I will be your guide as far as the coast of Hibernia and afterwards with your leave I will return to Britain.'

'Good!' Patricius exclaimed, clapping the monk on the back. 'I am sure that we could do with an extra pair of hands. Do you have any servants?'

Suddenly Seginus remembered Mog and Darach. 'I do, Father. I just don't know where they are at present. I haven't seen them since I was taken.'

'If they were separated from you when you were captured then very likely they have made their way to Nantes and are this very moment outside the palace walls in the main part of the town. I will send one of my guardsmen to see if he can find them. Do you have horses?'

'My servants should still have the horses.'

'Good. It is a long walk to the coast and I fear that without a horse you would not have much chance of joining us. I will meet you here an hour after dark. Until then I want you to rest and try to gather as much food as you can carry for the journey without anyone becoming too suspicious.' Then Patricius rose from his seat and shook out his cloak. 'I am sorry about the Hibernian who Julius saw fit to have murdered,' he said. 'Did you know him well?'

'He helped me to come through a very difficult time in my life,' Seginus replied, deliberately understating Cieran's role in the monk's escape from Eirinn. 'I owed him a debt of gratitude.'

EIGHT

 woman in her mid-twenties, dressed in the drab light-brown clothing of a servant, carefully spread blankets and large cushions on the flat-topped parapet of the rock fortress of Cashel in the Kingdom of Munster. Her queen, a tall lady with wild auburn locks tied up to keep them from blowing around in her face, leaned heavily on a walking stick. Her ponderous movements gave her the air of one who had seen many more seasons than was reflected in those bright eyes. The lady was clothed in a fine white linen shift of the kind reserved for women who are close to the time of giving birth. She observed her busy servant with detached disinterest.

The fine woven blankets befitting a queen of the kingdoms of Eirinn were quickly arrayed and the serving woman gently led her mistress toward the softest cushions. 'There you are, Lady Caitlin. The day is warm and dry and it may be the last such time before the autumn comes, so you should sit a while in the sun.'

'Thank you, Omra,' came the feeble breathy reply. Wearing the pallid complexion of one who is suffering great and constant pain, the queen bent her knees slightly to sit down. As she shifted her hold on the stick which supported her, the thin weakened fingers of her hand slipped and in that instant out of the corner of her eye Caitlin spotted a stranger standing on the top of the parapet not ten paces away. A sudden searing pain shot through her body as if an unseen hand had reached deep into her womb to snatch her unborn child away. The queen clutched her abdomen and retched violently.

The threatening stranger began to move with incredible speed around the battlements, darting this way and that so quickly that Caitlin could not focus her attention on the creature properly. Despite this she had recognised this being immediately and her heart began to pound wildly. Four times she had witnessed the coming of the ghostly stranger in the last eight seasons and on each and every occasion she had lost a baby before its term.

'She has come for my child!' Caitlin cried in distress and her hand slid further down the neck of the walking stick.

Seeing her lady's knees begin to buckle Omra reached out to catch the queen before she fell too heavily but she could not prevent Caitlin's legs folding under her and carrying them both tumbling forward. The queen came to rest on her side supported on her left elbow. A burning cramp shook her body from the base of her neck to the back of her heels. Her lower abdomen convulsed in spasms and Caitlin felt shudders pass up through her torso so that she thought her stomach would rebel against her, forcing up her last meal.

Though the pain was so intense that it seemed to last forever it ceased as suddenly as it began, leaving Caitlin light-headed as though she had drunk too much honey mead. The queen knew well that it was not strong drink that caused her discomfort. She was still a little giddy so she rolled gently off her side, keeping her arm under her for support. All the while she looked frantically about for the stranger, hoping to keep the creature at bay.

As Omra got up off the ground and stood at Caitlin's feet, an expression of shock spread slowly across her face. Puzzled, the queen followed her serving woman's gaze to find out what could have caused the colour to drain so quickly from the woman's cheeks. Omra's eyes were fixed steady and unwavering on a point near the queen's thighs. It was then that Caitlin looked down at her own body and at the white shift that she wore. In a deepening horror she saw what it was that had caught Omra's attention so completely. A bright red stain was quickly spreading over the bleached cloth of the shift around the area of her hips.

Blood.

Her throat closed in terror but Caitlin managed to scream at Omra and then wild-eyed the pregnant woman grabbed at her servant's sleeve tearing it open along the seam. 'Fetch Síla to me! Be quick!' Sweat began pouring from around her face and the shadowy rings around her eye sockets seemed swiftly to grow even darker.

'I cannot leave you, lady,' cried the serving woman in distress. Omra leaned forward to touch the queen's cheek. 'You are losing too much blood.'

Caitlin summoned all her resolve, realising that every second wasted now would diminish her unborn baby's chances of survival. The queen fixed her eyes on her maid and spoke in the most commanding tone that she could muster. 'I will be all right. If you bring my midwife to me now!'

A little blood appeared at the corner of Caitlin's mouth and her skin was suddenly cold to the touch. Omra pulled her hands back from her in dismay. In that instant the serving woman saw that she had no alternative if her mistress was to have

121

any chance of living through this birth. Hitching up her skirts so she could take greater strides, the maid turned toward the main part of the settlement quickly deciding that Síla the Druid healer would most likely be in the kitchens preparing a midday meal for the queen. She made off for the houses at the centre of the fortress calling out the midwife's name at the top of her voice.

A moment after Omra had run off on her urgent task Caitlin rolled onto her back. She lay there for a long while staring into the sky and willing herself not to cry out, but the spasms were building in intensity again, remorselessly shuddering through her weakened body. Each new convulsion was like a kick from a merciless assailant. She willed herself to relax, repeating to herself that all would be well once Síla came to her aid.

Without noticing it, though, she was beginning to drift gradually into unconsciousness. She could still hear Omra's calls—they echoed in her skull, sharpening the throbbing pain in her head—but the cries were very distant as though the serving woman were on the other side of the valley rather than within the fortress walls. Caitlin's stomach started to burn. The contents had begun to boil like molten iron in the smithy. She became painfully aware that her back seemed to be bruised in many places.

As her consciousness lapsed Caitlin discovered that she could no longer sense the warmth of the sun on her skin and she could not even bear to open her eyes to look on its brightness. Never before, not even after four failed pregnancies, had she ever felt this ill and weak.

'I am dying,' she mumbled to herself and her thoughts were cast back to the time long past when she had been badly wounded in a great battle. She bitterly recalled how close she had come to death on that occasion.

Her memories gave way to a desperate disappointment. Until now there had been no indication that this unborn infant would be so hard for her to birth. Everything had gone so well and the child in the womb had not been unusually active until the appearance of the ghostly spectre.

Just as this realisation came to her Caitlin sensed a shadow passing across her closed eyelids, shading her face from the bright sunlight. Caitlin ventured to open her eyes expecting to find Síla leaning over her. Instead, an immensely old woman was looking down at her with a sad grey otherworldly expression. About her face the old crone wore a dark blue veil that was thin enough that her white hair was clearly visible beneath it and she was dressed in the flowing blue-green robes that Caitlin had glimpsed many times from the corner of her eye but never been able to observe closely.

'You will not pass over yet,' the figure whispered reassuringly, and as though the old woman commanded the spasms they ceased once more and Caitlin was able to breathe more slowly and deeply.

'Who are you?' the queen gasped.

'I have many names. Some call me Cailleach, the blue hag, and some call me the gatherer of the changelings.'

A great weight pressed instantly down onto Caitlin's chest as the creature spoke and the queen's breathing quickly became laboured again so that she could hardly draw the air into her lungs with the great stress that seemed to lie on her ribcage. The old woman still smiled sweetly as if all were well. 'Some name me Anu the Destroyer. Yet others recognise me as the washer at the ford.'

Caitlin's vision suddenly became blurred and she realised that the old woman had dropped the veil from her haggard face. The ancient fingers deftly worked to bind the cloth tightly over Caitlin's eyes. Without the benefit of her sight the queen began to feel panic rising in her. All her strength sapped away, drained like the blood of a pig slaughtered for a festival.

She was acutely aware of fleshless knuckles gently massaging her throat. As she moved to brush them away the fingers unexpectedly tightened their grip. The queen battled to draw the life-giving air into her lungs and in that moment a memory-vision played itself out in her head.

An old hag was bending down in the middle of a stream trying to wash bloodstains out of her clothes. The picture became clearer as Caitlin recalled the buried memory of an unearthly figure that had once haunted her. That had been at the end of the war between Laigin and Midhe. She had first seen the washer at the ford nine winters before, after the siege of the fortress of Rathowen.

'You have nothing to fear, lady,' Caitlin heard the hag say in a reassuring tone. 'Ease your body. Let your soul dissolve into the land of sleep.' Some strange quality in the creature's voice brought the queen quickly to the point of dismay. She fought hard to see through blinded eyes into the misty web that clouded around her, fearing the consequences if she did not fight. Though she strove with all her willpower to utter her distress she could not prevent her eyelids from shutting and once shut she could not will them to open again.

'I have come for the little baby that you carry within your womb,' the Cailleach whispered, 'not for you. So there is nothing for you to fear.'

At that moment Caitlin felt her whole being jolted again as if a bright fireball of lightning had struck her on the top of her head setting her whole body aflame. She gathered her strength to scream and in a high-pitched gurgling cry she called out for the Druid woman, Síla. The old hag laughed at her, adding a wheeze to her cackle that was like the dying gasps of a plague victim. The Cailleach coughed wet phlegm to clear her throat then she began lowly chanting the queen's name over and over in a strange song that was made up of only two or three notes.

'Cait-lin, Cait-lin,' she crooned softly, 'do not fear,' but the song did not put the queen at ease.

Caitlin blocked out the lullaby, singing another air in her head so that she would not hear it. Her thoughts cleared a little then. After a short while the queen was able to open her eyes once more. When she did so she was able to breathe without restriction. Caitlin's vision took a long time to focus but when she was able to see clearly again the ghastly hag had been replaced by another figure equally as strange but without a trace of malevolence.

The woman who now met Caitlin's gaze had unkempt dark hair that sparkled with bands of silver cleverly woven into the plaits to hold them together. She had tanned skin and a beautiful triple spiral tattooed into her left cheek. Around her neck on a plaited leather thong, this woman wore a sliver of deer bone carved into the shape of a crescent moon.

It was Síla.

'Caitlin,' the woman said softly, 'do not fear. I am with you now.'

Síla's words fell on grateful ears and the queen finally allowed herself to lapse into unconsciousness. Before she lost all sense of what was going on about her Caitlin heard the Druid healer calling for water and the herbs of healing. She felt a hand under the back of her head giving support and the touch of some tasteless liquid at her lips and then she slept.

When the Queen of Munster woke it was the middle of the night and there was a roaring fire in the central stone hearth keeping the royal chambers warm. As soon as Caitlin stirred she heard Omra's familiar voice talking lowly to one of the other servants, though she could not clearly hear what was said. Nevertheless the queen caught an urgent bidding in the message that startled her. A moment later the door to the room slammed shut as the other servant sped off on her errand and Omra came to the queen with a bowl of weak barley broth.

'I am happy to see you awake, lady,' she said softly. 'Are you feeling well enough to take some food?'

Caitlin lay back for a few moments and tried to remember how she had got to her bed chamber for she could not recall having come there of her own free will. Disoriented, she breathed deeply to clear her head. A strange odour hung about her room that she immediately recognised but could not so easily name. Her eyesight was still a little blurred so that she had to stare for a few seconds before she saw anything clearly.

Omra put the bowl under Caitlin's nose and as the smell of the broth reached her nostrils the queen became aware that her belly was empty and that it ached. She was always hungry these days for the child within her belly was becoming larger and stronger. Caitlin lifted her hand and signalled for Omra to help her to eat.

'This one will grow to be a warrior king if he goes on eating like this!' she exclaimed, patting her belly.

The serving woman giggled, relieved that Caitlin was in good enough spirits to joke with her. Omra propped the queen up with a few cushions and then the serving woman settled down beside her mistress on the bed, placing a small piece of white bread and a cup of watered mead on a wooden tray nearby. She dipped a large wooden spoon into the bowl and fed Caitlin as though she were a sick child not a grown woman. After the queen had taken a few spoonfuls of broth and a sip of mead the maid soaked some bread in the soup and carefully placed it in the queen's mouth. Caitlin chewed slowly, enjoying the taste of the seasoned broth mixed with the flavour of fresh yeasty bread.

When the queen was finished chewing Omra wiped her mouth with a piece of white linen and filled the spoon again but Caitlin signalled that she had eaten enough for the moment. Satisfied that her mistress had at least improved sufficiently to take some sustenance, Omra left her and went to build up the fire.

The small amount of warm broth made Caitlin very sleepy again and as she watched her loyal servant the queen's mind began to drift off into daydream. She let her thoughts meander this way and that, passing over trivial matters quickly and only dwelling on any subject for a few short moments.

It was only when she lifted her hand to scratch the top of her head that Caitlin noticed that she was wearing a brown servant's shift instead of her white robes. Throughout each of her pregnancies she had worn the Druid-white, donning a fresh, clean shift every morning and making sure her bondswomen scrubbed out the dirt from each one until their knuckles ached. But neither the Druid-white, nor various herbal potions, nor the ice-baths, nor all the advice of the wisest of the midwives in Eirinn had ensured that any of the children that she carried had ever lived very long.

In the eight seasons since she had been wedded to Murrough she had lost three babes at birth. One feeble infant had been born early and as a consequence he was too sickly ever to take solid food. He had died quietly in his sleep after the space of only eight moons. Of all the children that had formed in her womb only one had proved strong enough to survive a difficult birthing and the first years on Earth. That one survivor was the very first child that the queen had ever borne and the girl was now seven summers old.

Perhaps Caitlin loved this daughter so much because she was such a rare gem. She had what all her siblings had lacked, the essence of life. 'Brigid was a good name for her,' reflected the queen, 'for Brigid who is the Goddess of Fertility and Fire watches over her and keeps her from all harm.'

No-one at the royal court of Munster would have guessed that there would ever have been any but healthy children, and many for that matter, from Caitlin's union with Murrough. But their failure to produce a healthy heir cast doubt on the future of the Eóghanacht dynasty. The child Brigid had lived but she was not strong of body and it was more than could be hoped for that she would ever wear the feathers of a chieftain and the seven colours of Munster or carry the staff of ruling as a queen in her own right.

'Eight summertimes have passed since I came to live here,' Caitlin recalled. 'Eight winters since I left the Holy Well of the daughters of Brigid to become Queen of Munster.'

She was not a woman to display her emotions openly to many folk, so when Caitlin felt a tear well up from within her threatening to roll out of her eye, she checked quickly that Omra's back was turned and that the servant was too busy with tending the fire to notice.

'What is it that tortures me so?' she asked herself. 'I live a life that any person dwelling in the five kingdoms of Eirinn would envy. I have servants and good food and mead and the best of clothes. I have a husband who loves me like no other man could. And yet there is something wrong with all of this.'

She had known from the moment that she decided to become Murrough's consort that to share her life with him was what she wanted with all her heart. Despite this there was some great mystery that needed to be resolved within her. No matter how hard she strived Caitlin could not pinpoint the cause of her uneasiness. In the months after the Battle of Rathowen she went to spend a long while meditating at the Well of Brigid with the high women Druids. Many were the discussions she engaged in on philosophy and healing and magic and ritual but she left after seven changes of the moon without an answer to her own puzzle, the riddle of herself. Upon her return she had consented to wed Murrough hoping that he could resolve the turmoil within.

As she drifted in her thoughts a mild shudder rocked her from within. It was another of the little spasms that had become more frequent in the last few days. As was her way Caitlin had not mentioned them to anyone. She did not want her servants to become unnecessarily concerned about her.

'It is normal to feel some discomfort at this stage,' she reminded herself. 'If only Murrough were with me now perhaps I could bear it a little better.'

The king, her husband, was away in the north attending the Great Council of Chieftains at Teamhair and most of the Munster court had gone with him. Caitlin recalled bitterly how she had demanded to be allowed to accompany him but he was as ever worried for her health and so wouldn't hear of it. 'I want you to stay here and govern in my place,' he had told her.

'I am not a weakling!' she had regaled him, hurt by what she thought was his patronising sympathy. 'Do you think that I am not up to the journey? Or that I have grown feeble with child and will become a burden and an embarrassment to you at the court of the High-King?'

'I know too well how strong you are! I have had to share a bed with you for the last eight months,' answered Murrough in a biting tone. He had immediately regretted his words. 'But if you will not listen to me then at least hear what Síla your midwife would advise. I do not want you placing your life in danger for the sake of an unimportant trip to Teamhair and six days of tiresome rituals.'

Síla, of course, had begged Caitlin to remain at Cashel and rest, warning her that the slightest fall could threaten the life of the child in her womb. So the queen had finally agreed to remain behind and did not argue when Murrough asked Síla to stay in the fortress to keep her company. Síla's soul-friend, colleague and lover, Gobann the Poet, was also heading north to Teamhair and Caitlin felt guilty at being the cause of their separation even if it was only to be for a short while.

'She has been good to me,' the queen admitted to herself. 'And she is as skilled as anyone alive in the healing arts.'

Caitlin gazed out from under the covers at Omra as she finished sweeping up the dead ashes that had overflowed from the fireplace. The queen rolled on her side a little to get into a more comfortable position. The slight movement was enough to give her the strange sensation that she was falling from a great height and in a moment she felt as though she could bring up what little she had just eaten. Caitlin tried to suppress the feeling of tightness in her gut, brushing off the discomfort as one of the many symptoms of her condition. But then her instincts caught hold of something that set her sharply on the defensive. She distinctly felt the disturbing presence of someone unfamiliar standing close behind her bedhead.

Straining to turn to see who it was who would creep up behind her, she was shocked to discover that she could not move any further than she already had. None of her muscles would answer the summons to shift. Her arms and legs felt as though they held dead weights made of stone. Caitlin broke into a sweat in her effort to free herself of the bonds on her weakened body. Calling on all her strength she struggled to stir her lifeless limbs but no part of her would budge.

A numbness began to gnaw at her fingers like the numbness that comes of spending too long in the wintry weather at snowfall. It spread steadily through her arms and over her chest in a wave of shuddering coldness. And the strange presence behind her bedhead came ever closer, hovering cautiously like a wild animal setting to steal some tasty morsel from a hunter's camp in the middle of the night.

It was in that moment that the queen remembered her encounter with the hag. Caitlin felt her heart begin to pound faster and louder, sure that the phantom who had confronted her earlier was preying on her again.

On the other side of the room the door opened and Síla came in greeting Omra first and only then heading over to Caitlin's bed.

'I am told that you are awake and with us again,' she said to the queen as cheerfully as she could but Caitlin was unable to reply, stricken as she was by an awful terror that the Cailleach could strike at her at any moment and steal the child from her womb.

The queen's distress was immediately evident in the greyed features of her face but Síla did not fully understand why Caitlin was shaking. Thinking that some complication had arisen from her fall the healer went to the fire and brought back a dish of warm water. Síla then took a flask from her belt and mixed a little of the liquid into the water in the bowl which she then pressed to Caitlin's lips. 'Drink some of this, lady. It will ease the pain.'

The queen opened her mouth eager to drink some of the mixture. She swallowed hard, making a loud gulping sound as the mixture went down. The concoction burned her tongue and throat and she felt it seeping down through to her gullet reaching to every part of her body with warming tentacles.

'It is one of Origen's healing liquors,' Síla explained and Caitlin instantly relaxed. The potions that the foreigner brewed were renowned for their restorative qualities. Satisfied that the queen was calming down the midwife began subtly to check her mistress for any pain or bruising that may have resulted from her fall. Síla was relieved to find there were no previously unnoticed injuries but she was well aware that the passing of so much blood at such a crucial time was not a particularly good sign. Considering the difficulty Caitlin had experienced in the past with birthing she seemed to be well and not suffering any obvious pain. The Druid healer presumed that the queen's anxiety was probably only a natural concern for the life of her unborn child.

'That is understandable,' she reasoned to herself, 'but I have never seen her quite so jittery. If I did not know better I would say she was paralysed with fright.' No sooner had that thought crossed the healer's mind when there was an almost indiscernible shuffle in the darkest corner of the room. Síla immediately noticed that Caitlin's breathing began to strain desperately when she heard the sound.

The Druid stood up from the bed and peered into the gloom. 'Is there someone over there?' she said, sensing a presence but unable to determine if her eyes were playing tricks on her. There was another jostle like that of feet scuffing the floor and the whites of Caitlin's eyes widened grotesquely in fright.

Síla did not waste another moment. She grabbed a candle and lit it from a burning twig at the edge of the fire. Then she steadily approached the queen again mumbling a chant that had the power to banish all evil. Drawing on all her Druid training she took care not to show any panic for she had been taught that malevolent spirits fed on fear. Treading softly, Síla made her way around to the foot of Caitlin's bed.

Suddenly there was a flash of movement close to where the queen lay. Síla held the candle high in the air to get a better look at the cause of the disturbance. What she witnessed was unlike anything of this world or the other that she had ever seen. Reflected in the light as if it existed within a frosted glass beaker was a grey hand, the fingers of which ended in long dark-brown claws. To her horror she plainly saw that there was no arm attached to this grisly palm. Síla knew that otherworld creatures could take on any form that they wished, even that of flesh and blood if it suited their purpose.

Omra, who was still near the hearth, also saw the phantom limb and gasped with fright. Such strange things were too much for her superstitious mind, though, for she swooned and fainted, falling forward into the middle of the floor, mercifully away from the fire. Síla ignored the serving woman, for the moment intent on observing the strange apparition. The fingers had set themselves down upon the white bed linen and begun to walk a strange insect-like walk toward Caitlin's swollen belly.

'It is the Cailleach,' the Druid muttered.

Moving quickly now that she knew what she was up against, Síla set the candle down on a table and removed the stopper from the flask of Origen's healing liquor. Then she silently unsheathed her black-handled Druid knife, the scian-dubh. Swiftly, she passed the iron blade through the flickering flame, heating it a little.

The ghostly hand crept steadily closer toward Caitlin's womb and for a moment Síla despaired that she would be able to heat the iron blade quickly enough to stop the creature before it reached its target. After what seemed an age the blade was hot and glowing orange at the tip. The Druid gripped the black wooden handle of the knife in her teeth, careful not to touch the blade. With the flask in one hand and the candle in the other she leapt onto the middle of the bed.

The clawed hand stopped its progress immediately and the body of an old hag appeared to grow from the severed wrist until it was a whole figure crouched over Caitlin. Síla did not waste a second. She threw all the liquor in the flask toward the hag then cast her candle at the apparition, muttering what she could remember of an ancient magical verse against Faery attacks.

There was a bright flash as the liquor ignited and then it burned in an intense deep-blue flame. A spark caught in the Cailleach's hair, instantly shrivelling it as the strands caught fire. With the hag distracted Síla was ready to strike another blow. She took the scian-dubh from her mouth and, grasping it firmly by the hilt, swung it at the Otherworld being, plunging the point of the blade into the middle of the hand that only seconds before had been making its steady unearthly progress toward Caitlin.

There was an eerie shriek as the dagger bit into the ghostly flesh. The door to the room swung open as a great gust of wind rose from where the hag knelt, scattering the queen's bedclothes and tearing at tapestries. The force of the gust rose to be so great that it almost extinguished the fire, scattering sparks around the chamber in its fury. Síla threw her body over Caitlin to shield her from the force of the gale. The wind tore at their hair as if there were hundreds of tiny hands trying to pluck their scalps bare. Then as suddenly as the tempest had materialised the heavy chamber door swung shut again. The gale ceased and Síla and Caitlin were left staring at each other in disbelief.

It was the queen who managed to speak first. 'Is it dead?'

'No,' answered the Druid, catching her breath, 'not dead but injured enough to be frightened off for the time being.'

Síla went immediately to every corner of the room checking them and casting a blessing on the house. Only when she had seen to the still unconscious Omra did the healer sit down again beside Caitlin.

'What is that creature?' the queen asked.

'She is one of the many Danaan folk who did not agree to live by the treaty between our two peoples. I have met one of these hags before when I was a young novice in the land of the Cruitne.'

'What does she want?'

'Your child.'

'Why my children?' Caitlin cried, and Síla realised that this was not the first time that the queen had seen the hag.

'Cailleachs will appear only at times when their victims are very weak. Perhaps you were grieving or sick or living among strangers and missing your home when she first stumbled on you.'

'I saw a woman washing at the ford at Rathowen just after the battle,' Caitlin admitted. 'When I looked closer she transformed into the lifeless body of a king stag. I can see the woman's face in my mind clearly even now and it had the features of that beast that came for my children.'

Síla looked at the queen in amazement. 'I think it is time for you to tell me everything that you know about this creature from the very first time that you saw it until the attack this night or I am afraid it may return again. I may not be able to prevent it taking the life of your unborn child if it should come again.'

Caitlin nodded slowly, her eyes opened wide with the wonder of all that she had just witnessed.

'I will tell you,' she began.

NINE

s the season of long icy nights drew to a close, cold northern winds persisted around the coasts of Eirinn, carrying with them the threat of late snow. This winter had been the harshest in living memory but, as with everything that has its time on the Earth, it could not last forever and the season's chilly edge gradually dulled. With each day that passed, the warming sun gained more strength. Fresh buds were already pushing up through the moist soil in sprinkles of green and yellow. The creatures of the wooded lands had taken to walking abroad during the daylight hours gathering food to nourish their young ones.

In the secret depths of an ageless forest in the kingdom of the Ulaid, the trees were unfurling their delicate shoots, pushing out their buds though the frosty air threatened to shrivel them in one last bitter attack. Under the spreading branches of those boughs, where no-one could observe them, a middle-aged man and a youth sat cross-legged beside a small fire built from sticks of fallen deadwood.

Both of them, master and student, were lost in deep meditations, eyelids gently closed to shut out the disturbances of the world around them, as perfectly still and silent as the mighty trees who stood around about. With relaxed hands and feet folded tightly under them neither man showed any sign that he was affected by the damp of the chilly ground or the light dusting of white cold that had arrived with the dawn. The two Druids could have been members of the forest clan.

The trees of the oak grove did not shudder when they felt the frost. They merely brushed it off as though it were some trifling annoyance. The icy part of the year did not hold the same fear for these venerable boughs as it did for other creatures. Oaks did not spend the dark months dreaming of the sun's heat and life-giving glow nor did they fritter away their days storing food in case it might one day become scarce.

Ice was not their enemy, nor snow, nor the wintry northern gales. These insignificant disturbances were just a benchmark of the passing of time, evidence of seasons flitting swiftly by. Winter, the time of sleep. Summer, the time of growth. Autumn, the time for discarding that which was no longer useful. Spring, the season for new buds and new endeavours. Time ran a different course for the oaks than it did for most Earth dwellers. Winter and summer were to them the same as night and day were to other beings.

In the gathering place of the sacred grove the mighty trees built their community close enough to one another to delicately touch the tips of their twigs, offering shelter, protection and companionship to each other throughout the turning of the seasons. The great oak tribe stood like a living fortress massed around two elderly boughs who were the mortal ancestors of every individual in the grove.

At the furthest outskirts of the assembly, younger trees clasped their branches together in a mighty chain. They kept out all who were unwelcome. They caught almost every shred of light before it had a chance to reach the forest floor. None entered their sacred space without their leave to do so. None was allowed to depart who had wronged the clan in any way.

To the animals who sheltered in their shade the trees were immortal and unmoving. The oak tribe knew better. Though the passing seasons had yet to bring death to any one of them, the great family taught their young ones that nothing lasts forever. As sure as the winter gives way to spring each of them would surely one day succumb to age and to death.

There was a circular open space in the midst of the wood where no tree grew. In that place there was enough room for a man or woman to walk twenty paces without having to bow down to low-reaching branches or step over the tangled roots. To that clearing there came, once in a while, the only visitors who ever dared penetrate the leafy silence. These two men seated by their little fire who followed the life of the travelling Druids were among those rare guests.

Evening had not drawn on the shadows in the outside world but the oaks effectively blocked out the rays of the sun from above and all sound from the land beyond their home. Night came so early to this wood that the creatures of the dark hours went about their business, though in fields not far away their kindred still dwelt in daylight. The light took on an eerie green hue tingeing the skin of the men so that their faces looked deathly.

The older of the two Druids stirred and slowly opened his eyes. He wore his long jet-black hair plaited. The strands shone with fragrant oils so that the tiny streaks of grey were not noticeable. Accustomed to the self-discipline of his vocation, he began to check his breathing, taking in deeper drafts of air to bring him back from beyond the edge of the Otherworld to a state of consciousness.

With the palm of his hand Gobann the Poet stroked his brow, touching the top of his forehead where a patch of hair from one ear across to the other was freshly shaved in the fashion of the Druid kind. Then he stretched both his hands out to the fire, cracking the joints and warming them. As he did so he searched the face of his student. The young man was still walking in the world of the soul-trance. The firelight danced across the student's gentle features distorting his peaceful expression. The poet watched, startled as the shadows played their tricks. For a fleeting moment the student took on the appearance of a contorted and monstrous ogre but the poet could see easily through such simple deceptions.

The mischievous flames danced on and despite their pranks Gobann quickly discerned that all was well with the younger man. He had never been more certain that the lad would turn out to be a fine bard. With that, Gobann of the Silver Branch allowed himself to relax a little more. Silently he tucked his blue robe under both his feet to keep them warm. Once he was comfortable he sat and recalled when he had first met his student, not long after Mawn had celebrated his first nine turnings of the seasons on Earth. Gobann realised that another eight cycles of the seasons had come and gone since then.

A breeze rustled the high branches of the grove and all the trees sighed. For the oaks, eight seasons was a fleeting moment hardly marked by any event of significance.

The poet's thoughts began to stray from recollections of the past to the question of what was yet to be. He knew that the beginning of Mawn's quest also marked the end of his own.

The youth stirred a little and a strand of his long fair hair fell across his face. The poet prepared to observe his student as he awoke from his trance. As he unfolded the woollen pleats of his long blue robes from around about him, Gobann straightened his legs ready to rise. He pushed the soles of his feet toward the fire as he did so, stretching the muscles of his thighs.

The poet's restlessness seemed to spread instantly to his student. The novice bent his head forward as his eyelids slowly parted. As soon as his eyes were wide open Mawn smiled broadly at his teacher, a simple gesture that said that all was well. His golden yellow hair was thicker than Gobann's and he was not yet shaved with the mark of an initiate, but there was a spark in his bright green eyes that showed he was ready for the ways of the holy ones.

Gobann waited patiently for his student to shake off all the effects of his trance. When he was satisfied that Mawn was fully conscious, the poet reinforced the day's lesson.

'We only travelled as far as the doorway of the Otherworld this time,' he began. 'One day soon you will be expected to open the door and pass through on the voyage of the Imbas Forosnai. No-one can tell you what to expect or how to find your way back from the place beyond. I can only teach you how to make your way to the portal. You already know that you need hold no fear of opening it.'

'I have not heard you use that term before,' Mawn observed, his bright eyes glistening with the possibility of learning something new. 'What is the Imbas Forosnai?

'There are many paths that lead to initiation,' the poet began. 'First and foremost among them is the trial of the Imbas Forosnai. So ancient is this rite that the very words Imbas Forosnai belong to another age. No-one living now knows their true meaning. A candidate seeking the Forosnai must have exhibited three vital qualities. First, the wisdom to be able to see beyond and behind the world that we know. Secondly, an ability to collect knowledge from a teacher without placing judgments upon the value of that learning. Thirdly, the gift of inspiration. You have all these and so you are eligible to eat of the salmon of knowledge that has feasted on the hazelnuts of wisdom that fall into the well of Segais.'

'I will eat the salmon?' Mawn asked shocked. For eight winters he had been allowed very little animal flesh. Now it seemed that restriction would be lifted.

'The Danaans have made you and Sianan a gift of the salmon caught at the holy well of Segais which lies within their domain. The hazel tree that grows by that well bears nuts that are the source of all poetic inspiration. When the salmon eat the nuts that drop into the well their flesh becomes sacred. Throughout your life the gift of inspiration will be your greatest ally. The Danaans are doing you a great honour in providing this meal before you set out on your journey to the Otherworld.'

'And what would happen if I could not find my way back from the Otherworld?' asked the lad in a tone that did not completely conceal his anxiety.

'You will find a way, Mawn,' the teacher assured him, 'though you may be sorely tempted not to return to this land. The world beyond is full of many wonders that will beckon you. Once you set out upon that Road you will not rest unless you have travelled it, length and breadth. Remember that the Road is somewhat like a Brandubh board. There are innumerable wonders waiting to be discovered as you traverse it and a thousand answers to every dilemma. I have never heard of anyone who has managed to explore every possibility that is on offer. In fact, the greatest danger you face is that you may occasionally be tempted to investigate one of the countless tributary paths that branch out from the main route. Be warned that most of these tracks lead to no worthwhile destination. They are no more than distractions, though you might learn something of value from a few of them. Remember that retracing your steps to the Road can be a tedious and time-consuming task. So you must always choose your path well, seeking constant confirmation that you are walking along the true Road.'

'When you passed through the doorway between the worlds at your initiation were you tempted to remain on the other side?' Mawn asked.

'I was,' replied the older man quickly and sharply. His eyes flashed for a second as he considered telling his tale, but in the end he bit his tongue and only said, 'When you are weary you must always seek to find the most direct route home.'

Gobann was well aware that if he told the story of his own trial the tale could lead his student into unnecessary danger. Every initiate experienced the Otherworld differently, no Druid could advise another of what to expect. Gobann would have to hold his tale until after Mawn's rites of passage.

The young man sat up straight and cocked his head in anticipation of what Gobann might add, but the poet merely coughed a little into his cupped hand and did not expand.

'Will you play?' Gobann asked eventually, indicating the gaming board that lay ready near the fire.

'I will,' answered Mawn.

The two of them rose and moved to sit at opposite sides of the board. Gobann carefully spread his cloak of Raven feathers in the place where he was to sit. When he had straightened the feathers so that none would break, he kneeled on the cloak in the ritual gaming posture. The moment that he was settled Gobann took up the chant that opened every contest between those of the Druid kind.

The monotonous song-chant told the story of how, when the first Gaelic people had come to Eirinn, their chief bard was challenged by the three queens of the Tuatha-De-Danaan, native peoples of Eirinn, to a game of Brandubh. At this time the Gaelic people did not know very much about their foes. They were certainly ignorant of the Danaans' skill in the arts of enchantment. The Brandubh board on which the three queens challenged the Gaels was under magic bonds so that it was mystically connected to the land of Eirinn. So it was that Amergin the Bard was really playing for the ownership of Eirinn, though he was probably unaware of it at the time.

Despite the Danaan enchantments, the Gaelic bard showed such skill at the Brandubh that he defeated each of the queens. In turn, they rewarded him with their prophecies. The queens foretold that the kinfolk of Amergin would soon rule all of Eirinn and that the Danaans would disappear to their strongholds below the ground.

The song-poem then went on to describe the playing board itself. 'Seven ramparts on each kingdom's quarter,' Gobann sang, and this referred to the row of seven squares along each side of the board. 'Three Ravens quarter each kingdom,' for the three dark pieces that were assigned to each of the four sides, making twelve pieces in all. 'The High-King in Teamhair,' for the white king who began the game in the centre space of the board. 'The kings of Laigin, Munster, Ulaid and Connachta around about him,' for the white King's four pieces. 'Four houses of sanctuary; they aid his flight,' referring to the white player's objective in getting the High-King past the Raven pieces to safety in one of the four corner squares.

When he had finished reciting the litany the poet's eyes met with Mawn's and the two of them turned their attention to the game. Out of respect for his teacher the young man waited for Gobann to open play. Because it was the custom that the first contender to move should take the white kings, Mawn began to think out a strategy for the Ravens.

There was a long pause while the poet considered his move carefully. He finally chose one of the white kings, abruptly shifting it into a new position on the board. Mawn relaxed a little and spoke.

'I had a vision while you were singing the chant. I heard Sianan calling out to me as if her life were in great peril. I thought that she was about to die.'

Gobann looked up sharply from the Brandubh board. 'A vision of death merely means that a great change is about to take place. And it has not been foretold for her that she will die,' he assured his student. 'Neither will the great death come to you as far as the diviners can tell.'

'Then what is foretold for her and me if not the great death?' countered Mawn. 'There have been too many times during our training when you or some other teacher has hinted to us about the future. Our questions are always either glossed over or answered in such a way that no solution is really given at all. Are you ever going to tell us why Sianan and I have warranted the special attention of the Druid Council for almost nine full seasons of our lives?'

Gobann coughed again louder than he had before. Mawn looked at the board and remembered that by convention the poet should not speak until it was his turn to move. The student hastily grabbed a Raven piece and moved it, taking no notice of where he lay it.

'Part of the story you know already,' the poet began, 'but you have not been told the tale behind the tale.' Gobann picked up a white piece and turned it over between his thumb and forefinger as though he were examining it.

'It is the responsibility of the Druid kind to keep safe the heritage of our people—the songs, the music, the stories, the Brehon law, the records of genealogy, herb lore, healing wisdom, the making of sacrifices, the reading of omens, the names of the deities and the interpretation of the prophecies.'

Mawn nodded. He had heard this list of duties many times. Gobann went on. 'It is for all these tasks that you and Sianan were chosen. A prophecy brought you to our attention, an insight into the distant future.' The poet took a breath, carefully preparing what he was about to say so that he would not give away too much too soon. 'Lorgan the Sorn, who was my teacher, often travelled in the spirit world. On one of his many journeys he learnt of a great conflict that is brewing in far-off lands.' Gobann smiled, putting the piece he held down on a square that he had selected. The poet waited for his student to move.

'When you speak of far-off lands are you referring to the Saxons who invaded the lands of the Britons?' Mawn asked. Then he impatiently chose another Raven piece and shuffled it quickly into a new position, freeing Gobann to speak once more.

'It is not just the invaders from across the sea we need be concerned about. The fabric of our society may be threatened by other invaders. If our ways are to survive we must be prepared for the difficult days that are to come. It is obvious that we need to ally ourselves either with the Saxons or with the Roman Christians if our land is to be safe from invasion.

'The Druid Council came to the conclusion that, though far away, Rome was in a strong position to aid us in any disputes that may arise with the Saxons. On the other hand the Saxons would probably prove to be unreliable allies if the Romans ever decided to take Eirinn by storm. Within the next few seasons a Roman will come here wishing to convert this island to the ways of the Christians. The Council has decided to offer nominal resistance to his religion at first but to succumb eventually to the doctrines of Christ in order to gain the sympathy of the Church and of the Holy Roman Empire. We believe that if the Saxons ever invade Eirinn the Romans will be more willing to send legions here to defend the homes of fellow Christians than those of uncivilised heathens.'

Gobann stopped for a moment. 'You are playing rather carelessly, my boy,' he observed. Then the poet picked up his High-King piece, lifting it to a new position on the other side of the board. In the same sweep he removed one of Mawn's Ravens that he had just surrounded.

Once again it was the student's turn to speak. He did not seem to care that he had lost a piece.

'Do you mean to tell me that we will be following the ways of the Romans out of fear for what might befall us if we don't?' he asked appalled. The poet was silent, unable to answer until it was his turn to move. Mawn did not even bother to look at the board as he shifted another Raven. He only stared straight at Gobann, waiting for an answer.

'It has been foretold that this whole island will one day be Christian, no matter what we do. It has also been prophesied that when the rest of the Roman world has fallen back into barbarity Eirinn will send Christian monks to the old empire. In this way folk from the five kingdoms will bring the Romans to the path of peace. The prophecies are not to be questioned,' he added.

'So it seems to me that we have little choice. Either we fight against both Rome and the Saxons, so risking the loss of all that is of value to our people, or we work from within the Roman church to keep our traditions alive for the generations that are to come. Our customs have never been under such a threat but this is only the first of many tests that will be put before our people.' As the poet made his next move he slowly said, 'What would you rather see, an Eirinn that still values music and storytelling or a future that belongs to war and death?'

The young student picked up another piece, staring all the while at his teacher. 'I am not sure that I would leave the future of our people to the likes of those black-robed fanatics who stirred up the whole of the kingdom of Laigin to rebellion when I was a boy. Is there no danger that the wisdom of our ancestors will be perverted if it is mixed with the doctrines of the Christians?' Having finished speaking he put the piece he was holding down in a new position.

'You are right,' Gobann admitted. 'So it was Lorgan's plan to educate two Druids in all the ways of our kind. Once they passed the tests of their novitiate they would act as emissaries to the coming generations, carrying with them a pure interpretation of the Druid ways. You and Sianan are the two the Council of Druids decided upon. Mawn, you were chosen for your talent for the future-sight and because your ancestors were of the Druid path. Sianan was chosen because it was foretold of her at birth that she would perform this task. It just so happens that she also comes from a long lineage of Druids. As you know her grandfather is Cathach the advisor to the High-King.' Once more Gobann carefully selected a playing piece and moved it across the board.

'I do not understand what you mean when you say "emissaries to the coming generations"?' Mawn asked, quickly shunting another piece across the squares.

'I will try to explain,' Gobann began, his hand brushing a white king. He had been avoiding this subject for many seasons unsure of how to present it to the lad. Now that the secret was coming out into the open he was relieved to be able to discharge this responsibility. 'You are aware, I am sure, that the Tuatha-De-Danaan were one of several races that inhabited this land before us. They have continued to exist alongside our people by separating their world from ours with a veil of enchantment that no Gael may cross uninvited. Their folk know how to produce many marvels that you and I cannot even begin to imagine. For example, their Druids brew a potion that is able to stave off the scourges of old age and sickness indefinitely. Just before Sianan and yourself came to the attention of the Druid Council the Danaan princes offered to pass this secret onto us, for although they have many magical skills it has been foretold that they will one day die out if they do not share their knowledge.' The poet stopped for a moment to make sure that Mawn was taking in all that he said.

Gobann reached out his hand to pick up the white king but before he could do so Mawn grabbed his teacher's wrist to prevent him. The young man's eyes begged Gobann to continue the tale.

The poet withdrew his hand, placing the little white king on a new space on the board. 'Three of the Danaan Druids came to us ten seasons ago having heard of the prophecies about our people. They offered to give of their wisdom in order to aid us. Some of the Danaan folk refused to support this alliance. Indeed, many were violently opposed to any plan that involved our peoples working together. A large number of the Faery folk remember with bitterness how our Gaelic ancestors invaded this land. Whether it was by chance or by design on the part of those Danaans who refused to work with us I cannot say, but a great civil war began at that time, reaching its height soon after I came to your village to lead you off on the life of a bard. The greatest casualty of that war was the Quicken Tree. On that rowan tree there grew the berries that give the Danaan healing concoction its special qualities. Murrough, the King of Munster, and Caitlin his queen, managed to save enough of the berries for our uses but the supply is much more limited than the Council anticipated. Within the turning of this moon the Druid Council are due to meet with the Danaans who will provide us with the necessary help to produce their secret brew of life.'

'And Sianan and I are to drink this potion when the Danaan have prepared it?' Mawn interrupted, at the same time recklessly laying a dark piece down in a new square without any regard for strategy.

'If you are willing to take the initiation that Síla and I have prepared for you and if the Danaans consider you worthy, then you will be given the Danaan gift. You two have been chosen to be the Wanderers,' Gobann admitted, glancing around the clearing to avoid his student's gaze. All the poet could think of was that his pupils would be cursed to walk the Earth long after their old friends had passed on.

When he was sure that Mawn was sitting calmly the poet returned his attention to the Brandubh board. 'You have not been watching your game,' Gobann observed and then he picked up the High-King piece and nudged it into one of the corners. 'We should not remain here after sunset for though we are trusted in this place, we do not belong here. I do not wish to encounter anything that you are not yet properly prepared to witness,' he added enigmatically.

With that Gobann took up the corners of the gaming cloth and emptied the Brandubh pieces into the little sack he usually tied at his waist whenever he was travelling. Once that task was done he began to throw loose earth over the fire in order to put out the flames and smother the coals. With the fire extinguished there was not enough light to discern the details of the forest but the outlines of the individual trees seemed to be much sharper.

'I have always known something of what you had planned for us,' Mawn admitted eventually. 'Lorgan the Sorn came to me on the very night that he died to tell me what I could expect from all this training. Sianan was with me that night and she also heard his words. So you see we have both been waiting for our duty to begin for the last nine summers.'

'When Lorgan came to you in the spirit form he must have been feeling an immense guilt for having cheated you both out of your death,' Gobann explained. 'He would never have revealed to you the full nature of your duties unless he had already passed over himself. I also spoke with Lorgan just before his journey to the halls of waiting . . .' Gobann stopped himself realising that he had already said too much.

'He came to me in the spirit form. I knew that he was not of flesh and blood,' Mawn agreed. 'I still experience the visions that I had when I was a child. Now I have learned how to conceal them from my elders so that I do not suffer too much for them.'

'You need not conceal anything from me,' the poet cut in.

'Nor you from me. But tell me truthfully now, will Sianan and I never know the great death?'

'You will always have the choice to do so,' Gobann answered carefully. 'As long as you have a supply of the Danaan berries you will live. One day you may feel that your work has been completed. All you need do then is stop eating of the fruit that the Danaans give you. In time you will age and pass over as was intended for you at your birth. No-one would dream of asking you to continue on endlessly without any rest. That would be worse than locking you in a tower for all of eternity. Tuan of the Partholonians lived from the time of the great flood until the reign of Cormac Mac Airt. In the end he chose to pass over peacefully and rest in the halls of waiting. Tuan simply decided to it was time to die. You too will have that choice.'

Mawn looked down at the ground to prevent himself betraying true thoughts on the matter. 'When will I be ready to take initiation?' he asked. He was instantly ashamed of his impatience but he felt as though the preparations for this rite of passage would never end.

'You will be ready soon enough,' Gobann smiled, 'soon enough, my lad. You still have a few tests to undergo before you will be admitted to the holy company. Fear not. You are doing well, much better than any of your teachers could ever have expected. Your time will come. The greatest test that you may ever undergo is the Imbas Forosnai.' Gobann bent down to pick up his sack, removing his little black-handled knife from its scabbard as he did so.

'I wish to cut some leaves and roots before we go back to the settlement,' the poet explained. 'You must learn about the properties of some plants if you are to fulfil your life's quest.'

'I have spent the last nine springtimes learning how to administer the herbs of healing! Tell me more about the Forosnai,' Mawn retorted, again regretting that his tone may not have been very respectful.

'In time, my boy. You are right. You have spent what must now seem a long time studying,' the poet agreed, 'and you have become very adept at gathering and preserving and dispensing the herbs. But now it is time to teach you of the few plants that have very little use in healing. Today we will be gathering the herbs of seeing and of death.'

Mawn stared into his master's face for a few moments. However, his restlessness did not melt away. The student signed assent to Gobann and in a few moments was standing beside his teacher with his own tiny sack shouldered. He gathered up his teacher's cloak of black Raven feathers which had cushioned Gobann as he sat at the Brandubh. Delicately the student shook the dust out of the garment. Then he draped the black coat over the poet's shoulders and brushed some more dust from the feathers with his hand.

Then Mawn grasped the leather strap of Gobann's harp case and slung it over his left shoulder ready to bear the instrument wherever his master willed. He had been performing this duty ever since he had left his home almost nine seasons before.

Gobann adjusted the fastenings on his feathered cloak, pinning it in place with a circular brooch pin that incorporated a design of a two-headed Raven. The Raven was his totem animal. The great black birds were his kindred in the spirit world.

As he finished with the cloak Gobann suddenly noticed that the boy beside him was taller than he had realised before. The poet took careful note of his own posture and understood that perhaps it was because he himself was bending to the will of time that the boy seemed to have grown. He slipped his staff through a loop of leather in his pack. The poet reassured himself that he was not so old yet that he needed to lean on a stick.

'Let us go,' Gobann declared, 'we have a long way to walk and much more to discuss as we travel.'

Mawn nodded assent as they set off, not along the well-worn path that connected the grove to the outside world but in amongst the tangled branches and roots. Soon they were stumbling through the gathered leaf-fall of a thousand autumns.

TEN

n the flat deeply pitted stones at the seashore below the settlement of Bally Cahor in the Kingdom of Munster, Moire the old teacher and the three young women who were her students were spread out in a line gathering mussels. The morning was bright and clear and the sun was already high over the eastern ocean heating the air. A soft easterly breeze gently swirling up the beach and over the hill enticed seabirds landward and gradually warmed the rocky headland.

The thick cloud of hearth smoke, which clung to the summit of the coastal hill-fort each morning in a choking haze threatening to smother all those who dwelt within the mound of stones, stirred in the wind. The haze suddenly began to lift, rising in long curling fingers that reached high into the sky, as if the gods had emptied their lungs in the effort to clear it away. One of the women, Niamh, a thin girl of eighteen summers with pale gold hair and freckles, looked up from her monotonous toil and spotted a ship far out beyond the breaking waves.

She gasped a little in surprise and called to her friends. The other two students, stopping work to take in the rare sight, gathered together at the edge of the lapping tide. Though the ships were still a long way off the excited girls counted a total of four vessels making their way under sail and oar directly toward the beach.

'Mother, come and see the ships,' called Niamh.

Moire had lived almost sixty winters at Bally Cahor. She well knew that no man would dare come to that place, for only Druid women were permitted to land, so she did not even bother to look up from her back-breaking chore. 'They are passing by on the High-King's business. You well know it is forbidden for men to come here on pain of banishment. Now bend your backs to your work or there will be less food upon the table this evening than you have come to expect.'

'But Mother,' called another of the young women, 'they are surely going to land on our beach.'

'Still your tongue, Feena!' bellowed Moire sharply, losing her patience, 'No matter how hard you wish it they will not land. The time for dreaming about menfolk is when you are in the privacy of your own bed and your day's work is done.' Then she laughed a little to herself, remembering how it was for her, just after her eighteenth birthday, when she first had come to Bally Cahor. 'Oh how I missed the men at first,' she recalled, levering another mussel away from its anchorage on the rocks. 'But it is many years since I had such thoughts.'

'Don't listen to me then, you silly old mare,' the copper-haired girl murmured under her breath. She loved her teacher and respected her but she bristled at the way Moire always seemed to be laughing at younger folk, mocking their ways. Then Niamh called out again and Feena was even more indignant that Moire was willing to listen when it was her favourite who spoke.

'But they are coming very close to the shore, mother,' exclaimed the tall, fair woman. 'And they are rowing very fast toward the beach. They must be going to land.'

'No Gaelic man would dare,' began their teacher with a laugh as she struggled to straighten her back to see what all the fuss was about. Her old eyes, when they were able to focus properly, nearly popped from her head at the sight that befell them and for a moment she lost her breath and the power of speech. These craft were obviously not those of the High-King of Eirinn.

Three longships with high prows, full of jeering warriors steadily dipping their oars into the bright blue sea, were approaching the headland. The wooden underbellies of the boats were already scraping at the rocks that lay just offshore and one or two of the men had thrown off their heavier armour, plunging feet first into the sea and swimming toward the rocky beach as their comrades hauled their oars aboard to bring the boats closer to shore.

'They are not Gaelic men,' the black-haired girl called Sianan said softly, so that almost no-one but Feena heard her.

'Who are they if they are not from the land of Eirinn?' Feena demanded.

'They are Saxons,' Sianan answered simply, shading her eyes with her hand. 'I saw them once when I was very young and I will never forget the look of them.'

When she heard Sianan's words, Moire's face lost all colour. She did not wait to hear any more. Quickly assessing the situation she turned to the girls to issue instructions. 'Feena, run to the main house. Take the great horn that hangs above the lintel and blow the gathering call three times.'

The girl stood frozen with fear. Moire quickly understood that Feena was in shock. Seeing that there was nothing else for it the old teacher walked straight up to the girl and slapped her hard across the face. 'Do you hear me, girl? Three times!'

A bright red welt spread across the girl's freckled skin. 'Yes, Mother,' Feena stuttered, jolting suddenly into action. She turned on her heel and immediately set off to clamber over the rocks as quickly as she could, making for the path that led to Bally Cahor.

Seeing Feena was making good speed over the difficult ground, the old teacher turned to face the ocean, raising her hands in the sign of invocation, both palms facing the intruders. She mustered all the strength of her voice into a piercing cry that hurt the other girls' ears so that they had to cover them to shut it out. Sianan, who was herself a singer, would never have thought the slightly built old woman capable of making such a powerful sound.

Niamh moved instinctively closer to her dark-haired friend, genuinely frightened now but too fascinated by the strangers to run from them. 'What is Moire doing?' asked Niamh.

'She is bringing down a cursing upon them,' came Sianan's swift reply. Niamh noticed then that there was a strange light in the depths of her friend's black eyes that she had never seen before. It was the light of great pain and fear, and bitter memories. Sianan's hands were wrenched in anguish for what was unfolding. The sweat was breaking out across her brow in long beaded lines.

Seeing Sianan's usual calm shattered, Niamh too began to feel afraid. Her knees started to shake, so she bent over to splash sea water up on to her face hoping that no-one would notice her face flushing bright red.

In the moment that her fingers touched the water, a flight of arrows sped across the short distance between the Saxon ships and the shoreline. What happened next was so swift that neither Sianan or Niamh had time to think clearly about what they were doing.

The first iron-tipped arrow shaft struck Moire hard, deeply puncturing her chest. The old woman reeled around in terrible pain, her hands grasping desperately at the wooden shaft, her eyes draining of their life, her lips moving noiselessly in a last warning to her students. The teacher had already breathed her last as her ancient body fell back upon the sand at the water's edge.

Before the other two women could reach out to Moire the next arrow slashed the air, splitting Niamh's long green shift just above the knee, narrowly missing her leg. She screamed, thrashing at it as if it were a bee that had threatened to sting her rather than a deadly weapon that could well have have crippled or even killed her. Sianan moved to fling her arms about her friend as the next arrow struck a patch of sand between them. It stood like a sapling in a gale with the shaft shaking from the force of impact.

Both girls stared at the arrow for a second then turned to make a run for the trees. By this time, however, one of the strange warriors had reached the water's edge and was already rushing up the beach, grabbing for Niamh with huge hands. The frightened novice was too dumbfounded to struggle with him. His cold calloused hands on her arms brought her to her senses, but she could not escape his grasp for he was a big man, standing at least a head and shoulders over Niamh, who was tall for her eighteen summers. The foreigner was heavily built and darkly tanned from many days at sea, and dressed in roughly sewn animal skins. The stench of decaying fish clung to him so strongly that Niamh felt the overwhelming impulse to retch when the smell reached her nostrils. It was well for her that she had a weak stomach, for that may just have saved her life.

Leaning forward in straining coughs her guts began to convulse and the Saxon let go his hold of her for a second so that he would not be covered in her vomit. In that moment Sianan saw her opportunity. Grasping the arrow that was sticking up in the sand, she swung it at the warrior in an upward arc that was perfectly aimed to connect with his groin. The iron-tipped prongs slipped under the man's light leather jerkin and bit deep into the cloth of his light leggings and the flesh underneath.

His great square jaw dropped in disbelief. He bent forward slightly but did not immediately fall over. Sianan found to her horror that she was looking up at his face, staring eye to eye with the fearsome warrior.

For a brief moment she felt her resolve fading. She saw the ugly creature smiling painfully back at her through his unkempt beard. Her soul quivered, but in the next instant she had managed to regain control of herself. With all her strength she wrenched the arrow back toward her, twisting it slightly as she did so.

She heard the sound of skin tearing on the tiny metal barbs and then the foreigner threw back his head and screamed so loud that the veins on his neck stood out. When she had fully withdrawn the bolt, the Saxon fell to his knees doubled up. For a moment Sianan stood still, her bloody fingers shaking as they grasped the weapon tightly.

Then she turned her eyes to scan the sea in front of her. Sianan quickly estimated that there were at least thirty more men exactly like the one she had just mortally wounded, wading through the tide toward shore.

In a futile gesture she flung the bloody arrow shaft toward them, wiped her hand on her long blue shift, grabbed Niamh by the arm, and dragged her across the rocks toward the ditches.

In just thirty steps they were over the most rugged part of the rocks and running on soft, open ground. They had got as far as where the grass encroached on the beach when they heard the high-pitched note of the gathering call echoing across the surrounding hills.

Despite her shock, or perhaps because of it, Feena had managed to inject an urgency in the signal that stilled the valley beyond. Every woman within earshot ceased her work at the call and in moments the whole community came running in from the hills and fields to defend their home.

By the time the two novices reached the top of the outer ditches, a dozen of the foreigners were already crossing the short expanse of sand below them. Sianan wished her legs were longer so that she could cover the ground as quickly as the taller Niamh, who was now outpacing her.

The women who were within the defences let go some of their own arrows over the heads of the two girls. Sianan's sharp ears heard several men cry out in pain, but she did not dare to look behind her to see how many had fallen. Niamh had stopped to grab Sianan's arm. Now she was dragging the black-haired girl behind her, frantic to reach the safety of the inner defences.

The morning smoke that was raised from the hearth fires and the three walls of well-laid turf were all that separated the women of the settlement of Bally Cahor from the world outside. Three walls thrown up from the digging of the ditches that enclosed this gathering of a dozen or so stone houses. Three walls each the height of a tall standing stone, embracing each other in a triple spiral that ensured all access from the outside of the enclosure to the dwellings within was tedious enough to keep away the eyes of the curious.

But the defences were not designed to keep out determined intruders, for this was a place of learning and of initiation, not a military camp. Despite the protective walls it was only a long tradition that prevented the uninvited from straying into the sanctuary. Druid women had built this place and the lands all about were reserved for womenfolk who had embarked on the life of the Holy Orders. No living Gaelic man would go there, nor had any set foot within the fort in nearly a thousand years.

Niamh pulled her friend close behind her, up and over the next walled ditch. Together they rolled to the bottom of the sloping bank, quickly regaining their feet ready to scale the next earthen wall. Each bank was wide enough and the slope steep enough that Sianan was swiftly exhausted. Niamh was beginning to panic that they did not seem to be moving very fast. In her distress she was sliding in the collected mire at the bottom of each ditch. The mud from the recent rains had made the sides of the bank very slippery so Sianan had to help her anxious friend back to her feet more than once.

The dark-haired novice began to think that they would not be able to escape the invaders but as they got to the top of the wall they glimpsed the ditch beneath them. Almost every woman in the community was there, labouring to drag all the dry timber they could find into the ditch.

At the sight of so many others of the Druid kind, Niamh seemed to come to her senses, rushing down the other side of the bank to join them. She had no sooner reached the bottom when she was helping to stack the timber in a huge wall.

Sianan could not be sure of what the plan was, but she knew that her elders would not give in without a fight. In moments she had joined her friend, filling her arms with bracken to pile on the heap. Far behind her from the direction of the beach Sianan could hear the sound of men's deep-voiced shouts, so she worked harder hoping to block the noise out. This was not the first time in her life that she wished she was taller and stronger for she was soon exhausted from the back-breaking labour.

Behind the women frantically building the fire, two wagons appeared loaded with four barrels each and drawn by stout broad-shouldered ponies. Sianan noticed them only as the women were finishing their work and retreating up the last embankment toward the central defences of the settlement. She could not even begin to guess why they had all worked so hard to build a wall of dead wood. She had seen the warriors and she was sure that it would not stop them for long.

In the throng of women Sianan somehow managed to find Niamh. She grabbed her friend's arm again. Once again the fair-haired Niamh dragged her friend up the embankment and down the last ditch into the settlement.

'We must find Feena,' Sianan reminded her before they had gone much further.

'She will be in the hall where the horn was hung,' replied Niamh confidently and they made their way then through the rushing defenders toward where they hoped to locate the girl. When they got to the hall one of the old blind Druid women was bolting the door.

'Is the girl called Feena within the hall, mother?' Niamh called to her just as she was about to lock them out.

'No, my child, she left a while ago saying that she was going to help Moire,' the woman answered. Both Sianan and Niamh sank down on the floor, deathly pale and looking at each other in alarm. When they had caught their breath Sianan cried out, 'She does not know that Moire is dead! We must try to catch her before she gets too far.' Then she made as if to rise and start the search for Feena.

'Are you mad!' shrieked Niamh in shock, tugging at her friend's sleeve then spinning her round to grab her shoulders and pin her down. 'We cannot go back. There are Saxons everywhere. We barely made it up the beach alive as it is!'

'But she will be captured if we do not help her,' countered Sianan, brushing her hair from her face with a sweep of her arm and gently pushing her friend's hands from her shoulders in the same move.

'She will realise how dangerous it is. Maybe she will think that Moire escaped with us,' Niamh countered, 'and then she will come back to the sanctuary.'

Sianan could sense that her friend was probably right but she still felt that she had to try to find Feena. She stood up quickly and brushed the dirt off her shift. 'Very well, if you won't come with me I'll go alone, but I simply must see that she is safe.'

Then before Niamh could grab at her again, she ran off through a gap in the barricade and disappeared from view.

For a moment Niamh wavered, nearly following straight after her friend, but black cold fear held her rooted to the spot until one of her teachers saw her. The woman took Niamh to the safety of the stone storage houses. In that place once all were inside, the entrance was sealed from within by heavy rocks and beams of roof timber that were kept there to season in the dry air. There Niamh waited with the greater part of the community for the storm to pass over them.

ELEVEN

here was little to distinguish early spring from midwinter on the west coast of Britain. The abbot of the monastery of Saint Ninian's often remarked this fact to himself on his daily pre-dawn journey to church. This morning was colder than most. As he walked along the secret passageway that led to the chapel he avoided touching the walls wherever possible, knowing that the stones would be damp and that would aggravate the muscular pains in his fingers.

When he arrived at the place where the tunnel emerged at the rear of the altar, he swung the tiny wooden door aside and peeked into the chapel to make sure there was nobody about. Then he squeezed his body through the narrow gap in the masonry, pulling the door securely behind him again. With breath steaming out of his mouth in the cold air he placed a stone over the door to seal the entrance securely.

The granite-walled chapel was just large enough to seat all the thirty monks and nuns of the abbey during mass. However, that often meant that the novices were forced to stand or were squeezed close against the moist stone pillars that supported the roof.

As the spiritual leader of a renowned monastic house it was a rare thing for Abbot Declan to have any privacy in his devotions. That is why he rose every morning an hour before the dawn and lit candles and incense around the altar. Often he remained there alone to pray in peace until his other duties summoned him.

Stretching the stiff muscles of his back, he slipped off his cloak, letting it drop to the floor near the chair that was set aside for him. Freed of the bulky garment he approached the grey stone altar. A few paces away from it he knelt to make the sign of the Cross. Then he quickly rose again and lit a tapered candle from the glowing embers in his tinderbox. Even though his fingers ached and rebelled against him he managed to find a small piece of charcoal in his pocket. He gripped it tightly, holding it in the midst of the flame until it began to smoulder.

He was just arranging several beads of precious incense around the slow-burning charcoal when he heard excited shouts coming from the direction of the abbey courtyard. Annoyed that his sacred time had been interrupted, but resigned to the inevitability of such occurrences in a large religious community, Declan placed the incense burner down on the altar. Once more he crossed himself then he gathered his long robe up around his knees and headed as quickly as he could for the outer door of the chapel. He was beginning to regret having accepted so many young novices this year. Some of them were proving to be a disruptive influence on the older brothers.

By the time he reached the wrought-iron handle of the church portal Declan had decided that he would have to punish this breach of the community peace with some severity. The abbot had hardly made that decision when he heard a chilling scream. The deep hearty laughter of several men followed the cry and with that Declan realised that the situation was far worse than he had suspected.

'They are here again!' he gasped as he swung the church doors open. 'Please God, not again. Not so soon.'

Moments later the abbot stepped out through the church portal to see a group of about a dozen armed fighting men milling about in the courtyard, cursing and laughing. Every one of the warriors had a flaming torch in his hand that dripped melted resin on the cobbles at his feet.

'This time the Saxons have come to burn down the whole abbey,' Declan surmised and his heart sank.

Across the neat square, near the bare apple tree that stood by the gatepost, Declan could just make out the form of a young monk being manhandled onto the bare back of a large war horse. There were shouts and curses coming from elsewhere in the dark but the abbot could not hear any female voices among them so he was quickly satisfied that all the nuns had been able to conceal themselves before the arrival of the raiders.

'If ever the savages find out that there are women amongst us . . .' he shuddered at the pos-sibility of what would happen and did not continue the speculation. Declan cleared the steps that led to the church in the next few seconds and started toward the young monk whom the Saxons were harassing.

The war horse was now being placed directly under the bare apple tree. The lad's hands were tied tightly in front of him and though he struggled violently he could not break free of his captors.

A large and particularly ugly warrior who stood closest to the horse deftly lobbed a rope over a sturdy branch of the tree. When the end fell again he quickly knotted it into a makeshift noose. Then leering he held it out before the terrified monk.

'Bloody heathens,' Declan cursed under his breath, 'why can't they leave us in peace?'

The young man, seeing the frightening loop, screamed out once more in terror to any who would hear. 'Help me! They're going to hang me!'

'Be still, Keenan,' Declan called back, pushing his way through the laughing warriors. 'They only want to see your terror. The more you struggle with them the worse they will treat you.'

'It is good to hear someone talking sense at last,' mocked one of the men, a slightly overweight fellow with a heavily matted dirty brown beard. 'Now maybe we'll get some of what we came for.' His voice was hoarse and throaty. Declan found his tone deeply disturbing but he refused to be intimidated. If he had learned anything about Saxons it was that one should never show them fear.

'Where is Eorl Aldor?' the abbot called back, trying to disguise his distress and to preserve some of his authority. 'I wish to speak with him.'

The bearded warrior turned to face Declan, squinting to get a better look at the abbot in the pre-dawn gloom. 'He is in his hall with the women-folk,' stated the warrior. Declan took careful note of the derision in the Saxon's voice and the grumbling of the other warriors. 'I am Eothain, his servant. What you would say to the eorl you may say to me.'

The raiders now converged on the courtyard from every corner of the monastery, forming a ring around the horse on which the young monk called Keenan was perched. The brothers of the abbey gathered as closely as they could to their abbot, all except those few who guarded the nuns' refuge.

'We have paid our tax to the eorl,' Declan snapped. 'Why have you returned?'

'Aldor wants more,' the brown-haired Eothain retorted.

'We have no more,' Declan lied, suspecting correctly that Aldor had nothing to do with this raid.

Eothain aimed a skeptical smile at the abbot, a toothless half-drunken smile full of menace. 'Very well,' the warrior said meekly. He turned to grin toward the man standing at his side who still clutched a makeshift noose. Then Eothain suddenly shouted, 'Hang the boy!'

The gathered Saxons raised a great cheer as though they had one voice. A few of the warriors pushed at the nearest monks, jostling any of the defenceless brothers who stood close enough to fall victim. The Saxon war leader, meanwhile, pushed his way through the heaving crowd making to leave.

Declan stood with his mouth wide open for a second as chaos erupted around him. But the abbot refused to allow himself to be distracted by the wild heathens. Declan knew that he had only moments to find a way of solving this dilemma. Any longer and Keenan would be the latest of his flock to be murdered by these raiders.

'Aldor, at least, I could reason with,' he said to himself, 'but not this one.'

Keenan squirmed about on the horse desperately trying to avoid the rope being placed over his neck but strong hands came down on him and held him firmly in his place. 'Help me!' he bawled and Declan breathed a sigh of defeat. 'Very well,' he bellowed over the jeering warriors. 'Eothain, servant of the eorl, what does Aldor charge these days for the life of a young man?'

'You are a sensible fellow,' jibed the Saxon, yelling from the back of the crowd in his thick guttural accent. 'Today the price is ten sacks of oats and twelve cheeses.'

'I have only four sacks of barley and five cheeses to give you,' Declan declared without the need for much calculation. 'That is all we have. Aldor took everything else from our storehouse less than a moon ago.'

Eothain sniggered and shook his head, then he walked over to where Keenan was mounted on the war horse and tapped at the underside of the monk's boot with the flat of his hand. 'A fine offer,' the warrior breathed roughly, 'but not fine enough. Hang the boy!' His men broke out into fresh cheers.

The noose was tightened around Keenan's neck and the slack tautened enough so that he could no longer even squeal in anguish. His breathing was becoming increasingly laboured.

Declan willed himself to remain perfectly calm and not to show the Saxons any sign of panic. 'Five sacks of barley and six cheeses from the south downs,' the abbot offered in a tone of defeat.

The brown-haired leader smiled again. This time there was genuine delight in the expression though his face contorted oddly, as though he was not accustomed to showing his joy. 'Five sacks, six cheeses and four barrels of ale,' the Saxon demanded, taking a perverse pleasure in having the advantage over his victims.

'Very well,' answered Declan immediately, 'so be it.' The abbot called to his monks to fetch the ransom, but he noticed with growing unease that Eothain made no move to free young Keenan.

'You are a hard man to do business with, brother abbot,' sneered Eothain. 'In the Saxon lands to the south of here, folk are paying for the privilege of being hanged on good strong rope like this. A quick end to their misery,' he added, and made a noise in his throat that was meant to resemble the gruesome sound of a man slowly choking.

'Eorl Aldor assured me there would be no more looting on this peninsula,' Declan began.

'Very well, so be it,' answered Eothain, mimicking Declan's earlier words.

When the grain, cheeses and ale were brought out, Eothain's men loaded them onto the backs of their horses and then began to file out of the gates of the abbey. All the while their leader leaned against the mount on which Keenan was sitting, although he still did not make any move to release the boy.

'And what of my brother?' Declan finally asked, suddenly afraid that the danger to the lad was not yet passed.

'You may cut him down, of course,' answered Eothain in sham politeness, 'but I have urgent need of the horse.' And with that he took the reins. Declan stopped breathing in shock. Without once looking back, Eothain began to lead his mount through the gate.

Keenan desperately struggled to keep his seat, kicking and gasping, but the noose tightened even more. In a few short seconds the rope had dragged him off the horse's back. Almost immediately he swung back violently on the rope and began to choke. A Saxon standing by the gate hauled on the line and tugged him up almost out of reach. Then the foreigner secured the end of the rope on a low branch.

Declan rushed forward to support the boy, trying to stop him from strangling on his own weight. Three other monks joined him in moments but Keenan was just high enough that their efforts were ineffective. The brothers grabbed at the soles of the young monk's feet trying to form a platform for Keenan to stand on. This, however, only slowed the steady choking of the noose; it did not prevent it.

By the time one nimble monk had climbed the tree and hacked away at the rope Keenan was in a deep state of unconsciousness. Despite all their efforts he died later that evening without ever regaining his senses.

'Without confessing his sins, without the comfort of the last unction,' Declan remarked to himself. 'Since those savages came to Britain there has been naught but war, rape, raids and the death of innocents. When will it end?'

The abbot did not sleep that night. As leader of the community he was responsible for every life within the monastery walls. Declan felt that he had failed in his mission: he was beginning to understand that he could not hope to protect his people from the raiding foreigners.

Next morning Keenan's body was laid out in the chapel ready for his funeral. For this reason Abbot Declan did not take the secret passage to attend his private devotions at dawn. Instead he wandered down to the edge of the sea and looked out over the waters that heaved and rolled in the southwest.

The sun rose behind Declan giving him a glimpse of a grey-green sliver of land on the far horizon between the Mull of Gallaighe and Inis Mannan. 'Eirinn,' he muttered under his breath, and a flood of fond recollections came back to him banishing all the feelings of despair that had begun to haunt him. Though he tried hard to hold back, tears soon welled up in his eyes and he found himself sobbing.

'Is it possible that I am homesick for Hibernia?' he asked himself. 'A place where I was not born and where I was not even particularly welcome.'

He continued to reason with himself even though only the lapping waters of the Hibernian sea could hear him. 'Though I was a stranger I felt more at home on that island than anywhere else on Earth.'

He found a seat on a rocky outcrop, resting his chin in his hands. He recalled a prayer that he had learned from one of the eastern Christians he had met at the High-King's court.

'If I had the Sun to wear like a shirt,' it began,
'And, the Moon to cover my shoulders like a
  cloak,
If I could sail in the boat of the Sun,
So that it would keep all evil from me,
If I could carry in my hands all the stars
And all the space between them,
Then I would be worthy of seeing your face.
Grant to me the glory of the Sun,
You of the great number,
That it may keep me from all evil.
Dip your pen in the black ink
And write upon my tongue.'

When he had offered up the prayer, he stood for a long while looking out over the Hibernian Sea. He remembered the eastern monk called Origen who had made Hibernia his home. He ran through everything in his mind that had happened since they parted.

Declan had aged, his dark hair showed the grey of age and duty. His belly was beginning to become noticeably rounded and his knees ached slightly in the cold weather. There were wrinkles on his face that had not been there nine years before and he was finding himself completely exhausted at the end of each day. He wondered whether he would live long enough to visit Eirinn again.

Abbot Declan was still sitting on the rock looking out over to the west and the morning was well advanced when a novice came to fetch him to attend to the rites for the dead. He rose with a sigh and promised himself that he would visit the kingdoms of Eirinn just once more before he died. First, he reminded himself, he had to finish work on the task at hand. Somehow he had to find a way to deal with the bullying Saxons who regularly raided the monastery.

'We are too weak to fight them. They will not listen to reason. They have no conscience or any understanding of their evil deeds. No sooner has one of their chiefs given his solemn word not to harass us when another comes along to hold us to ransom again. If only we had some warriors to protect us.'

The novice waited at a respectful distance concerned that his abbot seemed to be holding a conversation with the ocean. 'The local Dal Araidhan king does not have enough armed men to protect his own settlements so it is too much to expect that he could defend my community as well. Perhaps I could train the monks to fight,' he mused. Declan looked around at the boy who was standing nearby.

'They are mostly farmers' sons and fresh-faced boys. Even if I knew the first thing about training soldiers these lads are too young and weak to put up any sort of resistance to war-hardened seafaring savages. If only I could get my hands on a handful of battle-trained warriors. What a difference that would make to our lives.'

A wild thought struck Declan. For a moment the abbot was not sure if it was a voice that had spoken to him from above. 'Hibernia!' he called out at the sea. 'I will return to Eirinn and beg the help of the High-King.'

The abbot's whole expression instantly changed. Forgetting that he was due to say Mass for a dead brother, Declan turned to the novice, slapping him on the shoulder and grinning brightly. The boy could only stare back in disbelief. Within seconds Declan was marching off toward the monastery of Saint Ninian's loudly whistling a dance tune.

The novice stood staring after his spiritual leader, dumbfounded. It was a few moments before Declan noticed that the boy was not following him but when he did the abbot turned around and called out, 'Come on, lad, pick up your feet. There are many matters to settle here in the community before we set sail for Eirinn.'

TWELVE

he party of Patricius Sucatus escaped from the hospitality of Bishop Julius without any losses other than the loss of much precious time in locating Darach and Mog. They were eventually found skulking in a tavern in Nantes. Seginus was, to say the very least, unhappy with their desertion but they came up with a convincing story about being robbed by travellers and hounded by warriors in green. Patricius convinced Seginus to forgive their misdemeanours, arguing that they would be very useful on the voyage.

The party boarded their ship just as the master was making ready to leave on the tide. The ship's crew had only just set the vessel's sails, cast off their mooring lines and drifted away from the shore out of reach when the bhisop's warriors arrived at the docks. The green-suited soldiers were close enough for Seginus to be able to see the furious expression on the face of the officer of the guard. The monk was suddenly very glad that he had elected to join Patricius.

The merchant ship followed the coast for seven days out of Nantes during which the ship experienced fair weather but only a minimal breeze to fill their sails. On the morning of the eighth day they left sight of land heading northeast toward Britain. Two days later they passed close to the place that the Gaels called Inis Mannan, an island peopled by fishermen who spoke a language similar to the refugees from Britain.

This was a poor island, continuously raided by the Saxons for the past three years. The burned-out shells of houses and storage huts were scattered over the land. The Mananns never fought back against the strangers though, for they knew they could not overpower such warriors. In time they had developed a better strategy to deal with the ferocious raiders.

On certain parts of the island there were ancient caves and underground storehouses built of stones and interconnected by hundreds of narrow passageways. These rooms were constructed an age ago by an unknown race who had left their dead in the corridors bedecked with flowers. The chambers were generally so dry and cool that the bodies remained perfectly preserved, conditions that enbled the Mananns to store butter and cheese there through the summer.

When the islanders realised that they could not defeat the Saxons they simply moved everything they had into the complex of caves and passages. Cows, sheep, pigs, chickens, oats, wheat, all were stored safely out of reach of the thieving Saxons.

Then the people themselves moved underground, taking all their furniture and belongings, their weaving looms, the stone slabs used for making the fabric called tweed that these islands were famous for, their millstones and all their hearth tools. They took their tiny four-man fishing boats, the curraghs, made of calfskin and tar stretched over a wicker frame. Every bucket, spade, plough, knife and axe on Inis Manann disappeared. The inhabitants remained in their new refuge all day long, only emerging during the night, taking their light curraghs to the water to fish until dawn.

Patricius and his party of missionaries came into contact with the folk of the island only by chance. During the night they almost ran headlong into the large Mannan fishing fleet. The Christians were at prayers when the ship lurched over to one side as the vigilant helmsman pulled the rudder around to miss the tiny fishing craft. The owner of the trading boat that Patricius had hired roused the clerics from their devotions.

'The ship is surrounded,' he informed them, 'by hundreds of flimsy round boats but each one holds four fierce warriors. They mean to put us all to the sword.'

Patricius remained perfectly calm when he heard the news. He was not sure whether or not these fisher folk were from Hibernia. Determined that his first contact with the people of the five kingdoms would be fruitful; he was careful not to show any sign of panic. Patricius climbed into the bow of the ship where he could see the fishing boats in the torchlight.

The cleric at first tried to communicate with the fishermen in the Hibernian tongue but was greatly disappointed to find that they spoke a dialect of the British speech. This meant that he and his party were still a long way from landing in Eirinn.

Patricius had spent seven years working as a cleric in the British city of Eboracum so he did not find it difficult to hold a conversation in the fishermen's dialect. It was not long before he convinced the islanders that this ship and its passengers were not hostile to them. Hearing him speak, the Mananns decided not to attack but instead greeted the missionaries as friends and offered to lead them to a safe harbour.

Patricius accepted the offer of hospitality and by morning the ship was anchored in a sheltered bay of Inis Mannan. When the missionaries ventured ashore they were presented with food and water in great quantities.

They accepted the food but did not eat due to the restrictions of Lent which required all Christians to fast for the forty days before the feast of the Resurrection. The Mananns did not understand the custom, coming as they did from an island where food was scarce and hard won. Fasting was a luxury they could not conceive of. They naturally felt that their hospitality was being insulted by these Christians. Despite his suspicions, however, the chieftain of the island gave the missionaries freedom to travel across his domain without restriction.

Patricius decided that it would to their advantage to try to convert as many people to the faith as possible. 'We cannot know what the future holds,' he told his companions, 'one day we may be in need of a safe haven close to Hibernia where we will be welcomed as fellow Christians.'

On the evening of their first day on the island many people sat to listen as Patricius preached the message of Christ. He told them the tales of the evil deeds of the Devil and of the way Christ resisted the temptation to abandon his God. The Mananns appreciated the stories that the missionary related to them and like all Celts they respected the words of an engaging tale-teller, but it was difficult for them to accept that the Satan of this tale was very likely living amongst them in the guise of one of their own gods.

The Mannan tribespeople had always lived close to the sea and to the seasons. For them it was unthinkable that any of the deities who so graciously supplied their needs could be in any way as evil as the missionaries suggested. Patricius spent most of that night repeatedly explaining his point of view to those who had not gone out with the fishing fleet. He answered all the questions put to him and adapted parables for the sea folk but in the end not one of the Mananns would be swayed to take the Christian faith. He finally went to bed frustrated at his own lack of success though he resolved to try again in the morning.

When Patricius woke the next day he found that a great storm was rising to the east. The Mananns took this as a clear sign from their gods of their displeasure with the missionaries. Following their custom, the islanders immediately began to shun Patricius and his party so that the legate decided that it would be better if they all went back aboard the ship.

All the remainder of that day the gales blew and the rain pelted down rocking the trading ship in the harbour. Seginus did not mind being confined to the vessel if they were under sail, for he could pitch in and help the sailors with their tasks. That was usually enough to take his mind off the ever-present motion of the sea. Sitting idle in harbour there was nothing to occupy his mind, and he began to feel quite ill from the constant movement of the ship on the tide.

So without telling anyone of his plans, he slipped into a curragh shortly after midday and made his way towards Inis Mannan. It was better, he reasoned, to face hostility from the islanders than the eternal rocking of a ship at anchor on choppy water. On a foul day like this he knew that there would be little chance of Saxon raiders coming from over the sea to pillage the island. Even the reckless foreigners stayed at home in such rough weather so he did not feel too nervous about venturing ashore alone.

Seginus rowed the little curragh around to an inlet where there was no sign of any inhabitants and when no-one came out to challenge him he landed, pulling the boat up onto the rocks out of reach of wind and wave. He sat down when he had secured the curragh to look back over the sea in the direction where he imagined Gaul might lay.

The monk understood only too well how lucky he had been that Patricius had found him. If it had not been for the legate's intervention Seginus would have stayed in the bishop's cell until death took him. His fingers found the cross that Cieran had given him inside the leather pouch that also held Murrough's seal ring.

For a moment Seginus considered throwing both items into the sea to rid himself of them forever but at the last moment he stayed his hand. He was still haunted by the terrible nightmare that had come to him in Julius' cell.

He sensed that there might be a degree of truth in the message that his brother's ghost had given him in the nightmare. 'It was not my brother,' he corrected himself. 'I must stop believing that any of what happened in that cell was real.' Hearing himself speak common sense did not convince Seginus that he had imagined speaking with Linus. And for that matter Cieran's story about one of the other monks being his brother's murderer was also plausible to Seginus. 'I will never know the truth for certain.' he grunted, 'so there is no use in wasting my time worrying about it.'

His eyes strayed to the northeast where he knew the island of Hibernia lay. 'I would be a fool to risk returning to that land. The High-King would have me put to death for my part in the war with Laigin and the cutting of the great rowan tree. The only reason I came this far was that it was preferable to being locked in the bishop's prison.'

Palladius had sent him to Rome. Now he had been diverted from his duty. He had retraced his steps almost as far as the island of Britain. He had lost his master's letters and all the gold that he had been entrusted with to pay for the journey. Worst of all, somewhere along the way Seginus had started to see his master Palladius in a new light. And he did not like what that new light revealed.

The Roman lay back on the rocks listening to the sea. He brought to mind all that Patricius Sucatus had recently told him about how the Roman world was splintering due to the barbarian invasions and the greed of the more powerful bishops.

Seginus then allowed his thoughts to stray to the members of the party that Patricius had gathered about him. Tatheus the centurion was about the same age as Seginus. He had joined the army when he was sixteen, working his way swiftly through the ranks due to a combination of valorous deeds and pure luck. He was an approachable person and the men in his command respected him greatly. And just like Seginus he was a half-breed. The centurion's mother had been a Gaulish slave girl, his father an officer in the Hispanic legion. As a result he had an olive complexion and the bright grey eyes of a Gaul. Tatheus was a devout Christian, attending Mass whenever it was said and shunning the company of women. Seginus could not remember ever having heard him speak to the only female in the party.

Tullia reminded him of a woman he had met just after he had left the army. She was strong-willed, honest and simple in her tastes. 'Too simple,' Seginus decided. He admitted to himself that he found her attractive but she was too much like the girl he had fallen in love with when he was still a fresh-faced lad. He did not want to be the victim of another female as he had been then. The monk wondered what had possessed Patricius to allow someone like her to stay on with him. Then he remembered overhearing someone talking about a great store of wealth that Tullia's father had discovered in an old statue. 'She must have brought some of her father's gold with her,' he reasoned. 'That is why he tolerates her.'

Secondinus was not the sort of man that Seginus ever gave much time to. The Roman had decided very early that he was a mindless follower who had no ideas or ambitions of his own. The young priest's conversation rarely extended beyond religious matters and he had very little experience of the world outside the church. Of his own free will Secondinus had chosen the life of celibacy and he had always made sure that everyone was aware of his decision, in the hope of avoiding any difficult situations. Despite his professed disinterest in womenfolk, the young cleric seemed to spend a great deal of time with Tullia. 'I would have made a much better priest,' Seginus reminded himself, 'but Palladius wouldn't hear of it.'

His master had steadfastly refused to ordain any of the monks in his community. In this way he kept a tight rein on affairs by being the only one among them who was able to perform the sacraments. It had always been an ambition of Seginus' to one day receive ordination as a priest.

'One day Palladius will ordain me,' he told himself. Then in his imagination he began to toy with the idea of returning to Eirinn. 'The Hibernian kings would be looking for a monk called Seginus not a priest. Even if I were recognised, ten years have passed since I last set foot in Eirinn. No-one would be able to say for certain that I was the same Seginus Gallus who had accompanied Palladius.'

It was only a few moments before the Roman banished these fantasies from his mind. There was no sense in his returning to Hibernia. He was duty-bound to go back to Britain and to face his master with the admission that he had failed to carry out his allotted task. Palladius would naturally be angry for a short while but that would pass in time. Perhaps the old man would see fit to give Seginus another chance to set out with new letters for Rome before the end of spring.

He turned his mind once more to Cieran who had been banished from his own country because he had aided Seginus in his escape from the High-King's justice. He marvelled at how the Hibernian had suffered his misfortune without blaming anyone else for the hardship that came to him. Cieran believed that he had acted honourably and he remained steadfast in his faith to the very end.

'Do heretics who are unwavering in their faith one day enter heaven?' Seginus asked the sky. He knew from all that he had been taught that such people did not dwell in the Kingdom of God unless they professed the true creed on their deathbed. The monk could not help but feel sorry for the misguided savage who he was sure must now be burning in Hell.

Cieran had insisted that it was one of the monks in his master's original group who had murdered Linus. From all that the Hibernian had said it seemed more than likely that it was Isernus who was the killer. Seginus resolved then to go to the monastery of Saint Ninian in order to confront Isernus. 'If he really murdered Linus then I will have my revenge on him and no-one else need ever know the whole truth.'

A ghastly vision of his brother's undead spirit flashed before his mind. It caused Seginus to sit up with his eyes wide open. 'I will make sure that there is nobody left living who can ever throw doubt on my brother's martyrdom. Do not fear, Linus,' he whispered, 'once I have finished this task you will always be venerated as a saint.'

Seginus spent the remainder of the afternoon planning exactly how he would rid himself of Isernus, Declan and anyone else who knew the facts about the death of his brother. 'I should have dealt with the abbot of Saint Ninian's years ago,' the monk hissed under his breath, 'when Palladius had wanted to eliminate him.'

Seginus suddenly found it easy to convince himself that Declan's demise would open the way for Palladius to return to Saint Ninian's as bishop and abbot. Once Declan was discredited Palladius would once more become the leader of one of the largest religious communities in Britain. The Pope would be more likely to sympathise with such a respected mentor than with an old man who had been exiled by his own flock. In time Palladius might even be able to return to Eirinn to finish the work that he had begun.

It was already growing dark when Seginus set out to make his way back to the ship. He had not rowed far when he made another decision. As soon as he returned to the vessel he would ask Patricius to ordain him as a priest. He told himself that this would be the perfect opportunity to enable him to help his master with some of the duties and responsibilities that the old man was no longer capable of. It would also ensure that he could take over from Palladius one day as bishop and abbot. 'The master has not been well for a long time.

Nobody lives forever. It is only right that I plan for the future of his community,' he reasoned.

By the time he had got within hailing distance of the ship Seginus had thoroughly convinced himself that he would actually be making a great sacrifice in following this course of action. After all, it would mean a life of dedication to his monastic community with little opportunity to pursue any personal interests. In the long run he was certain that he would be repaid for his toil. 'A position of respect within the church must be earned,' he reminded himself.

'Where have you been?' Patricius shouted at the Roman when the watchman spotted the curragh approaching.

'I have spent the day in prayer and meditation,' Seginus replied. 'And I have made a decision that will change my life.'

The waves were still topped with dancing white caps when the Mannan fishermen set out that evening, though the churning water did not seem to bother any of them. Patricius, aided by Secondinus and Seginus Gallus, said prayers over the fleet as they left the harbour. By morning when the little hide boats had returned the weather was perfectly calm. The fisher folk were unmoved by the sudden change but Patricius was satisfied that God had intervened on his behalf to help them on their journey. When the sun was high a southeasterly breeze picked up. As soon as the tide turned the sailors hauled their anchor aboard to set off once more for Eirinn.

With the weather much improved and favourable seas, they made much better progress than they had after leaving Gaul. Only two days after they departed from Inis Mannan a thick mist engulfed the ship and a gull crashed into the main mast to fall stunned onto the deck. Patricius took this as a sign that they were very close to land. Before sunset that day the coast of Hibernia appeared, looming unexpectedly out of the strange fog.

Though the sea was gentle it was not until the next day that the mist lifted. When it was clear, many good landing places were revealed all along the coast but Patricius was reluctant to land straightaway. They had enough food and water to last them for five or six days more, so the legate ordered the ship's master to follow the shoreline until they found a safe harbour where they could be certain that there were few inhabitants.

At dawn on their second day near the coast a horseman appeared on the sea strand. The stranger rode furiously to keep pace with them all day long. Whoever he was he made no sign to them though many times Secondinus called out to him to get his attention. Then, just before the sun began to set, he disappeared over a ridge and they did not see him again.

Patricius ordered that the ship be anchored off a sheltered beach for the night. The priest realised that when the mysterious rider reported their arrival to his chieftain someone would be dispatched to investigate them more fully. He decided that if they had not been confronted by morning they would land.

The bay where they moored was almost entirely surrounded by wooded hills and rocky cliffs. This place would surely prove to be a safe landing spot. According to the chart of Hibernia that he had copied in Rome, they were not far from a place where the borders of the kingdom of Midhe touched the sea. Patricius calculated that it would probably take them two or three days of walking to reach Teamhair which he knew was the seat of the High-King.

For most of the evening Seginus Gallus paced the short deck of the ship or stood looking out at the dark outline of the hills against the star-lit sky. He had no intention of landing in Hibernia, but as he waited offshore within two bow shots of that land he could feel it calling to him. The cool breeze rose a little and passed through the rigging and the scent of rich soil and fresh water was carried to his nostrils.

Though he had stayed a long while in the lands of the Dal Araidhe and the mountain country of the painted people, he had never visited a place quite like Eirinn. Seginus closed his eyes and remembered the first time he had seen this land. He recalled the great storm that wrecked the little wooden vessel that Palladius had purchased in Britain, and the many times afterwards when he was sure he would perish at the hands of the heathen Hibernians. He remembered the first time that he was taken to one of their settlements and the terrible day that he found himself on the battlefield of Rathowen.

He thought once more about all that Cieran had said regarding the death of his brother. Seginus suddenly felt very dirty, as if he had not washed properly in many years. It was as if he was caked in the residual filth of his own sins. The sin of selfishness, the sin of unrighteous behaviour, the sin of cowardice. He knew the list was much longer but these transgressions were the ones that struck him hardest. He did not want to end up like his brother Linus whose whole life had been governed by sin and who in death was paying dearly for his wrongdoing.

The monk was distracted from his contemplations as the little ship lurched in a sudden squall. Seginus lost his handhold for a moment and staggered close to the vessel's side. He quickly regained his balance but realised that if he had fallen overboard he might have perished with all of his crimes unrepented. An urgent need to confess all of his offences and be shriven of evil came over him. He resolved to find Patricius and beg to be ordained but before he had moved he discovered that someone was standing close beside him.

It was Tullia. Seginus had not seen her since just before they came to Inis Manann for it was the time of her moon bleeding and Patricius had insisted that she keep herself secluded from the men. It was usual during the time of Lent for all nuns to remain apart from menfolk but Patricius had been forced to concede a little on that point since Tullia was needed to help with the daily tasks of the mission. She had, after all, only just commenced her novitiate so Patricius considered it sufficient that she merely remain below decks for the duration of her bleeding.

The first thing that Seginus noticed about her was that she was pale and drawn. No-one was spared the Lenten fast, especially not those who were perceived to be physically weakened by illness or by the moon bleeding. There was a smile on her face that gave Seginus the uncomfortable feeling that she knew his thoughts.

Tullia moved closer to Seginus and leaned heavily against the gunwale of the boat. 'Is this land as dangerous as they say?' she asked.

'There are parts of this country that are more beautiful than any land on Earth,' Seginus answered, relieved that she had asked such a harmless question. 'Danger originates with the traveller not with his destination,' he answered, surprised at his own enthusiasm.

'And what of the people here? Are they as wondrous as I have heard?'

'They are savages,' Seginus said, his tone changing to bitterness.

'Your brother was murdered by them, was he not?'

'My brother met his death within half a day's walk of one of the Hibernian strongholds.' Seginus paused for a moment for he no longer believed the story that Palladius had dished out concerning Linus' death and he could not repeat it again. 'The natives are savages,' he stressed as easily as if it were the litany of the Mass.

'Tell me about them.'

Seginus turned away from her so that she would not see his face. 'You will know about them soon enough and you may wish you had not run away from your father's comfortable villa to live amongst these folk.'

'Are there many Christians in Hibernia?' she persisted.

'A few. There are more heretics than true believers. They are Arians mostly. Arianism fits well with the Hibernians. Many of their ways are similar.'

'What ways?'

Seginus took a deep breath. He really was not in the mood for all this talk. 'The Gaels believe, as do many heretics, that once the body dies, the soul passes into another form and lives again on the Earth. I have read that the Arians and Pelagians also hold that heathen belief. The Hibernians also allow women to hold rank in their society much the same as the Arians ordain women as priests.'

'There are women priests among the Arians?' Tullia gasped.

'Yes, that is one of their greatest heresies. For did not the blessed Saint Paul preach that we should not suffer a woman to perform the holy sacrament?'

'The Hibernians have women priests also?'

'Not only priests, but chieftains and warriors and blacksmiths and queens who rule as the Emperors of Rome once ruled!' he scoffed. Suddenly he noticed that Tullia was giggling under her breath so he turned his head to face her. She was holding her hand to her mouth, drawing her breath in gasps of mirth but Seginus could not be sure if she was laughing at the absurdity of the Hibernian ways or at him.

He never had the chance to ask her for at that moment Patricius appeared from below decks, blessing each of his party as he saw them. The legate quickly came to where Tullia and Seginus were standing. Taking a deep breath of sea air he looked to the heavens, reciting a prayer under his breath.

As soon as it was clear that he had concluded his prayer Seginus took hold of the legate's sleeve. 'Father, I have been a monk for twelve years now,' he began.

'And you feel it is time that you made a deeper commitment to God,' Patricius interrupted.

'Yes,' Seginus replied. 'I feel that it is time that I took on the duties of a priest.'

'I am very happy to hear it,' Patricius exclaimed. 'There is bound to be more than enough work for Secondinus and myself in Hibernia. We could do with an extra pair of hands.'

'I do not wish to travel with you on your mission to Eirinn, Father,' Seginus protested. 'I am under banishment from this country by orders of the High-King. It would be very dangerous for me to return. However there is still much holy work to be done in the lands of Britain. That is where I intend to go.'

'Whether you return to Britain or come with us to evangelise Hibernia, one day you will have to face your God and make an account of your life. One day God will force you to look on that part of yourself that you fear the most. Is it not better that you are amongst friends when that day comes?'

Seginus wrinkled his brow in a frown. 'I wish that it were possible for me to come with you, Father, but if I were discovered in your party all your lives would be at risk. No, it is better that I do not return to Hibernia.'

Patricius smiled at the younger man, then nodded. 'You must do as you see best, Seginus, but if you discover that you have any doubts about this decision then I suggest that you leave the matter in God's hands. I would not ask you to do anything that was contrary to what your conscience demanded.'

Seginus stared out at the green hills before him and as he knelt down he said, 'I will ask God to be my guide.'

'Then I will ordain you as a priest of the Holy Mother Church,' Patricius confirmed. 'Go and bathe. When you are washed I will clothe you and anoint your forehead. Then we will say a Mass of thanks and of farewell.'

The legate turned to the rest of the party who were gathered on the deck. 'In four days' time it will be the festival of the Crucifixion and Resurrection of Christ. This feast marks the end of the fasting time of Lent. I would like to be in the court of the Hibernian High-King before Good Friday so that we may share the message of our Lord with the people of this land.'

Lupus, the ship's master, was relieved at this news. He was unwilling to wait around until they ran into a Saxon raiding party. 'This good weather will not hold. By sunset tomorrow there will be a great tempest and we could well be blown back out to sea. I cannot tarry here for fear that my ship will be smashed to pieces in this bay or else meet danger in deep water.'

'I have paid you handsomely,' Patricius reminded him. 'We agreed that you would wait offshore for word from us before departing for we cannot be sure of the warmth of our reception at Teamhair.'

Lupus offered the palms of his hands as if to prove he had nothing to hide. 'I will wait of course,' he assured the missionary. 'But I must also consider that there are many Saxon pirates in these waters. What if I am attacked? Then you and I will both be stranded in this land.'

'Very well,' Patricius conceded. 'Wait here as long as you feel it is safe to do so. But leave us a sign where we may meet you in an emergency and return to this bay every three days to see if we are waiting. If after three weeks you have had no sign from me then you may set sail for your home port.'

Lupus silently touched his hand to his breast and bowed his head slightly in agreement.

'We will land after morning prayers,' Patricius announced. 'Gather your things tonight so that we can be ready to leave after dawn.'

Secondinus went below decks straightaway to pack his master's gear and Tullia joined him soon after. Seginus went to wake his two servants, Darach and Mog, to help him prepare for his ordination.

The ceremony took place on the foredeck beneath the carpet of the stars. It was a simple affair attended only by Tullia, Secondinus, Tatheus and the master of the ship. Patricius formally asked Seginus to relate the events of his religious life to attest that he was ready to wear the robes of a priest. The Roman convincingly related to those present all that had happened to him since he had entered the monastery of Saint Eli.

Patricius blessed him for his honesty and then asked him about his understanding of the duties of a priest. Seginus curbed his cynicism sufficently to reply in terms that he thought Patricius would want to hear.

'I am an example to the Lord's flock. A servant of Christ and his Holiness the Pope. I hold the responsibility for the sacraments and the spreading of God's word. The people will come to me for guidance, I must learn to be able to give them wise counsel.'

The legate seemed pleased with all the answers he received. 'You have spent many years as a holy brother in the service of God, so I am confident that formal training is not necessary in this case,' Patricius announced to all present. 'The best lessons in riding are learned in the saddle. Kneel before me, Brother Seginus Gallus, and receive your commission into the ranks of the priesthood.'

His black monk's robe was removed, leaving him naked before all those present. Seginus was just starting to feel uncomfortable that there was a woman present when Patricius handed Secondinus the folded mantle of a priest made of plain unbleached linen. The Roman glanced around to look straight at Tullia. She was smiling broadly back at him. He was not sure why she seemed so amused. Secondinus helped Seginus to his feet, then assisted him in putting on the long hooded gown and finely embroidered vestments.

Once the Roman had put his boots back on Patricius touched oil and holy water to the new priest's forehead. Then the company said the Pater Noster together. With that part of the ceremony over, the Mass was said. Seginus took the bread and wine for the last time as a monk. From this day on he would be empowered to give the sacraments to others and he would be respected and honoured in the same way that Tatheus was esteemed by his soldiers.

At the end of the Mass Secondinus gave him a missal with the order of the Mass for him to learn. Tatheus gave him a small piece of cloth embroidered with the 'Chi Rho' symbol, the Greek letters that stood for the name of Christ. Tullia, still smiling, handed him a roll of parchment, some ink and a beautifully carved writing stylus. Then all except Patricius dispersed to go to their sleeping places saying their congratulations and their goodnights together.

The legate waited with Seginus out on the deck until everyone had gone. 'I am sorry that the ceremony was not very grand,' he said when he was sure that no-one would hear.

'Thank you, Father,' Seginus replied. 'I have dreamed of this day for a long time. Now I am certain that I will be able to make something of my life.'

'It is God who fashions our lives as He wishes,' Patricius corrected. 'We only imagine that we control events.'

'Yes, Father.'

'I would like you to consider joining this mission to Hibernia once more, Father Seginus,' the legate went on. 'I have a feeling that you would be very valuable to the church with all of your experience.'

'Believe me, my lord, I have considered my actions very carefully. My presence would be a liability to you and your people. I am glad that I was able to accompany you this far. I will always remember you and look to you for my inspiration.'

'Very well,' said Patricius, 'but if ever circumstances lead you to Eirinn I will be able to find plenty for you to do. I know that you do not value yourself very highly but I have a feeling that you could yet be a very successful evangelist. I have a gift for you if you will take it.' The legate passed a small parcel to Seginus who quickly unbound the leather straps that were wound around it. Inside was a cross cast in silver and very simply decorated.

'It is one of the many that I have brought with me for the consecration of native priests,' Patricius explained.

'It is very beautiful,' Seginus lied, looking at the plain design with distaste, 'but I already have one to wear.' He pulled out the decorated cross that Cieran had given him.

Patricius examined it closely when the Roman had put it on. 'That was made in Eirinn,' he observed. 'But I think that it was once a heathen symbol. All the better that it is put to the Lord's work. It suits you well, Seginus. Since you already have a cross please accept another gift from me.'

'It is not necessary for you to give me anything more than you already have,' Seginus cut in.

'The truth is that I have nothing else to give you but my blessings,' the bishop admitted. 'May God guide you and keep the Devil's servants from your door. I am going to take rest now. I will see you before I leave in the morning. I have decided that

I will leave the matter of your penance in God's hands.'

'Good night, Father,' Seginus said. He waited until Patricius had gone below decks before he offered up his own prayers for the future. 'From now on things will change for me,' he promised.

Tatheus had his men ready for the landing after first light. 'No weapons are to be drawn,' he ordered. 'I want the spears buried in a safe spot when we get ashore. Every man is to wear the brown cloaks that you were issued with at the monastery of Lerins. We will march at ease and in broken ranks. The Hibernians must not think for a minute that we are part of a military expedition.'

The centurion wrapped his helm in its leather case and slung it over his shoulder, his men covered their military leggings with the folds of their trouser legs and carefully packed short swords and bows and arrow bolts amongst their other gear so that the weapons would not be conspicuous, neither would they be too far out of reach if the need for them arose.

Then Lupus and his crew prepared to take up the anchor. Four of the sailors pulled on the oars that were used for manoeuvring in shallow waters. They would soon attempt to move the ship to a spot directly over where the anchor was caught in the rocks. They edged the vessel forward using the force of the incoming tide to drag the anchor up from its mooring. In moments the ship lurched free of its restraint and the oarsmen began their battle to keep it from being swept too close to shore.

At the very instant when he felt the ship break free, Lupus began to swing the tiller around, expertly bringing the vessel to within less than three galley-lengths from the beach. Two of his sailors dropped weighted lines over bow and stern, calling out the depths that were marked on the ropes. It was immediately apparent that they were far enough away from the shallows that there was no great danger but the ship's master was eager to land his passengers so that he could head for deeper water.

Tatheus organised a boat to be lowered into the water with all the party's essential gear and food loaded into it. A sailor climbed into the rear of this boat taking hold of a large oar which was used to push the tiny craft through the water while also acting as a primitive tiller. He pushed off and within a remarkably short while he reached land. He jumped out as soon as the boat struck sand to pull the tiny vessel ashore. When he had got it as far as he could above the high tide mark the sailor began to unload it.

'The rest of you will have to swim while the boat is being unloaded,' Lupus announced. 'There will be no time before the tide turns for us to load it again.'

Seginus said his goodbyes to Secondinus and Tullia as the soldiers were splashing into the sea with all their gear tied to them. Patricius was the last one to speak with him. 'Remember, if you ever decide to join us you would be most welcome. I must go now, Father Seginus Gallus. May your journey be short and may God bring you swiftly to your destiny.' With that Patricius lowered himself over the side of the ship for the short swim ashore. Tullia and Secondinus were the last to disappear over the gunwale but Seginus did not see them go. By this time he was deep in prayer, his eyes raised to heaven.

'Bring him safely to his destiny, O Lord, and lead me to mine.'

Mog and Darach stood behind their master both shifting uncomfortably from foot to foot. Finally Mog could stand the silence no longer. He did not want to be standing about all day. He had not eaten this morning and he noticed that most of the supplies had been loaded in the boat. 'Master,' he ventured, 'are we leaving now?'

'No,' came the reply.

'Are we returning to Gaul with this ship then?' Mog retorted with a hint of alarm in his voice.

'No.'

'Then what are we to do?'

'We are going back to the land of the painted people and the good bishop Palladius. God willing we will work to convert all of the wild Picti to the way of Christ.'

'But master,' Mog interrupted, 'I thought we were going to land in Hibernia with everyone else.'

'Don't you listen to anything you are told?' Seginus barked, losing his patience. 'We are going back to help Palladius in Britain.'

'Forgive him, lord,' Darach cut in, 'we did not know that was your wish to stay aboard the ship when we packed your gear into the boat.'

Seginus spun around to confront the two men. 'What do you mean you did not know it was my wish? Were not my instructions clear?' he yelled.

'Father Patricius told us—' Darach began but he did not get a chance to finish the sentence. The ship's master was calling out to Seginus and pointing toward the seashore. The Roman was distracted for a moment from his anger.

There was a great commotion out on the water. One of the swimmers had been swept past a sandbank toward the open sea. Whoever it was could been seen struggling about in the water helpless and exhausted. Seginus could not make out at first who it was because of the violent splashing but when he recognised the man he did not stop to think of his own safety.

Before Mog or Darach could convince him otherwise, Seginus had stripped off his linen tunic. He dived into the sea, re-emerging after a few moments to make directly for the drowning Patricius. The two servants stood watching for a few moments but finally decided to follow their master and lend what aid they could.

Lupus the ship's master did not waste a moment once they were all in the water. He bellowed out the order to raise the sails and head for the open sea. He was not even going to wait around to see the outcome of the rescue. By the time Seginus had dragged Patricius ashore the ship had picked up its supply boat and was gone past the headland almost out of sight. Seginus was distrubed by an uneasy feeling that Lupus and his merchant vessel would not be returning.

Patricius lay for a long while on his back breathing hard and trying to calm himself after swallowing so much water. Seginus stretched out beside him in the sand and as he lay there his first landing in Hibernia came vividly to mind. He recalled how, after safely reaching the shore, Palladius had lain on his back for a long while, seemingly dead. It seemed to Seginus that the first test that this land levelled at each new bishop was an ordeal of water. Hibernia continually tried all Christians who came here until the day arrived when they failed the trials and so were forced to leave.

Seginus got up onto his knees to look seaward but the ship was gone. With that vessel went his only hope of returning to life in Britain. The two servants draped blankets over both Patricius and Seginus, skirting around their master to stay out of the range of his blows. By now the Roman was resigned to his fate. He had asked God to bring him safely to the fulfilment of his destiny and the good Lord had done just that—in a most spectacular and unexpected fashion. Now all Seginus could do was to submit to the will of God and pray that he survived the trial that Eirinn was sure to lay at his feet.

Some force had pulled Seginus ashore against his better judgment, of that he was certain. In the back of his mind a nagging worry began to surface that this same unholy power could dress itself up to look convincingly like God at work. He thought for a second that he heard his brother laughing at him as he had in the prison cell. He turned to find the source of the giggling. It was Tullia with her hand over her mouth struggling to stifle her mirth. The Roman was acutely aware that he had been tricked into coming ashore.

'You're bloody mad!' Seginus barked at her, and then he got to his feet and stormed over to where the baggage had been unloaded. He quickly found some dry clothes and his spare boots. Without another word to anyone he wrapped his faded scarlet cloak about his shoulders then went to sit on the grass at the edge of the beach to wait until the legate had fully recovered.

When Patricius could stand, Secondinus and Tullia helped him up the beach to where the woodland met the sand. The legate stood beside Seginus as he lay on the grass. 'Thank you, Brother Gallus. I knew that God had marked you to help me in my work but I had no idea that you would do so before we had even reached Eirinn's shore.'

Seginus dragged himself to his feet ready to accuse the legate of engineering the whole situation so that he would have no choice but to accompany the mission. The outraged priest opened his mouth to speak but before he could say anything Patricius put a hand to the Roman's lips. 'I think it is better that we discuss this in private, my son.'

Secondinus brought the legate's chasuble, a long sleeveless mantle cut in the style of a Roman Senator. This robe, though faded and tattered, marked Patricius as a bishop. Seginus helped the missionary to put it on over his other clothes which were still wet. When that was done Patricius leaned heavily on his shepherd's staff and waited for the holy books to be unpacked. The altar vestments were arranged over a long stone that perhaps had once stood with its point to the sky as a centre for heathen worship. The great granite rock about the size of a fully grown man had lain on its side for a long time and now resembled a low table. Patricius was satisfied that this would be the perfect place to give thanks for their arrival and to say Mass for the first time on these shores.

The service was as brief as possible. Its main purpose was to give Patricius an opportunity to restate his objectives. He emphasised that the Pope had authorised him to come to this land as bishop to all the Hibernians who followed Christ.

Seginus listened attentively while Patricius made his speech and could not help smiling at the clever phrasing of the bishop's declaration. There was a subtle but significant difference between a mission of conversion such as Palladius had set out on, and one of ministering to a recognised and established Christian community.

When the Mass was ended the stores were laid out and divided amongst the soldiers and other members of the party. Each ended up carrying a good size pack, but even so it was clear that there was barely enough food to last the party more than a few days at the most. Tatheus had the spears and a small amount of food buried in the event that they should stand in need of them in an emergency. All the amphoras of wine—twenty jars in all—were also hidden with the other stores as it would have been highly impractical for the party to try to carry them inland. Once they reached Teamhair Patricius intended to send the soldiers back to retrieve the wine as a gift for the Hibernian kings.

By the time the sun had reached its highest point in the sky the party was ready to set off in search of the High-King's citadel. To the east lay the sea, to the south impassable cliffs and to the north a dark forest. Westward the trees thinned out and flowed into rolling downs, so the party marched off in that direction. Patricius did not know this part of the country but after referring to his chart he was certain that if they headed west they would eventually reach a road that led to Teamhair.

As they walked Seginus pondered his fate. He quickly came to the conclusion that it would prob- ably be safer for him to pose as one of the legionnaires until he had a better idea of how the Christian mission would be greeted. At the end of the day when Patricius called a halt to the march Seginus approached the bishop with his idea for anonymity. At first Patricius tried to reassure his newest priest that it would be unlikely any Hibern- ian would recognise the Roman after so many years. But Seginus could not be calmed and Patri- cius soon realised that the Roman had not revealed to him everything that had taken place during his time as an assistant to Palladius. On reflection the bishop agreed that Seginus should melt into the ranks of the soldiers. He insisted, however, that the Roman should pose as the bishop's personal bodyguard so that he could be present during all discussions with the Hibernian High-King.

'You are very valuable to me,' Patricius insisted. 'You have been to Teamhair and lived for a short time within the citadel. You could easily find your way around if the need arose. Also you have dealt with their warrior class and are conversant with their etiquette. I rarely had anything to do with the warriors. I spent all my time tending sheep in Dun-Gael which lies to the northwest.'

'I am afraid that someone in the High-King's court will surely recognise me,' Seginus repeated.

'Who could possibly remember you after all these years?' Patricius snapped back, surprised at the other man's nervousness.

Knowing that it would not be long before they were discovered, Seginus decided that it was no use trying to conceal the past from Patricius. If the bishop knew why he was so nervous, he might be able to help him when the need arose.

'There was a woman who was a chieftain,' the Roman blurted out, 'she was accompanied by a prince from the southern kingdom. The two of them were taken captive by the Saxon mercenaries I fell in with after the battle at Rathowen. I believe that the prince has since become king of the southern kingdom though I do not know what became of the woman. I am sure that either of them would just need a glimpse of my face to remember all that took place while they were captives.'

'What did take place while they were captives?' Patricius inquired suspiciously.

Seginus turned his face away, wiping his brow with his hand. 'They were hard days. None of us knew for certain whether we would live to see the next dawn. Many things were done which in hindsight might seem unjust, perhaps even brutal, but we all had our own survival to think of. I did my best to follow the orders of my bishop Palladius.'

'And did his orders extend to murder and to other such savagery?' Patricius pressed.

Seginus caught the hard cold tone in the other man's voice. 'Yes, Father. There were times when he required great sacrifices from his followers.'

'And from those whom he considered expendable. Palladius was a bloody-minded fanatic,' Patricius stated. 'I have read reports from the High-King of Hibernia that give a full account of the crimes he committed in the name of Christ. He executed many folk whose only misdeed was that they got in the way of his advancing army. He turned a blind eye to the destruction of villages and crops. He encouraged the rape, murder and enslavement of innocents. He attacked the dignity of the Hibernians, constantly seeking out new ways to provoke them. He created false saints for them to venerate over their own Gods. I believe he was responsible for the destruction of a tree that was cherished by one of the ruling clans of the south. This was done out of spite alone. It served no purpose in the task of converting the Hibernian people to Christ. I am certain that he would have gladly organised the annihilation of all the ancient holy places in Eirinn if his bishopric had not been cut short by his own arrogance.'

'You speak as if you hold some respect for the heathen sanctuaries,' Seginus gasped.

'Yes, I suppose you could say that I do respect the holy places of this land,' Patricius retorted. 'I recognise that if we stomp about the countryside uprooting beliefs that have existed here for a thousand years or more we will not gain the sympathy of the Hibernians. All we will earn is their bitterness and hatred. If we are to convert these people to the Word of God we must work slowly. In time, by our own living example, we will convince these savages that our God is greater in his majesty than any of their heathen statues. Eventually we will be able to turn the use of their holy wells and sacred groves to our own purposes so that their original function will be forgotten. We will gain nothing by marching around smugly declaring that our ways are better than theirs. My experience of the Gaels is that they are a proud people who cannot be readily browbeaten into accepting new ideas. If we are not careful they will simply stand and fight against us. At the least they will certainly refuse to listen to anything we might say no matter how well reasoned it may be.'

Seginus was stunned. 'They are heathen!' he stuttered. 'Their religion is inspired by the Devil.'

'Arrogance, haughtiness, fear, violence and vanity are inspired by the Devil,' Patricius corrected. 'These people are largely ignorant of the message of Christ and the ways of civilisation. Once they have heard the Word of God I am sure they will respond to it. They were created by the same loving Father who made you and me.'

Seginus was aghast. 'The best of them are still savages!'

'These folk have been misled, that is all,' Patricius insisted in his clipped Latin. 'Have you never been misled?'

Seginus thought immediately of Palladius. It was possible, he conceded to himself, that the old bishop had misled him in representing his brother's death as a true martyrdom. His old master had also insisted that the only way to bring the Hibernians to Christ was through a purging by the sword. 'I was misled once,' the Roman finally admitted.

'You have an opportunity now to undo the misdeeds that you were forced to commit under the false guidance of Palladius,' the bishop soothed. 'You cannot hold yourself entirely to blame for the outrages that were a feature of his bishopric. You were led to sin by one who was himself misguided. It is time that you sought a way to ease your conscience, my son.'

'I will do what I can to make amends,' Seginus promised.

'Good,' Patricius exclaimed, 'then you can make a start by admitting your guilt to the High-King and humbly asking for his forgiveness.'

Seginus coughed violently, a sudden tightness in his stomach. 'They will kill me.' he cried.

'Not if you make your admission with sincere remorse for the crimes you committed. If you are brave enough to admit your faults to those who are your enemies then God will stand beside you and protect you.'

Patricius spoke with such confidence that even Seginus believed him. For a moment.

thirteen

nce Sianan had crossed the settlement's ditches she made straight for the beach. If Feena had not been able to find her companions she would probably have doubled back along the path that the old women used when collecting driftwood for the hearth fires. That track had a gentler incline than the steeper path but it was a much longer way up the slope to Bally Cahor; almost twice the distance in fact. Where the lower end of the gentle path reached the rocky beach it was overgrown with bushes. So to someone standing on the seashore it would not be too obvious. Sianan hoped that the invaders had not discovered it yet.

As she rounded a corner that led to a lookout post, Sianan heard voices not far ahead of her on the track. Men's voices. They were not speaking any language that Sianan understood so she surmised that they must be Saxons.

Instinctively she came to a complete standstill, as unmoving as a tree. She listened. The sounds were definitely getting closer so she sought cover beneath the low branches of a hawthorn bush at the side of the track. As she lay shivering under the dense leafy branches waiting to be discovered she began to lose hope of ever finding her friend. If the raiders had found the alternative path to Bally Cahor then Feena had no means of escaping them.

Sianan closed her eyes and concentrated on her friend. This was a talent inherited from her grandfather, Cathach the High-Druid. If she set her thoughts on a person she would nearly always get a clear picture in her head of where they were and whether they were safe. It took only a few breaths for a scene to unfold in her mind. Sianan clearly saw Feena standing bound to the mast of a ship with thick ropes. Her friend was turning her head frantically this way and that straining to look back toward land. Feena's shift was torn open revealing a breast, there were tears in her eyes and her face was badly bruised. Sianan could only hope that this was a view of what might be and not of what had already come to pass.

'If I do not act now Feena will be gone from us forever,' she told herself, but, recalling the brutal warrior raiders she had seen as a child, she could not find the courage to move from her safe hiding place. It was as though her feet had taken root in the sandy soil and like the hawthorn bush, she could not move from where she was lying.

It was only at that moment that she noticed that the harsh voices had passed by and were now much closer to the settlement. Sianan realised that she was near to the spot where the steep path passed just below the gentle path and the two tracks nearly joined. As long as the raiders kept to the steep track she would probably not been seen. With renewed hope she slowly edged her way toward the tufts of grass growing around the bush and peeped out from her hiding place. The way seemed clear to her so she got to her feet and bolted down the path toward the beach. Within seconds more voices could be heard behind her but she was sure that no-one was following her.

Within fifty paces she came to a place where she had a clear view up and down the beach all along the little inlet. The first thing she noticed was that Moire's body still lay at the water's edge but it took her a few moments more to discern that there was a figure kneeling down beside the corpse. The mourning figure who bent over the old woman had copper hair and wore the green shift of a novice. It was Feena.

Sianan was about to call out when she saw two Saxons rushing up behind the girl. They grabbed Feena roughly, dragging her toward their boats through the salt water. Sianan was powerless to do anything save watch and pray that her friend could break free.

The foreign voices behind her were shouting now and a great pall of black smoke rose into the air close to the main part of Bally Cahor. At first Sianan could not take her eyes off the boat that had taken Feena but when she came to her senses she began to think of her own survival. Her heart sank at the sight of smoke rising on the sea breeze from the direction of the settlement. The only thing she could think of was that the Saxons must have set the houses on fire, until she noticed a familiar taint to the smoke. It was the smell of burning fat.

The barrels that the women had placed near the great barricade must have been full of fat used for making candles. They had set the dry tinder wall alight with oil and fuelled the fire with candle fat in the hope that this would hold back the invaders. There was no other way into the centre of the main settlement but by that ditch and by the gentle path that she herself had used.

Suddenly Sianan woke up to her own predicament. She was trapped. It was only a matter of time before the Saxons found this path and used it to get around the fire.

In the ditch behind her she heard a branch snap and she stifled a scream. Her pulse began to race again. Without waiting another moment she turned to run off toward Bally Cahor as fast as her legs would carry her, hoping against hope that she would not meet any raiders on the way.

She had gone no further than twenty paces when she heard the distinct sound of footfalls behind her. She was being followed. Sianan glanced back but could see no sign of a pursuer even though the footsteps behind her were close enough to be heard loud and clear.

Realising that she would not be able to outrun a determined Saxon warrior Sianan stopped in her tracks and searched hurriedly for somewhere to hide, but there were no bushes this far up the path.

Just as she decided to risk being seen and climb the ditch, a Saxon appeared behind her, charging up the path directly at her. When he caught sight of the girl he bellowed in triumph. Sianan's blood turned cold. She felt her legs begin to shake. This foreigner was exactly like those she remembered from her childhood, except that he was probably the largest man she had ever seen in her life.

The warrior hastily shoved his axe in his belt as he approached her. Sianan knew by that action that he meant to take her alive. The thought of what would happen to her in the company of these barbarians was enough to spur her suddenly and determinedly into action. Sure that she could not outrun him she stood her ground as he barrelled toward her. Then, deciding there was no way out of this terrible predicament save to fight, she picked up a rock and ran directly at the man who was now only ten or twelve paces away. Sianan let out a high-pitched war cry like those that she had heard when she was young. It was a simple call but the effect was devastating. The Saxon did not expect such a reaction from a woman. He stopped in his tracks in wonder at what he heard and saw.

Then he began to laugh. He was still laughing when Sianan reached him with the rock high above her head intending to strike him. He simply put up his massive open palm and snatched the stone from her before she had a chance to use it. Then he grabbed her by the hair and began to snigger again.

Sianan lashed out at him with her fists, hitting at him with all her strength but he was immovable. He took as little notice of her as he might a fly that buzzed around his face. In a long sweep of his arm he swung the girl around and began dragging her back to the beach. Sianan dug in with her heels and resisted as best she could. Finally she managed to land a kick that connected with the man's knee-cap and he grunted more with frustration than with pain.

The Saxon took her wrists, holding them with one mighty hand over her head. With the other he tore at her shift so that it split along the seam at the side. Desperate, Sianan wormed a hand free and punched the back of her fist into the raider's face, hitting him squarely on the nose. Almost immediately he let go of her and his hands covered his new bruise. Then, unexpectedly, the warrior's eyes glazed over so that he was staring strangely into the distance.

Sianan dropped to the ground and rolled away from her captor. He stood motionless before her, swaying slightly. All mirth had drained from his features and the tone of his skin changed swiftly from a healthy pink to a light grey-blue.

Sianan had no idea what had happened. She found it hard to believe that she had brought a raider down with her bare fist. Suddenly the Saxon jerked forward onto his knees and hovered there for a moment with glazed eyes before toppling forward onto his stomach. His bulk shook the ground as he collapsed, raising a cloud of dust, and Sianan saw clearly there, deeply embedded in the Saxon's back, the thick shaft of a hunter's arrow.

'Sianan!' a woman's voice called. 'Sianan, come quickly, we must find a place to hide.' Down the path closer to the beach stood a sun-tanned figure with long matted hair tied in a knot on the top of her head. Her light blue eyes sparkled against her dark complexion.

Sianan did not immediately recognise the woman as Aileesh, the chief herb-gatherer, for she had only met her once. She had certainly never spoken to the woman at any length. The herb-gatherer spent most of her days out roaming hills and fields seeking out the leaves and stems of plants which she then passed on to her students and assistants. They in turn produced the many medicines, tinctures and salves that were used by the community.

Sianan did not waste another second. Already the shouts of more Saxons could be heard nearby. The girl hitched up the bottom of her shift and ran toward Aileesh.

'We best get off this path,' the herb-gatherer exclaimed, taking Sianan by the hand to lead her up over the top of the ditch.

Once they were over the ditch the two women ran for a long time, so long that Sianan's legs ached and her breathing became strained. The pace did not seem to have any adverse affect on Aileesh, however. They crossed twelve square field enclosures, jumping the low dry stone walls that bounded them and not once looking back. Finally, when Sianan felt that she was about to collapse, they came to the ancient ruins of a broch. This broad round tower had once been a defensive building that had stood on the very edge of the coast. It had been many generations since the broch had been in regular use. The sea had retreated a great distance in the intervening seasons. Now the tower lay well inland far from the sound of the waves and smell of the salt. The walls were largely intact and the whole structure was about forty paces across, standing almost as high as a young yew tree.

The great boulders which were the foundation of the low tower were as solid as the day they were lowered into position. The herb-gatherer let Sianan lie down to rest while she nimbly climbed onto the top of the broch. Aileesh stood on the roof for a long while, motionless, staring off in the direction from which they had come. Eventually she was satisfied that they had not been followed. She slowly bent down out of Sianan's sight to drink some water that had collected in a small depression in the surface of the roof stone.

Sianan was still leaning against the tower trying to calm her breathing when Aileesh appeared again. The older woman put out her hand to the girl and helped Sianan to climb up the steep weather-worn stairway that led to the roof. Once seated on the flat surface Sianan drank deeply of the collected rainwater. Then she lay on her back refreshed, hoping that Aileesh would tell her what was happening.

When the other woman did not speak, Sianan had to break the silence. 'Were we followed?'

'No,' snapped the herb-woman as though the question had been extremely foolish and unnecessary. Aileesh clutched tightly at a small bag hanging on a leather strap round her neck and she shut her eyes. In the back of her throat the herb-woman started to hum a low steady note under her breath. Sianan did not dare interrupt her. It was obvious that Aileesh was using all of her senses to determine whether they were safe.

'They have not picked up our trail yet but we cannot be certain what they will do next. I have precious little experience of these people but it stands to reason that if they don't find the plunder that they are seeking then they will widen their search.' The herb-woman then started to run her hand through the thick grass that grew on the top of the broch as though she were searching for something precious she had misplaced on the roof.

Just as suddenly as Aileesh had begun this strange behaviour she stood up and put out her hand to Sianan. 'I want you to gather as much dry bracken as you can find to cover the entrance to this broch,' she ordered. 'Only the driest of leaves and branches, mind you. We want this place to look as if it has not been touched in a long long time.'

Sianan did not immediately understand what the herb-gatherer's plan was but she climbed off the top of the tower and went to do as she was asked. In a short while she had returned with as much bracken as she could carry.

While Sianan had been gone Aileesh had cleared a large space around the one door to the broch. Working quickly the two formed the bracken into a covering for the entrance that would not look as if it had been placed there too recently but instead had built up with time. When that work was done Aileesh motioned for Sianan to enter the tower.

'I'll come back to collect you tomorrow,' she casually informed the girl.

'You're going to leave me?' Sianan asked in a panicked voice. 'I thought you would be staying to hide with me.'

'It's too dangerous for both of us to remain concealed here. I'll be able to cover up all traces of our footprints but I think it is unlikely that the savages will search this far inland.'

'Don't leave me,' Sianan begged.

'I am going to climb into the southwestern hills tonight. It is a long journey and you will not be able to keep up with me. Believe me, it is better this way.'

The herb-gatherer handed the girl a candle made from fat and a small tinderbox made of iron. 'Only use this if you desperately need light and then only for a short time for there . may be gaps in the stonework. One chink of light can be seen for many miles over open ground.' Aileesh put a small hand-woven bag just inside the entrance and a leather bottle of water. 'Eat and drink sparingly. That is all the food I have with me and I may not get a chance to collect more before morning.'

With that she pushed Sianan inside the tower and withdrew from the entrance to start packing stones over it. The afternoon light began to recede from the interior of the stone tower as the door was closed off. Sianan took a last look at the walls of the place before it was too difficult to see what was around her. The stones were shiny as though they were wet, yet they were not damp to touch. The surfaces had been polished so that each one was as smooth as a fine silver cup. Sianan ran her fingers over the rocks and was surprised to find that every one was carved with spirals and zigzags and many other signs that formed a great picture of some sort.

The light was entirely gone before Sianan could make any sense of the carvings. When the last chink of sunlight disappeared she heard Aileesh piling the bracken over the entrance. Soon afterwards the room became terribly cold as though all the warmth of the outside world had departed with the light and Sianan could no longer hear the herb-gatherer moving about outside.

Not knowing what else she could do, she lay down on the floor using the bag of food as a pillow. Though she slept a little Sianan could not stop worrying about Feena. The vision she'd had of her friend tied to the mast of a ship, bruised badly from a beating, came back to haunt her. Feena seemed to call out to her again and again until the girl's voice was so hoarse from crying that she could only whisper through her strained throat. Sianan tried to reach out to her friend to give her some reassurance but her hands never quite reached Feena. Her fingers brushed at the cloth of the other girl's dress where it was torn but Sianan could not move the folds or make any contact with her friend.

In frustration Sianan rolled over to get more comfortable, aware on some level that she was merely dreaming but not willing to wake up and break the spell of the vision. She stretched out her left arm above her head as she turned and felt another hand grip her fingers tightly. Her eyes flew open. At the same moment Sianan heard a breathy voice call out her name.

The interior of the broch was very dark. There was no sound but the startled beating of her own heart. Sianan knew that she had been alone when Aileesh left her. Nevertheless, she distinctly felt the body warmth of another being nearby but she was so unsettled by the presence that she could not bring herself to investigate it. Finally, after many long moments, she could no longer bear the tension. Determined not to sound frightened she summoned the strength of her voice. 'Who's there?'

The words landed dull against the stone walls as though the earth that surrounded the tower had swallowed them up. She instantly regretted her rash decision to speak. 'What if the Saxons were near?' she reprimanded herself silently. 'You fool. Keep your mouth shut as Aileesh told you to or the raiders will take you to be a captive with Feena.'

After that she lay wide awake for a long long while. Her senses were now acutely aware of every little noise and each tiny draft. When she had stayed perfectly still until her legs and arms had grown numb she began to notice a burning hunger in her belly. She had not eaten since that morning when she and the other girls had sneaked a tiny meal of mussels behind their teacher's back. It was surely the middle of the night by now.

Stretching her limbs Sianan carefully moved her body until the cramps were relieved a little. Then she searched around for the bag that Aileesh had left her. Once or twice Sianan thought that she heard sounds outside but when she lay still again waiting to see if her suspicions were correct the noises ceased.

In the end she found the bag and put her hand inside to ascertain what the herb-gatherer had left her to eat. Her fingers touched some bread and some dried meat, but Sianan never ate the flesh of animals so she pushed that aside. Suddenly something pricked the skin of her hand. She swiftly pulled her arm out of the bag to put her burning fingers in her mouth, breathing a muffled sigh of exasperation.

Stinging nettles. Though they caused a bad itch if the leaves were not cooked, once properly soaked and boiled the nettles would make a good meal. Sianan was bitterly disappointed that she did not have the means to cook them. With her fingers stung once by the poison spines of the nettle leaves she was very reluctant to put her hand in amongst them again but her belly ached with hunger. She knew her restless stomach would not let her sleep unless she ate something soon.

In a flash of inspiration she remembered the candle and the tinderbox that Aileesh had left her. Once more she searched about until her hands found the little iron box. She pried open the lid and found the flint that was kept inside. There was also some dry grass, a few dead leaves and a short twig. In a few moments she had struck the stone against the roughened iron inside the lid of the box and blown the spark into a little flame. Patiently Sianan fed the tiny fire so that she could light the wick.

Being made of animal fat and not of wax the candle sputtered a bit at first but soon held a steady flame. Its bright orange glow lit every crevice of the stone broch. Sianan set the little light in the dirt where she would not bump it over accidentally and then unpacked the food bag, laying out the contents on the floor.

There was a great variety of roots and herbs in the bag besides the food that Aileesh had mentioned. Sianan wrapped her fingers in the hem of her skirt to separate those herbs that she was unfamiliar with. She did not wish to be stung again. Once that was done she took the little loaf of oat bread, breaking a piece off and stuffing it straight into her mouth. She washed it down with some water from the leather bottle.

There was a good serving of butter wrapped in a cloth and there were also some blackberries. A few of last season's chestnuts dried for making flour were at the bottom of the bag. Together with the butter and berries, the nuts made a tasty, if rather small, feast.

Satisfied by the small amount that she had eaten Sianan carefully packed the herbs back in the bag laying the remaining bread and blackberries within easy reach so that she could find them again in the dark if she was hungry. Then she leaned back against the wall, took another mouthful of water and studied the stones in the candlelight, looking for an excuse to keep it burning as long as possible.

From the outside the broch had seemed circular. Sianan could now see that this was not so. The interior of the tower was made up of nine walls that formed a shape similar to a circle but afforded a series of flat foundations on which an artist had crafted intricate designs. Strange and ancient patterns were carved in deep relief on every surface. Swirling parallel lines enveloped the stonework flowing over joins in the rocks and melting into one another.

Three great double spirals large enough to take up a third of the entire surface marked the point where all the patterns on the wall converged. Each of these spirals was surrounded by diamond-shaped blocks of lines picked out in countless tiny dots. These diamonds in turn were joined to zig-zags which linked with snake-like curves. These designs were everywhere but for the wall directly behind Sianan.

She followed the patterns around the chamber, gasping in admiration for the artist who had created such an awesome work. The wall behind her was constructed from a single stone easily the same size as one of the dwellings at Bally Cahor. It was dotted all over with star shapes, circles and strange little designs that looked like large tadpoles swimming in a clear pool. A large cluster of these creatures, most with oversized heads, some with half circles encasing them, swarmed up toward the roof, whirling around to the left of a large circular motif. Hundreds of tiny spirals filled the centre of this design, bordered by a hundred tiny lines that jutted out from it like rays of the sun.

From some invisible gap in the ceiling where the weather had eroded the packed earth outer shell of the tower there was enough space for a draught of air to find its way inside. The fresh breeze flowed down toward where Sianan sat on the floor awe-struck by the designs laid before her. Her candle caught the draught and the flame flickered slightly. As it did so all the patterns on the walls came to life, dancing in the yellow light.

Shadows began to pulse before Sianan in a way that she had never witnessed before. It was if the whole of the interior of the mound were a living creature that breathed and stretched, rolling its body around like a cat walking circles before it found a comfortable position in which to settle.

So entranced was Sianan that it was a long while before she became aware of a low hum that roared through the earth beneath her. When she first noticed the sound it was less a noise than a sensation. Her knees and shins were vibrated slightly by the strange resonance as she knelt on the floor.

The hum rose in intensity in the fluttering candlelight and the patterns began to undulate wildly, moving in time with the undercurrent of its pulse. Like clouds scattered before the rising breeze, the motifs twisted across the wall. Sianan thought that this was what the wind would look like if she could see it. She was acutely aware now that the floor beneath her had begun to heave as though she were standing in a boat far out at sea. She felt dizzy and disoriented. Her skin became sweaty. The small amount of food that she had eaten felt like a stone in her stomach. With great effort of will she forced herself to close her eyes and shut out the strange sensations. But closing her eyes only made her other senses more attentive to what she was experiencing.

When she stopped looking at the walls the chamber seemed to spin violently. Sianan was forced to lie down on the earth with her face on the cold dirt. The humming sound grew steadily louder and louder until she thought her ears would burst with the intensity of the reverberations.

Then the girl heard something that made her open her eyes for a second. Somewhere in amongst all the shuddering wailing drones Sianan was sure that she could hear the high-pitched music of the war-pipes. The tune was not a sombre march as Sianan would have expected to hear from such an instrument. It was a merry dance played impossibly fast; too fast for any dancer to tap out the rhythm with her feet. Yet Sianan was sure that she could hear a dancer.

It was not long before she realised that there were many voices calling out encouragement to the performers. There were heated debates and laughter emanating from every corner of the room. She could hear cups colliding in countless blessing toasts and occasionally a word raised above the others in anger.

With eyes half shut Sianan let her imagination fill in the details of what the folk were wearing at this imaginary gathering. She could see through a cloudy haze shapeless forms that brushed against her. It was clear that a fine feast was being consumed in this ancient hall. Sianan could smell the meat cooking, the bread baking and the mead being spilled. A piper stood on a chair against one wall and played a dance on the war-pipes. She shut her eyes tight again to concentrate on the scene for it was unheard of in Eirinn that an instrument of war would be played at a celebration.

As she was losing herself in her imagination the merry feast became more vivid until she swore she could overhear one or two of the conversations taking place in the room. The language was similar to that spoken by the folk of the far west of Eirinn—archaic and full of witty observation and double meaning.

Sianan thought she heard her own name spoken. Then there was uproarious laughter as though everyone at the feast had caught some joke that she had missed.

'Why won't she dance with us?' an old woman jeered. 'Aren't we good enough for her?'

'She's of the Druid kind,' another voice reprimanded. 'Now hush your foolish talk and let her be.'

'If she's going to walk the Great Road she should dance a little first so she gets used to lifting her feet,' a male voice pronounced solemnly and this brought all the assembly into fits of laughter again.

'Get her up,' they all began calling out. 'Come and dance, Sianan.'

The piper struck up another tune and with her inner eyes Sianan saw a musician with a wide round goatskin drum join him. She could feel the floor pounding with many feet dancing in a great circle all around her. The rhythm melted with the great rumbling that she had felt earlier.

'Come and dance!' they repeated over and over.

In her mind the room was suddenly lit brightly by many candles and lamps. Each little light was a different colour, blues, greens, reds, bright golden yellows and purples, not just the common orange glow of firelight. Sianan wondered at the beautiful scene that was playing itself out in her head. She had never experienced such impossible visions.

Suddenly she had heard a male voice, gentle but firm and very close by. 'Now you must dance with us, Sianan.'

She knew in her heart that she must answer this man out of respect for his position in the assembly but she could not be certain if her senses were playing tricks on her so she held her tongue.

'Sianan, do you hear me? You may look on us. We would like you to come and join the dance.' A hand brushed against hers. It was big and rough and calloused like that of a farmer and the shock of the touch banished all doubts from Sianan that this experience was a product of her imagination. Startled, she snapped her eyelids open to see who was addressing her.

The scene that presented itself to her was exactly the same as the one she had seen in her mind. The figure who touched her hand was immense and was bent over double to fit within the confines of the chamber. His head was huge and his nose was puffed up so that it looked swollen. His eyes were wet and black without any whites to them, rather like the eyes of a deer.

Though the room was illuminated by many candles it seemed that only Sianan's little light caused any shadows to appear on the walls. The huge creature who bent over shuffled a little so that he

226

loomed even larger bordered by the darkness behind him. Framed around the outline of this strange creature's head Sianan could plainly see the shadow of two dark antlers though there was none actually growing from his skull.

When he noticed her staring at him he awkwardly bent his knees to get more comfortable. Sianan was able to see then that he did not have the feet of a human at all. Where there should have been toes there were great hooves like the feet of a king stag. She had heard tales of Danaans who were half beast and half human. This she reasoned must be one of those folk.

As he settled again Sianan caught a little sparkle amongst the thick hair of his chest. It was a tiny jewel clear as the covering of ice on a freshwater well and it dangled around his neck on a chain of silver. She could not hold back any longer, overcome by a desire to ask the man who he was. His booming voice cut her off before she had filled her lungs to speak.

'All right, then,' he grizzled like a child who has been refused a treat and is retreating to a corner to sulk, 'don't dance with us. Now you'll have to wait till Beltinne.' He leaned forward and with a great breath he blew out the candle that Sianan had stuck firmly in the dirt nearby. Instantly all the voices, all the music, all sound ceased and the hundreds of tiny lights in the tower went out as though they had never been lit. Suddenly Sianan was left sitting alone in the dark.

'Perhaps it would not have hurt to dance with them,' she thought and an old woman's voice answered her: 'One day you may, my girl, one day you may.'

Sianan could still smell the scent of roasting meat and her body was tingling from the rumble that had filled her consciousness. The sweet dance music echoed in her head as though it had never stopped. All through that night it returned to haunt her but the feasting Danaans did not return no matter how she begged them to.

FOURTEEN

he leaves of this plant when infused in a pot of boiling water can be very dangerous. Indeed the Cruitne use it to poison the water of their enemies,' Gobann warned. 'But if applied in the right quantities it is useful in bringing on visions of the Otherworld and warding off extreme pain. You must be careful never to handle this leaf with bare hands especially when it is freshly gathered. I am not sure what effect it may have on someone like yourself or Sianan once you have eaten of the Danaans' potion of life. I cannot guarantee that it will not harm you. At the very least the herb could make you very ill.'

Mawn studied the leaves on the cloth before him carefully. 'What colour are the flowers when they bloom?'

'They are dark like the night sky,' answered Gobann. 'Deep blue-black, the same shade as the trees of the Otherworld that grow along the road beyond life.' The poet paused to gather up the corners of the cloth and conceal the leaves. 'Soon you will take the journey that leads along that road. You, however, will return to the Earth as others do not. Afterwards you will remain here when all of us, all your teachers, all your friends, everyone you have ever known or will ever meet have gone down that path to the halls of waiting. Only Sianan and yourself will remain when the world changes again. Are you sure that you are prepared to wander along this lonely path?'

Mawn shuddered. 'Can anyone ever be ready?' Gobann made no sign that he intended to answer so Mawn continued speaking. 'If Sianan will consent to take on this task then I also will take the Road of Life.'

'As the law requires me to do, I have asked you three times whether you are ready to become a Wanderer. Now it is time for us to return to Teamhair. Before the moon changes the rites of passage will be celebrated at the hill of initiation. Then the next step on your journey will begin.' As soon as he had finished speaking Gobann spun round on his heel, walking directly into the forest without looking back.

Mawn was caught unawares and had to gather up the baggage quickly to try to catch up with his mentor. In a short while the poet was clear of the woods and was crossing the fields toward the Druid school that was established nearby. There master and pupil spent the night. At dawn they loaded their horses and set off for the citadel of Teamhair, the seat of the High-King of Eirinn.

At the same time, unknown to Mawn, within the High-King's stronghold a great gathering of Druids was taking place. Never in living memory had so many of the holy ones been summoned. Not even the council that celebrated Gobann's initiation had included so many renowned and learned folk. Druids, Brehon judges, bard-harpers, Senchai and singers. Filidh historians came from Britain and the lands of the Cruitne. Learned men and women from Gaul and from the Western Isles of the Pretani tribes. Others came from Iberia and the Kingdom of the Dal Araidhe, all making their way to the hill that was the spiritual centre of Eirinn.

There were also three strangers who came to the assembly but did not mix with any of the other Druids. They were deliberately billeted apart from all the folk who dwelt in the citadel. The High-King placed his personal guards around their quarters to ensure that no-one entered who did not have his leave to do so.

None but the inner circle of the Druid Council knew for certain who these strangers were, though it was said that they had come as emissaries from the kingdoms of the ancient folk, the Tuatha-De-Danaan, the mysterious tribes whose world was beyond the reach of mortal people. Rumours were rife that these three were the chief Druids of their people. Skilled in all the arts were their clans, renowned in war, tall and fair of face. It was also said that they were immortal, for they brewed a drink from the juice of the rowan berry that gave them leave from all sickness and pain and staved off death forever.

Druids rarely pay any attention to gossip but the rumour of the Danaans had been passed among them encoded in a secret language used in the greatest necessity. It was a sure way to prevent the uninitiated from learning what was being said.

To affirm any suspicions that the delegates might have, the Danaans had arrived in a double chariot fitted with four stout wheels and covered with black leather. The wagon was wheeled directly into the midst of the large green tent on the field of initiation which had been reserved for them alone. Throughout the first night of their stay the guards outside the Danaan tent could smell strange sweet aromas of cooking. More than one of the soldiers was tempted to lift open the flap to beg a morsel of the food that they had prepared. None did. Leoghaire had given all the sentries a clear warning that he would not tolerate any breach of hospitality toward these guests.

At dawn of the first day after their arrival at Teamhair the whole citadel was shrouded in a veil of music unlike any that had been heard there for at least five hundred winters. Within the strangers' tent someone struck the brass wires of a harp, if indeed it was a harp, for the melody and the tone of that instrument was unlike any that the other gathered Druids had ever heard. The tune was so full of sadness and joy and yearning all at once that there were some among the Gaelic and Breton Druids who could not bear to hear it. Others sat still, striving to memorise the strains of the Faery music, hoping to be able to remember enough of what they heard to one day re-create its magic.

By this stage even the chief sentry was tempted to see what manner of folk were dwelling behind the tent canvas on the hill of Teamhair. The whole citadel was buzzing with talk about the Danaans, for such wonders, common ten generations ago, had become as rare as frost on a hearthstone in recent times.

Gobann and Mawn reached the citadel on the third day after the Danaans had come to the gathering. The poet deliberately led his student past the tent on their way to the Star of Poets, the hall where all the Druid kind met. As the two of them approached, Mawn caught the scent of an unfamiliar fragrance in the air which put him in mind of Origen the white-robed Christian monk from the country at the edge of the wasteland.

'These perfumes are not sweet like those of Origen,' he said aloud as they passed the sentry. 'The aroma reminds me of the first day of spring but there is something else in it that I cannot place even though it seems familiar to me.'

'You may soon ask these Druids about their herb secrets. We will be called to visit them in a few days. Be warned though, they rarely give a direct answer. They talk in riddles when they do not wish to pass on a recipe.'

'Who are they?'

'They are born of this land but they live elsewhere now. They are spirits of air and water who dwell within fiery caverns in the earth. They will tell you their tale all in good time.' Struggling to read the hidden message in what Gobann said Mawn realised that his teacher also made use of riddles when it suited him.

'Will you tune my harp this evening?' the poet asked as if the request were nothing special. Mawn nodded. It was the first time that he had been asked to do the tuning for his master in the whole nine seasons of his apprenticeship.

'Tonight you may leave your battered old harp with the rest of our baggage,' Gobann went on. 'This evening you will perform for the Druid assembly so you should have a good instrument to play.'

Mawn acknowledged his master's wishes simply, letting no sign of his excitement show for that would have diminished the great honour that Gobann was giving him.

'I shall polish the wires before I tune her,' the pupil said, 'and then I will pare back my nails.'

Not only Druids had gathered at Teamhair for the festival of Beltinne which was about to be celebrated across the land. It was customary for people of all walks of life to take part in the public rituals.

233

It was also usual to send one member of each family to collect a burning ember from the Need Fire that was lit at this time.

In the hall of the warriors, Murrough Eóghanacht the King of Munster and Enda Censelach the King of Laigin were waiting to meet in conference with their overlord Leoghaire in order to discuss the worsening situation in Britain.

The two other kingdoms were represented only by princes who were not able to take part in the High-King's inner council. The king of the northern Ulaid sent his nephew Oileel Molt as his stand-in while he was away in the land of Dal Araidhe assisting his cousins to drive back an incursion by Saxon and Jutish warriors.

The King of Connachta refused to sit under the same roof as Enda Censelach. He had still not forgiven the King of Laigin for invading his land and laying waste to his country. The people of Connachta had always struggled just to survive on the harsh, bleak west coast. After the war with Laigin their situation had worsened a hundred fold. Unable to muster enough strong hands to bring in the harvest, the kingdom of Connachta was suffering the most devastating famine in living memory. Cúnla Og was to have represented Connachta in council but he had fallen ill with a mysterious illness just after his arrival at Teamhair. He was confined to his bed most of the day.

So it was that only two kings of Eirinn sat with Leoghaire in the hall of the Ard-Righ. As it happened Murrough and Enda had no fondness for each other.

The King of Munster was chosen as ruler of his kingdom because his elder brother Morann had stepped down from that responsibility to take the Druid path. He had been the only person left in the clan who was eligible to rule according to the strict requirements of genealogy. Murrough could have chosen not to take the kingship but if he had done so then it would have passed to another clan. That of course was unthinkable to him. His family had been the elected kings of Munster for at least ten generations. They were descended from the legendary Eber who was the first king of the south and the son of the ancestor of all the Gaelic people, the chieftain called Míl.

Enda Censelach, on the other hand, had not been born to kingship. He had been nominated as caretaker king of Laigin by Leoghaire after the great revolt of Dichu. His one qualification was that he had chosen not to become involved in the resulting civil war. Enda had worked to ensure that after his year as caretaker king he would be certain to be elected by the Council of Laigin. That is how he secured for himself and his descendants all the rights and privileges due to those who rule. He had started a war in Connachta for no other reason than to gain prestige among his people. Later Enda had paid the lesser chieftains in the kingdom from his personal fortune to ensure their support.

Many Laigin men had died in Dichu's war and many more went into voluntary exile with their former king. Throughout Eirinn the shortage of harvesters had meant that there were not enough folk left to bring in the produce. Most of the crops rotted on the stalk. Enda had come up with a solution that made him very popular in his kingdom. He organised raids all along the coasts of Britain to take captives. Like Niall of the Nine Hostages, his agents demanded ransoms from their captives. Before long Enda had amassed enough gold to provide food for his kingdom by purchasing it from the more fertile south. In the end he won election to the kingship easily and he was revered as the saviour of his people. Enda Censelach had done more than feed his subjects, he had restored their honour after the treachery of Dichu.

Enda's rise to kingship had been slow and fraught with unending difficulties. This was why he resented Murrough, whom he felt had been born with the four-coloured cloak wrapped round his shoulders and the golden torc of kingship fastened to his neck. What was more, the King of Munster seemed to have no desire to be king at all. Even though the people of Munster loved their king and re-elected him each summer without fail, Murrough was largely indifferent to their faith in him.

Leoghaire was well aware that the two men had no respect for each other and he was not looking forward to having them seated in the same hall for the evening. They often spent days petulantly fighting over trivial matters or broke up the meetings with their traded insults. The High-King liked Murrough well enough and had been good friends with his father but when Murrough got together with Enda the pair of them seemed to be able to ruffle each other's feathers like no two other men on Earth.

Enda and Murrough sat on opposite sides of the central hearth fire which meant they were as far away from each other as possible. In absolute silence they waited for Leoghaire to arrive. Murrough had dismissed his guard and his chamberlain to go to their dinner but Enda forced his two servants to stand beside his chair until the High-King arrived. However, Leoghaire was extremely late.

It was uncharacteristic for the High-King not to be on time for any appointment; in fact, he was usually to be found waiting around for his guests with the cup of welcoming warmed by his own hands. So this was an unusual position for the two kings to be placed in.

Enda was happy to sit out the wait without a word to the other king. Murrough, on the other hand, began to get restless and it was not long before he had invited Enda to play at the Brandubh with him.

The King of Laigin hesitated for a moment. He was famous as a champion of the ancient game. Quite possibly there was no greater player in his lifetime in the whole of Eirinn. He rarely refused a challenge. To defeat the younger, less experienced Murrough would certainly not present much of a problem to one such as him. It might even be enjoyable to thrash the King of Munster in a quick match.

Murrough took the ravens as was the custom for a challenger. This gave Enda the first move. The warrior king gripped one of the white kings in his bony sword hand, placing it down on a new square as though it didn't really matter where he put it. Murrough watched him all the while.

The King of Munster could plainly see that Enda had lost a lot of weight since he had last seen him in the autumn. The Laigin king's arms were very thin as though the muscle had melted away to the bone. And Enda was now greying where once dark brown locks of hair had fallen across his shoulders. His eyes also seemed to be drained of their colour, no longer the dark orbs they had been. There were little red lines all across his nose and cheeks that had not been there a season ago. Even the eastern king's beard had turned almost completely grey and it had become extremely untidy.

Murrough began to wonder how much he himself had aged since he became king of Munster. Had his red hair gone grey without him noticing? Had his skin turned pallid and waxy? Did he still have the body of a warrior? Or had he grown soft with all the life at court?

As if his body were answering him Murrough felt a sharp pain in his shoulder. He had taken a wound there before becoming king and the old injury troubled him now and again. The sudden recurrence of the cramp made him decide then and there to go riding every day again. That way he would be able to keep fit as he aged. It was obvious that it had not been necessary for Enda to engage in any strenuous activity for a long time. Murrough did not want end up a weak old man. He had been thinking about joining his warriors in their training each day. The man before him was a good case for doing so.

The two men played out the game with Enda smugly winning the first round without a sound having passed his lips. Murrough watched his opponent closely. So matted was Enda's beard that it was hard to tell whether he was scowling or smiling. Murrough had often thought about cutting his beard back as the younger warriors did but somehow he had never got around to it. Caitlin, his wife, often begged him to remove it for when they had first met he had no beard or moustache. It was only when he became weary with his office that he neglected to shave.

Murrough thought of Caitlin again, reminding himself to send a rider to Cashel at first light to see that all was well with her. Though he knew that she was in good hands with Síla, none of her pregnancies had been easy and he worried about her.

Suddenly he noticed that Enda was standing in front of him and that there was another figure beside the King of Laigin. His gaze wandered to this other man. It took a few moments for Murrough to realise that it was Leoghaire. The King of Munster had been so lost in his own thoughts that he was not aware that the High-King had entered the hall. He stood up quickly, knocking over his chair and scattering the playing pieces on the floor.

'I am sorry, lord. I did not see you—' he began but Leoghaire cut him off.

'Don't worry, my boy.' He always addressed Murrough as if he were still very young. 'I see that you did not finish your game,' he added with an insinuation that the Brandubh had been knocked over deliberately.

'This game will not be finished,' Enda confirmed full of accusation. 'It is a pity that you are more clumsy than you are skilled at the game. It would be valuable for you as king of Munster to be able to win a match without spreading the pieces all over the floor.'

Leoghaire burst out laughing at Enda's comment but Murrough snapped back. 'I would be honoured if the King of Laigin would teach me all the tricks that he has learned.' Once again Leoghaire began giggling.

Enda and Murrough both looked at each other for a moment, then straight back at the High-King, who suddenly understood that he had acted a little strangely. He immediately took a serious tone again.

'How is Queen Caitlin? And the child in her womb?'

'All was well, lord, when I left Cashel a week ago. I have heard no more news since. Síla the Druid is with her and there is no better healing woman in all of the five kingdoms. She feels confident that this child will certainly come to term.'

'Excellent!' exclaimed Leoghaire, slapping Murrough on the shoulder. 'That is very good news. And what about your wife, Enda?'

'What about her, my lord?' Enda replied rather bewildered.

'How is she?'

This caught Enda off guard. He wasn't expecting to be questioned about his wife since it was well known that they were living apart. 'I am told that she is very well, my lord. Much happier now that she is staying with her family on the coast,' he stuttered, noticing that the High-King was beaming again.

'Good. Well, let's sit down and have something to eat, shall we?'

Enda and Murrough nodded in agreement but as soon as the High-King's back was turned they threw questioning glances at each other. The King of Laigin made a sign with his hands that indicated Leoghaire was probably suffering from exhaustion. Murrough lifted his hand to his lips holding an imaginary mead-cup while raising his eyebrows implying that mead might be the culprit for this strange behaviour. Then both men looked back to their lord, not sure which suggestion was correct.

The two provincial kings took their seats at opposite sides of the fire once more while Leoghaire sat himself down where he could see both of their faces. Food was brought in on great wooden platters and a large iron cauldron full of warm mead was laid at the High-King's feet. Before the dishes were touched the High-King took the silver cuaich cup from one of his servants and dipped it in the cauldron of mead. When he drew it out again it was full to the brim. This was the cuaich of welcome. Though these cups were common in the five kingdoms this was the most beautiful example that Murrough had ever seen. This cuaich had been passed down from one High-King to another ever since the Gaels had been in Eirinn. It was said to have been a gift from a queen of the Danaans.

'Blessings on the five kingdoms of Eirinn,' Leoghaire said as he sipped from the cup. Then he passed it to Enda who in turn took a gulp and passed it over the fire to Murrough. When he had taken a mouthful from the cuaich Murrough passed it back to Leoghaire, who put it on its stand beside him. This way the High-King could be sure that he could drink from it whenever he pleased. As this was probably going to be a long night— meetings between Murrough and Enda always seemed too long—he expected that he would be needing the cuaich quite regularly.

'I hope you are not offended,' Leoghaire said still smiling, 'I have asked Cathach to join us this evening after he has attended to his duties in the Hall of Poets. He has received some news from a Druid of the Cruitne that we should discuss urgently. I felt it would be better if he reported the matter to us himself.' This was actually just a thin pretext to have Cathach attend the royal council without prior notice being given to the other guests, but neither the King of Laigin nor of Munster protested.

Leoghaire reached over to the low table nearby and chose a piece of roast pork to chew on. He was not particularly hungry but it gave his guests the message that he would not be offended if they began their meal.

Enda immediately launched himself into the food before him with enthusiasm. Murrough was surprised that one who ate so well and so often could still be so thin. He realised then that Enda must have been very ill during the winter. The King of Munster picked at some bread and some meat but his mind was not on food, it was on Caitlin. He was concerned that he had not yet received any word about the birth. He could only think that perhaps it had not gone well with her.

'As you know, for too long now the British tribes who call themselves the Cumri have been unable to agree on a new High-King for their peoples,' Leoghaire said eventually, getting down to business. His smile was gone and he seemed to be himself once more. Both Murrough and Enda relaxed. 'Ambrosius, who was their last elected High-King, died just before we suffered the revolt in Laigin. That makes it nine seasons since they have been without a leader. The situation has become more desperate for them since the Saxons invited more of their people to help with the invasion of Britain.'

'Ambrosius and his rival Vortigern were stupid to trust those savages,' Enda commented. 'A child could have told them that the Saxons would not be content with mercenaries' wages and a small plot of land in exchange for manning the Roman wall in the north. When Vortigern was slain by Christian brigands, Ambrosius had no choice but to take to the Cross out of fear for the power of the black-robed clerics.' There was obvious distaste in Censelach's voice. 'They say that it was a Roman bishop called Germanus who poisoned King Ambrosius. While Palladius made war in Eirinn,

242

this Germanus was stirring up trouble in Britain. If only we had been able to lend a hand to our friends over the sea.'

'We were preoccupied with our own Christian uprising in those days or else the High Council would have been in a better position to give Ambrosius the help he needed,' Leoghaire asserted. 'He was a proud man but he was frightened for the future. In the last days of his life he probably would not have listened to anyone except the Bishop Germanus of Auxerre. That Roman had the old fool so scared that he refused to leave his fort.'

'Meddling bloody Christians always sticking their noses in where they're not wanted,' spat Enda.

The High-King grunted as if in agreement. 'After many seasons of internal squabbling the British kings have elected a new man to be a chief among their peoples. I believe that he is someone who may listen to what we have to say. He name is Uther, Son of the Dragon. The chieftains have not conferred the full status of High-Kingship on him because every petty ruler east of the Giant's Bridge covets that title. The internecine struggle that raged between Vortigern and Ambrosius was not so long ago that it has been completely forgotten. The Cumri Britons spent more energy during that time fighting each other for supremacy than fending off the Saxon threat. As a compromise they have awarded their new leader an old Roman office which they have specially reinstituted for the first time since the last imperial garrison departed. He is called war-duke.'

'So he is High-King in all but name,' Enda laughed. 'I have heard many tales of Uther the Pendragon. He has quite a reputation as a warrior

243

and leader of men. Most admirable of all he has refused the baptism of Germanus, the Christian traitor who was responsible for the deaths of Vortigern and Ambrosius. Uther is a good man by all accounts.'

'It is my plan to send a delegation to Uther as soon as possible,' Leoghaire cut in, 'to offer whatever aid we can to their cause and to negotiate a common alliance between our kingdoms. The Saxons pose as great a threat to our land as to the British. We can expect the savages to arrive here shortly after the conquest of Britain. Personally I would rather deal with them before they reach our shores if possible. Murrough, would you agree?'

The King of Munster was only listening with one ear. His thoughts were still with Caitlin. 'Yes, lord. They are a brutal people who do not seem to have any laws that we could recognise. If once they gain a foothold in Eirinn we might never see the end of them.'

'Then you think that we should send an emissary to Uther?'

'Yes, lord, of course,' Murrough agreed, not really aware of what he was assenting to.

Before he had time to admit that he had not been listening a guard opened the door to the hall and Cathach entered, walking very slowly and deliberately so that the three men had plenty of time to notice his arrival. This was an old-fashioned mark of respect that gave them time to conclude any confidential matters. The old Druid went to the High-King's chair so that Leoghaire could give him the cuaich. Cathach took his time with the mead, savouring the flavour and the sweet aroma of the brew. When he finally put it down the other men were sitting forward in their seats eagerly awaiting his report.

'I have news of the five kingdoms of Eirinn and of the kingdom of Dal Araidhe where our Gaelic brethren live and of the Cumri people who are our cousins,' the Druid began in the traditional manner.

'I beg you, speak to us of what you know,' Leoghaire intoned.

Cathach launched immediately into his report. 'I have been speaking with Fidach, Chief Druid of the Cruitne tribes who live to the north of Dal Araidhe. He has informed me that Uther, the war-duke of the Cumri, has just negotiated an alliance with Hengist, the King of the Saxons.'

Leoghaire, Murrough and Enda instantly stopped chewing their food, turning their eyes to Cathach.

'In exchange for territories that lie on the border between Uther's domains and those of the Cruitne, the Saxon king has promised there will be peace between their people and all the Cumri who support Uther.'

'And the Pendragon trusts them?' Enda gasped.

'Uther has extracted strong oaths from Hengist and promised to give Saxon raiding parties safe passage through his territory on their journey toward the lands of the Cruitne. The foreigners have already begun to harry the southern tribes of Fidach's people.'

'Uther has bought his own safety at the expense of the Cruitne,' Leoghaire sighed as though he had expected that this would happen.

'This is bad news,' Cathach admitted, 'but there is worse to come. The war-duke of the Cumri has laid open three of his harbours for the exclusive use of the Saxon ships. He is obviously trying to encourage them to seek new lands to pillage. Eirinn may be the first place many of the savages head for.'

'That is disgraceful!' cried Enda. 'Who does he think he is? We have stood by his people throughout all their troubles with the Saxons. We have supplied grain to his troops and sanctuary to his fleeing soldiers. Our blacksmiths have laboured to make battle harness and swords and spears for him. And this is how he repays us?'

'It has come to the stage,' Cathach interrupted, 'where I believe he has little choice but to ally with Hengist if he wishes to gain valuable time in which to rearm his people. There are scores of Germans arriving on the Cumri shore every day—Angles, Jutes, Franks, Bernicians and Frisians—lured by the tales of the rich southern lands of Britain. There are many more of them coming than Uther and his defences could ever hope to repel. For the moment he is passing them on to others to deal with while he builds his army for the fight that will surely soon come.'

'And he has left his brothers the Cruitne to fend off the onslaught in the meantime,' Enda hissed.

'It is not only the Cruitne who are in the front line of this German migration. I warned you that there was worse news to come. Now I have to report the most disturbing news of all. Two days ago a fleet of six Saxon ships landed near the Druid college of Bally Cahor. I do not know for certain how many of our folk perished in this attack but I have been told that many were taken hostage. The settlement was sacked and burned to the ground. My granddaughter is among those who are still missing.'

Murrough, Enda and Leoghaire let their jaws fall open in shock. If it had not been Cathach who had reported it they all would have laughed in disbelief at the tale. This was the ultimate proof of the Saxons' barbarity for no man who fully understood the significance of the women's settlement would dare set foot within the sanctuary. The fact that the raiders were Saxons and ignorant of Gaelic laws and custom did not seem to occur to any of them.

'Through the efforts of the women of Bally Cahor, the community at Inis Trá was warned of the presence of the Saxons and the day after the attack on the Druid settlement the fleet was surprised by a large force of warriors and freemen. Of the six ships they had brought with them two escaped. Both of these vessels sailed away before our boats could reach them. I believe they were loaded with captives from Bally Cahor. All the foreigners who were left behind on our soil chose to fight to the death and were eventually slain. For now the menace is past but it will not be long before they return. This was just a small party sent to test the defences. Next time they will certainly come in greater numbers.'

'Then we must strike first!' cried Enda, throwing a piece of pork fat into the fire. 'And the Druids who were taken by the enemy must be rescued as soon as possible.'

'The Morrigan alone knows how they will be treated by those bastards,' added Murrough. He remembered well enough how the Saxons handled their prisoners for he had been taken captive by Saxons shortly after the battle of Rathowen. 'Enda is right, we must send a force to deal with the savages.'

Leoghaire held up his hand to calm the two kings. 'There is no good rushing off and hoping that in all the wide seas you will have a chance of finding two Saxon galleys. We must consider carefully what action we can take or we could end up unable to defend our own shores. Was Sianan taken hostage?' he asked Cathach.

'I do not know as yet, lord,' answered the old man. 'However, my inner voice would have told me if she were in any immediate danger.'

'You said earlier, lord, that you would like to send an emissary to the war-duke Uther,' Murrough interrupted. 'I know the Saxons well enough. Let me go to the court of the Cumri and convince Uther to join in alliance with us.'

Cathach and Leoghaire exchanged glances. The old Druid rolled his eyes a little but neither Murrough nor Enda noticed. The kings of Munster and Laigin were already yelling at each other, arguing over which of them should be sent.

'You are still a boy,' roared Enda. 'And let us remember that the last time you met any Saxons you were privileged enough to be imprisoned by them. Unlike yourself I am in fighting condition,' he lied. 'My warriors are ready to ride at a day's notice. How long will it take for your army to mobilise?'

Murrough had neglected the training of his warriors. It was common knowledge throughout the five kingdoms. Unable to refute the veiled accusation he resorted to insults. 'Three Laigin men could not take the place of one Munster man whether he was trained or not, that is well known.'

'I suppose you think you could beat a Laigin warrior off with both hands tied behind your back. The Saxons trussed you up like that but you did not escape them unaided. If the Saxons ever invade the south we can be sure that their best rope-twisters will be in the front ranks.'

'The warriors of Munster do not submit easily to their enemies.'

'Is that so? Then why don't we test some of your champions against mine and find out who has the better soldiers?'

Leoghaire could see this rivalry ending in bloodshed. 'We have enough to think about in dealing with invaders from across the sea. Bickering amongst ourselves will not solve that problem,' he stormed. 'Now be quiet the both of you!'

The two kings sat down again, silenced and shamed by the High-King's anger.

'Here is my decree,' Leoghaire boomed. 'Since Conaire King of the Ulaid is in Dal Araidhe fighting with his kinsman and Fergal of Connachta is seeing to the famine in his country, I appoint Murrough King of Munster to oversee the defences of the southern coasts of Eirinn.'

Enda breathed a deep sigh. He was happiest when he got exactly what he wanted.

'Enda Censelach King of the people of Laigin, I appoint you to travel first to the court of Uther Pendragon. Publicly you will present our protest at his behaviour. In private I would like you to reassure him that we will support him should the need arise. When you have visited him you are to sail the length and breadth of Britain gathering as much information as you can about the Saxons. We need to know their numbers, who their kings are, and which areas they have already settled. You will send messengers to me at Teamhair every moon until your return. Do you understand?'

'I do lord,' answered the King of Laigin. 'I will need more troops.'

'Then you have my leave to raise them in your own kingdom.'

'And ships.'

'I will levy each of the kingdoms to place their fleets at your disposal.'

Enda could not have imagined a better opportunity being placed at his feet. He now had permission from the High-King to raise a real army, not just gather some warriors together to carry out puny raids. Well planned and executed, this expedition had the potential to make him a very rich man indeed. 'And to what extent am I constrained in the action that I decide to take in your name?'

Leoghaire turned to face the Laigin king directly. 'I leave all decisions regarding the practical aspects of this embassy up to you, Censelach. What you deem necessary I will not criticise.'

Murrough could not believe his ears. Was it true? The High-King was all but giving the famous pirate Enda a licence to pillage a land that was already suffering under the weight of foreign incursions. Something just did not seem right. 'He's worse than the Saxons,' Murrough snarled. The other men held their tongues as he spoke in case they provoked him to a deadly insult. 'Enda Censelach stormed Connachta only so that he would be popular with his people. That kingdom is still suffering from the deeds of his hand. Do you really think he will take the time to rescue a dozen Druid women when all the gold of the Saxons is begging to be pilfered?'

Enda's face turned bright red. Leoghaire was watching the situation carefully, however, cutting in before the King of Laigin could say anything. 'The King of Munster will be silent!' he barked.

Murrough stopped short, so dumbfounded that he sank slowly back down into his seat. The High-King had never spoken to him like that before and he did not know quite what to make of it.

'Murrough, you have your commission. You will ride immediately to Cashel and organise the southern defences from there. If you need anything send word to me. I will try to aid you wherever I can. In a few days I will be off raising the tribes of the

Ulaid who are my kinsmen to defend the north. Have you any questions?'

'No, lord.'

'Then you are dismissed,' Leoghaire snapped. 'You may leave my hall and make preparations to ride south. I will speak to you tomorrow before you leave.'

Murrough rose and bowed slightly to Cathach but he did not farewell either Leoghaire or Enda—he was still far too enraged by the High-King's edict. Enda rose from his seat at the same time to leave but Leoghaire stopped him. 'Censelach, I would like you to remain with me a while. We still have much to discuss.'

Murrough heard these words and it stung him to think that Leoghaire trusted a man like Enda to be his ambassador. At the door of the hall Murrough called out to his chamberlain, making sure that his orders could be heard by all those under the High-King's roof. 'Gather our warriors and saddle our horses. We leave for Cashel tonight!'

Cathach closed his eyes, praying to his ancestors that Murrough would not leave before Leoghaire and Enda had finished their business. The old Druid wanted a chance to explain the whole situation to Murrough.

'Thank you for asking him to leave,' Enda whispered to Leoghaire. 'I would prefer it if he were not nosing about in my private affairs.'

Leoghaire made no gesture of acknowledgment at this comment but motioned for Cathach to take a seat in the place where Murrough had been.

Cathach addressed the King of Laigin as he covered his knees with his long blue cloak. 'Have you considered the matter which I raised with you this afternoon, my lord?'

Enda did not look at the old man. 'I have,' he replied.

'And may I ask what your answer might be?'

'I have thought the matter over at great length and decided that should the High-King wish to marry my daughter, Mona, then I would be happy to give my consent. Unless of course . . .'

'Yes,' Cathach said, 'go on.'

'Unless of course she does not wish to wed. Then I am afraid that a much larger dowry would need to be offered her, in the event that she might ever wish to divorce.'

'You have been offered a dowry that any queen of the five kingdoms would be more than happy with,' Cathach pointed out.

The King of Laigin seemed wounded by the Druid's words. 'But my daughter is not yet a queen and I have not broached the subject with her. It is possible that she may resent my making arrangements for her future like this without consulting her.'

Leoghaire knew that Censelach was lying. Mona had always done what her father ordered her to. That was the way Enda ran his family affairs: in everything his children obeyed him. Mona was the only one among them who had ever dared to stand up to him. When she became a Christian neither begging, reasoning nor threats had been able to change her mind.

'So you see,' Enda continued, 'until I know her mind on this I cannot commit her to a marriage. Perhaps I will speak with her tonight. Tomorrow I may be able to give you her answer.'

'I think I can save us all a lot of trouble and put your mind at ease in one blow, Censelach,' Leoghaire interrupted.

The King of Laigin was puzzled but it was only a moment before Leoghaire explained himself.

'I spoke to Mona just before we all sat down at this meeting. That is why I was so late. I asked her straight out if she would consider honouring me as my wife and queen. She immediately accepted my proposal, on the condition of course that I promise to protect the rights of all Christians within my kingdom. I am interested in learning more about the ways of the Cross. Who better to instruct me than my wife.'

A pall of indignation passed quickly across Enda like an autumn leaf carried away on the surface of a swift stream. His anger did not have a chance to surface either before it sputtered out like a lamp burning its last drop of oil as Enda realised he had already secured a very profitable assignment in Britain as a direct result of this union. Besides which, he had managed to rid himself of an otherwise unmarriageable daughter, for who in the whole of Eirinn would want to be tied to a Christian wife?

'In that case,' the King of Laigin conceded, 'it is not for me to refuse.'

'Then with your permission I will announce the wedding tomorrow.'

'By all means,' Enda gushed.

Cathach stood up and excused himself as soon as he was sure that no-one would be offended. Once outside he made his way as quickly as he could to the hall of the Munster king. He wanted to catch Murrough before he left Teamhair for his home.

When the chief Druid arrived at the house of Munster there were many horsemen milling about. The whole court of Cashel seemed to be preparing to ride. Hoping that he still had a chance of finding the king, Cathach darted between the servants inquiring after Murrough.

'He has gone to the Hall of Champions to speak to his best warriors,' someone called out.

Cathach did not wait another second to take the path that led down to that building. The old man cursed his feeble legs which, though strong for a man of his age, could not endure too much walking, especially when the nights were chilly. When he finally came to the Hall of the Champions he was forced to wait for several minutes at the entrance before the door-keeper came out to see to him. Once the Druid stated his business the guard decided to allow him to pass, though, according to custom, Cathach was obliged to leave his knife and staff behind. These were considered the weapons of a Druid. With the formalities of entering the warriors' hall complete the old man finally made his way to the feasting chamber.

In one corner of the great room thirty warriors were seated in a semicircle. Amidst them was Murrough explaining loudly the reason they were leaving early to return to Cashel.

'I have been ordered by the High-King to see to the defences of the south,' he informed them. This was greeted by general grumblings as his warriors had been enjoying their stay in the citadel, visiting comrades and feasting more or less continuously. 'It is up to us to make sure that no more Saxon war parties land further along the coastline.'

The warriors echoed general agreement with their king but there was little enthusiasm for the strategy. 'I had hoped to set out tonight but there are too many preparations to be made. We will ride at first light. Twelve of you will gallop ahead of the column with me so that I reach Cashel as soon as possible.'

Murrough dismissed his men to their duties though some remained behind in the hall to finish their supper. It was then that the king noticed Cathach pushing his way toward him. 'What is a poet doing in a hall of warriors?' Murrough exclaimed, putting on an air of friendliness.

'I am not such a stranger to these places. I, myself, was a warrior once,' Cathach replied. 'Many times I sat here in this place feasting with my comrades. It was only after the warrior fire burned out in me that I took the Druid path.'

'You did not come here to relive your days with Niall of the Nine Hostages, did you?' Murrough pressed him.

'No, I did not. I came to speak with you on an urgent matter.'

'It seems that there are no other matters but urgent ones in Teamhair tonight.'

Cathach ignored the comment. 'Are you going to leave in the morning?'

'Yes.'

'That is good. There is much to be done if the southern defences are going to be effective. Are you still offended that the King of Laigin is being sent as an emissary to Britain?'

Murrough stroked the strands of his red beard and turned away from the Druid.

Cathach did not wait for an answer. 'If you are still hurt I would advise you to banish such thoughts from your mind. We all know what manner of man Enda is but each of us has our part to play in the great plan. It may be that even he has some contribution to make. You must concentrate on your duties now. Trust that Leoghaire and I know what we are doing in this matter.'

'You always seem to be able to choose the best path,' Murrough conceded. 'Even when you were my father's counsellor you always knew more than you let on.' Murrough swung round to face Cathach. 'What is it that you are not telling anyone this time?'

The old Druid blushed. It was not often that anybody dared question his motives or his methods. 'I have known you since you were a boy and so I will not allow myself to be insulted by that question,' he stated.

'There is something, isn't there?' Murrough persisted as his eyes widened. 'Something that you have not even told old Leoghaire about!'

Cathach grabbed the king by the arm and dragged him to the corner of the room. 'Be silent, will you! This may be the Hall of the Champions of Munster but even in this place it is not safe to speak of some things too loudly.' The old man looked about, checking that nobody had noticed them. 'I will tell you one thing but not because you pressed me to. I am only telling you because it may be a long while before you return to Teamhair and by the time you come back things will surely have taken another turn.'

The Druid lowered himself gradually down onto a stool. Murrough noticed that the old man was visibly relieved to be able to rest. The king crouched beside Cathach, leaning in close to hear what he would say.

'Within the turning of one phase of the moon a man will come to Eirinn who we have long expected. All the preparations that we have made these nine summers past have been for this one's arrival.'

'You sound like one of Origen's monks who preach the imminent return of the Christ from the realms of the dead.'

'It is not wise to make light of this situation,' Cathach added soberly. 'This man has been sent by the chief priest of the Roman church to bring Eirinn into the Christian fold. Many changes are about to be forced upon our people. It will be during this dangerous time that we could so easily win or lose the fight for our identity and the survival of our ways. You must see to it that the Wanderers are kept perfectly safe during the next four seasons. Even they may not be safe from all that is about to come upon us. Our world will be thrown into chaos for a period of time. They will be most vulnerable until the kingdoms settle down again. The only thing that I can tell you about the future is that the Christians will strike out at everything that they do not understand. They will attack the oak groves, the rites of our clan and anything that represents the old ways of our people.'

Murrough lowered his eyes to the floor. 'Mawn and Sianan were given into my care. I understand that is the reason why I may not go to lands of the Cumri as envoy. But tell me, why has Leoghaire decided to send Enda Censelach?'

'So that his hatred for the ways of Christians will not get in the way of their plans to evangelise the five kingdoms. Also of course there is the possibility that with all the Saxons running about in Britain he will not survive long enough to cause us any more trouble. Enda's untimely death would put paid to his ambition for the High-Kingship.'

Murrough raised his eyebrows slightly. 'I was not aware that he had such an ambition.'

Cathach smiled indulgently at the king, preparing to elaborate, but something caught his attention on the far side of the hall. A warrior dressed in full riding gear was striding through the door making straight for Murrough. The man still wore his sword about his belt. The door warden had noticed him too late and now was calling out to him to halt. He did not pay the man any heed. Three of the king's guards stepped out from the crowd to launch themselves at the man. He was larger than any of them so had no trouble fending them off and continuing on his way.

The King of Munster stood up to get a better look at the warrior. He had never heard of anyone breaking the rule of the hall by carrying his weapons into the feasting chamber. Murrough had only his bare fists to ward off any blow from an iron sword. Cathach reached toward his boot, instinctively searching for his knife only to realise that he had left even that insignificant blade at the entrance.

The doorkeeper retreated to his quarters and emerged seconds later with an arrow strung tautly into the gut string of a bow. 'Halt, stranger,' he called out, 'or I will send this shaft to strike you.'

The warrior did not acknowledge the threat. Before the doorkeeper could let the arrow fly the man was within five paces of Murrough. There he stopped in his tracks before the King of Munster, breathing steadily and waiting to be recognised. The door warden aimed his weapon but in the next moment the rider knelt down before Murrough and bowed his head. Many other warriors now crowded around the king, blocking the doorkeeper's line of sight. He had no choice but to let the tension on the bow drop since he could not be sure whether or not he might strike an innocent target if he let the arrow fly.

'Forgive me, lord,' the rider began once all the other warriors were quiet, 'but the fool at the door would have kept me all night with his rules and ritual. I was ordered to come to you with the greatest speed.'

'What is it?' Murrough demanded.

'Queen Caitlin has given birth to a son.'

The whole chamber erupted into cheers and Murrough was suddenly engulfed by many comrades congratulating him and thanking the gods that all was well, but the warrior who had brought the news was not finished. He pushed his way through the throng to reach out for the king. The messenger struggled to yell over the top of all the other voices but Murrough could not hear what he said. In a moment the king raised his hand and his soldiers began to fall silent at the command.

'I said,' the rider bellowed, 'that the queen has suffered badly from the birth. She was close to death when I left the fortress. You must return as quickly as your war horse will carry you. I pray that she still lives when you arrive.'

This news brought every eye in the chamber upon the king. Murrough stared at the messenger's face trying to discern if he was speaking the truth. It did not take long for the gravity of the news to hit him. When the words had sunk in Murrough spoke softly but firmly, addressing all his soldiers.

'I will leave this moment for Cashel. Twelve men of the royal guard will ride with me. The remainder will follow on in the morning.' The king took the messenger's hand to thank him and then forgetting all ritual and without saying another word to Cathach, marched directly out of the hall to find his horse.

'I have not told you about Leoghaire and Mona!' the Druid called after him but before the old man could catch him the King of Munster was gone. His escort of twelve warriors was so slow to ready themselves that Murrough, overcome by impatience, left the Citadel of Teamhair before they had begun to assemble all their gear. He rode hard that night, pushing his horse until he thought his heart would burst. His escort had no hope of catching up to him until late the next day though they also drove their horses on like the wind.

The news of the marriage of Leoghaire and the Princess of Laigin, who was called Mona of the Dark Complexion, swept through the citadel long before it was officially announced. Her father's appointment as emissary to the war-duke of Britain was also heavily rumoured but it was not until his commission to raise an army was endorsed that folk started taking the gossip seriously. Leoghaire's proclamation had no sooner reached the ears of the Druid Council than Enda sent one of his chieftains back to Laigin to start hiring troops.

Gobann heard of all that had come to pass from Cathach later the same evening that Murrough left for Cashel, for the two Druids met together in the Hall of Poets. He learned also of all that had happened at Bally Cahor and like Cathach he was deeply concerned for Sianan. Without her all the plans that they had worked on were worthless for they had no time to train another to take her place. That the Saxons had dared raid the shores of Éirinn was proof that all the events that had been foretold by the Council of Druids would certainly soon come to pass.

Leoghaire's marriage to a woman who professed a faith in Christ was a guarantee that the Christians would believe in the sincerity of the High-King's conversion. Both men agreed that now was the time to prepare the Society of Druids for the change that was about to come upon them.

'In Gaul the legions of Rome murdered many of our kind out of hand, as I am sure you have heard,' Cathach began. 'They burned the oak groves and cut the harpers' fingers off at the first joint so that they would not be able to play the songs. It was not long after that the stories ceased to be remembered.'

Gobann listened patiently though he had heard all of this before. Indeed, he also knew that the Romans had plucked out the tongues of all the storytellers and burned female Druids alive on pyres.

'That was long ago in the times of the Roman conquest. When Rome first turned to the word of Christ the new ways of the Empire existed for a short while at peace with the Druid path. That is until a small group of Christians began to preach against the old worship. Now the followers of Christ have as much power as the Imperial Senate of old. They resort once again to murder and destruction in their frenzy to convert everyone to their laws. The mistake that the Gauls made was to resist Rome openly. If once you resist the Romans they will instantly become the more resolved to crush you. That is what happened in Gaul.'

'Yet if we seem to be too eager in our adoption of the Christian doctrine they will not trust us and may be equally harsh,' Gobann rejoined.

'Yes, that is true,' Cathach confirmed. 'So I have a plan to convince them that not everyone is willing to accept the written word of their Gospels. As chief Druid and foremost advisor to the High-King they will expect me to speak out against them. So I shall. I will surround myself with fellow Druids who are fanatical and hostile to the Christian doctrine. If this new bishop is anything like Palladius was, his pride will lead him into a contest of the faiths soon enough. I will allow him to win that competition. When news of my defeat reaches the kingdoms it will be the signal for Druids all over Eirinn to start flocking to the banner of the Cross. For the sake of a good show I will go to my grave without accepting the Christian doctrine. Yet if we are careful we will ensure that the Druid Council is still able to direct the affairs of the five kingdoms. For every priest who follows blindly the orders of their holy books there will be ten who maintain the Druid path. It is just a matter of keeping their true loyalty a complete secret.'

Gobann was slow to reply. 'I think that you are right about putting up more than token resistance to the Christians, but we must ensure that the result is not a bloody war as it was when Palladius came here.'

'This Roman will not start a war. We have been watching him for a long time. He knows how to press followers into his service with eloquent speeches full of fear of the future. He is well-versed at using the weaknesses of individuals to further the Christian cause. To such a man war is a very crude tool indeed and seldom necessary.'

Gobann was suddenly struck by a thought for his friend from the lands of the great deserts. 'What will become of Origen and the white brothers once the new bishop has established himself?'

'I had not considered them,' Cathach admitted. 'I am not sure that they will be tolerated by the Roman Christians. The manner of Christianity that Origen preaches has its home in the sands of the far away southern countries. It is markedly different from the doctrines of the Europeans. I would

262

be surprised if Origen were allowed to stay in Eirinn once the new man has Leoghaire's ear.'

'You talk as if the High-King might one day turn against us!'

'Do not be surprised if a great change comes over our High-King in the next four seasons. With a young and beautiful wife to attend to who just happens to be a Christian herself, we may well see Leoghaire taking on the mantle of the Cross with more enthusiasm than we might have otherwise expected. Already she has insisted that the marriage ceremony be conducted by a priest of the Roman order.'

'And Leoghaire has consented?'

'So long as the traditional Beltinne wedding also takes place.'

'If Leoghaire becomes hostile to the Druid Council how can we be sure that Sianan and Mawn will be safe?'

'It is possible that Sianan is already beyond our help but you are right we should prepare for such a possibility. For now we should continue preparations for the initiation of the two Wanderers in the hope that Sianan returns to us before Beltinne.'

Cathach rubbed his eyes, yawned and looked about him. Everyone else had gone to bed and they were alone in the hall. 'Sometimes I see Lorgan's ghost walking through this room late at night,' the old Druid confided.

'So do I,' Gobann admitted as thoughts came to him of his long-dead teacher. 'So do I.'

FIFTEEN

hough the experiences of the strange night hidden within the ancient broch were unlike any that Sianan had ever had, she never felt that she was in any danger. In fact after the lights went out she sincerely regretted her decision not to join in the merry dancing of the Faery folk.

Occasionally throughout the remainder of the night a mysterious rumbling stirred her from her rest, though only once did she catch any more than its dying sigh. The noise shook the walls of the tower making her wonder what great force could be the source of such powerful sounds so deep under the ground.

The sunlight was peeping in through a crack in the roof of the structure when she first opened her eyes the next morning. Despite being woken several times during the night she had slept well and no longer felt weary.

The broch had once stood on a cliff by the sea so its eastern wall was weathered from many storms. On the western side the walls were largely untouched by the ravages of nature and the mortar still filled all the gaps between the stones. That is why the sun had not penetrated the tower at all on the previous afternoon when Aileesh was sealing the entrance. Now, however, the sunlight crept in from the eastern side to find gaps in the masonry that had been beyond its reach the day before.

The thin shafts of brightness were enough to help Sianan find her water bottle and bread so she broke her fast sparingly, hoping that she would be rescued before the food ran out. It was the water that she was most concerned for. There were only a few mouthfuls left and she had no way of knowing when Aileesh would return or whether the herb-gatherer would be in need of refreshment herself. Sianan finished her meal quickly, afterwards wrapping the bread in linen to keep it moist. Then she turned her attention to inspecting the walls of the broch once more.

The morning must have been far advanced when she was distracted from her study by a loud scraping sound that seemed to come from somewhere near the entrance to the tower. Sianan listened carefully but there were no voices to accompany the clamour. Sure that Aileesh would have called out to her if it she had returned, Sianan began to listen more intently to all noises from outside.

Even though she put all her attention to it for a long while she could not be sure whether the people who were digging her out were friendly or not. Sianan decided to keep perfectly quiet so as not to give any indication that the broch contained anything more than the carved stone decorations of the walls. Just as she made that decision a clod of earth loosed itself from the ceiling and the sounds outside grew in intensity. Sianan rolled aside as another piece of compacted soil crashed to the floor close beside her. Surely Aileesh would have been more careful if she were the one removing the rubble from the door.

For better or worse Sinan was about to be discovered but the more she thought about it the more convinced she was that it must be Saxons who were trying to break their way into the structure.

An old tale that her grandfather had told her came clearly to her mind then but unlike most of his stories it did not put her at ease.

Some of the tribes of the southern kingdom who still told tales about their people's first encounters with the Danaans reckoned that these towers were constructed to hold buried treasure. Many stories told how the Faery folk had built these forts to conceal all their gold and silver from the invading Gaels. A warrior had once spent the night inside a broch to emerge the next day with armour made of a metal that shone like gold and many jewelled armbands and rings and chains of silver.

She had heard of folk in her own lifetime who, led on by these legends, dug their way into the sealed brochs to seek the fabled treasure. This was despite the treaty between the Gaels and the Danaans which strictly forbade such conduct. Only if the entrance to a tower was already open were the Gaels permitted to enter it and only then when in urgent need of shelter. Sometimes these treaty breakers found a small number of trinkets. More often they returned to their families maddened by whatever enchantment had been created to protect the broch.

Sianan asked herself whether the celebration she had witnessed during the night was just a result of the insanity that gripped so many who dared to break the treaty.

'The door was already open,' she whispered, justifying her presence to any of the Danaans who would hear. 'The treaty was not broken. You have no right to punish me.'

She had just convinced herself that everything she had seen had been a cruel trick when a strand of her jet black hair fell into her eyes. She raised her hand to clear it from her face and her wrist brushed against her neck. She detected an unfamiliar object hanging at her throat from a thick silver chain. She felt around for the clasp and unfastened the clip so that she could get a closer look at the trinket that had appeared from nowhere.

When Sianan could see it properly she instantly recognised the jewel as the one that the half-beast Danaan had worn around his neck. She immediately put it in her pocket to hide it but in a few moments she had thought better of keeping it on her person. With a whispered apology to the generous Danaan she scooped out a little hole in the dirt of the floor and covered the jewel over with earth to hide it. Then Sianan began to pray that the Saxons had not heard any of the tales that she knew. If they even suspected that there was gold and silver to be had under the Faery forts they would excavate every tower in Eirinn to get at it.

The noise of excavation outside was much louder now and Sianan sensed that the strangers were getting closer to her. She began to sweat. Then she heard the unmistakable sound of an iron tool striking the dirt to drag it away. She knew that at Bally Cahor there was nothing made of iron that was any larger than a small knife for the rules of the community forbade it. This law was meant to encourage humility and resourcefulness among the Druid women. Sianan knew now that it was Saxons who were excavating the doorway. She looked around in case there was some corner of the broch that she had missed where she might curl up and hide. But the inside of the tower had nine plain walls and no niches or hidden doors.

Suddenly a shaft of light broke through the piled-up rubble. The golden beam began quickly to widen, spreading across the wall opposite. Sianan could see the shape of a head in the light but could not make out the face because of the intense sunlight that shone behind the figure. There were whispers outside. All digging ceased for a moment. Sianan was certain that she was in trouble. She shrank back against the wall, her fingernails clinging to the stone.

The figure advanced deeper into the newly created gap but was still partially obscured by light so that the girl could not see anything more than the outline of a wild hairstyle. Then Sianan heard her name being called.

It was Aileesh.

'Are you all right?' the herb-gatherer shouted.

'I think so,' Sianan answered, striving not to let on how scared she had been.

'We will have you out soon. A part of the tower doorway caved in during the night. We had to clear away the rubble before we could reach you.'

Without wasting another moment Sianan started to work on disposing of some of the smaller rocks that lay on her side of the door. Sitting on her knees she pushed all the stones behind her back deeper inside the chamber.

When the gap was finally wide enough Aileesh reached in through the doorway to grab Sianan by the hand. The older woman dragged the student Druid out of the tower as if she was no heavier than a sack of oats. Once the girl was out in the light Aileesh dived back in through the doorway as quick as an otter plunging into the lake to retrieve her food bag and the water bottle.

On the outside were several women, one of whom offered the handle of a wide-bladed Saxon axe to help her up. The iron weapon must have been taken from a fallen enemy. Before her eyes had adjusted Sianan began brushing the dirt from her shift but she stopped the moment she heard a familiar voice call her name. From her dishevelled hair and the burned edges of her clothes Niamh looked as though she had suffered a far worse night than Sianan. The two girls threw themselves into each other's arms and hugged for the joy of having come through such an ordeal with their lives.

Niamh took her friend's hand and looked deep into her eyes. 'Feena was taken,' she said sadly.

'I know,' Sianan replied, 'I was only a hundred steps away from her when it happened. If it had not been for Aileesh I would have been captured as well.' Then Sianan turned to where she thought the herb-gatherer was standing with the intention of thanking her but Aileesh was nowhere to be seen.

'Bally Cahor was burned to the ground,' Niamh continued. 'Every building was wrecked except the underground grain store where some of us were hiding. Twelve women were killed and at least another twenty taken. There are still five who we cannot account for, though their bodies may well lie among the ashes of their homes. I hope they escaped like you did by hiding in the hills and fields.'

'And what of the Saxons?'

'They are gone. They set sail before first light this morning after spending the night rampaging through the settlement. They drank every drop of mead they could lay their hands on.'

'Where did they go?' Sianan asked, but it was Aileesh poking her head out of the broch who answered her.

'South. Towards Inis Trá.'

'How do you know?'

'I don't for certain,' admitted the herb-gatherer, 'but the tide and winds would probably lead them in that direction. Inis Trá is the nearest settlement to here. It is a farming community. Though they have many cows they usually have no garrison to protect them. Just the sort of target the foreigners like. I knew that the Saxons would not get much food in Bally Cahor if the grain store was not broken into. I am certain they would be happy to find cattle to slaughter. I ran to Inis Trá in the night and warned the people to be ready at first light for the enemy ships. All the warriors from around about will have gathered there by now and be waiting to spring the trap. I would think that the Saxons will probably reach there around noon if this breeze from the north holds out.'

'So the captives will be rescued!' Niamh exclaimed.

'If the Saxons do as I guessed and all goes well,' said Aileesh without conviction.

'You ran to Inis Trá overnight?' Sianan interrupted, full of admiration. 'That is half a day's journey on horseback.'

'Is it?' Aileesh said, brushing off the comment. 'Well I have proved that even if you are barefoot and alone it takes no more than a full night to get there and back without a horse. Now we must get back to the settlement to see to the food stores and to the injured. I will need your help, Sianan, in collecting some herbs on the way.'

'I have been taught all about the healing herbs,' Sianan offered.

'I know you have,' Aileesh replied. The healer hesitated, noticing the way Sianan kept looking back over her shoulder toward the entrance of the tower. 'Have you left something behind?'

'I am not sure,' Sianan muttered self-consciously. 'I feel like I have already picked up more than I should.'

Aileesh's eyes widened. 'We will talk of this when the work is done. You were supposed to be leaving for Teamhair today but I am afraid it will be a few days more before we can spare you. Don't worry, I will make certain that you leave in time to prepare for the Beltinne fires. I will send word to your grandfather.'

As it happened things were not as bad at Bally Cahor as Aileesh expected. Many women had managed to conceal themselves from the fury of the raid. By sundown that day most of them had emerged to begin rebuilding. When Aileesh realised that Sianan was probably not needed she sent her north with a warrior to escort her.

At Teamhair the rumours regarding the three strangers lodged in one of the High-King's tents had grown in proportion by the hour. None but the Druid Council and the High-King himself were certain who the guests were. The common folk and the craftspeople could only speculate. And after five days during which no-one had even glimpsed the visitors, only heard their laughter and eerie music from a distance, the inhabitants were more than ready for a bit of speculation. A full account of the strangers' arrival had by that time expanded to include an immense army of Sidhe folk—that is people of the hills—who had come to escort their chief Druids. The Faery host were said to be camped within bow shot of Teamhair and the king of the Danaans was reputedly demanding a heavy tribute from Leoghaire.

Such are the ways of whispers. By the end of seven days there were many more exaggerations flying about, so many in fact that the original account of the three strange travellers whom nobody ever saw was buried deep under a mountain of rumours. A chieftain from the west arriving in the citadel after the seventh day of the Danaans' stay would certainly have been dismayed by what he heard at the gates.

It was common knowledge on the battlements that Leoghaire had been taken ill with love sickness brought on by Faery enchantments. By this time everyone knew that he was to be married to a woman less than half his age. The gossipers had to admit that the High-King's betrothed was above suspicion being the daughter of Enda Censelach and a Christian. That was until someone close to Leoghaire's clan claimed that Mona was descended from a Faery queen of Laigin. This was how the Danaans hoped to subjugate the Gaels, the theory ran, by breeding with the High-King of Eirinn.

When all the inhabitants of Teamhair had stirred the rumours up a little the stories began to take to the road on the tongues of the country folk. Travellers were greeted by strange stories at some distance from the citadel gates. So it was that Sianan and her guardsman interrupted their journey to hear of the marriage between Mona of Laigin and Leoghaire of the Ulaid. They heard too of the inhabitants of the green tent on the plain of testing. They listened unbelieving to the news of Caitlin's difficult birth-giving and a garbled report which claimed that the Faery folk had been haunting the Queen of Munster for many seasons.

Sianan was too relieved to be returning to Teamhair to be concerned by the idle talk of country people. The citadel was where she had spent most of her early life before Gobann had taken over her education. Soon she would enter the gates as a novice for the last time. From now on she would receive all the honour accorded to an initiated Druid. She could never pass the embankments unnoticed again.

As for the rumours of the Danaan people, there was a time when Sianan probably would not have taken too much notice of what the farmers said about Faery folk. But now things were different. As she rode her pony closer to the citadel walls she could sense the same tension in the air as she had experienced during her night in the broch. The road was clean in the aftermath of a rainstorm yet Sianan felt that there was something indiscernible in the atmosphere that had not been flushed away. Her guard obviously felt the same discomfort. His war horse strained at the bit turning this way and that, reluctant to approach the outer gates of Teamhair.

When the great oak doors of the gateway came into view Sianan began to tie her locks of black hair up at the back while deftly gripping the reins under one knee. Her nimble harper's fingers braided the strands and secured them about the top of her head in the fashion of a female novice Druid. In this way her rank and position would be instantly recognisable to everyone she might meet within the citadel.

As they were about to pass under the gates her guardsman halted. He waited until the young woman had crossed the threshold of the citadel then he immediately turned his mount around. With a quick word of farewell he set off again for Inis Trá to help with the defences should any more Saxons come raiding. Sianan went on alone.

Three hundred paces separated each of the seven fortified ditches that defended the citadel from attack. At a trot Sianan quickly passed through the first three where the servants and craftspeople had their homes. At the fourth gate, beyond which was the centre of Teamhair, she dismounted.

The guards held her at that gate for a long time, checking that she had a right to advance, so she took the opportunity to stretch her legs. The wooden palisade that surrounded the fourth enclosure was very old and had not been well maintained in parts. Sianan quickly found a gap in the woodwork and peeped through at the buildings on the other side. She scanned the small area that was revealed to her, trying to pinpoint a familiar house or workshop. Then a particular scent met her nostrils: sweet and strong, the essence of innumerable flowers. It brought back memories of her childhood, of helping the workers who tended the dying in tents of healing.

For the first time since those days she heard in her memory the strange songs of the white-robed Christians, who, unlike their counterparts from Rome, had always been friends to the Druids. It was then that Sianan understood that pungent odour must be the work of Origen the healer from Alexandria. Somewhere within the fourth enclosure the monk was brewing his delicate perfumes and strong elixirs.

Sianan lingered a few moments more at the wall before she noticed that the gate had been swung open. The gatekeeper was eyeing her suspiciously but nevertheless waiting patiently for her to proceed. She went to her pony, leading him quickly through under the square gatehouse and then out into the open again. Within fifteen paces she had come across many shelters, tents, wooden halls large enough for a dozen inhabitants, stone sweat houses and stables, all crowding in on the path. In this part of the citadel the master craftspeople who personally served the High-King were quartered. All the food was stored here also and all the horses and ponies were stabled. No beast of war or work was permitted beyond the confines of the fourth enclosure.

Sianan sought out the narrow path that led between the buildings to where she knew Origen had his large tent. She passed through the lane quickly, unnoticed by the silversmiths, gold workers, dye-makers and leather workers until she could smell the heavy scent of boiling liquor. A waft of the brew met her so that she could almost taste the nectar of the many flowers that had gone into its making. The aroma filled the air with sweet sickly spices.

After a brief search Sianan found the tent that Origen used as his workshop, close to the communal well. The cover of his dwelling was made of a bright white material that she recalled came from the seed pod of a plant that grew in the far-off eastern countries.

Sianan tied up her pony at a tethering stake and then without any hesitation she peeled open the flaps of the shelter to stick her head inside the tent. Origen was there, as always bent over a large iron cauldron, with his back to her. He had three Druid novices standing around him receiving instruction in the preparation of liquors and tinctures.

One of the students noticed the girl standing at the entrance. He tapped his teacher on the shoulder. Origen turned slowly around, scratching the top of his head and frowning.

'Yes, what is it now? Can you not see that I am busy? Whatever it is, it can wait until this afternoon.'

'I will come back later,' Sianan replied, ashamed that she had interrupted the lesson.

'Wait a moment. Do I know that voice?' Origen exclaimed. 'Is that the Druid Queen begging admittance?'

Sianan laughed, relieved and flattered that the monk had used his old nickname for her. She had not heard him call her that since she was very young. 'May I join you, master?' she respectfully inquired.

'Come in, my dear Sianan,' came the reply. 'I am sorry that I was so harsh but it seems that I am always being interrupted.'

When she had crossed the short distance between them she kissed the Christian's cheek noticing as her hands gripped his shoulders that he was much thinner than she remembered. The monk's hair was also greyer than the last time she had seen him. He looked as though he had aged much more than was natural in the passing of two summers. Sianan held him at a distance so that she could examine his face. What she beheld when she looked into his cold opaque eyes was the last thing that she had expected to find waiting for her in her old home.

'Yes, my dear,' Origen cut in before she could say anything, 'I have lost my eyesight.' He clapped his hands to curtly dismiss his pupils. 'The lesson is ended for the day.' All three young men quickly gathered their things. When they were gone Origen whispered to her, 'I have had a hard winter. I was very close to death from the cold. Come and sit for a while with me.'

Sianan held the monk's hand while they rested together in silence in the room that he used for treating his patients. She had been so excited about seeing him when she first recognised the incense that he made. She had wanted to tell him about the Faery tower and the little lights and the music and dancing and all that she had witnessed since leaving Teamhair. Sianan had even wanted to let him know all about the terrible Saxon raiders but now her tongue would not move in her mouth. She wanted him to see how much she had changed and grown but because he could not it was as though the monk had passed out of her world entirely.

She had guessed that a few things would have changed in the two summers of her absence, but she did not think that her old world could have altered so dramatically and so permanently.

'How is Mawn?' Origen finally asked, breaking the uneasy silence.

'I have not seen him yet,' Sianan admitted. 'You are the first person that I came to visit.'

Origen jerked his head, cocking his ears. 'Then we must go straightaway to the Hall of the Poets. Gobann and Cathach have been very worried about you. If they find that you have been hiding here I will never hear the end of it.' The monk stood up. His walking stick made of blackthorn and decorated with a carving of a man hanged on a cross was leaning by the door. 'I am permitted to come and go as I please these days,' he explained. 'It is strange that since blindness came upon me I have been allowed to see many more things than when I had the full use of my eyes.'

Sianan took the Christian's arm and they walked down to the fifth gate together, passing through without speaking at all but simply enjoying each other's company. The fifth compound housed the warriors and the weapon makers; a dirty and noisy place. The sixth enclosure was where the great hall of the Druids called the Star of Poetry was situated.

As they passed the gatehouse, two novices appeared bearing the long blue cloak of a judge. They came right up to Origen and draped the garment over his shoulders and would have taken his hands to guide him but Sianan would not let them lead him to the hall. She preferred to do that herself.

The novices went on ahead to prepare a place for the old monk and as soon as they were gone he whispered into Sianan's ear. 'Tell me something. What colour is the coat they have covered me in? I have been greeted with it ever since my eyesight faded but out of politeness I have never asked anyone. Now I would like to know.'

'It is the deepest blue.'

Origen straightened his back and lifted his head as though he could see into the far distance. He knew the meaning of the blue cloak. It was the highest honour that the Druid Council could bestow upon a foreigner. The honour was made the greater though because it had not been explained to him that each time he came to the Star of Poetry he sat clothed in a poet's cloak. Origen recognised this as Cathach's doing. He was quietly delighted that his Druid friends had chosen to respect his sense of modesty in this way, aware that the monk genuinely preferred a life of humility.

The door to the Star of Poetry was half open as the monk and his guide approached it. Sianan put out her hand to take the handle but it moved out of her reach just as she touched it. All of a sudden Gobann came rushing out from the hall without looking so that he almost knocked them over in his hurry. When the Druid recognised his friend he apologised profusely. 'Origen! Are you all right? I am sorry but I have just had word that Sianan is in Teamhair and I must be off to seek her out.'

'Look no further,' Origen replied. 'The blind man has found her.'

Then Gobann looked at the novice who held Origen's arm. There was something about her that was familiar to him but he had to look deeper before he recognised Sianan. Two summers had passed since they had seen each other and Sianan was no longer a girl. Her hair had grown, she was taller and she had an air of serenity about her that reminded Gobann of a much younger Caitlin. As soon as he realised that his mouth was hanging open in surprise the poet remembered his manners.

'Thank all the Danaans that you are safe,' Gobann muttered. 'Now we have much to do. You and the boy are to be initiated at Beltinne and that festival is less than four nights from tonight.'

Gobann led them into the hall where Sianan related to him and Origen all there was to tell of the fight at Bally Cahor. Both men listened intently, asking questions and making comments throughout until Cathach arrived to join them. Sianan greeted her grandfather and as always she deferred to his rank and did not show any unseemly emotion. Once he had welcomed her she began the whole story again so that he would know what had befallen the women's community. Gobann and Cathach exchanged knowing glances as Sianan brushed over her experience in the broch but neither man questioned what she told them. That did not mean of course that they had failed to note what had happened to her.

Other Druids gathered around them; some half listening to what Sianan said, others engaged in philosophical debates or tale-tellings of their own. After sunset the hall filled with many more folk the like of which Sianan had never seen before; people from the far-off lands whose tribes rarely sent embassies to Eirinn.

Throughout the evening Gobann and Cathach never once spoke of the great plan that was the reason for almost everything they did these days. Despite the honour that had been accorded him, Origen was still a foreigner and a Christian. There was no telling what he would make of the Druid Council's strategy to protect Eirinn from invasion. They held their tongues and let Sianan have the evening. Their time would come later when there were not so many idle ears about and they would be sure of an unprejudiced hearing.

It was long after supper had been eaten that a young harper took position near to where Origen was seated. He had a beautiful instrument on his lap which Sianan did not recognise as belonging to her master, Gobann. In all the time that she had known the poet she could never recall him allowing another musician to touch the wires of that instrument.

The harper turned his back to Cathach and Origen so Sianan could not see his face. He played a haunting lament that ebbed and flowed like the ocean tide and made the young woman think of Moire who had been her teacher at Bally Cahor. Before she could stop herself the tears were rolling down her cheeks. Sianan said a little prayer under her breath for the peace of the old woman's soul and for Feena who had been captured by the Saxons.

Then the harper changed his tune, ceasing the sorrow music and moving on to a piece from the strain of sleep. Origen gradually nodded off and began to snore, so two novices came to lead him to a quiet sleeping spot.

Sianan then looked at her grandfather, whom she had not seen for two turnings of the seasons. Cathach too was looking tired, more tired than she had ever seen him. She knew with the certainty that she always felt when these pictures came into her head that she would not have much more time with him before they parted company forever. Sianan knew that she would miss the old man but she was surprised to find that she was not sad. After all, he had worked very hard all of his life and soon he would truly be able to rest.

Silent Gobann was the next to draw her attention. He was sitting with his eyes closed, obviously enjoying the opportunity to hear someone who could play his harp well. The tune raised a pitch under the expert hands of the harper changing into a war melody. The poet tapped out a walking rhythm with his fingers on his knee and everyone in the hall seemed to start moving in time with the tune.

But war melodies are only one half of the third great category of music. The other encompasses all the airs that are dedicated to love. The young unnamed harper moved on quickly, using the same melody as the war tune but playing it more slowly as if to emphasise the close relationship between the two.

It was not until this point that Sianan realised that none of the tunes that this harper had played were known to her. They were played with great attention to the ancient rules of music, that was certain, but these were original compositions. It was not often that she had the opportunity to hear so skilled a performer. She was enchanted by his tunes. Thinking that he must be one of the foreign Druids who were scattered in the hall that night, she changed position to get a look at his face.

The harper was young, for his fair hair was not shaved in the fashion of an initiate. Sianan smiled at him thinking that there was something about the young man that reminded her of the Danaan who had begged her to dance in the Faery tower. The colour of his eyes reminded her of Lorgan the Sorn, Gobann's old teacher. This harper was different though. There was something special about him that she could not put her finger on. There was a special grace in the way his fingernails made contact with the harp wires. There was a gentleness about the way he swayed to the melodies. She had thought only the truly ancient airs could sound so wonderful. Then the truth came to her. Suddenly, as if the Otherworld sight had forced a veil away from her eyes, she knew where she had seen him before. His hands came to rest as he finished the love air and as soon as the instrument was completely silent he turned to look at her.

He seemed not to recognise her at first and Sianan could not believe that he could have forgotten what she looked like.

'Hello, Mawn,' she said. 'At last I'm home.'

SIXTEEN

urrough rode wildly down the Cashel road toward the ancestral home of his family, stopping only to change horses at the guardposts that were set at intervals along the track. He had made this journey countless times in his life and he knew every bend in the road, every hill, every glen, every place where the highway crossed a stream or skirted a valley, but this was the first time that he did not take notice of the mountains, lochs and forests along the way.

Easily anticipating any difficulties that the road could present, he leaned forward in the saddle and gripped each successive mount with his knees so that if any of the horses stumbled he would not fall from his seat. At that pace he had soon reached a place that he often visited in his worst dreams. At this place, after the Battle of Rathowen, a troop of horse soldiers that he had commanded was ambushed by Saxon mercenaries. That was where the Prince of Munster had become a prisoner in his own kingdom. He had lost a good friend on that day, a veteran called Ruari, who had fallen under his own horse in the panic and been killed by the savages as he lay helpless. Defenceless.

Murrough thought about stopping to pay his respects at the graveside but decided that respects could wait for another time. The fortress of Cashel was his target and he was an arrow let loose from the bow, flying to find its mark in that distant stronghold.

At dawn of his second day Murrough was joined by several of his guardsmen who had pushed their horses to breaking point in order to catch up with him. None of them had rested at all since leaving Teamhair. The King of Munster did not acknowledge their presence for at first he did not notice them. He had no way of knowing how long they had been riding with him so he decided that thanks could wait until they were within the walls of their own clanhold.

At sunset on their second day of travel the king and his escort, barrelling down the hill road, came within sight of the Cashel crossroads. This marked the northern most outpost of the kingdom.

On the plain where the road to the south crossed another paved way running from east to west, a great grey tree trunk lay shattered on its side. Around about were still scattered many branches that had been discarded as the hulk had fallen. Murrough always took time to halt at this place, paying his respects to the venerable Quicken that was now only a memory.

In times past this was the holiest of all the trees in Eirinn, revered by Danaan and Gael alike for the healing properties of its fruit. Under a treaty of withdrawal the Danaans had left the Quicken to the protection of the clan Eóghanacht, who were Murrough's people. When that older race disappeared into the mists of their Otherworld the Gaels became its guardians. Murrough and his ancestors used an ancient sign for the Quicken Tree as their royal seal. It was comprised of a stylised tree design made up of several of the old Ogham letters which only the Druids understood.

For many generations the tree stood without any threat to its life and when peril finally came there was no-one to fulfil the promise of protection. Murrough was present when the tree was slaughtered but at the time he was a prisoner of the Saxons who did the deed. Two of the savages had held him down in the snow and he watched helpless as axemen destroyed twenty generations of history. All to satisfy the whim of a Christian monk who had fallen in with the Saxon savages.

The murder of the Quicken Tree, though calamitous, had been a turning point in Murrough's life. It had brought him closer to Caitlin who at that time was also a captive of the Saxon captain. Murrough knew that he had failed his family and the alliance between the Danaans and the Gael in allowing the Quicken to be cut down. However, no-one ever openly blamed him for the disaster. Even so, in his heart he told himself ever after that he was solely responsible for the death of the tree and the dishonour of his clan.

Since that day he regularly returned to that spot to ask forgiveness of the Danaans and to pledge personal amends for his failure to keep the ancient treaty.

Where the branches furthest from the dead tree lay, Murrough reined in his horse. He slid from the saddle and made straight for the tree. His mount was as exhausted as he was so he knew she would not walk too far. After checking that his guardsmen were still with him, Murrough ran up to the great trunk, kneeling down on the grass beside the massive grey skeleton, his eyes to the ground and the palm of his hand flat against the fallen timber.

'I have come, though my wife lies with her life in peril. Even though she who is dearest to me on this Earth could pass away while I tarry here, I still came as I promised I would always do. I have come again to beg your pardon for the great wrong that I did to your people. I beg you not to punish her for my failing.'

The corpse of the tree did not answer him nor was there any sound anywhere on the plain save the far-off call of a black bird. Murrough recognised the breed immediately. The caller was a Raven, one of the giant ebony birds that had once used the tree as their gathering place.

The king scanned the hills around about but all he saw of the creature was a far-off shadow flitting over the hills. Night was drawing in and the presence of the Raven made his guardsmen visibly nervous so Murrough caught his horse and mounted ready to ride on. With a good road he was sure to be in Cashel by midnight.

If he had known that Caitlin still lay unconscious after the birth of her son perhaps he would not have stopped at the Quicken Tree at all. Then maybe his prayer would not have been heard.

Within the main tower of the fortress Síla sat a vigil at the queen's side for four days without taking any rest herself. Caitlin's women watched the child at her breast while she slept, in the hope that she might awake if she sensed the baby's presence. Síla took a different approach, regularly applying cloths soaked in herbal tinctures to the queen's feverish skin. Many times the healer forced her remedies down Caitlin's throat. When she was not nursing the sick woman Síla sat playing on Caitlin's harp, telling the queen old stories to try and reach through the shroud of her unconsciousness.

Síla did not possess a harp of her own. In Britain where she had grown up among the Cruitne, harps were much rarer than here in Eirinn. The Roman invaders had destroyed many of the finest instruments centuries before and with the harps they also destroyed the harp-makers, burning the craftspeople in funeral pyres constructed from the beautiful instruments they made. The Romans feared the magic spell that harp music could weave on an unsuspecting listener. Fear was the reason that they had eradicated the instruments almost completely.

Despite this there were harpers in the land of the Cruitne, though their harps came from Eirinn for the most part and the players had probably trained in the Druid schools in Gaul or in the schools in the kingdom of Munster. It was from Gobann that Síla had learned to play, not that he ever let her touch his harp.

From the first moment she had seen him, she always watched him carefully as he performed. And whenever she could borrow someone else's instrument without his knowledge she would patiently teach herself some of the techniques she had observed him employing. Síla only did this because she knew that harps are prone to the same foibles as any person. Most of all they are capable of great jealousy. She realised then that she could not be sure how Gobann would feel if he realised she had been looking on so intently.

Exhausted though she was, the Druid managed to concentrate on a melody that she remembered from her childhood, a lullaby to a sick child, a song of healing and of rest. It was night and the servants had built up the fire in Caitlin's chamber and were now gathered around the blaze listening to Síla's melodies. Omra hummed the tune under her breath as Síla sounded the bass notes, deep ringing chords that sounded like the musical drones of many bees.

The lullaby was so effective that it did not take long for the two other women in the chamber to nod off. Omra ceased her crooning soon after so that all that was left was the sweet ringing resonance of the brass-wired harp, each note chiming like a tiny bell.

The servants were snoring when Síla let her hand drop from the music wires. The air had suddenly become hot and clammy and it had a foul scent to it. The Druid healer scanned the room, searching for anything out of the ordinary. There was no movement, no sign of danger apart from the strange smell. Síla visibly struggled against the onslaught of sleep, yielding eventually to her weariness after a long fight. As the fire spat little sparks onto the hearthstone she gently closed her eyes. The healer's head fell forward until her chin rested against her chest, and the room fell utterly and eerily silent.

In the middle of the fire a piece of sap loudly exploded somewhere deep in the grain of one of the logs but the servants did not stir. Not long after that the chamber door slowly slid open a little way to let in a draft but all within the room seemed to be so deeply slumbering that the tiny breeze did not wake them.

A thin grey-green hand crept around the door near to the latch and shook the iron fittings. The rattling of the latch was loud and yet no-one in the room moved from their sleep. Satisfied that all were resting soundly the Cailleach moved quickly across the floor towards Caitlin's bed, skimming over the floor stones noiselessly as she reached her hands out to the' child that slept in the queen's arms.

In less time than it takes to draw a breath she was plucking gently at a loose thread of the woollen wrap that wound the baby in a soft warm cocoon. Once more the hag carefully checked the room. There was no movement, no sound, nothing. A broad evil smile passed across the Cailleach's face. Grey saliva dripped uncontrollably over her lips as she made the gesture.

The otherworldly eyes lit up with a white fire that made the black pupils stand out darker than ever. The creature leaned over the queen, lifting Caitlin's arm from around the precious package that the queen clutched so tightly even in her stupor. Patiently the Cailleach laid the empty hand back down on the bed again. She had stolen many children and knew that this was the crucial moment when a mother was most likely to put up a fight.

Across the room Síla moved in her seat to get more comfortable and the Cailleach froze, becoming almost invisible in her stillness. However, the healer did not wake and satisfied at last that all were asleep, the creature struck.

With a swift jerk the Cailleach snatched at the little parcel wrapped in wool and grabbed the child tightly to her breast. A second later she let out a great shriek that would have woken the hosts of the dead.

'I have the baby!' she cried jubilantly. 'I have him! Stupid Druid woman thought she could stop me coming here. Stupid Druid woman!'

'You are the stupid one!' Síla replied. The healer was standing at the foot of the bed.

While the Cailleach was distracted Omra leapt up and slammed the door to the chamber just as

Síla made a leap at the hag, tearing at the flesh of the creature's arm with her knife. Dark red blood gushed out of the wound like water from a spring. The hag retreated toward the door but Omra now had a flaming log in her hand and she waved it around before the monster, cutting off her escape.

'Let me out!' cried the hag in distress, 'or I will kill the child.' As she made that threat she pulled back the cover to look on the baby's face.

'You cannot kill that child,' Síla announced as the Cailleach's expression changed from triumph to rage.

The creature reached its hand into the clothes where the child's head should have been. The bony fingers closed in, squashing together, making a hideous sound as their strength converged on the area of the child's face. Suddenly the hand withdrew again to tear wildly at the baby clothes. Unable to believe her eyes the Cailleach spat a few strange words that sounded like a curse. The monstrous hands were full of straw.

'Where is the child?' shrieked the creature.

'He is safe,' Síla answered. 'Out of the reach of you and your kind.'

The face passed from grey-green to purple with rage. The fingers clenched. The straw baby burst into flames in the Cailleach's hands. 'Never mind,' the hag smiled through blackened teeth. 'Never mind.' Her ugly head rolled back and forth on her shoulders as her chest heaved up and down. 'You cannot guard the baby night and day. And even if you do the queen will surely have other children. I will come back for them.' Then the monster turned her gaze directly on Síla. The hideous body of the Cailleach ceased its heaving and became very still.

The hag leaned forward to touch Síla under the chin with one of her claws, speaking in a sweet manner that was an evil parody of the words of a loving mother indulging her favourite child. 'Maybe I will take you instead,' the beast cooed in her throaty voice. The saliva dripped from the creature's mouth down across her chin and onto her chest. In the corner Omra steadied herself against a chair so as not to faint.

Síla stepped back in disgust, gripping her knife, making ready to attack as soon as the hag came within striking distance again. Caitlin stirred in her bed, rolling on her side without waking. 'Then again the queen is still young and strong,' mocked the creature. 'She would be an excellent breeder for my two sons.'

As the Cailleach began to laugh there was a loud noise outside the chamber. Someone was banging on the door demanding to be let in. Realising she was trapped, the hag started to search about her desperately for a way to escape. There was none.

The creature toughened her resolve when she understood that this had been a trap. 'If I am going to die then this Druid woman will die with me!' she declared.

The Cailleach stormed over to Omra, growling at the servant with stinking breath. This was all that Omra could take. Her eyes rolled back in her head and she fell face first to the floor. The hag scooped up the fiery log that the serving woman had been holding and turned round to face Síla with it.

The healer could now plainly see the Cailleach's sharpened teeth. The rank breath that poured out of the hag's mouth turned Síla's stomach.

'Come to me, my pretty,' the Cailleach hissed. 'Let's have an end to this little game. One of you must come with me to the Otherworld, now who's it to be, the queen or you?'

In that instant the door to the chamber was broken down by three armed men who tumbled onto the floor as the wood splintered under their assault. One of them drew a sword from his belt as he landed on his companions. The clanging of a steel blade sliding against the iron scabbard ring caused the hag to look round in dismay. This was all the distraction that Síla needed. At that second she struck at the hag, slamming her little knife into the beast's side. Thick dark blood flooded out of the ugly body as the Cailleach turned to grab Sila's wrist.

Now the Druid was face to face with the monster so that their noses almost touched. From its throat the hag coughed a piece of bloody black phlegm, allowing it to ooze over her lips. Still the Cailleach smiled. 'It will take a great deal more than a tiny pinprick to kill me, my lovely,' she sang. Her breath was like the gas that rises from a rotting pig's carcass. Sharp fingernails cut into the flesh of Síla's arm like talons. The healer could feel a sharp burning sensation on her wrist and she called out in disgust and dismay.

'Stand away!' came a familiar voice. 'Stand away from that woman or you'll feel my blade fall against your neck!'

The hag looked back over her shoulder to mock the threat. 'Come any closer, brave warrior, and I will snap this Druid's arm off at the elbow and then beat her with the dead stump. Her harp playing won't be half as sweet with only one set of fingers to touch the wires.'

Then Síla heard the same male voice uttering an obscenity. A sword cut through the air slicing the space between her and the Cailleach, singing as it fell. Suddenly the hag's whole body jolted violently and the healer found herself covered in a wet substance that reeked like the sewers of the fortress. She had to study the substance for a few seconds to understand that she was soaked in coagulated blood. The vicelike grip on her arm was abruptly released and a heavy object thudded onto the floor before her.

Síla barely had enough time to discern that the hag's arm had been cut off at the shoulder when a great gust of wind blew the warrior forward and off balance. The foul hag leapt over him through the open door of the chamber, easily knocking over the other two stunned warriors who stood in her way. In seconds she had disappeared out into the night, leaving a severed limb thrashing about in spasms on the stone floor.

The healer ran straight for Caitlin to make sure that she was all right but the warrior was already at the queen's side lifting her face to his. It was only then that Síla was able to see through the warrior's muddied clothes and dishevelled hair to discern the face of Murrough the King of Munster.

SEVENTEEN

awn fasted for the three nights and days before the festival of Beltinne as all initiates to the Druid orders were required to do. Throughout that time he was not allowed to wash or dress in fresh clothes. He was permitted to drink rainwater collected by novices and each night an apple was brought to him so that his body did not rebel entirely. Because of the impending ritual he was exempt from manual labour. Throughout the period of cleansing prior to the ceremonies he spoke only to Gobann, setting eyes on no-one else who lived within the citadel of Teamhair.

Sianan too followed the same strict code except that she was allowed a little more food. Women who undertook the test of the Imbas Forosnai invariably had more intense visions and so were allowed more bodily nourishment. Gobann was also Sianan's only visitor. The poet resisted the urge to speak with either of them about their test. He confined himself to playing at the Brandubh with them whenever he visited.

The two initiates were housed close to each other but they had both been blindfolded before entering their confinement so that they could not be aware that they shared separate sections of the same hut. It was unusual for two novices to receive initiation in the same ritual; in fact, these ceremonies had not been performed in such a way since the great plagues of generations past when many Druids had succumbed to disease. In those days it was not unusual for twenty or thirty novices to be tested at one festival. Keeping the two of them apart ensured that they did not distract each other from the ordeal ahead.

The building in which they were housed was made entirely of earth tightly packed to form windowless walls. The top of the hut was covered in thick springy grass that grew out of the sodden roof. This gave the air inside a freshness that was unique to such a dwelling. The hut was divided across its length by a wall of earth newly added and dense enough so that sounds would not travel between the two rooms.

The festival of Beltinne traditionally began in the few days before the full moon marking the beginning of spring and the coming of new life to the world. Both Mawn and Sianan were aware of the deeper significance for them. They had been chosen to carry the light of the old ways into the new world that was soon to emerge.

The journey that they were about to undertake was the most dangerous of their lives. At the appointed time they would pass from this world into the realm of spirits. Whether they returned from the Otherworld would largely depend on how well they had learned their lessons and how good their teachers had been. They would have to rely on their learning, insight and foresight throughout the whole time that they tarried beyond this world.

Not everyone returned who undertook the test of Imbas Forosnai. Some fell victim to their fear long before the real testing had begun. Others returned from the Otherworld but their minds and hearts were evermore in the lands beyond life and so they were in a sense already dead. That is one of the reasons why this initiation was nicknamed 'the little death'. The other reason was that it centred on the entombment of the initiate for a period of three nights. After they were brought forth from their symbolic burial Sianan and Mawn would be considered to be reborn, plucked from the earth-womb that had been for a while their tomb. They would then begin their new lives in the keeping of a new clan all of whom were Druids. But unlike all other initiates before them who had faced this test, Mawn and Sianan would not ever have to face death again. If the Druid Council's strategy was a success.

When the fast had lasted three days Gobann came to visit Sianan. He asked her many questions about everything she had learned and all that she knew. Finally he asked her to speak frankly about the task ahead and whether she felt ready for the test.

'I have known since I was a child that my life would be spent in service to the Druid path,' she told him, 'but I did not know that my life could possibly be as long as you say it will be. The test that we are about to undergo is just the first step on the Road we have often talked about. I have always looked forward to travelling the Great Road.'

'You may encounter the Deities on your journey,' Gobann warned her. 'How will you know them?'

'If they choose to make themselves known by name and not otherwise,' she replied.

'Manann, protector of the seas, Brigid of the fires, Scathach of learning, Oghma of writing and knowledge, Macha of wisdom, Flidais of the animal world, Dagda of music, Aenghus Og of dreaming,

Boann of fertility, Goibniu of creativity, Dana of the Faeries, Miach of healing, Banba of Eirinn and the Morrígán of death. Each or any of them may take you under their wing. They are kings and queens among their own people, you must remember that, though they are generally modest.'

When the poet was satisfied that Sianan was ready he went to make similar inquiries of Mawn. 'How will you greet the Deities?' he asked the lad.

'As brothers and sisters under the stars,' Mawn replied with a sparkle in his green eyes. 'They are like us, just older and wiser.'

'When we are all gone, when the world has changed, what laws will govern your life?'

'The laws of the Druid path that you have imparted to me, which state that all major decisions are to be arrived at by consultation. The Druid Council is the guardian of tradition and so it is our duty as walkers on the Druid path to provide guidance to the kings, chieftains and people. Judgment is law. Advice is not. Our actions must always be governed by the laws of hospitality and courtesy.'

'Where will you turn for guidance when your elders and teachers are all dead?'

'I will always turn to them. If you live on in the heart of those you leave behind, then death cannot touch you. They will live in my heart and I will be able to call on their wisdom when need be.'

Both students had spent their time wisely reviewing the events and learning of their apprenticeships. Gobann judged that they were as ready as they were ever likely to be. He sent word to Cathach, giving him the go-ahead to make the final arrangements, then he went to sit by the stones near the Star of the Poets until word came to him that all was ready.

It was midday when novices came to paint ashes over the naked bodies of Mawn and Sianan. When that was done they were led blindfolded to the sweat houses. Despite the precautions Sianan caught a glimpse of her soul friend from under the edge of the binding as they were led out of the hut. She longed to call out to him. Somehow she managed to restrain herself.

The two stone sweat houses stood together amid the smoke of many open fires so that the rest of the plain of Teamhair was obscured from view. Inside the sweat house Sianan took off her blindfold but it was as dark as the Faery tower in the little stone building. Perhaps this resemblance to the broch was why Sianan was able to relax even though her mind was racing due the effects of her fast.

There were fresh leaves and roots infusing in a steaming stone basin. As she smelled them she found that she could name each one from her knowledge of herb lore. No-one had explained that these herbs were used in sweat houses. Indeed she had sat in the sweat house many times and this was the first time that she had noticed this combination of herbs in use. Then she realised that these must be the herbs of seeing.

Gobann had spoken vaguely of the recipe but had never explained exactly which plants or extracts were used for the bringing on of future-sight. Sianan guessed that she would be confined here until she began to feel faint. She sensed that she might lose consciousness and have to be carried out in that state and she was determined not to allow that to happen. 'I want to be aware of everything that is happening to me,' she told herself.

This was the first stage in the ritual voyage of the Imbas Forosnai. A journey that would take her along the spirit road. This is what all of her training through the turning of the nine seasons since she had become Gobann's pupil had been for. This one test would show her to be capable of taking on the duties of a Wanderer and of a Druid.

This whole exercise put her in mind of when she was a little girl and her grandfather had taken her on one of his trips to the south. She recalled vividly now how excited she had felt to be setting out for a part of Eirinn that she had only ever visited in her imagination. Sianan could not be sure of where this expedition would lead her but she hoped with all her heart that she would once more meet the Danaans who had danced for her in the broch at Bally Cahor.

Only a stone's throw away from where Sianan was sitting Mawn was walking his thoughts along more or less the same track as his friend. He brought to mind the day that Gobann had come to the home of Mawn's father to fetch him away to become a Druid. He recalled vividly how Gobann had fallen ill on the first night of his stay with the family. The poet had afterwards drifted into a strange dreamlike state where he sweated constantly and cried out in an unrecognisable language.

All of his young life Mawn had suffered from strange visions of the future so he had found it easy to sympathise with the poet's affliction. He was never scared of the apparitions that came into his head though they sometimes put him on edge. Sianan, too, suffered the future-sight and she and Mawn often shared common visions. Even when they were separated for their final two winters of training they had kept in contact with each other.

It was a kind of communication that Mawn experienced with no other living being. There was no real need for words in the language that they used to pass messages to each other. Rather it was a feeling that they shared; a feeling of security and safety, a sense of the other person's presence. When Cathach and Gobann were worried about what had become of Sianan at the hands of the Saxon raiders, Mawn had known for certain that she was safe. He could not explain how he knew, he just knew. In fact, as long as he could still feel her presence beside him, comforting him, he never worried about her.

Mawn let his hand drop gently from his lap onto the ground beside him. He had not removed his blindfold. He would not have thought to take it off in case it was essential to the process of his initiation. He sensed another hand reach out to enclose his tightly and he began to relax. He was sure that Sianan was with him.

Mawn had witnessed Gobann's initiation into the higher circle of the Druid Council when the poet had first brought him to Teamhair. He expected therefore to be confined within the sweat house for a similar amount of time as Gobann had been. But a long while passed and the only novices who came to the door were there to place hot stones in the cauldron to make more steam. None came to lead him away.

Mawn began to feel very sick in his stomach. He had not eaten more than apples for three days so he was already somewhat weak. Now he could feel his guts turning and growling and his head spinning.

When the next novice entered the little house to put more stones in the water Mawn was tempted to ask if everything was going according to plan.

The young male trainee skirted around the initiate as if he fully expected the question and his stern silence warned Mawn against speaking. Resigned to his fate, Mawn breathed deeply and surrendered to the temptation to remove his blindfold.

His eyes adjusted quickly to the dim interior and with surprise he noticed that the walls were painted with many symbols similar to the ones that covered Gobann's harp bag. Drawn to one of the motifs, Mawn began to trace his fingers along its elegant pattern. It was a huge double spiral, the outer arms of which were painted to represent the tails of two enormous dragons. The bodies of these two beasts twisted around one another swirling inward until they terminated in ferocious heads that bayed at each other, almost touching but not quite.

Mawn blinked, wiped the sweat away from his brow and when his eyes focused again on the two serpents they were moving in a strange dance across the wall. He blinked again and they were only a lifeless painting once more. Just as he convinced himself that a combination of the heat, the herbs and a lack of food had confused his senses, one of the serpents winked a large watery green eye at him and stuck out its tongue, dark red and venomous. The creature's whole body took on a verdant hue, shining like the bright moss that lives between the sunlight and the water's edge. There was an overwhelming air of maleness about this serpent which was reflected in its every move.

The other serpent started to mirror its partner, though she took on the colour of the dark blue ocean deep, menacing and mysterious. The two dragons cried out loudly in voices high-pitched and threatening. Then they began to dance ever more wildly together before Mawn's bewildered gaze.

Their undulating movements were the last thing that Mawn saw before the strong seeing-herbs took their toll. For a while he got the distinct impression that he had taken on the form of one of the serpents. He felt the skin of the other dragon rubbing itself up against his body, hard and hot. He felt himself seeking to push back, returning the attention that he was attracting.

Mawn imagined his whole being had suddenly become a scaly snake-like creature that moved sensuously around its mate in a courting ritual that was both arousing and disturbing. The experience was touching things in Mawn's consciousness that he had rarely allowed to come to the surface. He struggled to commit these feelings and thoughts to memory so that he could try to reason them out of his life at some point in the future, but even his mind had become a serpent mind and it no longer worked within the logic of human boundaries.

The other creature was caressing him now, coiling her tail about him and smoothing her long body into the crevices between the lines of scales on his belly. He threw his head back in ecstasy and from the pit of his stomach he brought forth a deep resounding bellow like the mating call of a stag. At once menacing and enticing.

EIGHTEEN

bbot Declan and his fellow monk Isernus arrived at the gates of Teamhair two days after Sianan returned from Bally Cahor. They were admitted to the fifth enclosure and housed with the Christian monks who followed the rule of Origen's order. No audience could be arranged with the High-King or any of the Druid Council for this was the season of Beltinne and each person who lived in the inner circles of Teamhair had some ritual duty to perform. Declan resigned himself to waiting until the festival was over before making any further attempt to speak with Leoghaire.

Origen was renowned for his generous hospitality. He opened his tiny Egyptian chapel to the two travellers from Dal Araidhe, begging them to worship with him and his small community. In fact Origen was relieved that Isernus and Declan arrived when they did. He had been asked as senior Christian prelate to perform the marriage ceremony for Leoghaire and Mona. The ceremony was to be before the moon turned again after Holy Week and the celebration of the Resurrection.

The daughter of Enda Censelach had specifically requested that the Roman rites be observed for the wedding but Origen did not know the first thing about Roman rites. He guessed that Mona had probably never witnessed a Roman marriage so she might not know that there was any difference between the eastern and the western ceremony.

On the other hand, however, she knew enough to have instructed that the festival of the Resurrection would be celebrated according to Roman dating and not that of the eastern church. Origen and his monks were making ready to celebrate the death and magical rebirth of Christ which as always fell at the same time as Beltinne. The eastern system of dating venerated the Jewish Passover festival but the Romans had modified their observances, not wishing to have them confused with Hebrew rites. Romans never like to directly associate their traditions with anything that might be interpreted as having foreign sources. This year, while the easterners celebrated the resurrection, the westerners would remember Christ's entry into Jerusalem.

Origen tried to be charitable in his estimation of Romans but it was often difficult for him to imagine that they were anything but an arrogant and ignorant people. The followers of the eastern church were taught that before a person took the Cross they were a gentile. Afterwards they could consider themselves converts to Judaism. Following that logic, Christ was merely the leader of a breakaway Hebrew sect. How could the Romans accept the teachings of many of the old Hebrew customs and yet refuse to celebrate the Jewish holy days? Over the years Origen had met many Roman Christians and he had come to believe that they still thought their Empire was all powerful. Some still held that, as Romans, they were superior to all the peoples they had once conquered.

It just would not do for them to admit that they had adopted the religious ways of one of their subject states. To a well-travelled brother like

Origen the only significant differences between the eastern and western churches were the minor issues of dating festivals. But he knew the split ran much deeper than that. The church of the west was Roman and always would be Roman. Many of their rites had been directly adopted from heathen Roman practices. The grades of their clergy were named after old military and civil ranks from the days of the Empire and they paid homage to the Pope as though he were the Emperor of old. Christ was restyled under Roman influence to be like one of the old Roman gods: a figure to be worshipped, feared and fed with sacrifices to placate his wrath.

Roman Christianity owed a great debt to the Empire. The church was organised along the same lines as the civil service. In fact monks were commonly called clerics which was the old name for the lowest rank of public office. Every aspect of a cleric's life was strictly administered by his superiors, right down to what colours he was permitted to wear. Their clothing harked back to the heyday of the Empire; bishops still wore senatorial garb. The language they spoke and the ritual that they performed each day at the holy offices were Roman through and through, calling on God on high to intervene in their affairs.

The easterners did not call on God to bring them prosperity or to keep them safe from marauders or to bring more converts to the fold. They called on God's attention in earnest thankfulness and awe. Declan could never remember hearing a Roman priest speak so intimately with his God nor so honestly as Origen did during the shared prayers.

To the eastern church Christ was a holy man chosen by the Deity for a specific task. He was to be admired and venerated but he was not divine. He had merely been a messenger sent from God.

Declan had showed a great sympathy to this view when Origen had first explained it to him.

The two men had spent long hours discussing points of difference when the Abbot of Saint Ninian's had last been in Eirinn. Declan had impressed Origen from their very first meeting and the Egyptian was eager to speak with him again. The abbot seemed just as enthusiastic.

It soon became evident that in the nine years since Declan had left Eirinn he had come to modify his strict Roman view somewhat. Amongst the Gaelic people he worked with there was an attitude which regarded all things on Earth as imbued with holiness. The abbot admitted that the older he grew the less important was the substance of the ritual that he performed and the more important the intention of the celebrant. The notion of the divine nature of Christ was not something that Declan could be swayed on, however. He had been instructed in the Roman concepts of divinity since birth. One of the main tenets of the Roman faith was that God chose special people to do his work. These chosen ones were undeniably at one with God while they remained in his service. In this way Christ truly was the selected Son of God.

All the arguments for and against the divinity of Christ did not seem to matter to Declan until he went with Origen to say the Mass or, as the eastern Christians said, to share the offering.

Origen had no church, only a little chapel in the stone hut in which he lived. The service was often said high on the hill of Teamhair among the standing stones. The wind blew over the top of the hill tearing at the monks' vestments, whipping their hair around their faces, but to Declan this was the greatest church he had ever visited. It was grand to pray under the roof of a rich basilica in Rome or in the chapels of the monasteries of Gaul and Italy but how much greater it was to kneel in devotion beneath the vault of the heavens that were built by God. To Declan the eastern rites were a simpler and more direct veneration of God. Compared to Origen's humble offering the Roman sacraments seemed dull, empty and insincere.

The day after his arrival Declan attended a Mass in memory of an Egyptian saint. It was then that he began to glimpse where the real differences between east and west lay. Origen gave the wine and the bread to all present. Declan did not refuse it even though the manner of making it sacred and one with God would not have been acceptable to any Roman bishop. Isernus crossed himself in the Roman manner and none of the Egyptians seemed to notice that his way was different from theirs. Had it been a Roman abbot giving the western rites to easterners there would have been an uproar at such tiny discrepancies. These humble men, however, were happy to be sharing their worship with others who knew Christ. It was almost as though it did not matter what form the praise of God took for it was all done in adoration of the one true creator.

The service of offering ended with a kiss on the cheek passed around the circle from the officiating priest until it returned eventually to him. Then the monks filed off down the twisting path of the hill, singing a chant of praise in their own language.

At the foot of the hill of Teamhair Declan caught up with the blind eastern abbot and took his arm as they walked. 'Thank you for sharing your worship with us,' he said.

'I am impressed that a brother abbot of the Roman tradition could bear to join in our heretical ravings,' Origen jibed.

'I have a great respect for your ways, Origen. I sometimes think that I would prefer to go to a heaven full of the joyful singing of your monks than to a paradise ringing with the stale liturgies of Rome.'

'Careful what you say, brother. Anyone might think that the two are incompatible.'

Declan raised his eyebrows in acknowledgment of his error. 'You have lived here for so long that you even think like an Hibernian.'

Origen laughed but added in a more serious tone, 'Why have you returned to Eirinn, brother?'

'I had come with the intention of asking the High-King to help protect my community from Saxon raiders but now that I am here I think that God led me to Eirinn for some other purpose. Perhaps it was to teach me something. I have a feeling that a new path is opening up before my questing feet.'

'That is good. I thought many years ago when we first met that you were ready for the life of a hermit but you ran away to Dal Araidhe before I could suggest it to you. I hoped that you would return to us one day. I am glad that I have lived to meet with you again.' He sought out Declan's hand and held it for a moment. 'God did send you to us for a reason.'

Declan smiled at the Egyptian, forgetting for the moment that the white robed monk could not see the gesture. 'What might that be?'

'He has not revealed the whole plan to me yet but I can tell you what I know over supper if you like. Will you and Isernus join my brethren at our meal?'

'We would be very happy to,' Declan replied enthusiastically. 'Very happy indeed.'

NINETEEN

I am sorry that the monster escaped with all of her other limbs,' Murrough admitted after the guards had secured the door to the queen's room. 'Had I known that she was the cause of Caitlin's troubles I would not have been content to strike at her only once.'

'The Cailleach has been dealt a severe blow,' Síla reassured him. 'She will need to recuperate before she sets about stealing any more children. It will be a long time before we see her again.'

'Is there no way that we can rid ourselves of her permanently?' Murrough pleaded. 'I can't help but feel that our two surviving children will never be safe as long as that creature haunts the fortress.'

'It is not the fortress of Cashel that this monster is bound to follow. It is Caitlin,' Síla explained. 'Sometime after the clash of arms at Rathowen this beast attached itself to your queen while she was in a weakened state and still suffering the shock of her injury in the bloody battle. I am not sure if we can ever rid her of its terrible shadow. The only ones who have any influence over these creatures are the Danaans themselves. I am certain that this hag is one of their race turned rebel. There were many of the Old Ones who never accepted the treaty with our people.'

'Is this monster one of the Sidhe-Dubh?' Murrough exclaimed. 'One of the Dark Faery kind?'

'I believe so,' Síla admitted. 'Only Druids of the Danaan race have the ability to hold sway over one such as this, for a Cailleach can never be killed by any means that you or I might devise. She is as immortal as are all of her folk but she is more powerful than most because she feeds on human flesh and frailty.'

'There were three Danaan Druids at Teamhair who arrived a few days before I departed,' Murrough muttered, remembering the rumour that he had heard from one of the High-King's guards-men.

'What's that?' Síla cut in. 'Are you sure?'

'A tent was laid aside for them and no-one allowed to enter. Sweet music could be heard play-ing within the enclosure after sunset and before the dawn. Not even Gobann handles the harp with such skill as the one who played inside that tent each night.'

'They have come to guide the Wanderers on their first steps upon the Road,' Síla realised. 'Then we do hold some hope of saving Caitlin from this curse if we can get her to Teamhair before they leave. How long do they intend to stay within the citadel?'

'I have no idea. Perhaps you should ask Gobann.'

'If only I could but he will be deeply involved in the ritual of initiation. By the time I get a mes-sage to him it may be too late. I would guess that they will stay until the day after Beltinne but no longer.' Síla pushed the heels of her palms against her eye sockets and tried to think of what to do. She had gone without sleep for four days while waiting to spring the trap on the hag. Now she was beginning to pay the price for her vigilance.

'I will sleep until daybreak,' she said finally. 'And then all must be ready for us to ride to Teamhair with Caitlin and her baby. If luck is on our side we will reach there before the Danaans leave the citadel for their own country. If we do not reach them it may be many seasons before they send another embassy to our world.'

'I will make the preparations for our departure,' Murrough assured her.

'Choose fast horses. The baby will ride strapped face-first to my chest. Caitlin will ride with you. The high point of the Beltinne festival is only two nights and two days away. That is between sunset on Beltinne eve and sunset the next day. According to custom no-one will be permitted to enter or to leave the citadel of Teamhair. Can we make the distance in that time?'

'We must try.'

'Very well then, we shall. Now I must go and take some rest.'

Murrough went directly to the stables where a troop of his warriors had only just arrived after patrolling the coast. The soldiers were brushing their mounts and cleaning their saddles, preparing to bed down for the night.

Murrough went amongst them organising them into small troops of mounted warriors and then sent them out to raise the kingdom for war in case the Saxons came again in force while he was away. That done he appointed one of the veterans of the guard to take command of the coastal defences to see to the security of the fortress. The man went to the task immediately without any questions as to why Murrough might be rushing straight back to Teamhair while there were foreign raiders on the doorstep.

However, not every warrior obeyed his orders without question. There were mutterings among the troops that the king was deserting Cashel to help defend the High-King and thus he was neglecting his duty to his own kingdom. Those words of disquiet did not reach Murrough's ears; if they had he might have thought twice about what he was about to do.

By dawn his mounted warriors were riding off to perform their allotted duties and Murrough had readied six horses for the ride north. Three guards were to go with them so that they would not be slowed by too large a retinue yet not too vulnerable to attack. There was one mount for Síla and one for himself plus a spare, since his horse would also be bearing Caitlin's weight.

Omra readied riding breeches for the queen and then she roused Caitlin just before the sunrise with fresh water and warm bread. Her efforts seemed in vain for the queen floated between consciousness and dreaming for a long while. Half sleeping and still suffering some degree of physical pain, Caitlin fought off all attempts to dress her or wrap her well for the ride.

Despite the difficulties with the queen and the hurried preparations for the journey they managed to set off an hour after dawn. They followed the road that led north. For Murrough this would be the second time he had galloped along this road in as many days but he did not spare the horses. With the possibility of Saxon raiders afoot in the land he wanted to get this first leg of the trek over with as soon as possible.

His impatience paid off for they made such good time that they reached the crossroads as the cattle were being led into the fields after milking from the nearby farmhouses.

Murrough paid his customary respects kneeling at the Quicken bough but to Síla's annoyance he did not rush through his private ritual. If anything he had much more to say on this occasion to the spirit of the bough than ever before and now he was more earnest in his request. He set Caitlin down on the grass beside him as he sought communion with the spirit of the tree. As if in answer to his summons she stirred from her sleep just as he finished his invocation. Slowly she reached a hand out to touch him on the leg.

Caitlin's eyes had brightened as if she had woken from a long and restful sleep and Murrough took another moment to thank the Quicken. The queen reached inside her shirt and withdrew a small black bag which she passed to Murrough. The king was a little puzzled.

'Open it and look inside,' she whispered.

When Murrough pulled the drawstring apart and tipped the contents into his hand he still did not understand what he saw.

'Those are the nine berries that I found in that little bag after the tree was cut down,' she explained. 'One of the Saxons had collected them. I have kept them with me all these seasons in the hope that they may aid me in time of need. But not even the seeds of the Quicken could protect me from the old woman.'

Murrough put the red berries straight back in their bag and tied the leather strap around Caitlin's neck without saying a word. Then he lifted her in his arms and carried her back to the horses.

By this time Síla was pacing her horse up and down the road impatiently so Murrough mounted reluctantly, even though he knew the stop had cost them valuable time. If they did not reach Teamhair before the ceremonial closing out of the winter they would likely miss a rare opportunity to meet the Danaans before they departed the citadel for their own country. And with their passing would perish any real hope that Caitlin would be freed of the demon that preyed on her.

As they rode up the steep valley sides toward the hill pass above the Quicken crossroads a light rain began to fall. Murrough was put in mind of the journey that he and Caitlin had taken nine Beltinne festivals ago. Then they had been riding to save the Quicken Tree from destruction. Caitlin was at that time still suffering from a wound to the leg that she had sustained in the defence of Rathowen. He recalled how she had drifted then into unconsciousness as they travelled south and how he had cradled her in his arms as they rode, in much the same way as he was doing now.

He wondered to himself if the state she had fallen into after Rathowen had less to do with her wound, which had healed well after the poison was drained, than it had to do with the Cailleach. He had always known that Caitlin carried a deep soul injury after the battle. Her lover and champion Fintan had been captured in the fight and he had been executed before her very eyes in a most gruesome manner.

Ever after Caitlin held herself responsible for Fintan's death, not allowing herself to forget that she had stood by and watched as he was murdered. Of course she had been powerless to save him. They were separated by two hostile armies.

Síla had explained to him that creatures like the Cailleach often fed on a person's feelings of frustration and guilt in much the same way as mortals feed on bread and mead. The healer also believed that such creatures were capable of consuming the flesh of their victims. Murrough was certain that he would rather be devoured in body than have his spirit gradually ingested by such a monster.

In fear of the possible consequences of their flight north Murrough had made certain that Brigid his daughter was perfectly safe. He had sent her away to a hill-fort that was owned by one of his relatives in the east. There she would be able to grow to womanhood without fear of being recognised by the Cailleach and abducted as a slave to the Otherworld.

The boy who had just been born to them, he had already decided, would be sent to North Britain to be given into the care of Murrough's brother Morann, who was a judge at the court of Conaire the King of the Dal Araidhe. With both his surviving children fostered Murrough would be able to concentrate on helping Caitlin to heal herself. There was nothing that he wanted more in the world.

The rain eased as they began their descent down the range of hills to the north of the crossroads and so they were able to pick up speed a little. Two black dots rose in the sky far off ahead of them. Murrough watched the Ravens as they made a wide circuit around the party. As they flew they gathered more of their kind until there were about seven birds travelling together. By the time the king called the riders to a halt at midday the rain was starting to fall heavy again but the birds were nowhere to be seen. This put his mind at ease a little.

Since the queen was now awake Síla fed the baby from Caitlin's breast. Afterwards the healer wrapped the lad again, securing him to his mother for the rest of the journey. Murrough lay under a tree which gave him almost no shelter from the downpour but he was deep in thought and did not really notice how wet he had become. His soldiers started a small fire, as veteran warriors will do whenever they have the opportunity to relax during a long ride, but they had no sooner warmed themselves by it than Síla was calling for them to mount and move on.

From habit the warriors kicked soil over the flames smothering the coals, but they need not have bothered for the rain was bucketing down by now. By sundown the rain was still pouring and in the distance there was lightning but Síla begged Murrough to ride on through the night so that they would be sure to reach Teamhair in time. Caitlin was soaked to the skin as they all were but at least she gave no sign of discomfort and Murrough was grateful for that small mercy.

When dawn came the sun did little to light the road before them for it was shrouded by black clouds. They rode on regardless so that by midday they had reached the southern borders of Midhe. From here on the going would be easier if only the weather broke. Murrough prayed that it would, otherwise their hopes of reaching the citadel before nightfall would be dashed.

He was relieved when the rain ceased for a while and overjoyed when the sky cleared not long afterwards. Soon they were able to pick up speed. Within an hour's ride of Teamhair the road became level. In parts it was paved and well drained. They came to this section of the road well before sunset but Murrough advised that they should not stop but travel on at an easier pace.

Eventually they could glimpse through the trees the outline of the hill of Teamhair itself. Síla voiced everyone's relief by giving a wild victory call such as her people often did when they rejoiced. The strange warbling song upset the mounts and they let their riders know that they were ready to break into a trot.

'The horses are keen to put an end to this ride,' Murrough cried.

'Then let's make the most of our ponies' enthusiasm,' Síla replied. She gave her mount a kick that sent him galloping out in front of the others. The last stretch of road was before them; horses and humans could smell food and warm lodging. Murrough most of all was keen to get back within the citadel for he had spent nearly five days on the road and his body was crying out for slumber.

Then he realised that Síla had slept very little in the last week, if at all. He came to the conclusion that Druid discipline had kept her going. Only that training would allow anyone to keep going for so long without collapsing.

When they passed a large party of travellers walking toward Teamhair they did not break their pace to greet them. There were obviously foreigners among them but Murrough did not wish to stop or waste time with words of greeting. He calculated that the walkers were still three or four hours' journey on foot from the citadel gates and by this reckoning they would probably not make it to the royal enclosure before the doors were shut at sunset.

The foreigners were soon far behind him. Murrough decided that they must have been foreign Druids arriving for Beltinne. If the strangers were hoping to collect a coal from the sacred fire for their hearths they would be able to get one after the rituals were complete, but he was glad that he would not be in their position. They would be forced to camp outside the citadel gates and due to the Beltinne restrictions they would be unable to light any fire for cooking or for warmth until morning. It would be a long hard night for them.

Seginus heard the riders long before he saw them. Many horsemen had passed the missionaries since they had discovered the road to Teamhair. One or two riders had stopped to speak with them but it would have been obvious by their build that some of the men in the missionary party were warriors. Those of the party who spoke Gaelic could not disguise their strange accents and so it was plain, too, that they were foreigners.

The word would reach Teamhair soon, Seginus thought, that there were strangers on the road to the citadel and there were warriors amongst them. From that moment on he was sure that there would be trouble waiting for them around every bend in the road and behind every bush.

The centurion of the guard, Tatheus Nonus, was also nervous, so nervous that he did not take his hand off his sword hilt through the afternoon, though he kept the weapon well concealed beneath his cloak. Tatheus was a veteran of the war against a particularly brutal tribe of Franks who had penetrated deep into the southern interior of the Empire. Once the barbarians had the rich lands of Transalpine Gaul in their grasp they had decided to start spreading their kingdom out toward Trier. It had been a long and bloody conflict but the Roman army had finally forced the heathen back into an enclave; not, however, without paying a heavy price.

The wide scar across the centurion's face was his personal memento from a barbarian warrior who refused to die. The rippling gash made his lower lip sag permanently so that even when he smiled there was cynicism in the expression which perhaps did not always accurately reflect his mood.

All of the guardsmen under the command of Tatheus had been hand-picked by Patricius for their loyalty to Rome and their profession of the Christian faith. They were all experienced warriors, each with a tale to tell similar to Tatheus'. All of them were extremely suspicious of barbarians. Nevertheless this journey to the far north was considered by many of their fellow legionnaires back in Ravenna to be an easy posting. 'If only they knew,' Tatheus kept repeating under his breath. 'If only they knew.'

It was plain to Seginus that they would reach the citadel some time after dark. He was loathe to travel in Eirinn at night. The newly ordained priest could not help feeling nervous about travelling after nightfall in a land where he and those in his company could be mistaken for invaders. His stomach turned as he thought of some of the things that happened to him the last time he had been in Hibernia.

As it turned out there was nothing that would have helped them to arrive before the shutting of the gates for Beltinne even if they had known about the prohibitions on entry after sunset. So it was that when they did finally arrive at the outer defences they found the great oak doors barred to them.

Patricius hailed the gatekeepers telling them who he was and why he was in Eirinn but nothing he could say would persuade them to open the way for the party to enter. Finally the bishop convinced the captain of the guard to send a message to Leoghaire stating that he was an emissary of the

Pope and that he was seeking admittance to the court of Teamhair. An answer was a long time in coming.

Patricius had almost given up hope of being granted an audience when he was summoned by someone standing high on the battlements.

'Patricius Sucatus, ambassador from Rome!' came the deep and crackling voice of an old warrior.

'It is he who answers your salute,' Patricius called back in his best Gaelic.

'The High-King of Eirinn, Leoghaire ú Niall, wishes you well this night, but he regrets that the custom of the land forbids him to allow you to enter here until the sun sets tomorrow.'

'Surely you aren't serious,' Patricius roared. 'I have travelled halfway across the Christian world to speak with him.'

'How many nights and days have you journeyed?'

'One hundred and seventy days and as many nights.'

'That was indeed a long journey but if you spent so many days on the road then one more night under the stars surely will not harm you.'

'I was warned of many dangers that would face me in coming to this land but no-one told me that the High-King of Eirinn was inhospitable,' Patricius yelled back.

'It is the time of Beltinne and no-one in the kingdoms takes in strangers after sunset. It is the custom. I assure you that Leoghaire will attend to your every comfort if you return tomorrow at nightfall.'

'Leoghaire insults the Pope and the people of Rome, and he insults me also who represents them.'

There was silence for a few moments. It seemed that the man on the battlement was searching for an honourable reply, 'Let it never be said that the High-King is inhospitable to his guests. Behind you there lies the hill of Slané. Leoghaire gives this place to you for your rest this night. You will find shelter among the stones or if you prefer you may occupy the long-house that lies to the side of the hill. This is a dwelling that is dear to Leoghaire and he would not allow his closest friend to lie under the roof of that house without leave. You are honoured that he invites you to rest there tonight.'

'I will take my followers to Slané but I demand to see the king tomorrow evening.'

'And so you shall. You have my word on it.'

'What is your name who speaks for the High-King of Eirinn making assurances in his name?'

'I am Leoghaire ú Niall. I am the High-King of Eirinn,' came the sharp reply.

Patricius allowed his eyes to widen in surprise. It was rare that he was caught off guard. 'God bless you then, Leoghaire,' he answered.

'And also you, Patricius,' Leoghaire replied in Latin.

The bishop smiled at the High-King's final words for they were lifted straight out of the Roman Mass. It was clear that the High-King of Eirinn had some knowledge of the Roman ways and rituals.

'What will we do now, Father? Where will we go?' asked Secondinus, who had not understood any of the discourse in Gaelic.

'We will rest this night on the hill of Slané as honoured guests,' Patricius announced. 'And tomorrow evening I will go to meet and to baptise King Leoghaire of Eirinn.'

TWENTY

hen Sianan began to regain her senses she was seated on a low cold stone out in the open air. She observed beside her the slumped figure of Mawn about an arm's length away. At least she assumed that it was Mawn for his hair had been cropped away by shears and as a result he looked very different. Where the blades had cut too close to his skin the pink of his scalp showed through the fair stubble. All his long hair was lying about him on the stone, in the grass and clinging to his wet shoulders in great honey-coloured tufts.

No sooner had Sianan noticed his abandoned locks than she felt her own hair being tugged. She clearly heard the sound of a sharp blades scything through the long black strands. From the corner of her eye she could see her ebony threads of hair falling like dark wheat sheaves at reaping. Once she had been proud of her shining locks but now she did not care if they cut it all off and it never grew back. She once more drifted into semiconsciousness, losing a sense of what was going on around her, no longer perceiving the novices as they prepared her for the next stage of the initiation. She did not even notice that she and Mawn were naked but for linen cloths that were draped across their laps.

Cathach finished cutting her hair and sheathed his small iron shears. As he did so he called on the attendants to come and wash the two Wanderers. As they were being led away he carefully gathered up all the pieces of their hair that were scattered about and threw the ball of mingled hair on a little fire that burned nearby. The dark and golden strands crackled and spat as they shrivelled in the heat and the air was tainted by the bitter smoke.

The novices took Mawn and Sianan toward a great stone basin hollowed out of a single piece of rock that served for the cleansing of initiates. This pool was known to all as the Cauldron of Life. It had been crafted in ancient times, generations before the Gaels had set foot in Eirinn. Legends said that the Tuatha-De-Danaan had made it, though some claimed it was much older than even their people. The stone was a wide basin, broad enough that a cow could stand in its midst and her shoulders not touch the sides. It was deep enough that the beast's head would not get wet when the basin was full to the brim.

Mawn was first to be lowered into the cleansing stone cauldron. His head slipped beneath the cold rippling waters for a second but two novices quickly dragged him back out to scrub him with sea sponges. When they were satisfied that he was clean of all dirt and hair they wrapped a fur about his shoulders and let him sit crouched on the basin's step.

The next thing Sianan knew was that she was cold and wet and everything had gone dark. She struggled to breathe but her mouth and nose filled with water. She had no sooner become aware that she was underwater than she felt strong hands pulling her clear of it. She coughed violently to clear her lungs. Though the weather was unusually warm for this season both the initiates began shivering almost as soon as they emerged from the cauldron despite the furs wrapped around their bodies.

With the ritual bathing complete Sianan and Mawn were half-carried half-led to a wattle and daub hut which was just out of sight of the cauldron in the centre of a tiny wooded area. This was where their bodies would be painted with the sacred signs.

The furs were taken from them and they yielded them up unresisting so that the painters could work unhindered on their cleansed bodies. Before the work began in earnest they were each given a bitter tea that tasted so strongly of herbs that Sianan found it hard to swallow. A novice made sure that she drained her cup then helped her to lie down on her back. Before she could take ten breaths Sianan had slipped into a state of deep relaxation.

As soon as their subjects were resting the artists went to work with urgent haste. They were aware that if they did not lay the sketches for the many patterns quickly the work would not be finished before sunset. With blue dye made from the stems and leaves of a plant known as the gorm, sometimes called woad, they outlined their designs with tiny slivers of wood chewed at the ends to make primitive brushes.

Not long after they had begun their work Gobann arrived with his harp bag over his shoulder. He silently entered the hut to seat himself by the central fire. This building was of a simple design. There was no chimney. Instead the smoke rose straight up to filter through the rafters, drying the roof and thus preventing vermin from infesting the thatch. A feature of this ancient plan was that guests who gathered around the central hearth were forced to face each other. Meeting houses and royal halls were still constructed after this fashion.

After he had settled and observed the painters' progress Gobann opened a small bag that hung from his waist and poured some of the contents onto the hot coals of the hearth. Billows of smoke spread throughout the room as the incense melted and bubbled before being consumed by the embers. While the fumes were dispersing into the roof Gobann unwrapped his harp and prepared to play.

At the striking of the first tuning note Mawn stirred into full consciousness. The ringing of the brass wires held a perpetual fascination for him; he had always listened intently whenever Gobann played. Mawn tried to rise on his elbows but he was restrained by one of the painters so he shut his eyes once more and lay his head back down on the floor.

Gobann began to dabble with the bones of a slow sleep melody as soon as he had finished fine-tuning the instrument. Striking only two wires together he built up a slow steady rhythm that soon became a droning hum as the harp warmed to Gobann's hands. The brass wires, if left to vibrate, would ring for as long as twenty breaths. When they were struck in combination with other notes the instrument would allow its voice to soar in volume and intensity like a series of mighty ocean waves washing onto the seashore.

This style of playing was named the sleep strain but it was not just meant as music for lullabies. This music was also performed to aid those who were in deep contemplation or about to enter the realms of the Otherworld. There was no strict tempo such as a Gaelic march might rely on. Instead a combination of the sounds of the harp and emotions of the harper were utilised to bring out the melody. This was the most powerful music of all. The old stories told of harpers who were able to put whole kingdoms into a deep trance to be wakened again only at the whim of the musician. While warriors were required to hand over their weapons on entering a king's hall, harpers were also forced to surrender their instruments to the door wardens. Only one such as Gobann who had earned the poetic honour of the Silver Branch could play when and where he wished.

The bearing of the Silver Branch signified that a musician had mastered the harp and vowed not to use its powers for any reason that might not benefit his host. Until this day Mawn had borne the little silver branch with its tiny golden apple-shaped bells wherever his master travelled. After the initiation he would be considered a Druid in his own right and it would no longer be seemly for him to carry Gobann's badge for him. The poet would have to find someone else to fulfil that duty.

The droning quickly became one long continuous hum that filled Mawn's head with an echoing cacophony of half-human voices singing in a low pitch. In his imagination a great choir of men stood crammed into the wattle and daub hut pushing out the walls to make room. Though the tiny house was already full of people he could envisage more of the choristers pressing at the backs of their comrades forcing their way through the doorway.

Then he heard a second group of higher-pitched voices joining in the chanting. Somehow a group of women had sneaked in through an open window to challenge the males to a duel of melodies.

Mawn became aware of a brush dragging slowly across the top of his shoulder. He could feel the wet paint drying quickly in the heat of the room. It contracted as it warmed, pinching the skin beneath it. At that point Gobann brought in a new element to the melody that he was playing and Mawn was surprised that he had never heard this form of tune before. He was determined to try to remember it but he could not concentrate. In the end he surrendered to the unfamiliar tones and allowed the music to wash over him. He felt the notes reaching out to lift him high into the air so he was almost touching the ceiling.

Mawn was sure that he was floating through the hut on a breeze. When the music dropped a little in intensity he was lowered onto the floor again as gently as a she-cat places her kittens in their sleeping places. He was briefly aware of the floor beneath him before he was once more lulled by the harp into a sound sleep.

Sianan did not wake at all during the painting of the sacred signs, instead she drew slow breaths and dreamt of a great hall where a hundred musicians were playing on harps made of gold and silver. Only once did she show any sign of stirring and that was when a novice was preparing the spiral designs for her forehead. She was as lifeless as any that had passed beyond the world.

As the shadows began to lengthen outside the hut the painters added the finishing touches to their handiwork. Gobann expertly brought the music to a gentle end, returning to the opening phrases of the piece. When he was done he allowed the harp to carry on its droning for a few minutes more. In the end he was unwilling to stop altogether for the instrument was in particularly good voice this evening, but he did not want to hold up the ceremonies. With one last stroke of his long rounded nails on the shining wires he ended the enchantment.

The novices sprang into action as soon as the room was quiet, gathering their tools and paint and all the templates of their designs. Everything they had used would have to be destroyed in flames and every fire in the land would be extinguished just on sunset so they had very little time.

Gobann was returning his harp to her bag as Cathach entered the hut. Once more the two initiates were draped all over in fur. This time it was the skins of two white deer that they wore. Cathach gently placed a new black-handled knife on the chests of both Mawn and Sianan. The novices who lifted the two initiates ensured that the sheathed blades did not fall to touch the earth. Borne by six apprentice Druids dressed in dark blue cloaks and hoods, the seemingly lifeless bodies were then carried out of the hut and through the little wood. There was smoke on the breeze as the party came out onto the plain for every fire in the citadel had been extinguished with the water of the holy well of Teamhair. The resulting haze filled the valley with an eerie purple mist.

Cathach went on ahead of the bearers to check that all was ready for the next stage of the initiation. Just over the rise and out of sight of the wood was the Mound of Testing where all new Druids were sent to undertake a trial of their worth.

It was not unusual for the whole population of the citadel to turn out to witness such ceremonies but on this occasion the audience was strictly limited to those of the Druid kind. The Danaans had specifically requested that the proceedings remain closed to all others and Cathach could not really refuse them after all they had done to help with the Druid Council's plan. However, Cathach had managed to convince the Danaans that Leoghaire should be allowed to attend the initiation because he was the symbolic guardian at the new year kindling of the Need Fire and because he was a trusted partner in the great plan.

Usually the ceremonies lasted through the long night and the lighting of the fire took place at sunrise. The weather was mild so it would not be too long a night for anyone except Sianan and Mawn.

When Cathach came to the great stone mound he gathered all the musicians together with a wave of his arm and silently sent them to their positions around the structure. Gobann arrived soon after Cathach, setting himself a stool at the entrance to the long passageway that led into the mound.

Three great brass cauldrons were placed on metal stands to the right of the entrance and Gobann placed a few drops of water in each before he finally settled beside them to tune the harp once more. The three Druids who were the keepers of the cauldrons then took their places behind the vessels. Each of them held a thick rod made of oak each about the length of a horse's foreleg.

On the opposite side of the entrance three groups of three more Druids stood bearing long ceremonial trumpets also made of brass but richly inlaid with gold. A group of nearly a hundred other Druids congregated around the entrance to the mound in a semicircle, awaiting the arrival of Mawn and Sianan.

Just as the preparations were complete the procession appeared over the lower rise of a hill nearby. The novices, with the initiates on their shoulders, followed a winding path toward the stone mound. They were soon joined by many other novices who chanted a low note in mourning for their comrades who were passing from the college of the novitiate into a new life as Druids. No torches flickered, no lanterns lit the way, for all throughout Eirinn there were no fires on this night.

At a certain point not far from the mound itself there were two tall stones of great antiquity standing sentinel at either side of the path. There the novices stopped their procession for they were forbidden to come any closer to the mound of testing until it was their time.

Out of the night came dozens of Druids in white robes covered by long blue cloaks and hoods. They gently relieved the novices of their burdens and then the procession moved on. The novices waited until the escort had been swallowed up in the darkness then they all silently returned to their hall where they would hold a feast in memory of their colleagues.

The path was silver in the reflected moonlight so Gobann could clearly see the shadowy procession slowly marching down towards the mound. He realised that anyone who did not know that this was a sacred initiation might have thought that a funeral rite was being enacted here this night. In some respects, he reminded himself, it was similar as this was a ceremony marking the passing away of two people from one world and their entry into the next.

'They will be more like Danaans than people of the Gael,' he said aloud. 'They will be like ghosts walking the Earth deathless and eternal.'

As if in answer to his words, three dark figures appeared at the opposite side of the entrance path to stand behind the trumpeters. Gobann felt his skin tingle. The poet knew that these three were the Danaan Druids who had come to take part in the ritual. He could not see any of their faces under their long hoods but he felt their gaze upon him and the power of their presence. He remembered the feeling that he got as a child when he sat beside the great Loch Nighe and listened to the sounds; they were everywhere about him. These three were ancient and full of murmurs like the wide loch. They were as dark and as immeasurable. He could sense that they were at once dangerous and tranquil, like the surface of a deep lake at daybreak. For the first time in many seasons Gobann felt real awe.

If the Danaans could hear Gobann's thoughts they did not acknowledge them. They stood effortlessly still like the oak trees of the sacred grove and like the oaks they watched everything that took place around them without emotion, fearing nothing.

Gobann heard a voice inside his head reminding him to attend to his duties and he wondered if it was one of the Danaans who was reprimanding him. The Druid touched one of the musicians on the shoulder as he stood by the three cauldrons. This was the signal that it was time to start playing. The woman lifted her wooden rod high above her head and her two companions followed the lead. Then she placed the rod on the lip of the cauldron in front of her, running it steadily around the raised rim of the vessel. There was no sound at first other than a gentle scraping. Then gradually the great brass pots began to sing in voices that were similar to that of Gobann's harp.

The lead musician touched her cauldron with the rod in such a way that the whole vessel moved slightly on its metal stand. This caused the few drops of water that lay at the bottom of the bowl to move around and affect the note that was produced. The resulting sound was unlike anything else on earth, eerie and haunting, like the wailing of a seal pup or the cry of a wounded stag.

At a certain point the drummers began to strike their goatskin bodhrans. The beat was slow and soft at first but they built the rhythm and intensity of their drumming as the procession approached the entrance. Then, at Cathach's command, the trumpets sounded. Like the drums their tones were gentle at first. Each instrument was tuned to complement those to either side of it so that the overall effect was of a great droning, a cross between the sound that the war-pipes made and the sound of the harp when the chords were repeatedly struck.

All these instruments blended together in an harmonious lilting hum that shook the bone marrow of those who stood nearby. It spread a veil of music over the entire citadel. The gathered Druids closed in behind the procession as it passed them, taking up a chant that underscored the trumpets and drums and the singing cauldrons. Gobann easily spotted Leoghaire and a guard among the many blue-cloaked figures, for non-Druids were required to bare their heads during such rites in order for the initiated to be able to quickly recognise them. These were the only two among the many who did not wear hoods. He gasped a little though when he recognised the guard as Enda Censelach. Gobann realised that this must be Cathach's doing.

As the procession came close to the mound only the Danaans seemed not to be singing and moving in time with the drumming. Instead they were as still as stone as if they were standing alone on the plain.

Cathach walked out in front of the marchers as they came level to the three cauldrons. He called the group to a halt by raising his staff in the air.

At that very moment the musicians ceased their playing and silence fell over the plain again. The bearers obeyed the silent order, lowering their burdens onto the ground and placing folded cloaks beneath the initiate's bodies.

The Druids who had carried Mawn and Sianan stepped back to allow Gobann and Cathach to examine the Wanderers one last time and the two chief Druids of Eirinn brought a bowl of water to both of their students. A little rainwater was placed in each mouth, just enough to wet their tongues, then Cathach looked toward the Danaans, offering the palms of his hands in a sign of respect.

The taller of the three Faery Druids stepped forward, touching his forehead and his heart in one smooth gesture of greeting. Then he pulled a leather bottle from under his robes, releasing the stopper with bony fingers as he knelt beside Mawn. He placed the neck of the bottle carefully up to the young man's lips as Gobann supported the initiate's head. Mawn did not wake but instinctively swallowed the liquid that was offered to him. The Danaan moved immediately to where Sianan lay and repeated the process with Cathach holding his granddaughter's head.

When that was done the tall Danaan retreated to where he had been standing earlier and the other two came forward. One went to stand beside Sianan and the other beside Mawn. They each held small leather parcels in their thin hands but they did not kneel to present the contents to the two initiates. Instead the Danaans unwrapped the parcels and daintily lifted the contents up to the heavens. Gobann could clearly see the pink salmon flesh they held, the flesh of the salmon of knowledge that had feasted in the well of Segais. The Danaans knelt down then and placed the morsels of food into the mouths of Mawn and Sianan, who swallowed the tiny pieces.

The tall Danaan took out another bottle and spread the contents of it on the ground. The scent of freshly turned soil and wet grass in summer filled the air. Everyone who caught a hint of it on the evening breeze suddenly felt completely refreshed and acutely aware of their surroundings. This was soil from the Otherworld. The two Danaans withdrew and Cathach signalled for the Druid bearers to bring the two initiates into the mound.

As they were lifted up off the ground Gobann struck the chords of his harp once more in a steady ringing drone. The other instruments joined in the cacophony of music but where their earlier recital had been constrained and reverent, now it was wild and erratic, building swiftly into a crazy dance. Some of those Druids who remained outside the mound began to sway to the rhythms.

The Danaans drifted off to their tent without anybody noticing and were not seen again that night. Gobann was surprised that Leoghaire and Enda followed after them as though they had been invited to join the ambassadors in their tent. However, before the two kings had made it to the door a messenger approached Leoghaire. After a few moments the High-King strode off with Enda and the messenger in tow toward the king's hall. Gobann wondered what could have been so important that it needed such urgent attention but he returned his attention to his duties for the time being.

A long passage led to the centre of the small man-made hill. Unlike most monuments of a similar nature, this one was large enough to allow a tall man to stand at full height as he walked toward the central chamber. Three warriors could comfortably walk abreast without their shoulders scraping the large stones that supported the ceiling. It was said that this mound was more ancient than even the Danaans because even they held these structures in awe and respect.

The passage was perfectly straight, ending at a rounded chamber which held a stone basin of similar construction to the one in which Mawn and Sianan had been washed, though much smaller. Nevertheless, both of them could have easily fitted within its smooth bowl. Moonlight filled the chamber from a specially constructed shaft directly above the basin so that the beams of silver light reflected on the surface of the water that filled it. This gave the Druids enough light to be able to place the initiates at either side of the stone.

Patterns covering the walls were dimly visible as sharp shadows. When Mawn and Sianan were set down and their furs removed, the designs on their bodies seemed to blend in with their surroundings. Cathach had the bearers place the bodies as though they were truly being entombed. Mawn was set on his left side, knees drawn up to his chest and right hand clutching his black-handled knife. Sianan was laid out on her right side with her head at Mawn's feet and her Scian-dubh in her left palm. Great care was taken so that their postures would resemble a giant double spiral.

With that task satisfactorily completed Cathach silently commanded everyone to leave him alone with the couple for a few moments so that he could perform his personal blessings. Four Druids returned soon after bearing baskets of flowers and red ochre. Cathach took handfuls of the ruddy dust and threw it over the naked bodies of his granddaughter and her companion. When that was done the initiates were banked with the flowers. Finally everyone, including Cathach, withdrew from the chamber.

At a distance of about ten paces along the passage three Druids had begun the process of walling up the tomb. Cathach squeezed through the gap and then lay the last stones himself. All had been prepared according to ancient formulae, with the help and blessing of the Danaans. Nevertheless the old Druid was deeply anxious as to whether he would ever see Sianan alive again. What if she did not pass the test? What if she never woke from the dream walk?

Ten paces further along the passage, work on the next stone seal was almost completed so Cathach retreated from the passage entirely and walked out into the night. He did not stop to watch the frantic dancing that had taken a hold of all the Druid company or to listen to the frenzied music that was filling the night with strange sounds and cries. Instead he went straight back towards his chamber in the Star of Poetry to sit alone until he was called for the dawn services.

TWENTY-ONE

t was past the middle of the night by the time that Patricius and his party arrived at the hill of Slané. The journey from the gates of Teamhair had involved a much longer walk than they had expected. Exhausted and hungry they virtually ignored the three guardsmen who greeted them at the entrance to the long-house.

If the sentries were offended they did not show it. They dutifully held the doors open for the High-King's guests. Once the whole party had entered the great hall, the Gaelic warriors closed the doors behind them and took posts at the far ends of the room. The Roman soldiers and their centurion arranged themselves beside the cold and lifeless hearth, squatting on their haunches as they were trained to do when they were on war footing. This posture ensured that they did not relax their guard too much and were ready to spring into action. Tullia, Seginus and Secondinus lay down to rest.

The interior of the building was dark but moonlight filtered in through the smoke hole above the central hearth to fill the air with an unearthly silver luminescence. Bishop Patricius knelt in the midst of a wide shaft of this light and offered up prayers of thanks for their safe arrival.

Seginus cast his eyes about him, surprised at how vast the interior of the hall really was. From the outside the building looked quite narrow with low roof beams but from the inside, where Seginus was stretched out on the floor, it was difficult to pinpoint the furthest walls. He could see the door through which the party had entered yet though he strained his eyes in the half-light he could not even glimpse any of the other supporting structures.

Seginus had not been able to calm himself since they had stumbled upon the Teamhair road. He was convinced it was only a matter of time before he was found. He noticed that he had broken into a cold sweat. His fingers quickly found the pouch that always hung round his neck and he clutched it as though it held a holy talisman.

Though he could not see the walls Seginus could feel them steadily closing in on him. Neither did the sight of three Gaelic warriors at such close quarters ease his mind. Seginus remembered too well the bloody slaughter that took place on the field of Rathowen. He knew what men such as these were capable of if their honour was threatened.

Though the tale might sound fanciful to anyone who had not been at that battle he had seen with his own eyes two hundred determined Gaels almost completely annihilate a larger band of berserker Saxons who had been in the service of Palladius. He reasoned that if Hibernian warriors could so easily face a force of barbarian raiders without any fear, what chance did a mere twenty-four Roman legionnaires and a handful of clerics stand? If any of these savages were to recognise him what terrible torture might their High-King have waiting for him?

Seginus heard his stomach grumble loudly but the outburst was prompted by nerves not hunger. Suddenly he decided that he could suffer the atmosphere in the hall no longer. He stood up intending to stride out into the night air. Tullia looked over at him when she heard him stir but did not rise from her task. In that same moment one of the Gaels who wore a small shield strapped to his arm jumped to his feet and headed across the chamber to cut Seginus off. The Roman felt for the little pouch around his neck, again holding it tightly as he quickened his pace.

Now the monk could feel his heart beating hard in his chest, hammering as though it were going to burst through his ribcage. He turned his face away from the warrior and looked at the floor as he walked, certain that he had been spotted as a fugitive from the High-King's justice. The air within the room was suddenly stiflingly hot and Seginus found that he was struggling to breathe. The sweat was running down his arms to gather in the fibres of his sleeves.

Before he had trod another step the guard called out something in an Hibernian dialect but Seginus did not catch what was said. He only knew that he had to reach the door and the cool fresh breeze outside before the warrior stopped him. The priest picked up his pace a little, desperately trying to ignore the sound of footsteps behind him. He glanced back and saw that the other two Gaels were now standing, watching him with interest as he crossed the short space that separated him from freedom.

In a few moments he had covered twenty paces of ground though it seemed to take him as long as it would to walk twice that distance. The Hibernian yelled out again and this time there was a hint of threat in the strange savage words. Seginus was so startled at the warrior's tone that he half turned to look back at the man and as he did so he tripped and fell forward onto the packed earth floor. In the next instant the Gael was standing over him with a hand resting on the hilt of the broad sword that hung from his belt. The Hibernian spoke but Seginus could not understand his thick accented speech. The priest's knowledge of Gaelic was not as complete as he would have wished in this situation.

Seginus twisted his head round so that he could look his enemy in the face and when their eyes met the Hibernian broke into a wide grin, offering his hand to help the Roman to his feet. Before Seginus knew what had happened the door was thrown open for him and he was ushered out into the night. There he stood for a long while staring out over the moonlit plain toward Teamhair, relieved and baffled by the Hibernian's behaviour. When he finally came to his senses he found himself entirely alone. The warrior had gone back inside the hall and shut the door again. The priest still had not realised that the warrior was warning him about being outside on a night such as this.

Seginus began to walk with shaking legs back down to the road that climbed the hill. He needed time to think. Eventually his heart calmed, returning to a slow steady beat and his thoughts began to clear. He reasoned that the Hibernian warrior had probably not been intending to threaten him at all but had only wanted to escort him outside. Seginus was ashamed to admit to himself that his own fear had led him to believe otherwise. For the moment at least he had not been recognised. If he had understood that the warrior was warning him of the presence of Faery beings in the woods at Beltinne, the priest might not have been so calm.

Seginus was sure that someone in the High-King's retinue would eventually put a name to his face. Inside his shirt his fingers searched for the little pouch that held the seal ring he had stolen from Murrough all those years ago.

He told himself it was stupidity to carry such a compromising item around with him. If he were searched such an item could balance the scales of fate against him. He fetched the ring out of the pouch and held it tightly in his hand. His fingers traced the intricate design of a stylised tree that was the motif of that seal. Then he realised for the first time that the design represented the Quicken Tree that Seginus had been instrumental in destroying.

His natural instinct was to dispose of this ring immediately. A voice from within reminded him that the royal seal had saved his life once before. Perhaps it would serve him again. His trembling hand slipped the signet ring back into the pouch and fastened the cord tightly.

With that decision made Seginus decided to put himself to some hard labour so that he would not have the opportunity to dwell on his predicament too much. He found the edge of the path and collected some tinder. Then returned to the long-house to see to the building of the hearth-fire.

When Seginus got back to the hall the three Gaels were now standing outside the door to the long-house leaning against the wall. The Roman priest went to open the door intending to enter the hall but the warrior who had helped him earlier now put a hand out to prevent him entering the building.

Seginus could not at first understand why they would not let him within the hall. One of the Gaels gestured at the tinder that the Roman carried. At the same time the Hibernian repeated the Gaelic word which meant 'no' several times. Seginus laid the dry kindling on the doorstep and the warriors swung the door open for him. He could only surmise that they already had a good supply of fuel laid in and so were offended that he had collected more. He had no way of knowing that it was forbidden to light a fire on this night.

The Roman put all his fear aside and quickly pushed past the guards to enter the long-house. It was empty but for Patricius who was still kneeling by the cold hearth. The rest of the missionary party had dispersed. Seginus did not want to disturb the bishop at his devotions so he found the wall and made his way around the hall by touch, searching for a supply of split timber for the fire.

He was almost back at the door when Patricius called out, 'If you are looking to start the fire there is no wood stored in this place. I have sent Tullia and Secondinus to bring some in. Perhaps you would like to help them.' There was a touch of annoyance in the older man's voice so Seginus did not answer but slipped out again as silently as he could. Only one warrior was by the door now.

Before long he had found the shack where the firewood must usually be stored but there were only a few splinters remaining within it. He thought it very strange that there would not be a good supply of fuel for such a large hall. Seeing no other way out of the situation he disguised his nervousness and prepared himself to approach the Hibernian who leaned against the outside wall.

'Where is the kindling and cooking fuel stored?' the Roman asked in his best Gaelic. 'We are weary and in need of warmth and food.'

The warrior did not even look up to answer but gestured for Seginus to wait while he went to consult his companions. A few moments later the priest could hear all three warriors speaking over the top of each other in a dialect that Seginus was unfamiliar with. Though the Roman missed much of what was said he gathered that they were all agreeing that no fires were to be lit on the hill for any reason.

A few minutes later the three warriors returned to where Seginus was waiting and the one who held a small shield on his arm explained the situation as best he could.

Seginus was still not sure if he had understood what was said though so he went into the hall to fetch Patricius. They returned a few moments later. Tatheus had appeared in the meantime and stood close by the bishop's side, his hand on the hilt of his sword but still concealed by his cloak. The question of firewood was carefully posed to the warriors once again, this time by Patricius himself. In a short swift reply one of the Hibernians gestured that the lighting of any fires was totally out of the question.

'We do not believe as you do that this night should be kept dark. We believe that the light came to the world at this time. Besides, how will we cook our meat?' Patricius reasoned. 'And would Leoghaire have us freeze to death during the night?' At that the Hibernian said something under his breath to his comrades then immediately left to mount his horse. In a few seconds he had charged past them in the direction of the citadel leaving the clerics wondering what was going on.

'Clearly there has been some sort of misunderstanding,' Patricius whispered to Tatheus. 'It might be a good idea to gather all the soldiers back here as soon as possible.'

Tatheus was about to carry out the order when shouts were heard on the road. The Hibernian warrior could be dimly seen trying to control his horse as he raised his voice at someone who would not let him pass. The next thing they all heard was Tullia's fearful scream and a cry from one of the legionnaires.

Before Patricius and Seginus could react Tatheus bolted off into the night. He had covered half the distance between Tullia and himself by the time the clerics realised what was going on. Then the noise of a violent struggle and an ominous clash of swords met their ears and Patricius and Seginus also moved to run towards the fracas. Their way was almost immediately blocked though by the other two Hibernian guards who threatened the clerics with their manacing broad blades.

In the distance another legionnaire shouted. Seginus could hear the footfall of men running in the night to answer the summons. Suddenly there were more frantic calls followed by an anguished cry of pain but the priest dared not try to break away from the two warriors who held himself and Patricius at bay. Neither of them knew if it had been a Roman or a Gael that had fallen.

All the noise ceased shortly after and seeing that he could do little else for the moment the bishop sank slowly to his knees in prayer. Meanwhile the two Hibernians spoke quickly to each other. One of them sheathed his sword and disappeared into the night. The other man, the one who had opened the door for Seginus, came up behind Patricius and grabbed the legate by the hair. Then he carefully lowered the edge of his blade to the bishop's throat, grunting something at the other Roman. The Gael made it very clear that he intended to slit his hostage's throat if anyone came too close.

Just then Tatheus returned with five of his soldiers closely packed around Tullia in a classic escort formation. The remainder of the soldiers could be heard in the distance securing the road and the path to the hall. All the legionnaires had their weapons drawn now and their cloaks thrown back to reveal Roman armour. There was no longer any pretence about them being mere monks. It was the centurion who first saw Patricius kneeling with a Gaelic sword at his throat. He swore loudly at himself for what had happened during his brief absence.

The Hibernian was almost surrounded by legionnaires when he made a snap decision not to wait around any longer to be captured. With a powerful arm he shoved Patricius face first onto the ground and leapt nimbly over the bishop. While all eyes went to Patricius the warrior darted off into the darkness. Tatheus ran straight up to to his master to make sure the cleric was unharmed and in those few seconds the Hibernian melted into the night.

As it turned out the guard had not run more than fifty paces before he blundered his way into three Roman soldiers. The force of the collision knocked the warrior senseless and in that state he was easily overpowered. Patricius was comforting Tullia when they dragged him back to the cleared ground in front of the long-house to throw him down before Patricius.

'Do not treat him so roughly. He was merely defending their custom,' Patricius chided. 'They believe that no fires should be lit in the whole land on this night. It is their heathen notion that only the High-King has the power to give the gift of fire and the magic ability to turn the cold winter months into the season of harvest and sunshine.'

'The man threatened to kill you!' Tatheus roared in outrage.

'It is my wish that none of these people be harmed,' Patricius ordered, 'not even if my life is in the direst peril! Do you understand?'

'Yes, Father.'

'Do not forget your place, Tatheus. Remember that I am in command of this expedition. This is not an invasion, it is a mission of mercy to those who have no knowledge of better ways. I know it goes against all your military training but you are going to have to try to be compassionate toward these people!'

The centurion dropped his eyes to the ground like the child of a nobleman who has been scolded for mistreating a servant.

'Bind his arms and legs for the time being,' the bishop conceded, 'but make sure he is not too uncomfortable!'

After a slight struggle the warrior was tied up, by which time the whole company had gathered around to watch. Patricius decided to take the opportunity to address them all and he motioned for them to sit. When they were all settled he spoke to them as though he were preaching to a congregation back in the Gaulish land.

'We have been through many hardships together,' he began, 'but this night the real test of our strength and determination begins. At sunrise begins the anniversary of the entry of our Lord into Jerusalem. Not long afterwards he fell into the hands of His enemies. In His infinite wisdom He has arranged that this night and the following day are also considered to be holy by the heathen of this land. On any other night of the year we would not be able to challenge their devilish practices so directly and effectively. Tonight we will reveal to these ignorant folk the light of the Lord and the radiance of His grace. Tonight we will do what no others in Eirinn would dare. We will light a great fire with all the timber and kindling that we can find. It will be a fire that can be seen throughout the countryside as far as Teamhair itself.'

Everyone present was perfectly still and silent though they knew that this action would place them all in great danger. Tullia and Secondinus crossed themselves and everyone followed their example, not the least Seginus.

'The flames that we fan will burn in the hearts of the Hibernians forever more,' Patricius continued. No-one doubted his words. 'We will show the heathens that their beliefs are nothing compared to the veneration of the Risen Lord. Once the idolaters have witnessed the glory of Christ they will surely leave their silly superstitious customs and unite with us in worship of the one true God.'

Seginus sat quietly in the midst of the others but he obviously did not share their enthusiasm. He knew too well that the Hibernians tolerated strangers only until the moment those strangers broke their obscure laws or insulted their traditions. Seginus himself had been the victim of one such act of intolerance and the memory of the humiliation it had caused him still made his blood boil.

'Tonight we will light a vigil fire to the glory of Our Lord's sacrifice. Throughout the night we will pray and at dawn we will hold a Mass in His memory.'

In a flash Tullia was off again to collect more timber and kindling. Tatheus quickly followed after her, calling for her to slow down. Secondinus went off to fetch some water for the Hibernian warrior. By the time he returned Patricius was already speaking to the young man in slow and deliberate phrases to be certain that his words would be understood. 'You have been led to us so that you may have the honour of being the first of your people to come willingly to the Cross.'

The warrior stared back at Patricius not quite sure what to make of his captor. He scrutinised the gathered Christians carefully and then unexpectedly he began to laugh. At first Patricius was a little shocked but then he began to laugh along. Almost immediately the Hibernian became very serious again, dropping all signs of mirth from his face.

'There is nothing to fear,' Patricius assured him, 'for the power of God is greater than that of any king or Druid. We are going to prove that by kindling a flame for our God though the heathen would threaten us with every demon and spirit of the air that they can conjure.'

The warrior's expression turned instantly to anger at this last comment. He struggled briefly to break free from his bindings but he did not have the strength to break them. In frustration he turned to Patricius and snarled, 'You will not see the sun rise again if you break the sacred laws of the land.'

The warrior spoke quickly and Patricius did not quite catch all of what he said but he understood the general meaning of the phrase. 'I will watch the sunrise tomorrow without fear,' the bishop answered, 'and by the grace of God I will see many more before my days are up. Through faith in the Lord who is my saviour I have no fear of the Druid kind and neither should you. Tomorrow I will ask you once again if you will convert to the Cross. Perhaps you will see things differently by the light of day.'

Seginus rolled his eyes and put a hand to his forehead to rub his brow. He had a distinct feeling that the whole situation had taken a nasty turn and that the next morning could hold the stark possibility of a bloody reprisal from the High-King's men.

Tatheus had made the same appraisal of the situation as Seginus. He was keeping one eye on the missionaries while he set guards around the perimeter of the hill in anticipation of an attack.

Soon afterwards Tullia returned with the kindling and an armful of fallen timber. She immediately sent Secondinus off to get more, then she set to work quickly constructing a sturdy frame of timber from the strongest logs that she had collected so far. Helped by a reluctant Seginus and two legionnaires she set about filling in the structure with smaller pieces of wood and kindling until it began to resemble one of the signal beacons that were used by the legions to pass communications over long distances.

Patricius went to fill a bucket with water from the nearby well. Just as he was blessing the contents a sound reached his ears that set the whole company on edge. Not far off in the direction of the road to Teamhair they could hear the unmistakable roar of war trumpets.

Secondinus appeared at that moment with more bundles of wood and he was visibly shaken. 'How could they have got word to the High-King so quickly?' he panted. 'The only warrior who escaped was on foot. He could not have possibly covered the whole distance on so short a time. It's too far away.'

'There will be a great battle this night,' Patricius declared sombrely. 'The Devil has seen that we will likely be victorious in our quest. Even now he is gathering the hosts of his demons to attack us.'

Tullia and Secondinus both fell wide-eyed to their knees, crossing themselves and muttering prayers for the protection of the mission. Even the two legionnaires who helped to stack the fire quickly made the sign of the Holy Cross over their chests.

Seginus was unmoved. He looked at Tullia and Secondinus with distaste. Palladius would never have tolerated this sort of undisciplined behaviour. And he certainly would have appraised the whole situation very differently. Seginus noticed that the Hibernian captive was laughing quietly at the Christians as they grovelled to their God and the Roman wondered what could be amusing him so much.

It did not take long for Seginus to realise that there was something very wrong with the assumption that the Hibernians were about to attack. This was not the way that Gaelic chieftains made war. He knew from experience that they usually gathered their troops silently, only declaring their intention to attack when they were fully ready to engage in battle.

Something else nagged at him about the legate's declaration of an impending fight. Seginus could only ever recall the savages playing war-pipes in battle. He had no memory at all of trumpets being used to rally the troops. He suspected that the trumpeting had more to do with the festival the Hibernians were celebrating rather than any preparations for an attack.

Patricius was about to light a fire in defiance of the High-King's law. To Seginus nothing was more certain than that as soon as the inhabitants of Teamhair saw the flames in the distance on the hill of Slané they would come to investigate and then punish all those who had broken their laws.

'Bring me a tinderbox!' Patricius called and though he was sure that he would regret it Seginus dutifully rummaged through his own pack until he found the little iron box that held flint and tinder. He brought the fire-lighting gear to his master and Patricius took it from him eagerly. The legate opened the tightly fitting lid to bring out a small piece of flint. He examined it as closely as he could in the moonlight to decide which edge would be the best for striking and then he searched in the box for a piece of pitch.

When he had located all the ingredients for making a fire he selected a few handfuls of dry twigs and then knelt down by the great pile of timber. He arranged the pitch and the twigs and some shrivelled leaves a little apart from the main mound of firewood. Satisfied that all was in readiness, he struck the flint against the roughened iron box to create a spark. The first sliver of flint flew across the bishop's lap in an arc of a falling star. It landed useless in the dirt and its light quickly died. But the next time he struck Patricius altered the angle of the blow so that the flint was directed downward at the fuel.

This manoeuvre worked immediately. A bright orange spark landed in the midst of the tinder and in a few moments the bishop had started the dry leaves glowing into a radiant little flare that he gently coaxed into flame with long slow breaths over the fuel. The very second that the leaves began to blaze he nudged the pitch closer to his new fire. Then he quickly added twigs and bracken gradually building the intensity of light and heat.

When he was sure that the small fire was going strong he took a thick twig and dipped the very end in a drop of pitch. Then he held it in the flames until it caught ablaze. With the flaming twig in one hand he stood to face Seginus, Tullia and Secondinus.

'Now we will see the plan of almighty God unfold before us. When this timber is lit every demon for a hundred miles around will be attracted to it like as moths. Unlike moths, though, they will come to extinguish the flame. We will more than likely have to fight to keep the fire going through the night until morning.'

Patricius used the wand of fire to make the sign of the Cross in the air before him then he set it amidst the pile of kindling at the foot of the stack of timber. It caught almost immediately. In moments the bishop had to step back from the fire that he had started to avoid the scorching heat.

Across the plain within the citadel of Teamhair the Druids had just completed the ritual sealing of Sianan and Mawn within the mound of testing when a tiny point of orange light appeared in the distance. At first many of the company of Druids and judges thought that it could only be the work of the Danaans for it seemed to be floating high in the air. But Cathach knew that there was another force behind it.

The chief Druid had already left Gobann and set off in the direction of his own hall when the light appeared. Once he noticed it he changed tack to head in search of Leoghaire with the intention of reporting this fire. It would be some hours now before the next part of the ceremony was played out and Cathach felt secure that Gobann could oversee the watch on the mound without his help.

It was a long walk from the testing field to Leoghaire's hall. By the time he arrived, Cathach's legs were aching from the exertion. He found his way to the High-King's chambers and summoned the steward to fetch Leoghaire to him urgently. Whilst he waited Cathach sat down by the cold empty hearth to rub his calf muscles, trying to push some of the dull annoying pain out of them.

A long while passed but still the slight tightness in the old Druid's chest and his breathlessness did not subside. His heart was still beating wildly as though he had sprinted the entire distance between the testing field and the hall. Cathach knew he needed rest this night before taking part in the dawn ritual. He did not want to be too exhausted to carry out his duties.

A mead cup had been set down for him so he drank a draught of the yellow liquid. As the brew warmed his throat he brought an old poem to mind that was a lament for the passing of youth. He spoke the verse out loud, smiling to himself that it applied so well to him. 'Once my hair was yellow-gold. Now my head grows a short grey crop. I would rather have hair the colour of a raven's wing than short grey stubble on top. I no longer court women. They do not see any colour worth acquiring. One day soon I will leave my house feet first and the last thing my neighbours will see is a balding patch of skin surrounded by a short grey crop.'

He had last heard that poem spoken by Lorgan just before he died. 'I do not have the leisure to pass away yet,' he reassured himself. 'There is too much to do.'

At that moment Leoghaire and two guards entered the hall. Cathach rose to meet them holding his palm to his forehead as a sign of respect.

'Greetings, my friend,' the High-King began, 'I am relieved that you have come. Caitlin is very ill and we are all frightened for her life.'

'Caitlin?' the old man exclaimed. 'Is she not at home in the fortress of Cashel with Murrough at her side?'

'The King of Munster has just returned from his kingdom with Síla, Caitlin and their newborn son. It seems that the Queen of Munster has contracted a wasting sickness. I am told that she is close to death. Murrough brought her here in the hope that the Danaans would lend their superior healing skills to help her recovery.'

This was the last thing Cathach had expected to happen during the time of the Wanderer's testing but as ever he was ready with a solution to the problem. 'I will approach the old ones to beg their aid as soon as possible. This thing has been with Queen Caitlin for many seasons now. Murrough was right to bring her here at this time,' the old Druid stated. 'But I have come to see you on another matter.'

As Cathach was about to continue a sudden pain shot through his left arm, forcing him to sit down again. 'Forgive me, lord, if I take a seat in your presence,' he wheezed.

Leoghaire frowned with concern and put his hand on his advisor's shoulder. 'What's the matter?'

'I am merely overtired, lord. These last days have been a great strain on me. I will rest after we have spoken.'

The High-King pulled up a seat beside the old Druid. 'I am more than happy that you take your ease when we are together. I will send someone to fetch you a draught of well water. I must admit that I too would like a short rest from everything that is going on.'

'I fear that you may have less of an opportunity to pause and recover than I have,' Cathach began.

'A signal fire has been spotted out on the plain in the direction of Slané in open defiance of the ban on the kindling of all hearths.'

Leoghaire frowned even deeper, covering his forehead with one hand as if he had been struck by a sudden headache. After a moment he placed the palms of his hands over his eyes, pushing the balls of his thumbs into the sockets. Finally he spoke, reaching slowly for a mead cup at the same time. 'I should have known that this would happen,' he sighed, disappointed at his own inability to foretell the future.

'You know who is responsible for this?' Cathach queried.

'A company of men came to the gates after sunset. Naturally under the circumstances they were refused entry into the citadel,' Leoghaire explained. 'Their leader claimed to be a Papal legate. I thought it best not to trouble you or Gobann since you were both busy with the rites of initiation. Murrough had just arrived with Caitlin. I was already late for the ritual. So out of hospitality I gave this man and his retinue the long-house on the hill of Slané for the night. It was my intention to send riders out there in the morning to formally greet the Romans. Their leader spoke our language well and so I assumed that he understood the Beltinne custom.'

'What is this man's name?' Cathach gasped.

'Patricius was his first name,' Leoghaire replied, 'and his other name was—'

'Sucatus,' Cathach cut in.

'Why yes,' Leoghaire mumbled, unsure how Cathach had known this detail, 'it was Sucatus.'

'He has come to our land much sooner than I expected.' The old man was staring off into the distance as though some great calamity had befallen him. 'By lighting the fire on Slané he is taunting us to take action. The Christian would like nothing more than for us to confront him. He is looking to openly challenge our traditions and laws.'

'He has succeeded on that point,' Leoghaire observed. 'If we react too strongly to this breach of custom he will be difficult to work with in future.'

'I am not so sure,' Cathach remarked. 'He knows also that a small spark often kindles a great fire. He will expect us to take action that challenges his flouting of the law.'

'We have been planning for many seasons for this moment. If we punish him too severely we could earn his enmity and that will be end of all our hard work.'

'Yet if we ignore this outrage he will certainly distrust us.'

'What am I to do?' asked Leoghaire.

'You should send out a force of warriors to Slané with orders to uphold your law in this kingdom,' Cathach said. 'We must not give them any special treatment at first or their suspicions will be aroused. As far as we are concerned they are renegade foreigners who have deliberately challenged the authority of the High-King of the land. Do not forget that the last man who came here as Papal legate nearly took your kingdom from you. Patricius knows that and so does every living soul on the island of Eirinn. You must put up a good show.'

'I will assemble my guardsmen.'

'I would advise you to put Enda Censelach in charge of the operation,' Cathach added. 'He will certainly convince the legate that we are all angered by this breach of custom.'

'That is because Enda will be genuinely enraged at the foreigners' actions,' Leoghaire gasped, realising that the situation could easily get out of hand.

'How can we be certain that Enda will not give rein to his prejudices and slaughter every mother's son?'

'You are right,' Cathach conceded. Then he had an idea. 'Send Murrough along as well. He will keep Censelach from overreacting if anyone can.'

'Neither of them will be able to enter the fortress again until after sunset tomorrow evening,' Leoghaire reminded the Druid.

'Excellent. Then Enda will be out of our way during the kindling of the Need Fire.'

'And Murrough will be unable to be with his queen.'

'I can think of no other solution to this problem. Murrough is a king. It is about time he started taking some of the responsibilities that go with that office. The kingdom needs him now more than Caitlin. Have no fear, I will see that she is cared for.'

'Very well,' Leoghaire agreed reluctantly.

'I should meet with Patricius as soon as he comes to the citadel,' Cathach added. 'I must go now and make ready to do battle with him.' With that the old Druid rose from his seat with renewed energy and strode off out of the hall without another word.

'Battle,' Leoghaire repeated under his breath. The High-King drained a wooden cup of mead in one draught before going off to organise the ride to Slané.

TWENTY-TWO

urrough was busy arranging his
queen's sleeping arrangements
when the messenger arrived summoning him to the High-King's
chambers. There had been no
room for Caitlin, Síla and the baby in the Grianan,
the women's house. For that reason he decided to
lodge them in the Star of the Poets. Both Síla and
Caitlin were initiated Druids though the queen had
abandoned the holy path when the duties of her
kingdom had become too great.

Murrough was exhausted by the long ride from
Cashel otherwise he probably would not have
barked at Leoghaire's messenger to leave him
alone with his worries.

'But, lord, the High-King has ordered me to fetch
you on a most urgent matter,' the messenger
pleaded.

'Can you not see that I am fully occupied here?'
Murrough bellowed. 'Tell the High-King that I will
be along when I am done.'

'He told me to say that the safety of the kingdom
was at stake.'

'The safety of my queen is at stake, boy! When
I am assured of her wellbeing I will see to the
kingdom.'

'What shall I tell Leoghaire?' the lad stuttered.

'Tell him that we will all be happy when he is
married so that he has a wife to keep him busy!'

The messenger did not give the King of Munster any further excuse to lose his temper with him. He scurried out of the path of the southern retinue, returning directly to Leoghaire with the reply.

The messenger was not long gone when Murrough realised that he had been somewhat unreasonable. He decided that it would be best if he got Caitlin settled in at the Star of the Poets as soon as possible, then he would make his way to Leoghaire's hall to see what all the fuss was about.

As it happened the messenger arrived at the High-King's chamber just as Enda Censelach was taking his seat so the King of Laigin overheard the lad's report. Naturally Leoghaire was outraged that the Munster king had seen fit to be disrespectful. That the message arrived when Censelach was present made the position all the more embarrassing. 'I will have to have words with that young Murrough,' he mumbled. 'Sometimes he forgets where he stands in the hierarchy.'

'I will not wait for the King of Munster. This is an urgent matter,' Enda Censelach butted in.

'Send one of your warriors, will you, Censelach? I think it would be best that both you and Murrough went out to greet this Patricius.'

'As you wish, my lord.'

It was a good while before the warrior returned with Murrough lagging behind him. The Munster king threw off his cloak as he entered the chamber nodding to Enda and Leoghaire. It had taken him much longer than he had expected to settle Caitlin down for the night. Weary as he was he sat straight down to reach for a mead cup.

'Is this the way that Munster men honour their High-King?' Censelach bellowed. 'You come and go when you please disregarding your overlord's urgent summons, then you do not even offer an explanation for your disagreeable manners.'

'Munster men are unaccustomed to being fetched by Laigin warriors to do the High-King's bidding,' Murrough snarled. 'Your ambition to the throne of Midhe is beginning to get the better of you, Enda.'

'I will not answer your taunt, Munster king. We have a saying in Laigin that trampling on dung only spreads it around.'

'You may die of wind, Censelach, but you will never die of wisdom.'

'Enough!' shouted Leoghaire 'I have had enough of your constant jibing.' Both men fell quiet. 'Someone has lit a fire on the hill of Slané. I want you two to lead a warrior band to find out who it is that has broken the law. You will bring them to me unharmed. Do you understand?' The High-King looked from one man to the other. 'You may make a show of force but there is to be no fighting except in self-defence. Do you understand?'

Murrough nodded then looked to the floor, remorseful. Enda Censelach stared down his nose at the King of Munster. 'Which one of us will have the final word on what action is to be taken?' he asked coldly.

'You will make all your decisions based on a consensus of opinion. You will have to consult with each other.'

'You can't be serious,' Enda protested. 'How can I reach consensus with a man who flouts the wishes of his lord?'

'After what I have seen tonight,' Leoghaire answered, 'I am not sure that you can, but I am ordering you to try.'

'I am sorry for my behaviour, lord,' Murrough began. 'I will do all that I can to co-operate with Censelach.'

'This is a matter of the greatest importance. I am led to believe that the man who lit the fire at Slané may be a Christian sent from Rome to oversee the conversion of our people.'

'A Christian priest!' Censelach burst out. 'I will teach him a lesson in humility before I bring him to you, lord.'

'That is exactly why I have asked Murrough to accompany you. To make sure that you don't teach him any unnecessary lessons.' Enda laughed heartily and Leoghaire was not sure whether the man had taken what he had said seriously. He decided not to press his point for the time being knowing that they would keep each other in check. 'Of course,' the High-King went on, 'you will not be able to return here with the Christian until after sunset tomorrow, so you have my permission to rest on the summit of Slané until you are ready to leave.'

'My lord,' Murrough cut in, 'Caitlin is very ill and needs me at her side. Could you not find someone else to take my place?'

'I was willing to ignore your impudent response to my messenger,' Leoghaire retorted, losing his patience, 'but I am not ready to let you decide when and whether you will follow my instructions. I am your elected chieftain! Sometimes the duties of a leader are painful and the decisions are difficult. As harsh as this may sound to you, I cannot put the comfort of one before the security of many. You will do as you are ordered.'

Murrough had never seen Leoghaire in this mood before. 'I will do as you ask,' he replied, quietly bowing his head again.

'As long as you are in my hall you will respect my orders!' Leoghaire yelled to emphasise his displeasure. 'Now go to the task I have given you! And no more needless bickering.'

Tatheus had a nose for trouble and he could smell a lot of it about this night; quite likely more than he could handle. As soon as Patricius had finished lighting his fire the centurion approached the bishop to make a report on the defences.

'If they come along the road we may be able to hold them for a short while. If they come over the fields we will certainly be overrun in a matter of minutes. Of course that is assuming the odds against us are no greater than three to one. If they come in stronger numbers we will be swept away like oats before a scythe.'

'You need not fear, centurion,' Patricius began, 'they will not dare attack us. We have God on our side.'

'Father,' Tatheus reasoned, 'I was at the fields of Trier. God was also on our side at that bloody battle but he could not stop three thousand men falling to the swords of the barbarians. You must understand that there is a very great risk the Hibernians will break through our defences and we will all be slain as a result.'

Patricius looked at the officer with understanding for the centurion's fear. After all this man had seen things in action that Patricius could only imagine. Tatheus, he knew, saw everything from a fighting perspective. 'You are right of course. I will leave the military decisions up to you, but I would ask you one thing. Set your soldiers in position so that they are not easily spotted by anyone coming down the road from Teamhair. We do not want to provoke the wrath of the Hibernians unnecessarily. If anyone does arrive from the High-King wait until they have made their intentions clear before you act.'

'I will set a guard on the road,' the centurion answered gruffly. 'But if events turn against my troops or we are outnumbered I will have the men fall back to this hall. We should be able to hold out on the high ground until long after first light.'

Seginus listened in on the entire conversation with deep concern and growing anguish. His own instincts confirmed what Tatheus was saying and he was sure they were too exposed here on the hill. Common sense told him that their survival depended on concealing themselves from the enemy until safe passage to Britain could be arranged for the whole group. He was about to say so when Patricius spoke.

'You were a soldier once, were you not, Father Seginus?'

'Yes, lord, before I took the monk's cowl.'

'Then it might not be a bad idea if you went along with Tatheus to appraise the situation for me from a military standpoint but report to me as a priest.' It was as though the bishop had heard his thoughts.

'I would be happy to go with the centurion.'

'Don't be long. I would like you to be present for prayers before we all take rest for the night. Where will your men sleep, Tatheus?'

For a moment the centurion was stunned by the question. 'They will not sleep this night, Father. They are on duty and awaiting imminent attack.'

'Oh, very well then. But you really should let them rest. We have a long day ahead of us tomorrow. Goodnight. Wake me if things get out of hand.' With that Patricius wandered off toward the hall. Mog and Darach followed, dragging the

Hibernian warrior. The bishop could be heard reciting a psalm in the Hibernian language.

Seginus looked sideways at Tatheus, unsure whether Patricius was in command of his wits. The centurion was obviously asking himself a similar question. Making eye contact they silently left the fire, holding their tongues until they were out of the bishop's earshot. The centurion was the first to voice his frustration.

'No disrespect intended, Father Seginus, but aren't you a little worried about what may come to pass if we are attacked by an overwhelming force?'

Seginus grunted, not giving any commitment. Tatheus took the noise to be a sign of the priest's anxiety. 'There are only twenty-four legionnaires in my company, Father.'

'Twenty-five,' Seginus corrected him quickly, 'including yourself. Then there are my two servants Mog and Darach who I am sure could handle themselves in a scrap. Secondinus is probably of no use. However, I trained with the twentieth legion so I can handle a blade.'

'Are you suggesting that we should try to put up a fight?'

Seginus breathed out loudly in exasperation. 'I do not see that we have any choice. If the Hibernians are coming to fight with us, then it would only prolong the inevitable to run away from them, unless we could be sure that a boat was waiting on the coast to pick us up. I think we can safely assume that master Lupus and his merchantman are far from Hibernia's shores at this very moment.'

Tatheus nodded, reluctantly admitting that the priest was probably right.

Seginus thought back to the time long ago when he had attempted to outrun a group of determined Hibernian warriors. 'This is their land. They know every hill and valley. They will find us no matter where we hide. If they are coming to attack it would be better if we can manage to surprise them before they have fully appraised the situation. At least we will have given them a taste of our steel. We may even earn their respect.'

'What are you proposing?' Tatheus asked.

'Patricius asked that you keep your soldiers well concealed, didn't he?'

Tatheus grunted in agreement.

'Then gather your men at the foot of the hill where the road ends. I will show you what I mean to do when you have them ready.'

TWENTY-THREE

obann waited at the hill of testing all through the seemingly endless night. Long after the dancing had finished, long after all the Druids save the sentinels had gone to bed, long after the tomb of the mound of testing was completely silent. He did not know how his two students were faring but he sent all his thoughts to them.

The poet had not known what to expect when they had locked him in the mound at his testing. Even when he had taken the higher circle of initiation in order to be ranked as an advisor to Murrough he had not been sure exactly what would happen to him.

'It is different for everyone,' he said aloud, although there was no-one but the rocks at the foot of the mound to hear him.

The poet turned his attention to the stars. Brightest of all the lights in the sky shone his old companion the Evening Star. He easily pinpointed her position in the night sky, setting his mind on her silvery sparkle. A moment later the poet was overcome by an intense feeling that he could not immediately explain. He closed his eyes to concentrate on the sensation and Síla's face appeared clearly in his mind.

As far as he knew, she was attending to Caitlin at the fortress of Cashel so he was concerned that she seemed to be so close to him. 'Some trouble has befallen the queen,' Gobann guessed correctly, but as he had not had a chance to speak with Cathach he could not know that Caitlin and Síla were sleeping in the Star of the Poets at Teamhair at that very moment.

The feeling of foreboding that came to him was so strong that Gobann almost succumbed to a temptation to leave his post. In the end he forced himself to think about something else to keep himself from worrying. He picked up the harp and picked out a gentle melody on it. As he played clouds blew in from the east on a sea squall. Before the tune was ended the stars were all gone from his sight.

Sianan woke when she heard the muffled call of the trumpets sounding. There was only dim light within the chamber so she could not see very much about her. Mawn was breathing with difficulty nearby and soon he whimpered in his sleep. Without hesitation she turned her body around, crawling over the top of him to snuggle into the small of his back. She found that she was not as drowsy as she had expected to be so she stroked the surface of his cropped scalp until her eyelids felt heavy. The trumpets had faded away; all the music and voices had ceased when she finally drifted off into a deep slumber.

The next thing Sianan knew Mawn was calling to her from what seemed a long way away. She could hear a harp playing out a beautiful melody nearby and she attempted to open her eyes but had great difficulty doing so. For a few more seconds Sianan struggled with her disobedient eyes before she realised with a shock that she could see perfectly. Amazed at the sensation she rolled onto her back.

The simple act of moving her body was suddenly unlike anything she had ever experienced. She scanned the ceiling of the chamber in awe. Directly above her head she noticed a silver grey mist swirling at the whim of imperceptible air currents. Her surprise deepened further when she eventually realised that the fog enclosed the features of a familiar face. It was Mawn. His golden hair had miraculously returned to flow about him as if he were lying on his back in a rockpool full of sea water.

This was the moment she and Mawn had both been preparing for throughout the last two cycles of the seasons. Sianan was at the brink of her initiation. Her first feeling was of disappointment that she had not remained conscious throughout the whole experience. Somehow she had allowed herself to fall asleep and so miss the moment of transition to the spirit form. But her inner voice told her there would be many more opportunities.

Sianan heard Mawn calling to her again. 'Rise up here with me. It is time we were on our way.'

'I am coming. Wait for me,' Sianan replied, observing as she did so that she was not really speaking to her companion at all. All she had to do was form a thought in her head and he was able to hear her. When he replied to her his lips remained motionless though his wispy smoke-like body gestured in the same way that he would if he were having a conversation with her in the Hall of the Druids.

'Do you hear the harp?' he called.

'Yes,' Sianan answered, becoming aware that the melody had been playing for some time.

'That is Gobann at the wires. I would know his harping anywhere.'

'Shall we go and find him?'

Mawn nodded assent. A few moments later the two of them had found their way out of the top of the mound. This puzzled Sianan since there did not seem to be any opening in the structure through which they could have passed. Before she had an opportunity to find a solution to this latest mystery the two of them were floating above their teacher taking in the gorgeous notes that fell from his fingers. They swallowed the music, allowing it to fill their ethereal bodies as if it were some rich food for their souls. Sianan bathed in the humming melody, soaking herself in energy and joy, nourishing her spiritual hungers.

Mawn reached out to to his companion's hand, but the gesture, simple in the flesh, was infinitely more challenging now they had taken the spirit form. After several unsuccessful attempts to make physical contact Mawn drifted toward the ground with Sianan following after. The two concentrated all their wills as they attempted to touch hands again. Each palm melted at the point where they should have touched, to pass through the other without making the slightest contact. Neither of them felt the slightest sensation at all. Astonished, Sianan encouraged Mawn to try again, determined to succeed this time, but their hands offered no more resistance to each other than a wall of feathers might to a war horse.

As though he sensed their presence or had witnessed the difficulty that they were having, Gobann ceased his playing. He searched all around him, then turned his attention to the sky, noticing that the clouds had hidden his star from view. A cold wind blew in over the mound, whipping up the edges of his Raven-feather cloak. The poet stood up to smell the rich scent of coming rain as it flew in on the breeze, then he quickly packed his harp away in her waterproof case.

Mawn and Sianan watched their teacher closely. Wrapped in his clothing of flesh the poet seemed heavily weighted down and lethargic. He moved incredibly slowly, fighting against the forces of nature with every twitch of muscle. They observed him with interest as he lifted the harp bag, straining to drag it onto his shoulder. Then, before he walked off to seek shelter from the approaching storm, he turned his face to look in their direction. He paused for a few seconds then he opened his mouth to speak.

'Feet that are not used to walking tread slowly on a new road,' he whispered.

Sianan realised that this was a last piece of advice from their teacher before they set off on their journey. Both of them understood him to mean that they would solve the problem of being able to touch each other when they were more used to this new existence. As Gobann departed they watched the rain begin to fall, bringing with it a fresh odour that washed away all that decayed in the world. The cloudburst, however, made no impact on their spirit forms. Before long they were both dancing around between the droplets, revelling in this new experience.

When the shower ceased they hovered above the mound of testing for a while unsure what was expected of them next.

'Where do we go?' Mawn asked.

'I thought perhaps that you would know what we were supposed to do,' Sianan answered.

'I guess that we should be looking for the door to the Otherworld.'

'What does it look like?'

Mawn stopped to think. 'Gobann took me to it many times but now that I try to recall it I find that it wasn't really a door at all. I don't have any idea what signs to look for.'

The same breeze that blew the rain clouds over Teamhair now brought distant sounds to their ears. A wailing skirl came in on the wind from the direction of the central enclosure of the citadel. Mawn and Sianan recognised the music of the war-pipes instantly. Without any sign to each other, but in mutual agreement they drifted up over the plain of Teamhair travelling side by side until they were suspended directly above the High-King's hall.

Down below them three pipers faced each other playing a stirring battle tune to the gathered warriors; Mawn guessed there were upwards of fifty men and women, their bodies painted with the broad stripes and spirals of war. More warriors were coming in all the time with their swords strapped to their belts and shields slung across their backs. Most of them had little other gear apart from their cloaks, which in itself indicated they were preparing for some action that was not too far away.

Sianan spotted Murrough in the middle of the troops. He had cut his beard off completely so that now only his thick moustache remained and he sported a bright blue and yellow knotted design on his right arm, his sword arm. The King of Munster was organising the warriors into groups of three ready for an impending conflict; each soldier to watch the backs of the other two in his group when the fighting really began. Twenty spearmen appeared as he was still organising the archers. They came running up the road to the hall to halt before the king. When Murrough stepped out in front of them they laid all their spears on the ground so that they could more easily sling their shields for a march. Every one of them had their faces painted with dark reds and bright whites for battle.

'What is going on?' Mawn whispered.

'A great emergency,' Sianan replied. 'It must be that the Saxons are upon us.'

Enda Censelach marched out of the hall at that very moment, calling the pipers to silence. The Laigin king wore the same armour that Dichu had dressed in at the Battle of Rathowen. When he had ascended the throne Leoghaire had given it to him as a spoil of war. The breastplate was obviously too large for Enda for he was much thinner than Dichu had been, but he wore the armour proudly nevertheless. He had his own trusty helm in his hand. Some serious conflict was obviously brewing.

As Mawn and Sianan were drifting above the soldiers a wind rose from the west, lifting them higher into the air. They both struggled against it, wanting to remain at Teamhair to see what was happening. Suddenly the gale gusted with incredible intensity, drawing the two of them apart. Sianan began to cry out, fearing that they would be separated, while Mawn swam against the flow of the wind as though it were merely the ocean tide that he was fighting. The inexorable force of the squall gradually pulled them apart until they could barely make out each other's form in the tempest.

Mawn refused to give up the fight. 'Come closer!' he screamed above the roaring storm. 'I cannot reach you if you do not try to get closer to me.'

'I cannot fight against this gale,' Sianan cried. 'Help me!'

The next thing she saw was a great ghostly hand twice the size of either of them that seemed to be a part of the wind. The mighty palm took hold of Mawn; the fingers tightened around him. When it had him securely fastened in its grasp the colossal hand tore Mawn away from her across the sky at such speed that before Sianan could even call out he was nothing more than a tiny spot on the horizon. For a little while afterwards she could hear his cries for help but then abruptly they ended. When the wind dropped away Sianan was left entirely alone.

Sianan looked down to study the scene around the High-King's hall wondering whether anyone had noticed her plight, but she was stunned to find that there was no longer a gathering of rooftops directly beneath her. Somehow Sianan had been transported beyond the walls of the citadel to another place in the middle of open country. The night was still very dark; nevertheless she found that she could see quite well. Directly below her there was now a hill with a large hall on top of it. Not far from the hall was a raging fire built up from masses of broken timber.

As she observed the scene a man rushed around the lower slopes of this hill through the underbrush, striving to remain concealed. Sianan could not see who he was hiding from so she allowed herself to soar down towards him to find out.

He was a strange-looking fellow. From his manner of dress, Sianan quickly decided that he must be a foreigner, though she was certain that he was not a Saxon. His eyes and skin were dark and he wore his hair cropped at the back with a circle shaved to his scalp. She had seen this hairstyle before though she could not immediately place where. By bending all her will to the task she lowered herself down to ground level, drawing closer to the man.

Within a few paces the foreigner slipped on the wet ground. Sianan noted then that he was very fastidious about his clothes. As he was brushing the mud off of his tunic she realised that he had sensed the presence of someone nearby. She froze, fearing even to think in case he overheard the echoes of her mind as Mawn now could. All of a sudden the foreigner turned directly to face her.

The stranger called out something in a language that Sianan could not understand. Then he spoke a few familiar but mispronounced words of Gaelic, 'Who is there? Show yourself.' When he got no reply he drew a sword from his belt, swinging it through the air towards Sianan. The blade passed through her without doing any harm. The foreigner slashed in her direction again before charging directly at her to pass on by, harmlessly. He ended up standing behind her. Sianan was sure that the foreigner could not have seen her but his behaviour had startled her a little. It was obvious that he could sense her presence.

The stranger turned around again almost immediately to continue his journey through the underbrush. As he passed Sianan noticed that he was wearing a Druid's sunwheel about his neck. This perplexed her for he was obviously not of the Druid kind. The holy ones rarely carried swords about their persons except in the most desperate expediencies of war.

Sianan recalled the warriors gathering at Teamhair. A conflict must have begun while she and Mawn were being tested. But then she remembered that Moire, her old teacher at Bally Cahor, had warned her that time runs differently in the spirit world. Sianan speculated that either she could be witnessing future events or she was watching something that had taken place in the past. Whatever was going on around her, Sianan was overcome by a desire to solve this mystery. She followed the stranger as he made his way down the slope.

Not far from the bottom of the hill the foreigner crossed a narrow road and jumped feet first into a ditch. Sianan flew above the road to get a good look at her quarry in his hiding place. What she stumbled on when she rose up over the ditch made her dizzy with dread. More than twenty warriors were cowering in the open trench with their weapons drawn. They were not like any men that she had ever seen in Eirinn before. Nor were they Saxons, that was certain. They were all too clean and uniformly dressed.

Sianan was fascinated by their distinctive armour. Rather than links of metal interlaced to produce a woven iron casing or a single breastplate that strapped around the chest and belly, each warrior wore several narrow breastplates that wrapped around their torsos to overlap like the wooden tiles of a roof. Their helms were all of a distinctive pattern too and exactly alike as if some blacksmith had cleverly beat them all out of the same mould. All the headgear had several back flaps that echoed the overlaid design of their breastplates.

Sianan was still trying to discover the identity of these soldiers when she heard the far-off skirl of the war-pipes. She turned her gaze over her left shoulder to see an army marching down the road toward this very spot. If she had been using the eyes she had been born with perhaps she would not have clearly seen Murrough and Enda Cen-selach riding at the head of this force. With her spirit eyes she could clearly make out the shapes of the two kings even at a great distance.

At the same time as she noticed the Gaelic warrior band, a great disturbance broke out below her. The foreigners cowering in the trench were readying their weapons for a fight, putting arrow to bowstring and setting shield against shoulder. The man who had first attracted her attention was now reciting a poem in his garbled language. Sianan decided that he must be casting a spell of protection over his troops. She had heard that many foreigners believed that magic could be used to win wars for them. These warriors were not taking any chances with the abilities of this sorcerer; they were also resorting to dishonour by laying an ambush.

How treacherous it was to be waiting to catch one's enemies unawares! Where was the skill in striking down the foe from the shelter of a ditch without giving him the chance to see your face? The man who wore the sunwheel ended his recital and then he did an astonishing thing. Raising two fingers of his right hand above his head he made an exaggerated sign in the air. It was the sign of the Cross. Sianan had seen Origen make this blessing many times in the past though he had performed it a little differently.

Christians. There was no doubt about it, for now the man who had made the Cross began to sprinkle water over his companions in the customary blessing of the followers of Christ. Each foreigner fought his way to the front to make sure that some of the holy liquid fell on him. One or two held their swords out under the falling droplets.

Were these the Romans that Cathach had spoken of so often? Was she seeing some event that had yet to come to pass? She had no way of being certain. She recalled that the last time she had seen Murrough in the flesh he had a full beard, now he was clean shaven. And Sianan knew that the King of Munster had left for Cashel before the ceremonies of Beltinne because of difficulties with his wife's child-birthing. So, Sianan reasoned, Murrough could not be at the High-King's hall mustering troops. There was one other thing that she had noticed that confirmed to her that time had begun to run differently. The hall nearby had a fire roaring outside its door.

'If it were still Beltinne that fire would not have been lit. These events are yet to be,' she said to herself. 'I am witnessing the future.'

By this time Murrough's troops had come almost level with the trap. While Sianan had been trying to work out what was happening they had covered a distance of nearly a thousand paces. When she noticed how close they had come she was overwhelmed by an urgent need to warn Enda and Murrough. A moment later she was standing before the small force of Gaels in the middle of the road in an attempt to block their path.

Time and again Sianan tried to get the attention of the two kings but they either could not or would not hear her. Desperately she attempted to obstruct their progress with a large branch that lay at the roadside but found that she could not so much as budge the timber. The Christian soldiers were whispering among themselves, preparing to spring their snare. Sianan could hear every word as loud as if they had all been shouting but this was a trick of the spirit form for Murrough rode on regardless, still unaware of the ambush that awaited his warriors.

Sianan by now was frantic with fear. It did not take the gift of future-sight for her to realise that a great slaughter was about to take place. Those riding out in front were most vulnerable to attack from the flight of enemy arrows. Enda slowed his horse to sniff at the wind as if he sensed that something was amiss. Murrough, however, rode on proudly ahead. Sianan was suddenly certain that the King of Munster would be among the fallen when the fighting was done.

Then Sianan noticed a remarkable thing. Further down the road, about a hundred paces on, a group of shadowy figures appeared, shuffling noiselessly between the trees at the side of the road. Their heads seemed to glow with a ruddy sheen in the darkness as if they were soaking wet. An old woman was amongst them, directing their advance. For a long while Sianan had no idea who these figures might be. It was only as they came closer that she grasped what manner of creatures they were.

Redcaps. These were the Faery folk who traditionally haunted battlefields seeking out the corpses of slain heroes. Once they had hold of a dead warrior they would collect his blood with which they would dye their headgear bright red. It was said that in times of prolonged peace the redcaps were responsible for any fighting that broke out in Eirinn for they could only devour the flesh of a warrior slain in anger. The blood of the innocent was of no use to them. Redcaps took great pride in their freshly coloured hats. They would go to any lengths to ensure that the supply of gruesome pigment was plentiful.

Seeing those ugly creatures nearby with their great protruding teeth and repulsive features stirred a reaction deep within Sianan. A cry welled up in her soul, rising through her very being in an attempt to escape through the top of her skull. Her whole spirit shook as her eerie call took to the wind, becoming part of the night, bouncing off the trees all around and setting the leaves to shivering. Sianan put threat, sadness and urgency into the wail, and they combined into one blood-freezing shriek.

The effort that she expended in her desperate bid to warn Murrough cost her an awful toll. Within moments Sianan was sapped of all her energy. When she could cry no more she lay on the road thirty paces ahead of the Gaelic army. Their horses neighed wildly, rolling their eyes at her but the riders still did not heed her presence or stop their march. She was completely invisible to the warriors.

The redcaps had advanced by this time so that they were now very close to the ambush point but they stopped near the Christian soldiers, sniffing at the breeze. Sianan wondered if they had heard her cry. That possibility spurred her on to gather her strength to raise another call. This time her roar held the fury of a wild sow protecting her offspring from the hunters. The scream was fierce and unrestrained. The redcaps faltered. Some turned to retrace their steps unsure of what sort of creature they might be competing with for the bodies of their victims.

The old woman who led them berated their cowardice, beating at her ugly companions with her walking stick. Sianan noticed that though she seemed almost human in most respects there were two distinctive things about this old woman that were memorable. First of all her skin had a green glow about it, like the slime that grew on the top of a pond in summer. Secondly she had only one arm. Just above the elbow her left arm had been severed. Sianan thought that she could see blood oozing from the stump as if the wound were new.

The warriors under Murrough's command marched on heeding none of this. They had already passed Sianan when a huge figure loomed out of the forest at the side of the road to stand squarely blocking their way. The man was easily twice the height of any of Murrough's warriors and broader than an ox. At his shoulder sat a massive black bird the size of a hunting hound. The beast stretched out its wings to fill its lungs with air. Then the Raven sang in a language that Sianan could almost comprehend but not quite interpret fully. Somehow Sianan got the impression that the Raven was calling in all the creatures of her kind.

Awe-struck by the appearance of these two unearthly figures, Sianan momentarily forgot Murrough's plight. The Gaels had by this time marched on past the enormous man-creature without any sign that they had seen him either. This convinced Sianan that the giant was a Danaan, very likely in league with the redcaps. Her hope faded. It seemed certain to her now that the kings of Munster and Laigin would be slain with all their troops. Alarmed at the clarity of the vision, Sianan could almost picture each man and woman among the Gaels being devoured in the carrion greed of the Faery host.

The Raven's cry ceased abruptly as Murrough's men came level to the ditch where the foreigners were concealed. As if they had rehearsed this move many times, twenty or more Christian soldiers stood up in their trench. Most of them had bows drawn with iron-tipped arrows ready to strike. The Gaels marched on.

Sianan cried out again in a desperate last bid to get the attention of the two kings. To her relief Murrough turned in his saddle as if he had heard her. He was looking over his right shoulder directly at Sianan when the first flight of arrows struck the front ranks of the Gaelic force. Murrough gasped, clutching at a shaft that had entered his chest near the collarbone through a tiny gap in his armour. Instantly the whole scene was filled with flying arrows that whistled through the air, raining death upon the Gaels. Men and women fell with their shields still slung for marching. They were totally unprepared to fend off such a vicious and unexpected onslaught.

Sianan lost sight of Murrough as dozens of men and women sought shelter at the side of the road or fled across her path. Most of the warriors panicked as the second and third flights of arrows fell down upon them. In the confusion that followed Sianan willed her ethereal body to seek Murrough out. At least twelve of his warriors were lying on the ground killed or wounded after three volleys of arrow bolts. Enda Censelach was nowhere to be seen. His horse lay dead and unattended in the middle of the road.

Then, in less time than it would have taken her to cough, Sianan's view of the fight was blocked by the enormous figure of the giant. The Raven at his shoulder took off, flying directly toward the hill where Sianan had seen the hall. Suddenly the sky turned pitch black. No cloud or star could be seen at all through the trees. At first Sianan had no idea what could have caused such a dramatic change but then she heard what could only have been the beating of many wings.

Ravens. Hundreds of them. They had been sitting in the trees at either side of the road, waiting to strike. An old woman's voice cackled, mocking Sianan's worst fears. 'The Faery hosts have joined with the Christians to drive the Gaels out of Eirinn forever,' the hag sang.

The huge man-creature spun his body round to face Sianan as soon as the old woman had spoken. She could clearly see that in one monstrous hand he held the slumped figure of a warrior, an arrow jutting out of the poor fellow's neck. In the other he carried a great bronze axe bloodied and notched.

'Do not listen to her, Sianan,' the creature boomed. 'My folk have come to drive the Sidhe-Dubh out of this kingdom once and for all. It is the redcaps who are our enemies, not the kings of your people.'

Only now was it plain to her that the Ravens were sweeping down to peck ferociously at the remaining redcaps and at the old woman who led them. As she was observing the birds taking part in the battle, the man-creature disappeared silently among the trees with his burden. He was long gone when Sianan remembered him as the Danaan who had tried to persuade her to dance in the broch near Bally Cahor.

Sianan longed to run after the giant but the Christian soldiers chose that moment to make their charge. Up over the ditch the strangers came, screeching unintelligible war cries at their enemies. But the foreigners had not gone far when they faltered for a brief moment. Every man among them could see that the situation was not as favourable as they might have hoped. Though they had severely damaged the Gaelic defence they were still outnumbered at least three to one. The Gaels formed a battle line linking shields as men and women aligned themselves into their groups of three preparing for the first clash of arms.

Just as the Christians got within spearcast of the Gaelic line forty long shafts were slung at them. Two of the Romans were knocked over by the force of the flying spears. For the most part, however, the weapons rattled against the Christian's segmented armour and were deflected safely away. Then the Romans also linked shields, overlapping them in a pattern that echoed the design of their breastplates. Rather than stand a moment longer exposed to their foe's spears, the Christians raised another cry in unison rushing forward as if they were suddenly one massive creature with an armour-plated hide.

The Romans built up enough speed before they crunched into the Gaelic line that many of the High-King's warriors were knocked over, winded by the collision. The foreigners stuck their short swords in under the guard of their enemy's shield wall, wounding many warriors. Faced with such a fearless and determined assault, all the Gaels could do was begin to withdraw with some semblance of order and with as few casualties as possible.

Sianan raised herself high above the battle to get a better look at the overall situation. She had just spotted a large group of redcaps skirting around behind the hill to outflank both the Gaels and the Ravens when she heard a familiar voice summoning her. The words were seasoned with urgency and despair.

Completely forgetting about Murrough, Enda and the bloody fight that was taking place below her, Sianan lifted her attention to search the horizon in the general direction of the coming dawn. Nothing was as important to her now as locating the one who was begging her help. No other person in this world or the other for that matter, could have drawn her focus so completely at such a calamitous moment.

The voice that rang in her head was that of her companion Mawn.

TWENTY-FOUR

obann reached the Star of the Poets just as Cathach was drifting off to sleep. The poet was only too aware of how exhausted the old man had become in the last few weeks so when he noticed the chief Druid dozing in a chair rugged up in animal furs he let him be. Gobann then sought out a corner where he could be by himself and get some much-needed rest of his own. All he wanted was a quiet sip of mead and a bite to eat to see him through to the dawn.

A large chair carved out of a single yew trunk was unoccupied so the poet collected a cup of brew and some oat bread, and then settled down between the spreading arms of the seat. The unease that he had experienced on the testing field had not dissipated, indeed the more he tried to relax the more fretful he became. His students, he told himself, were on their own now. If they were worthy they would pass the testing and go on to be accepted into the ancient society of Druids. If either of them failed then it would be due to some weakness that neither Gobann nor Cathach had the talent to identify. Their teachers had prepared them as best they could.

Despite the calming draught of mead Gobann still sensed the presence of Síla and this also worried him. Resigning himself to a difficult night, he closed his eyes, covering his body with the cloak of Raven feathers that was the symbol of his rank. He forced his mind to concentrate on something other than his students or his beloved Síla.

A sharp clear memory came to him then of his own initiation to the circle of the silver branch nine summers earlier. He imagined that the venerable old Raven who had sat beside him on the branches of the Quicken Tree at the gathering of the birds was there with him now in the Hall of the Druids. Gobann did not open his eyes—he did not want to spoil this vision. The smell of wet feathers drying in the body heat of an old bird met his nostrils. The poet marvelled that he could recall such tiny details of his experience.

The part of Gobann that always sought explanations tried to discover a reason for the clarity of this distinct memory. It was easy enough to remind himself that he was wearing a cloak made of Raven feathers and he had just come in from the rain. The familiar scent that met his nostrils was therefore probably that of his own coat. Amused at the trick his senses had played on him, Gobann pulled the cloak up to his chin and tucked his legs up under it to keep them warm.

As he finished getting comfortable the poet heard a loud shuffling sound like that of a clawed creature crossing the floor. In his imagination he saw Lom-Dubh the bird who had introduced him to the Raven Queen.

'It is almost dawn,' the bird croaked, 'and a great calamity has come upon the Children of the Gael.'

The poet had lain down when the night was just past its zenith so he reckoned that sunrise was a long way off yet. Nevertheless he opened his eyes to make sure that this was only a trick of memory.

When he saw that the room was lightened by the coming sunrise Gobann panicked that several hours had passed by so quickly. 'How could I have overslept?' he rebuked himself. The cloak fell off his shoulders as he grabbed for his harp bag and got up out of the great chair. He turned to where Cathach had been sleeping but the old man was already gone—to attend the rituals, no doubt. 'Do not let me be too late,' the poet prayed.

Gobann would have rushed out of the door then without waiting another second but a strange sight materialised out of the shadows in the corner of the chamber. A short dark figure with a large body and very thin legs waddled out of the darkness to stand in the middle of the floor. At first the poet could not make out who or what it could possibly be, but then he recognised the shape as being that of a large bird easily twice the size of a cat. The creature had a yellowed beak and tattered feathers and its legs were covered in sinewy skin.

'Lom-Dubh?' Gobann whispered, seeking out the Raven's deep pool-like eyes.

'Do not fear,' Lom-Dubh answered in his familiar cracking tones, 'you will not be late for the rituals. I have urgent news for you but it will not keep you long.'

'Tell me on the way to the mound of testing,' the poet answered.

'I cannot go there. I must return to the battlefield as quickly as my wings will bear me for I fear that there may be more evil afoot this day.'

'Battlefield?' Gobann gasped. 'What battlefield?'

'Only a skirmish really,' the old bird corrected himself, 'but Murrough is badly wounded and the Christians may yet gain the upper hand.'

'The Christians have attacked the fortress of Cashel?'

'No, no. Are you still half asleep? The Christians who lit the fire on Slané.'

'Is Murrough not in Munster with his queen Caitlin?'

'Where have you been?' the Raven screeched. 'Murrough returned to Teamhair yestereve on an urgent errand. Leoghaire commissioned the King of Munster along with Enda Censelach to arrest the Christians who are at the royal residence of Slané.'

'And Murrough is badly injured?'

'But safe for the time being. He is well enough hidden but the warriors that were with him are now scattered. Our folk did all we could to aid the Gaels. Unfortunately we were faced with an old foe of our own that demanded to be dealt with. Smelling a blood feud, redcaps gathered from all over Laigin and Midhe for a feast of dead soldiery. My people beat them off only with great losses to our own forces. As a consequence we had little opportunity to help Murrough and Enda.'

'Who are these Christians?' Gobann inquired. 'I had not heard of their arrival.'

'I was hoping that you would be better informed than I am about the strangers. I can tell you only two things; first that there is one holy man among the Christians whom no redcap would dare go near. He is a strong one and has stayed behind in the High-King's hall while his soldiers sprung their trap. And second, the one who led the Christian soldiers is known to me.'

'Known to you? What is his name?'

'I never heard it spoken,' Lom-Dubh admitted, 'but I saw him with my own two eyes nine summers ago. Strangely he is not a Saxon, though he was with those savages who cut down the holy Quicken Tree. He dresses now as a Roman priest.'

'I believe that I have heard of this man,' Gobann flashed, his eyes widening with horror. 'If it is the same Roman that Murrough and Caitlin have spoken of then he was one of the chief henchmen of Palladius. The fellow must be a fool to return to Eirinn in defiance of his banishment.'

'These matters are for you and your kind to settle,' Lom-Dubh cackled. 'My queen will be less than happy that one of the Quicken killers is abroad in the land. It would give our folk great assurance to know that your people were going to deal with him swiftly.'

'I must inform the High-King before I can make you any promises as to what action will be taken about this outlaw. I expect that Leoghaire will be outraged that he has dared to return.'

'Urge him to act quickly, my friend. There is a tide of unrest swelling in the ranks of the Danaans about the manner in which your people are handling the many threats to Eirinn. An influential minority are openly opposing the old alliance with the Gaels and calling for war once more between our two kinds.'

'Thank the gods that Sciathan-cog, the leader of the rebels, failed in his aims after the Quicken was destroyed.'

'None of the Raven kind would have stood beside him after he sided with the Quicken killers. There are more vocal and persuasive advocates for war now. The old queen of my people is not as strong as she once was. I fear that she may have been influenced by the Sidhe-Dubh to lean toward the advocates of war. The redcaps have been hoping for a situation such as this for a long time. Now it seems they have got the strife they wanted.' The Raven coughed, touching a wing to his bald head. 'That is enough talk. If you are to make it to the Need Fire it is time to go. I have made my report and I think we have an understanding. I will send word of Murrough when I can be sure that it is safe to move him.'

'And I will go straightaway to inform Cathach and Leoghaire of this terrible news. Many thanks, old friend.'

'You are welcome, fellow Raven.' With that the ancient bird hobbled out through the open door. Gobann followed close behind. As soon as there were no walls to hem him in, the bird spread his wings, taking to the sky. He was circling high above Teamhair in less time than it takes for a bowman to draw an arrow. Meanwhile the poet set off with the same determination if not the same swiftness to find the High-King.

As soon as Gobann and his visitor were gone one of the guests in the Star of Poetry stirred, throwing off the blankets that covered her and dragging herself slowly to her feet. Caitlin had been sleeping not five steps from where the poet had spent the night. She had rested soundly until she was woken from her slumber to witness the entire conversation between Gobann and Lom-Dubh. Wisely she had not revealed her presence to either of them, preferring to hear all the news that Lom-Dubh imparted to the poet.

Now, with great urgency, Caitlin searched around in her pack until she located her knife. She tied back her long chestnut hair, slipped her riding boots on over her trousers and tucked the blade neatly into her boot. Then she made her way quickly and quietly out of the door of the hall, making sure that she had not disturbed Síla in her haste. The healer was too exhausted from the ride to Teamhair to have been woken easily.

Down through the several enclosures toward the main gate of the citadel Caitlin stealthily trod with her dark green cloak drawn over her head to hide her face. At the fifth circle she visited the stables, selecting a good riding saddle before untying one of Murrough's horses.

When she approached the gates of Teamhair she threw back her hood and declared herself but the sentries were very reluctant to let her pass. In the end she had to press her authority as Queen of Munster. Even then the captain of the guard sent a runner to Leoghaire to make sure that the High-King knew what was happening. He did not want to disobey the queen but neither did he want to be held responsible if any harm came to her beyond the walls. Everyone near the gates was aware that a small force commanded by Murrough and Enda had departed during the night. It was rumoured that they were setting out to engage a company of marauding Saxons.

The captain stalled Caitlin at his sentry post as long as he was able. However, by this stage it was dawn; he had received no word requesting that she be kept within the citadel, so against his better judgment and at her insistence he let the mighty oak doors be swung open for the Queen of Munster. Almost as soon as she had passed by, the captain regretted his decision but it was too late to stop Caitlin. The queen swung up onto the back of the war horse and was soon galloping swiftly down the road away from Teamhair.

Caitlin did not look back. All her attention was on the road in front of her, secure in the knowledge that Slané was no more than several hours' ride away. Her first thoughts were for Murrough. The Raven had said he was very badly wounded and in need of assistance, and she prayed over and over that he was safe. She knew she was not up to this ride—her body was still weak from the ordeals of the last few weeks—but Murrough had often risked his all to help her and now it was time for her to come to his aid.

But Murrough was not the only one on her mind. The Raven had said that he had seen one of the Christians who had been at the cutting of the Quicken Tree. The bird had also stated that this foreigner was no Saxon. An olive-skinned face appeared before her mind's eye. It was a face that she would never forget. Caitlin had first met him when she was still the chieftain at Rathowen and he had insulted her. Fintan, her champion, had punished the arrogant Roman and later paid for that action with his life.

The feet of the queen's horse pounded on the even surface of the road, keeping up a regular beat. Caitlin took up the rhythm in her head, drumming out the hated syllables, strengthening her vengeance, filling her heart with venom. And when she could no longer confine her rage to her thoughts alone she intoned the despised name, invoking her enemy, daring him to meet with her in an open challenge.

'Seg-in-us Gall-us,' she cried. 'Seg-in-us Gall-us.'

By the time that Gobann made it to the mound of testing, the rites for kindling the Need Fire were well advanced. Now he feared that he might be too late to catch the High-King and the chief Druid before they became too involved in the ritual. His conversation with Lom-Dubh had obviously lasted too long. Now both Cathach and Leoghaire were performing in the most crucial part of the ceremony.

The poet took a place at the rear of the gathering where some of the Druid kind from over the sea were adding their own touches to the ceremony, whispering prayers in their various languages or casting grain upon the ground. One couple who were Cruitne from North Britain were plucking the strands from a long white feather to scatter the pieces on the wind.

Throughout Eirinn all the fires, save the one notable exception, had been extinguished. It was up to the High-King and his counsellor at this time to create a spark, feed it, fan it and nurture it until it became a larger fire. For this purpose they used two of the oldest tools known to the Gaelic people: a bow and an arrow. It is said that when the Gaels first set foot on the soil of Eirinn all their possessions had been soaked through by rain and storms sent by the Tuatha-De-Danaan to confound them. At the first place where they made camp it was necessary to kindle a fire from a spark rather than from a coal as was their usual method.

In remembrance of that first night in the land of Eirinn, the ritual of the kindling was re-enacted each Beltinne.

Cathach held the arrow in his hand symbolising the steadying force of the Druid kind: always ready with words of wisdom, advice and legal precedent. Leoghaire wrapped the string of the bow once around the arrow and set the wooden point of the shaft into a piece of dry oak bark. As he drew on the bow, the arrow spun around in Cathach's hands caught in the grip of the bowstring, gradually warming the bark. Skill and teamwork were required to perform this task effectively.

If the arrow did not remain in constant motion precious heat would be lost, in turn prolonging the whole exercise indefinitely. Leoghaire kept the arrow moving steadily though, while Cathach blew on the bark as it began to smoulder with the heat of the rubbing. Within a remarkably short space of time a spark jumped out from the piece of bark to land smoking on the ground. Cathach picked it up, cupping it in his hand and puffing gently over it. Just as he did so the sun crept up over the far horizon, edging its fiery disc skyward.

This act of blowing on the flame was called imparting the breath of life. Before long a small pile of hay was smoking. Then the dried-out barley stalks from last summer's harvest were stacked around the base of the ember. Leoghaire and his counsellor had once again proven themselves to be an excellent and reliable team. This was a clear example to the chieftains of the land that the High-King and his council could be depended on to furnish the needs of the people of Eirinn.

When the fire was well lit it was transferred with infinite care and solemnity to a specially constructed pit full of dry timber. Those Druids who were to be the fire wardens until the next festival were responsible for this task. When this fire had died down sufficiently the embers and coals would be distributed throughout the five kingdoms to every hearth and smithy.

At sunset this day the bone-fire would be ignited to cremate the remains of all those Druids who had passed away within Teamhair during the winter. Seasoned wood was already being stacked near the mound of testing. When Gobann had been initiated into the circle of the silver branch the timber was stacked over the mound in which he was buried. Mawn and Sianan were receiving initiation only as far as the first circle of the Druid path, so the bone-fire would be close by but not constructed around the tomb in which they lay.

Once the main part of the fire ceremony was ended Cathach retired from the front of the gathering to sit on one of the sacred stones. Gobann could clearly see that the old man was sweating profusely even though the morning was brisk and cool. The poet wondered at the chief Druid's sudden weakness, for Cathach had seemed in the best of health the previous evening.

The sun climbed quickly over the hills and the grey half-light blossomed into the gold of early morning. Leoghaire strode through the crowded field near to the mound making straight for Gobann. The poet realised that he had been seen and began to push his way back towards the High-King. They met in the midst of the throng, both looking as though they had not slept for many days; both with ill news to impart.

'Murrough has fallen at Slané,' Gobann reported before Leoghaire even had a chance to greet him.

The colour drained from the High-King's cheeks. This was the last thing he had expected Gobann to say. All he could manage to stutter in reply to the poet was the one word he dreaded to hear. 'Dead?'

'Not as far as I know. He is in safe-keeping for the time being. The Christians have fought a pitched battle and routed our warriors.'

'When did you learn of this?'

'All this took place a short time ago, just before the sunrise.'

Leoghaire sighed heavily and tugged at his beard in despair, searching his mind for an answer to this new problem, but he did not question how Gobann could have learned of the battle so quickly. 'We have been very foolish. None of us expected that they would dare attack our troops. Now I will have to go to Slané myself with more warriors. That will mean calling on Murrough's guardsmen and some of the soldiers of Laigin as reserves.'

'If you leave Teamhair you will not be able to return again until sunset,' Gobann observed. 'Not even the High-King may break the ban on entering the citadel gates during the rites of Beltinne.'

'My main duties are finished with here. I doubt that anyone will miss me for the rest of the day. Tell the assembly that I have retired to my hall. It is unlikely that I will be able to clear up this mess by sunset so the prohibition on re-entering the gates will not affect me. I will need a Druid law counsellor in my party. Will you accompany me, Gobann?'

'He will not,' Cathach burst in. Neither man had noticed the old Druid approach. 'I am the High-King's advisor and I am the senior Brehon judge in the land. It is my duty to ride out with the military expedition to Slané.'

'I mean nothing but respect to you, Cathach,' Leoghaire answered politely, 'but it is obvious to me that you are somewhat overtired. I noticed last night that you were in pain when we met and that you were having difficulty breathing. Now you are drenched in sweat.'

'I was suffering a minor discomfort last night. That is to be expected since I am an old man. When you have attained my age you will understand that it is important not to let every trivial passing ache rule the outcome of your entire life.'

'I have a feeling that what I witnessed last night was more than simple discomfort,' the High-King pressed. 'In any case there are duties that need to be attended to here, such as the care of Queen Caitlin.'

'Caitlin!' Gobann interrupted. 'Is she in Teamhair?'

Neither Cathach nor Leoghaire answered. The chief Druid was already busy reinforcing his view to the High-King, 'Gobann is more than capable of dealing with the Queen of Munster's ailment. The poet is a skilled negotiator and a learned judge but only I can face Patricius with any hope of achieving the results that we want.'

Leoghaire looked to the poet and then back to Cathach. Gobann cast his gaze toward the ground. It was obvious to the High-King that Gobann would not dare gainsay the chief Druid of Eirinn. 'Before you give your final word on this subject—' Leoghaire was about to suggest that Cathach remain in the citadel while a war band fetched the Christians to Teamhair but before he could do so one of his messenger's shoved past a guardsman to touch him on the arm.

'Lord!' he called. Leoghaire refused to be distracted. The young man reached out again, lurching forward to fall face first in the dirt at the High-King's feet.

Leoghaire leaned over to help him up. 'You have burst in on the council of the High-King, lad. This is the second time since sunset that you have disturbed my peace. It had better be with good reason.'

'The gate captain of the citadel begs to report that Queen Caitlin passed through the first circle and out of the citadel just after sunrise. She was alone but mounted on a war horse.'

Leoghaire covered his face with his hand, groaning under his breath. 'Did he not think to question her?'

'She convinced the gatekeeper that she was acting under your instructions, lord.'

'Was she armed?' Cathach snapped.

'She was unarmed, lord Druid.'

'Then the matter is settled,' Cathach declared. 'Caitlin is under my protection as a guest of the Star of Poetry and she is a queen of this country. No-one less than the High-King and myself should be seeing to her safety.' He did not wait for Leoghaire to protest before calling to the messenger.

'Boy, go to the stables and have them prepare a war horse for me, no more than twelve hands high, mind you. I do not want to come away from this experience crippled by cramps from sitting on a huge beast.'

Leoghaire waved the messenger on, giving his consent for the lad to carry out the errand. 'Will you join me now for bread and honey cakes? It would be a good opportunity for us to discuss what strategy we will employ at Slané.'

'There'll be time enough for talking when we're in the saddle,' Cathach barked. 'I will be waiting for you at the first circle after you have broken your fast. I leave Gobann to take over my duties as chief Druid.' The old man looked sternly at the poet. 'Do you understand what I am saying, brother Druid?'

The poet nodded gravely. With that assurance the chief Druid forced his way back through the assembly, making toward his sanctuary in the Star of the Poets. On the way he picked out two younger Druids to accompany him on the ride to Slané.

Patricius Sucatus had been disturbed from his prayers just before dawn. The holy father was no warrior but he recognised well enough the awful din of weapons clashing in anger. Screams of the wounded, the dying and of those in flight met his ears, sending him out of the hall into the night to seek out the source of the disturbance.

'Keep your prisoner well minded and watch over Secondinus and Tullia while I am gone,' Patricius commanded Darach. 'But you,' the bishop gestured toward Mog, 'you will come with me. I may need a guard.'

'I am no warrior, your grace!' Mog protested. 'I am a humble servant, the son of a farmer. I would not be much use to you, your grace, I am a little slow.' Mog waved his hand around at the side of his head to show that his brains were not arranged in any recognisable order.

'You may have very few wits but you are carrying a sword. I'd guess that your master would not allow you to bear it if you did not know how to put the blade to some use.'

'This?' Mog protested, pointing to the weapon that hung at his side. 'This is all for show, your grace. I mean to say, it's not even sharp.' To prove that he was speaking the truth he drew the sword from its scabbard and ran the edge of the blade over his forearm. The weapon left a nasty welt but it did not cut the flesh. 'See, your grace, this old poker wouldn't cut a scar on a bowl of oatmeal porridge.'

'I am perhaps not as foolish as you might think,' Patricius retorted. 'The blade of a stabbing weapon is rarely honed for slicing. Now come along, I am in need of you!' With that Patricius stormed out of the hall toward the fire. Mog looked to Darach for support but his companion pretended to be too busy to notice.

A few moments later Mog left the hall, sheepishly following the bishop at a safe distance. 'Wait, your grace! I can't keep up with you!' he called but Patricius did not slow down. The cleric was making straight for the bottom of the hill where he assumed Seginus, Tatheus and the soldiers had been standing watch.

The clamour of fighting filtered up through the trees as the two men made their way toward the road. However, long before they reached the scene of the original clash the struggle had shifted further back up the road. Patricius heard eerie anguished shouts from that direction followed by a long wail that chilled his heart. He sensed that there was some force at work here that was not of this world. Determinedly he set out to find the source of the disturbance with Mog desperately trying to keep up.

Patricius had run about a hundred paces along the road when he stopped to wait for the servant to draw close again. The cleric looked about him checking that there were no marauders waiting in the bushes. It was then that he noticed several dark shapes lying to the right of the path. Patricius approached one of them carefully not quite sure what the shadow might be. The night was still too dark for him to see clearly so he used his staff to prod gently at the shape.

The bishop had heard many stories concerning the Otherworld folk of Eirinn. He had been told that they could take on any shape to confound their victims. He touched the object cautiously with his staff. It had a solid form like the body of a human. A fallen warrior.

These dark shapes were not enchanted spirits. They were dead Gaelic warriors.

'What has happened here?' Patricius wailed. 'How did these men die?'

Mog caught up with the bishop as he asked that question. The servant was panting and wheezing from the run and his eyes were wide with the horror at seeing corpses scattered about. He had hardly stopped long enough to catch his breath before strange footsteps could be heard running up the road from the direction of the hill.

'That is not the footfall of any Roman soldier,' Patricius observed. 'Legionnaires have iron studs in the soles of their boots to give a better grip on rough terrain. That is the slapping of the leather-soled shoes of Hibernians against the packed earth of the road.'

Mog swallowed hard, signing the Cross with lightning speed. The footfall was becoming much louder now. From the tremendous noise that the Hibernians made Mog was certain that there must be at least twenty warriors in the approaching party. Darach would have said, if he had been there, that this meant there were probably only about five. Mog, with characteristic pessimism, decided that his days on Earth were finally up. 'I'll never hold them all off, your grace!'

'Nonsense!' Patricius bawled. 'Don't let them see that you're frightened. The Hibernians respect bravery but they roast cowards over their festival fires.'

'Roast?' the servant repeated but before he could exercise his first instinct, which was to run as fast as he could, the enemy was upon them. Mog had accompanied Seginus throughout all his many travels; from Alexandria to the Saxon lands he had served his master, coming into contact at one time or another with every race that inhabited the mighty Roman Empire. But he had never seen any folk that matched this handful of warriors.

Their dress was very simple, rather like the peasant clothes of the Cumri, but their arms were incredibly long, dragging almost to the ground as they ran. At first Mog thought they were wearing leather boots but when he examined them more closely he realised their feet were covered in thick matted hair. His back started to feel as though it was turning to jelly. There was something unnatural about these warriors.

They were ten paces away from the cleric and the terrified servant before Mog saw the bright red hats that they all wore. The strange headgear reminded him of the Emperor's Persian guards that were stationed in Ravenna. So entranced was he by the pretty hats that it took a few seconds longer for him to notice what Patricius was gasping at. Mog looked to the bishop and then back at the soldiers, then his eyes nearly popped out of his head.

Each man, if they were men at all, had two long broad protruding teeth that stuck up like the tusks of a boar. Indeed they looked more like wild pigs than humans. Mog felt his knees tremble. The next thing he knew Patricius was lifting his staff in the direction of the warriors.

'Be gone, demons! Return to the Devil, your master!'

The pig-faced creatures laughed. Mog heard the evil cackles and would have blocked his ears but something inside him was strangely enraged by this demonic behaviour. If they were going to kill him well and good but this mockery was too much to bear. All of a sudden his outrage erupted, overcoming his fear. He lifted his sword to charge at the beasts, coming to within only two paces of the largest one before stopping. He could smell a foul stench like rotten meat that seemed to have soaked into the devil's clothes. The smell made him falter for a second.

Then he closed his eyes, screaming a loud battle cry at the top of his lungs, and in a mighty downward sweep brought his weapon crashing toward the nearest demon's head. The next thing Mog knew was that his sword had stuck fast in something and would not budge. The servant dared to open one eye. He looked at the point of his blade. It was wedged in the damp surface of the road close by the demon's feet. Mog reached down to release the spear point but as he did so his hand seemed to pass through the legs of the creature as if it had no more substance than smoke.

Mog froze and slowly moved his gaze up again toward the grinning face of his adversary. The servant's mouth dropped open a little as he realised what he was up against. A split second later he was running panicked in the opposite direction, passing Patricius without a thought for the bishop's safety. He heard the cleric raise another challenge to the demons, 'So it's a fight you're after? I think that I'll prove more of a challenge than a servant. God stands with me!'

Mog had run about thirty steps when he ascertained that he was not being followed. After that it was not long before his conscience got the better of him. He stopped to see what had become of Patricius. The demons had advanced on the cleric but Patricius still held his staff up in defiance. Mog could hear the bishop reciting the 'Our Father'.

The devils were within striking range of their victim when Mog decided that he could not bear to watch Patricius sacrificed to such evil spirits. He took a few steps back toward the monsters and then he shut his eyes and prayed earnestly. 'O Lord, do not punish the good bishop for my cowardly behaviour. Drive off the demons and protect your servant Patricius.'

Mog heard unearthly screams. When he opened his eyes again the devils were all standing with mouths agape, slathering foam over their teeth. One of them turned to run screaming into the trees. Then another bolted off and another, until only their chief remained. Mog's heart filled with gratitude and, more surprisingly, valour. Secure that God would protect him he charged back toward the last remaining beast with his fists raised above his head yelling every obscenity he had ever heard.

The creature saw him coming but its attention seemed to be on a point far above the servant and to his rear. Whatever the monster saw terrified it enough that before Mog had got close enough to land a blow it had scurried off into the dawn after its comrades.

Mog collapsed in relief on the road beside Patricius, unable to wipe the grin from his face. He imagined good Christians telling their children the story of Mog the demon slayer long after bishop Patricius was a forgotten legend. But his triumph was short lived. As the bishop gave thanks to God Mog heard a mighty thump behind him. It was closely followed by another. If he had not known better he might have thought a giant was stumbling around. Mog turned to get a look at what was happening behind him. He had to blink twice before he believed what he saw.

Thirty paces away a huge man-like creature slipped into the cover of the trees. The giant held a warrior in one hand and an enormous axe in the other. This shock was a little too much for the delicate sensibilities of Mog. But before he collapsed the servant realised that the red-hatted demons weren't fleeing from him or Patricius or even the wrath of God; they had been running away from yet another hideous beast of the night.

Mog did not come around until a soldier threw cold water on his face. There were warriors all around by the time he regained his senses, some with bloodied bandages around their skulls, others covered in the gore of their enemies. Patricius was talking loudly and sternly above all the other voices.

'And knowing what this would lead to you still disobeyed my orders!'

'They meant to put us all to the sword,' Tatheus protested.

'How do you know that?' Patricius bellowed. 'Did you take the time to ask them what they intended to do? No. Did you give them the opportunity to appraise the situation or to face you honourably on the open field of battle? No. You saw fit to slaughter two dozen men—'

'—and women,' Seginus added. 'There were wild women with the other warriors.'

'Yes!' Patricius threw his arms up in dismay. 'As Father Seginus has noted, both men and women were killed. What excuse can you give me for this barbaric, unChristian, unRoman behaviour?'

Tatheus held his head upright and proud. 'I am a soldier. I came to do a soldier's job. To protect the life of your good self from the ravages of the heathen.'

'In future do me the courtesy of letting me perish at the hands of the savages!' Patricius chided. 'Better that than for me to see heathen who do not know the word of Christ behave in a more civilised manner than any of the so-called Romans that I keep company with. You are a disgrace to your uniform, centurion. I will see to it that you are formally charged when you return to Ravenna. And if you are shocked by my anger, just wait till you are brought before the Emperor. I am told that the latest fashion sweeping the Roman court is the public castration of traitors.'

'This debacle was not my doing,' Tatheus cut in, visibly shaken by the threat.

'What did you say?' bellowed the bishop. 'Are you trying to shift the blame onto another?'

The centurion made a conscious effort to lower his voice, hoping that this would calm Patricius a little. 'It was not my fault.'

'You are the commander of these troops, aren't you?'

'I command them, but I acted on the advice and urging of Father Seginus.'

Patricius closed his eyes, dropping his head forward until his jaw rested on his chest, trying to control his rage. When he raised his head to speak again, his voice was so subdued that Tatheus had to move closer to hear the question. 'How many are dead?'

'Seven legionnaires perished, Father. Twenty-eight of the enemy were killed or wounded.'

'They are not our enemies, centurion,' the bishop reminded him, 'they are our flock. Was the leader of the Hibernians slain?'

'We have not found a chieftain among those who died or among the captives, lord.'

'Have you considered for a moment that their chieftain may have been very badly wounded? Even now he could be bleeding to death in a ditch somewhere.' Tatheus by now wore a helpless expression on his face. 'Don't just stand there,' the bishop whispered menacingly, 'send out soldiers to find survivors. You will bring any Hiberenians to me unharmed. This may be our only chance to make amends.' As an afterthought he added, 'And see that all your prisoners are fed and their wounds tended to.'

Tatheus hesitated for a second then clasped his right hand to his left breast in a Roman military salute. 'Yes, lord.' The centurion about-turned smartly to face his men. 'Form ranks and listen here you slovenly lot! I've got a delicate job for you.'

Patricius put his hand down hard on Seginus' shoulder. 'Let us go back up the hill to stand by the fire, my son. I think you owe me an explanation.' The bishop walked off along the road without waiting for the priest.

Seginus hesitated but eventually followed obediently. Mog came along after he had managed to dislodge his sword from the mud. Along the way the bodies of slain warriors lay dispersed on the track. Seginus pretended not to notice them but Patricius stopped briefly to bless each corpse.

As they came close to the fire outside the hall Patricius raised his voice slightly so that Secondinus and Tullia would hear that he was back. 'What manner of man are you, Gallus? What made you convince Tatheus to fall on the Hibernians in ambush?' Patricius glanced at the other man's hands, noticing with disgust that they were covered in dried blood.

'You don't know what those savages are really like,' Seginus answered quietly. 'I have seen action against these folk. They ask for no quarter and they give none. They are vicious in dealing with their foes. After they have killed a man on the field of battle they slice his head off to hang in their feasting hall as a trophy.'

'I never saw any evidence of that practice,' Patricius exclaimed, 'except in the exaggerated telling of their far-fetched stories. I think you may have read too many questionable accounts of the Gallic wars. You have come to confuse reality with the garbled reports of Julius Caesar. What led you to believe that these warriors would treat us as enemies?'

'They were marching in a battle formation ready to attack,' Seginus explained. He knew he was stretching the truth a little here for though he had experience fighting against the Hibernians he really didn't understand any of the tactics they employed. He took the chance that Patricius would not know any better. 'I acted with the good of the mission at heart,' he added.

'I believe that you behaved out of fear for the consequences of being captured and brought to trial by the very people whose husbands and sons you butchered during the time of Palladius. You may have saved my life when you dragged me ashore, Seginus Gallus, but deep in your heart you are a bloody coward, unworthy to wear the vestments of a Roman priest or even of a holy brother.'

'If I had not ordered our troops to attack when I did you would all be dead by now,' Seginus asserted.

'If you had not ordered the attack there would be sixteen men and women still cherishing the sacred gift of life!' Patricius tore the hood from his head violently to reveal his face full of wrath. 'You will do penance for this crime. I will not let you get away with anything that your former master would have applauded. Now you are a priest, not a mere monk with loose vows to bind him. You belong entirely to the Holy Mother Church. Body and soul you have sworn to do the bidding of the

Pope and his ministers. I am the chief of the Holy Father's servants in this land and so it could be said that you belong to me. With God's help and my firm hand there is still a chance that you may one day learn to discipline yourself.'

'We beat them soundly,' Seginus said lowly.

'I have heard enough!' Patricius stormed. He waited a moment before he spoke again, trying to keep his voice calm. 'Are you so blind to the truth that you cannot see it when it stands plainly before you? If the High-King can send seventy warriors to this place at such short notice, how many more will he dispatch when he really means to do us harm?'

'They will think twice about coming here to fight with us now that we have so completely thrashed their finest warriors.'

'How do you know that these were their best soldiers? Even if they were the finest in the land, their kindred could well raise the whole kingdom in order to avenge the deaths of these warriors. How long did you say you lived in this country with Palladius?'

'A little more than three years.'

'Is it possible to reside in a land so long and never hear the stories that the common folk tell?'

'What do you mean?' asked Seginus.

'All the Hibernian warrior myths deal with the betrayal of honour and the steady inevitable path that leads back to revenge. Folk who tell such tales to their children do not expect their High-King to sit back and let a few insignificant Romans walk all over them. Lighting the fire was a challenge to the authority of the Druids, in the hope that they would come here and confront us in a contest of words and ideology. However, fighting a pitched battle was an open invitation for the High-King to institute harsh reprisals. Didn't you learn anything from the dreadful mistakes of that mad old bishop, your former master?'

Seginus suspected that during his bishopric Palladius had acted beyond his mandate in stirring the country up into a civil war. But he sincerely believed that everything the old man had done had been for the good of the barbarians. He was about to say so when Tullia, Secondinus, Darach and the Hibernian prisoner came out of the hall.

The captured warrior looked around the circle until his eyes fell on Seginus. His expression turned immediately to hate when he saw the priest's bloodied hands for he had also heard the sounds of battle and had surmised what was taking place. He grunted loudly, muttering an expression that none of the Christians could understand, then he squatted by the fire with Darach standing close behind him.

'I am going to pray and to meditate on all that you have said, Father,' Seginus lied, making ready to get away by himself for a while; but before he could leave, Tatheus and two legionnaires appeared with the body of an Hibernian warrior slumped between them. A richly woven cloak covered most of their prisoner.

'We think we've found the leader of this expedition,' Tatheus reported. 'Alive but wounded. The sentries discovered him buried under leaves at the foot of this hill not long ago.' Tatheus gave a curt hand signal and the two Roman soldiers set the Hibernian down near the fire. The other warrior still being guarded by Darach took an immediate interest in the other prisoner.

'Do you know anything about him?' Patricius inquired.

'Nothing,' Tatheus began, 'other than the fact that he has a Roman arrow embedded above his collarbone and that he has lost a lot of blood.' With a flourish the centurion whipped back the cloak to reveal a red-headed man wearing a golden ornament of exquisite beauty around his throat.

Seginus took a sharp breath as the full horror of recognition hit him.

'You have got yourself quite a catch, centurion,' the bishop observed, taking careful note of Seginus' reaction. 'I would say that you've caught yourself a king by the look of that neck-piece and by the war paint that he is wearing. What would you say, Father?'

Seginus Gallus looked from one face to another, trying to conceal his panic. 'He is a petty chieftain, no more,' he asserted. 'At least I would be surprised if he were anything more than that. We will have to wait until he regains consciousness before we find out for certain.'

'Nonsense!' Patricius cried. 'We don't have to wait till then. We have a man in our midst who will be able to identify the captive. Darach, bring your prisoner here.'

The servant jumped to his feet dragging the Hibernian warrior over to the bishop. Patricius asked the warrior slowly and clearly, 'Do you recognise this man?'

The warrior answered immediately. 'He is Murrough the King of Munster.'

Seginus proceeded to turn a log over in the fire pretending not to hear what was being said.

'You knew a man called Murrough once did you not, Seginus?' asked the bishop.

'I did my lord.'

'Was he not the king of the south?'

'Did I say he was a king? No the man I knew was a prince when I met him.'

'Is this the man?'

Seginus took a long hard look at Murrough. 'I don't think so. Murrough had black hair,' he lied. 'That man,' he pointed at the other Hibernian, 'is trying to deceive us.'

'So you are certain, are you, that this is not Murrough, King of Munster?'

Seginus glanced once more at the unconscious prisoner. 'I have never seen this man before in my life.'

'Thank you, Father Gallus,' Patricius declared loudly. 'I knew that I could depend on your infallible memory.'

Tullia allowed a sound to escape her lips which perfectly expressed her disgust.

'With your permission, lord, I will go to check the road for more Hibernians,' Seginus requested, determined to ignore Tullia's scorn.

'I would like a brief word with you before you go. In private if you don't mind,' Patricius stated.

As soon as the two of them were out of earshot the bishop's tone changed dramatically. 'When we stand before the High-King of this land, as surely we must, you will tell him everything. Everything! Do you hear? If you cannot deceive Tullia then what makes you think that the High-King will swallow any of your lies. You will beg his forgiveness and submit to his punishment. When your secular penalty is paid I will set a spiritual penance on you that you will never forget. I was told that Palladius could be hard on those brothers who broke the rules of his congregation. I can be much tougher when the need arises.'

Seginus acknowledged the bishop with a nod. 'Will that be all, Father?'

Patricius stared into the priest's dark eyes. 'From now on you will work to make sure that this mission is a complete success.'

'Yes, Father.'

'Swear it.'

'I swear that I will do everything in my power to ensure the success of your mission in Eirinn,' he stated formally, though as usual he placed his own interpretation on the phrase.

'One last thing,' Patricius added, 'is that the king called Murrough?'

Seginus thought about lying; he considered denial but he had no fight left in him. The bishop was right. It would only be a matter of time before he had to face his God with the burden of his sins. 'He is the one called Murrough.'

'Then I think we can be sure that when he is missed his kinfolk will march here with a much larger force than he had at his disposal. And when they do you had better pray that this king does not have such clear memories of you, my son, as you seem to have of him.'

'Yes, Father.'

'Go now and bring the rest of the soldiers in. I would like us all to be praying together when the heathen arrive to take us.'

'As you wish, Father.'

'And for God's sake go and wash the blood of battle off you,' Patricius added sternly. 'I wish to say Mass in a short while. If you are to beg the Lord's forgiveness for your deeds it would be better if your hands were not soaked in the gore of your victims.'

Seginus did not bother to reply. Grabbing his old red cloak from where he had left it inside the hall he stormed off toward the spring that fed a stream at the bottom of the hill.

Mog followed his master for a little way until Seginus noticed his presence. 'Get your useless arse back to the rest of the company!' Seginus barked. 'I don't want you getting in my way this time. Wait with Darach until you hear from me.'

When he was sure that his servant had obeyed him the priest made for the stream where he washed his hands carefully, scrubbing them diligently until there was no trace of blood. He splashed the cool water on his face, inspected his sword for notches and then when he was sure that no-one was about he made his way quickly into the cover of the trees. From there he walked parallel to the road back towards Teamhair slowly formulating a plan of escape.

From his hiding place among the undergrowth Enda Censelach watched all the Christians as they gathered on the road with their leaders after the attack. He noted that three men walked off back up the hill. He would have followed after them in the hope of striking an effective blow but the main body of Christian soldiers still blocked his path. So he waited.

When Murrough had tumbled off his horse pierced by an arrow, Enda had been riding beside him not an arm's length away. Without hesitation the King of Laigin had rolled off his mount to find cover from the falling shafts of death. This was an old tactic that any seasoned warrior would have resorted to. Once on the ground, though, Enda saw that Murrough was badly wounded and that several other warriors had also been grievously injured. By the large number of arrows that still rained down Censelach quickly judged that his force was probably heavily outnumbered. He had no way of knowing that his opponents were a small number of highly trained Roman legionnaires. So rather than stand to fight and very likely be killed in the affray he crawled through the darkness to the edge of the road. After that he made his way into the trees to hide until the assault had finished.

From his vantage point he watched the road, taking careful note of all the soldiers who passed by. He was surprised to find that he could only count about twenty Christians in the whole contingent. Enda had been convinced that there were many more enemy warriors than that small number. He rebuked himself for acting rashly in retreating when he did. Perhaps if he had stood his ground he might have been able to defeat the intruders by rallying his troops.

Unsure what to do, the King of Laigin covered himself with bracken and leaves to wait until an opportunity arose for escape or better still to rescue his honour. That chance did not present itself until long after the sun had climbed into the sky.

He was brushing the leaves away from his head when he heard the horse approaching but it was a long while after that before he actually saw the animal. He reasoned that the Christians probably did not possess mounts so this was most likely a Gaelic warrior. The rider did not seem to be in any hurry, however, letting his war horse wander at a gentle pace.

Not long after the mounted warrior came into Enda's view, the horse drifted over to the side of the road and began munching on some juicy green grass. The rider leaned forward in the saddle a little, covered in a rich green travelling cloak which completely concealed his head.

Enda wondered if the warrior was wounded or whether he had simply fallen asleep. Unable to make out who this rider could be, the King of Laigin was forced to wait for some sign. That came when the mount turned around to show its right flank. There on the fleshy part of the leg Censelach could clearly see the stylised form of a tree inscribed in the secret ogham symbols. This was Murrough's personal sign and all the horses of the kingdom of Munster were branded with it.

Until that moment Enda had considered approaching the rider but seeing the seal of Munster made him hesitate. It was that moment of indecision that gave him the upper hand in the next few seconds.

Not ten paces away a man in a long tunic covered by a scarlet cloak rushed out of the trees with a drawn sword making straight for the mounted warrior. This fellow was obviously not a Gael for his head was shaved so that a circle of skin showed at the back of his scalp.

'A Christian,' Enda mumbled.

This was the king's chance to make up for his unfortunate retreat, perhaps even an opportunity to look somewhat honourable again. Censelach drew his own sword, a long tempered blade that had once belonged to Dichu, the previous king. He raised it in the air and sprinted out across the road with his leather-soled boots lightly touching the earth. He knew that the quieter he could be the less the chance that he would scare the enemy off.

The Christian was very close to the mounted Munster man by the time Censelach had made any gain on him. However, to the king's surprise, the warrior on horseback did not react to the foreigner who was charging straight at him. The horse took a few steps backward as the enemy came close but other than that there was no sign of life from the mounted man.

The Christian had also reappraised the situation by that stage, sheathing his short sword so that he could use both hands to grapple the warrior to the ground. Without any difficulty he dragged the man off his horse, lying him on his back in the road. He was still checking the warrior for weapons when he noticed Enda Censelach rushing toward him like a wild boar in a blood rage. The Christian clawed vainly at the hilt of his sword but by that time the King of Laigin was already bearing down on him.

Enda grunted as he swung his blade toward his enemy, but somehow the Christian rolled out of the way managing in that split second to draw his own sword. Censelach pressed his advantage so that the foreigner had to shuffle backwards quite a long way before he could stand properly. By that time Enda had also unsheathed his hunting knife, holding it in his left hand to parry any blows from his adversary.

The Christian's eyes darted this way and that searching for an escape route. The King of Laigin could read the panic in his enemy's face and laughed at the nervousness of the man. 'I'll make you wish you'd stayed at home in Rome, Christian,' he cried.

To his surprise the man answered him in broken Gaelic. 'I already wish that I had never come to this land.' As he spoke the foreigner let loose a stroke of his sword that Enda easily deflected onto the ground with his hunting knife.

'You'll have to do better than that if you hope to ever see your home again!' Censelach mocked. The

416

King of Laigin could see the Christian back off from the attack searching for a reply.

'I'd rather perish here now than live another moment in a land full of cowards and fools.' The foreigner swept his sword around in a wide arc that cut through the air gracefully. Enda easily anticipated the blow, slipping beneath the man's guard so that the Christian's blade ended up falling wide of its mark. While his enemy was off balance Censelach used his sword hilt enclosed in his right fist to land a ferocious punch on the underside of the Christian's jaw. The man teetered on his feet for just a moment before falling backwards unconscious.

'I may grant you that wish, Roman.'

Enda advanced to stand over the man, making sure that he had done a good enough job. Behind him the King of Laigin heard a shuffle. He spun around to level his sword at the warrior who had appeared behind him. It only took a matter of seconds for Enda to realise that this was the Munster man who had been riding the horse.

'So you've come round have you?' the king said gruffly. 'What's the matter with you?'

The warrior pulled back the green hood to reveal long chestnut brown locks of hair and a face that though very pale was one that Censelach instantly recognised.

'Have you seen Murrough?' Caitlin asked.

TWENTY-FIVE

awn's voice continued to summon Sianan long after she had left the battlefield at the foot of the hill. She felt no guilt about leaving Murrough fallen on the roadside. She was only too aware that there was nothing she could do to help him while she remained in the spirit form. Sianan was being drawn up into the sky to a point just below the clouds. From there with the sun close to rising she could make out the details of the countryside around about. To her right far in the distance she could see a bright expanse of water. She reasoned quite correctly that this must be the eastern sea.

To the north was a landmark that she knew quite well. The white stone surrounds marked the hill known as the dwelling place of Aenghus Og. Sianan strained to glance behind her to the south and there she spotted Teamhair.

'I was never far from home,' she told herself, committing the events that she had witnessed to memory so that she could relate them to Gobann on her return.

She had not quite worked out exactly where the battle had taken place before a wind rose in the west distracting her. Like a giant feather she was lifted higher on this breeze until she rose far above the grey clouds. Sianan could still hear Mawn calling to her in the distance but all she could see about her was the gaseous cloud tops. Not long after she had begun this flight she felt herself dropping toward the earth again at an alarming rate.

Stretched out below her when she emerged through the clouds was a wide expanse of white-capped water. She felt herself swinging forward toward a stretch of coastline far in the distance and for some reason that she never understood for she had never travelled beyond her native land, she recognised the place as Britain.

In the next instant Mawn was beside her. 'Where have you been?' he called. 'I've been searching for you.'

'I was with Murrough when he fell in a great battle,' she answered.

'Murrough is gone as well?' Mawn cried. 'Come with me quickly. Gobann is also in great danger.'

Sianan did not have a chance to find out any more details from her companion. Mawn whisked away in a flash toward the rocky coast. She caught up with him near a strange white building set in a snow-clogged landscape. When she reached him he was trying to force his way inside the white hall but to no avail.

'What are you doing?' she inquired. 'Where is Gobann?'

'The poet is over yonder,' Mawn indicated, 'trapped within the hill-fort with the other people of Dun Righ. We must stir the brothers into action. They may be able to save the situation.'

'What are you talking about?'

'The Saxons are attacking!' Mawn shouted.

'Gobann is in Teamhair,' Sianan insisted. 'He can't be in Britain at the same time. This is not happening yet. We are glimpsing the future.' She

419

grabbed his arm and found that she could grip it as if it were still made of flesh and blood.

Mawn paused, startled by the sensation of Sianan's touch. At that moment a man opened the door of the stone house but it was clear that he could not see either of them. The stranger pulled the cowl over his head to cover himself against the frosty wind and Sianan noted that the back of the fellow's head was shaved in the fashion of a Roman monk.

'These are Christians!' she gasped. 'We must be careful.'

'It's no use, I can't get their attention,' Mawn cried.

'Never mind. Take me to Gobann. Maybe he'll recognise us.'

Mawn turned toward the hill-fort, speeding off like a spark rising from a fireplace. Sianan could only hope that he would not go too far before she caught up with him. When she located him again he was floating above a ruined village built at the top of an enormous enclosed earth fortification. The whole complex was much larger than Teamhair though the defences were a great deal simpler in their design. The first thing that Sianan noticed was that the thatch roof of almost every building within the enclosure was on fire. Darting among the flaming houses were warriors whose manner and dress were instantly recognisable to her. Saxons.

Men, women and children were desperately striving to keep out of the way of the marauders as they dodged between the buildings.

Mawn suddenly dived earthward to end up beside the body of a man dressed in a long blue robe. Sianan noticed that the fellow had a large pillow made of Raven feathers supporting his head but it took her a few seconds to identify him. It was Gobann. His face had been badly cut and bruised but his hair was cut in the fashion of a Druid and besides she would have recognised his harping hands anywhere.

'What is happening?' Sianan cried, confused. 'Why did the master come to Britain?'

'I am not sure. But it seems that he was staying here when the Saxons raided this place catching all the warriors unawares.'

Gobann opened his eyes. It was obvious that he saw them there. 'I thought I sent you away, you foolish lad! You've brought Sianan back with you! All is lost! You must run now while you still can. Before you are taken by the enemy.' Then their master coughed and closed his eyes again. 'Find your way to Declan's house,' Gobann murmured. 'He's the only one who can help you now.'

'We must do as he says,' Sianan insisted, still confused. This all seemed so real to her. How could it be the effects of future-sight? She had never heard of anyone sharing their visions with a companion. Then a thought came to her. 'There is something about this place that I do not understand,' she said.

'There are many things happening that I do not understand,' Mawn replied.

'Our initiation is taking place at Beltinne,' Sianan observed, 'and yet the ground here is covered in thick snow as if it were the season of Samhain. This must be happening in another time.'

'Let us go,' Mawn suggested. 'Let's return to Teamhair if we can.'

'Yes,' Sianan agreed. 'I don't like it here and I do not want to risk being betrayed by Christians so I would rather not go to Declan's house.' She concentrated all her thoughts on her home and on the mound of testing, quelling her senses until she could feel that some shift was taking place. The change that occurred did not feel as though it was a very great one but something dramatic had happened that made Sianan feel much more relaxed about her surroundings. When she turned her attention outwards once more and listened again to her senses, she found that she was not inside the mound of testing but in the great hall of a magnificent feasting chamber.

Mawn was seated beside her on a massive oak chair that would have been big enough to fit two more of their kind. Such a seat was obviously not intended for the likes of them. Innumerable candles lit the room lending a golden glow to the walls, which were cleverly constructed so that streams of water cascaded over their crystal-clear surface. At the bottom of each wall the water collected in deep gutters that channelled the flood back out through a sewer.

The ceiling of this chamber was very high, reaching into a darkness which barely concealed a host of small, winged creatures. Sianan could hear them flapping about as they darted between their perches but she could only glimpse them.

Sianan recognised that this was very much like the vision she had in the broch, except that this hall was a much grander version of the one in the tower. A fireplace was erected in the centre of the room with a brass grate for cooking. A huge cauldron, decorated with many inlaid figures and designs, was hanging on the grate. The fire had obviously not been lit for a long time; the coals were cold and lifeless.

No sooner had Sianan noticed the dead fire than a figure pushed his way into the chamber through an opening in the wall near Mawn. The flowing waters parted for this peculiar creature who would have been no more than four feet tall and was completely covered in snowy white fur. At almost the same time another creature appeared from a similar opening to the right of Sianan. This figure was also covered in fur though it was jet black in colour, and it had more of a rounded head than the other.

Both figures approached Mawn and Sianan, walking with great solemnity, each bearing a shining brass box before them. As soon as the figures were in front of the two initiates they halted, faced their guests and flipped open their boxes.

The creature that stood before Sianan looked exactly like a large black cat that had taken human form to stride on two legs. Its eyes were long yellow slits that blinked with double eyelids. Mawn's attendant, however, had the form of a silver-white stag whose horns had grown to become intertwined like the knotted patterns carved on a standing stone. Both of the strange animals sported human hands and feet that sprouted tufts of fur.

'I have never seen a white stag before,' Mawn remarked.

'I have never met a Wanderer,' the attendant snapped, much to Mawn's surprise.

Sianan reached into the little brass box that was held out before her. Inside there was a tiny red berry which she removed to examine more closely. Mawn found an identical fruit in his box. Once the attendants had delivered their gifts they withdrew through another door about forty steps in front of the great chair and beyond the central fire.

'Rowan berries.' Almost before the words had left Sianan's mouth the fireplace sprang into life and flames licked the ceiling, causing all the creatures living near the roof to flutter about noisily in a panic. Another great racket rose behind Mawn and Sianan, but when they turned to look they could see nothing stirring.

They looked at each other questioningly then turned around to face the fireplace again. It was then that both initiates realised that the whole chamber had suddenly filled with people. Musicians, dancers, ladies dressed in fine long gowns, fierce warriors, servants carrying platters of food, guards, young women with deep blue eyes and old folk who, despite the weight of many seasons, moved in a remarkably sprightly fashion. The whole company danced through the room chattering, laughing and singing.

Sianan recognised the music as being exactly the same as that which she heard playing inside the tower at Bally Cahor. A dozen little bells rang out the time as a piper and bodhran player performed a formal set piece. Jugs of drink were passed around the chamber, thrust energetically from one hand to another, meeting many dry mouths. Eventually a wooden jug was handed to Mawn.

He hesitated for a second before placing his lips against the rim of the finely turned container. The brew inside smelled earthy and sweet like ale that has been allowed to mature a little too long. The odour filled Mawn with a burning thirst. He tipped the jug back to let the liquid drain into his throat but before it reached his parched tongue the vessel was knocked out of his hands to land shattered by the wall. At the same time the whole chamber went silent. Everyone stopped what they were doing to look at Mawn.

Mawn was stunned that the jug had been so violently thrust away from him but he was more shocked to find an enormous man standing before him with a massive bronze axe in his hand. 'Did your teacher warn you not to drink of the brews nor eat of the food while you are in this place?'

Mawn could remember someone saying something like that to him once but he couldn't recall if it had been his teacher Gobann or some other Druid. The lad sat dumbfounded before the giant, unable to answer.

Sianan, on the other hand, recognised the giant immediately. 'You are the king who I met at the broch,' she said, 'and who I saw at the battle between Murrough and the Christians.'

'I am,' the king admitted. 'And you are the two who will wander the eternal Road as we do. Welcome to our Beltinne festival. I have brought a coal from Teamhair to light our hearth. This feast is being celebrated in your honour.'

'Now perhaps we may have a dance together,' Sianan said hopefully.

'It is not permitted that you and I should dance together tonight. Rather it is Mawn who should dance with you to our music.' The giant clapped his hands and by some magic the two initiates were instantly standing in the middle of the floor facing each other. The king sat back on his great chair to watch.

Sianan reached out to Mawn and clasped his hand. Where this simple act would have been impossible at the start of their journey it had now become as easy to them as talking. Mawn delighted in the tingling sensation that crept up his arm from where their fingers touched, numbing him as far as his shoulder.

They stood for a few moments as the piper filled his pipes and began his wild tune. The music seemed to take control of their feet as the two of them began to whirl around the room in a jig. They passed through the thronging crowd as many well-wishers patted their backs or passed on helpful snippets of advice.

An old man almost bent double whispered, 'Row with the oar that is within your grasp.'

Another fellow who seemed youthful but spoke with an ancient crackling voice said, 'The youngest thorn is the sharpest.' He was soon pushed out of the way by two young women who spoke in unison, 'Speak but little and speak it well.' Then the whole room erupted into a cacophony of Otherworld wisdom, well-intentioned but bewildering.

'Don't show your teeth till you're ready to bite,' one fellow yelled. Another tiny man boomed in a deep voice, 'The sweetest mouth is the silent one.' Mawn began to laugh at the irony of that proverb coming from one who could not help being heard.

The piper picked up the tempo of his dance so that his notes skipped across the chamber like flat stones cast at the surface of a lake. Without warning, all the people in the room took up the jig at once, forming a whirlpool of surging bodies all vying with each other to be closest to the two visitors. The whirlpool became an enormous spiral with two arms that reached to the walls of the chamber. Sianan was spinning around in the centre rapidly becoming dizzy though she was enjoying the hearty dance.

As she whirled around to catch Mawn's arm through hers she caught a glimpse, out of the corner of her eye, of an old woman who stood still, silent and alone at the edge of the crowd.

There was something that immediately disturbed Sianan about this woman. Every time Mawn swung her around towards that side of the room Sianan could see the hag laughing. Her face was grey like candle wax that has been re-used too many times; her eyes were like those of eels—dark and empty.

Sianan was fascinated. When she came round the room on her next little circuit she searched for the hag but the old woman seemed to have disappeared.

The next thing that caught her attention was Mawn crying at the top of his lungs, 'Stop! Leave me alone.' The hag had caught hold of him and was tugging at his long golden hair. It was then that Sianan noticed that the old woman had but one arm and she suddenly remembered the hag who had been with the redcaps at the battle.

In an instant the old woman caught hold of Sianan's black hair also and was screeching a few words into her ear. 'The oldest Gael that ever lived found death at last.'

Mawn shrieked again but rather than heeding his distress the dancers seemed to take it as a signal to pick up more speed. Without warning a voice boomed out across the assembly, shaking the floor with its intensity. Abruptly everyone in the hall went deathly still and quiet. 'Enough!' the giant ordered. 'They have had enough.'

Mawn and Sianan were lifted up by the crowd and deposited on the edge of the great chair again as the giant stood to make room for them. 'It is far easier to scatter seed than gather the harvest,' the man-creature said finally. 'Our blessings go with you, Wanderers. Call on me in your need.'

The door at the end of the hall swung open as the crowd parted, indicating that they should leave. Sianan searched quickly around the chamber but could not see the one-armed hag anywhere.

Before either of them had moved from their seat Sianan could sense that she was taking the spirit form again. The next thing she knew she was floating down from the chair to skim across the floor.

'We do not know your name,' Mawn realised. 'How are we to call on you if we don't know your name?'

The entire hall erupted in raucous laughter. In the next instant the candles went out and everyone disappeared. 'I am Aenghus Og,' a voice boomed, 'and there is a price to be paid for our goodwill.'

The Wanderers passed out of the chamber then and into the light. The stone door shut heavily behind them.

When Sianan tried to get her bearings she reckoned that they were high above the white-rimmed hill known to the Gaels as the House of Aenghus Og. Teamhair was outlined on the horizon to the south and they were being drawn back to the mound of testing. Sianan was dizzy and tired from the ordeal, which is probably why she made the mistake of assuming that it was ended.

It was immediately apparent to Enda Censelach that Caitlin was very ill. Besides the unusual paleness of her skin, her eyes were surrounded by dark circles and her tongue had a yellowish tinge.

'What are you doing out here on your own, queen? Do you not know that there are savage Christian warriors about?'

'I came to find Murrough,' she answered still dazed. 'I was afraid that the Roman would kill him.'

'I will get you back to Teamhair,' Censelach announced, 'but first I must tie our prisoner down to the back of your horse for the journey.' Enda stripped the warrior's cloak off him and threw it in the dust at the side of the road. Then he took off his waist belt and bound the man's hands over his head. In desperation he took a strap from the saddle gear to tie the Christian's feet together. When that was done he stood up to ask Caitlin to give him a hand in lifting the Christian over the back of the mount, but he was amazed to find her kneeling by the side of the road with the foreigner's cloak held close to her breast.

'What's the matter, lady? What ails you?'

'It is a fine cloak,' she muttered. 'I have found him at last. I knew he would come back one day. By the blessed goddess Brigid he has returned.'

'What are you talking about?' Enda snapped. 'There is nothing fine about that filthy rag. Who is this man who has returned?'

'The Roman. The one who led the assault on Rathowen,' she replied. 'The one who hanged Fintan by nails from a tree. The one who made the Saxons cut down the holy Quicken.'

'Where is he?' Censelach asked, confused. Now he was deeply concerned that Caitlin might be sinking into a semiconscious stupor.

'There,' she pointed to the warrior tied up on the ground. 'His name is Seginus Gallus and he has defied the High-King's banishment.'

The King of Laigin followed the line of her finger until his eyes fell on the Christian. Caitlin the Queen of Munster was sitting in the dirt weeping quietly to herself and babbling about some stranger who had cut down the Quicken. Enda looked from the Christian to the queen and back again. It had been a hard night. He had lost a battle and a fellow king. He had not slept at all. Now he was afraid that he had a mad queen on his hands. 'I must get you back to Teamhair,' he announced finally.

'Not without Murrough,' she replied.

'The King of Munster fell to an arrow.'

'He is not dead!' she cried at the top of her lungs.

Enda leapt at her to close her mouth. If the Christian sentries heard her making a din they would be down from the hilltop in a very short time. 'Be quiet!' he whispered, trying to calm her. 'You must be quiet or they will find us.'

She settled down a little bit then, turning her head as if she could hear something that was beyond the range of Enda's ears. 'A company of horse warriors is approaching,' she said quietly.

Enda froze where he stood but if there were soldiers approaching he could not hear any evidence of it. The King of Laigin was now more convinced than ever that Caitlin was terribly ill, then he heard a far-off call followed by the dim sounds of war gear rattling as a company of horse approached from the direction of Teamhair.

'There is nowhere for us to run, Lady Caitlin. So we will wait here and hope that it is a contingent of the High-King's warriors come to assist us.'

Caitlin did not acknowledge Enda. She just sat holding the old cloak close to her, allowing her memories of the battle at Rathowen to return to her in a flood of grief.

TWENTY-SIX

Leoghaire and Cathach spurred their horses on when they saw that it was Enda Censelach waving to them in the distance. The forty or so mounted warriors in the war party packed closely around their leaders offering what protection they could. No arrow would penetrate this human shield. Seventy foot-soldiers in the company ran as fast as their legs could carry them to keep up with the advance guard. A great cloud of dust was stirred up by the High-King's relief force as they passed by.

'The Christians will know that Leoghaire has arrived!' Censelach observed.

The High-King dismounted as soon as he spotted Caitlin sitting on the road beside the King of Laigin. 'Thank the Danaans you are safe! Queen Caitlin, whatever possessed you to hide out here alone!' he cried.

'Murrough sent a message to me,' she answered calmly, 'that the Roman had returned to Eirinn.'

Cathach, who had stayed in his saddle, looked down at her with pity. 'She was unwell when she arrived in Teamhair but now I fear she has worn herself out. We must hope that the Danaan Druids can cure this ailment of hers.'

Leoghaire turned his attention to Enda, now urgently asking for an explanation. 'What happened? How could so small a force of soldiers defeat so many Gaels?'

'Treachery,' Censelach replied, 'and surprise. They stayed hidden until we were almost on top of them. Early on I saw Murrough fall to an enemy arrow. After that I led my troops as best I could but was separated from the main group. I tried to find the surviving warriors but discovered that there were Christian soldiers swarming through the whole area. I thought it best to lay low for the night. This morning I came across Caitlin being attacked by this fellow.' Enda gave Seginus a kick to signal his disdain for the Christian.

The Roman stirred groggily, sitting up as best he could. The sight of so many Gaelic warriors surrounding him sobered him up quickly. He tried to stand but Enda pushed him over again before he had the chance to rise.

'You did not come to Murrough's aid?' Cathach asked.

'I could not. There was too much confusion and too many arrows flying.'

'So what then became of the King of Munster?'

'I have no knowledge of what happened after I was split from my warriors.'

'You have killed him,' Caitlin muttered. 'You are a coward.'

All the warriors present fell silent, some averting their eyes from the King of Laigin. The queen had spoken the thought that had crossed all their minds but which none of them would have dared give voice to.

'I saved your life, Queen Caitlin,' Censelach reminded her. 'If Murrough fell it was because he was not skilled enough as a warrior to survive the skirmish. I had nothing to do with his death.'

'Enough!' Cathach insisted. 'We will search for the King of Munster after we have dealt with this

Patricius and his soldiers who dress as monks. Who is this fellow you have tied up?'

'He is Seginus Gallus,' Caitlin replied. 'He was one of the Quicken killers, and a follower of the tyrant Palladius.'

'That was a lucky catch, Enda,' Cathach observed. 'His capture adds a slight sheen to your otherwise tarnished image.' The King of Laigin was careful not to show any sign that he acknowledged the implied insult.

'Two warriors to help the queen into her saddle!' Leoghaire ordered sharply as he mounted his own war horse again. 'We will bring Caitlin and the prisoner with us. It is likely there are more Christians lurking hereabouts. I will not risk her safety by leaving her in the open. Enda Censelach, you will take up the rear guard of this column. There is no-one I know who could do that job so well.'

'Careful,' Cathach whispered, 'do not stir him up too much. You may have a need of him one day.'

Leoghaire smiled at his advisor, acknowledging the warning. 'May the ocean freeze over before that day dawns,' he breathed so that only the Druid heard him.

Cathach and the High-King spurred their horses to ride on ahead of the column while Caitlin was helped onto her horse. Seginus had his legs unbound then he was fastened by a long rope to the straps of Enda's saddle for the walk back to Slané.

'This may be the last opportunity that we have to speak openly with one another. There is much for you to remember,' Cathach stated when they were far enough ahead of the others that they would not be overheard. 'You must not argue too much with Patricius. It is my task to challenge the intruder. This Christian will try to drive a wedge between us. Do not bite too quickly at the bait he sets for you. Show him your strength by all means. Let him know that you are not to be trifled with, but deal with him as if you already know much about the Christian doctrine and do not object to its principles.'

'I have been a good student,' the High-King stated. 'You would be proud of me. The Christian tales are well known to me. Origen has explained much to me.'

'I am also sure that Mona was a good choice for you. Doubtless she has helped see to your education,' the old Druid smiled. 'I told you that there would be no need of Druid tricks for you to win her. There is only the planting of little seeds which may grow each day as we care for them. Now you must nurture the sapling so that it becomes a strong tree. No matter what else happens you must play out our strategy to the very end.'

'As if it were only a contest of the Brandubh I was competing in. In fact, I am gambling the whole future of the five kingdoms of Eirinn,' Leoghaire observed.

'The land of Eirinn and the Brandubh are linked together in many subtle ways that you and I cannot even begin to comprehend. You are the High-King. Much of what comes to pass in this land relies on what moves you decide to make. I have only this one last piece of advice. In the Brandubh it is often better to skirt around your enemy, avoiding confrontation until he is blocked into a corner and unable to retaliate. If you capture too many of his pieces too early in the match, you give him less troops to worry about and more room in which to manoeuvre.'

'I am not sure that I will be able to carry this through without you to guide me.'

Cathach turned his face. 'Gobann will be at your side for a little while after I am gone. However, he is not destined to be your advisor. That duty will fall eventually to Patricius. For the time being the Druid Council will supply you with a Brehon judge. Trust no-one other than Gobann, Murrough, Caitlin and Síla. But if anyone, including any of them, clings too closely to the old ways or openly opposes the adoption of the Christian doctrines, they must be swiftly declared outlaw. Your adoption of the Christian ways will give the Druid Council an excuse to object. This may stir unrest in some of the chieftains. In order for Patricius to believe that a real resistance was exerted to his ways you may need to act at times contrary to your conscience. You must be stern and unshakeable if the plan is to succeed. Anyone who criticises your reforms must be dealt with severely. Others who pose a threat, like Enda Censelach, can easily be thwarted so that they have no opportunity to nip the flower in the bud.'

'And what of the Wanderers?' Leoghaire queried.

'Their fate is also, to a large extent, in your hands. Murrough may be their guardian and sympathetic to our aims but he is nevertheless as potentially dangerous to the cause as Enda. The King of Munster is too headstrong and quick to anger. He often draws attention to himself unnecessarily. If we find him still alive it might be a good idea to think of some excuse to send him off on an embassy before his bold unbridled tongue gets the better of him. Eirinn could become a very dangerous place for the Wanderers if Patricius even gets the slightest hint of our plans. Murrough and his charges might be much better off if they were concealed somewhere in the kingdom of the Dal Araidhe.'

Leoghaire took all of this in though he could not imagine a situation where he would have to send his most loyal and reliable subordinate king away from Eirinn. The mounted guards caught up with them a few moments later, surrounding the two men like a curtain so they were unable to discuss the subject any further. Within a short while the horse warriors had reached the foot of the hill of Slané. Leoghaire rode about busily organising the advance toward the hall.

When the foot soldiers arrived the High-King sectioned them off in groups of three teams each made up of three warriors. Every cluster of nine fighters was part of a larger company made up of three units just like the first. This gave the High-King four companies of twenty-seven warriors. He decided to send two foot companies around to the side of the hill to climb up and outflank the enemy. Of the other two, one was partly foot soldiers, all of whom were bowmen, and partly warriors on horseback. He marched this company immediately off up the road toward the summit. The mounted troopers rode behind Enda Censelach, Caitlin and Leoghaire. The footmen led. Seginus was still bound behind Enda's horse.

It was midday by the time the whole army assembled near the top of the hill. The Roman centurion had by that time formed his legionnaires up for battle in front of the hall, standing in line as if ready to receive a charge. At first there was no sign of Patricius or the other members of his party.

Leoghaire and Cathach rode out together to the front of the column, daring the Christians to run out at them. The chief Druid stopped beside the fire that Patricius had lit. Turning in his saddle he called back to the High-King's army.

'These flames were kindled contrary to tradition and the laws of Eirinn.' The old man waited a few moments then faced the Roman soldiers. 'Who is it dares to mock the hospitality of Leoghaire and the customs of this land?'

The Christian soldiers stood fast with grim faces. All of them expected to perish in a Gaelic attack but not before they had done some damage themselves. None among the Romans moved or made a sound.

'Who dares bring war to our country?'

Still no-one spoke from the enemy lines.

Cathach turned to the Gaelic army again and waved his hand toward the fire. 'Put it out!'

Instantly five warriors rushed out of the ranks kicking at the flames and covering the coals with earth. The air filled with smoke from the smothered embers and amidst that smoke Patricius appeared, emerging from the hall adorned in the full vestments of a bishop. The Roman ranks parted to allow him through. Tullia followed carrying the Gospels open to show the word to the heathen. Secondinus was beside her bearing a casket and a silver cross.

Even Seginus who should have been used to this sort of spectacle was taken aback by the courageous gesture. Patricius had not shown anyone the vestments he intended to wear at this first meeting; they were a complete surprise to everyone in the party. The bishop was draped in the white robe of a Roman senator, the edges picked out in dark red embroidery. On his head he wore a tall two-pointed hat similar to the one that Julius of Nantes had sported, except this one was pure white with senatorial red trimming. Seginus remembered that this new style was called a mitre. To complete the magnificent picture Patricius held his staff in one hand and a censer full of wafting incense in the other. His beard was combed and his boots washed clean of travel dirt.

Cathach eyed the bishop with a certain amount of admiration. 'He knows how to put on a good show for his followers,' the Druid whispered to Leoghaire.

Behind the bishop and his two attendants came two men, whom Seginus recognised as Darach and Mog, bearing a body on a makeshift stretcher. When they were in front of the Roman soldiers the bishop halted and the two servants laid their burden down, withdrawing quickly again to the safety of the hall.

Patricius faced the Gaelic warriors waiting for some word of challenge. It was Leoghaire who spoke up. 'Lay down your weapons and submit to the will of the High-King of Eirinn.'

Patricius looked up at Leoghaire speaking to him in the language of the Gaels. 'Are you the High-King?'

'I am. And this is my chief advisor, Cathach mac Croneen.'

'I am called Patricius Sucatus,' the bishop announced without acknowledging the Druid. 'I have been commissioned by Pope Celestine to answer personally the letters that you sent him regarding the misdeeds of his former envoy, Palladius the Unworthy. The Holy Father has charged me to bring the word of God to you and to help those Christians already living in your kingdom to follow the Roman example. To that end I have been ordained as bishop of this land and legate of the Empire.'

'Eirinn has dealt with one bishop already,' Cathach jibed, 'and that was one too many. You have come here uninvited and misdirected. Go back to your master. Tell him that the people of this land do not want to hear the word of your Roman God.'

'Before I go on I have something to present to you to prove my goodwill. King Murrough of Munster was found wounded this morning after the unfortunate fight between my troops and his warriors. I have removed an arrow bolt from his chest and treated the wound as best I could. I wish now to return him to his kindred.'

'How bad is the injury?' Leoghaire asked.

'With proper care he will live.'

Caitlin ignored the two men. She dismounted, running to the stretcher where Murrough lay. The King of Munster was still unconscious so she remained at his side kneeling in the dust brushing his hair with her hand until two of the High-King's men came to take him to the rear of the lines.

'The Pope has ordered me,' Patricius continued, 'to examine the doings of the former bishop Palladius so that a fitting punishment may be devised for him. It is in your interest that I be allowed to pursue my investigations unhindered.'

'If that is your true purpose in coming here, then why do you need a small army to protect you?' Cathach asked. 'It seems to me that you have already proved how many philosophies you share with Palladius. He too brought a dishonourable war to Eirinn. There are common folk in mourning today for the cruel hand that you dealt their kin.'

'The soldiers in my retinue were meant to be protecting me as I crossed the treacherous territories that lie between here and Ravenna. I did not sanction this action and I am ashamed that it came to pass. My bodyguards acted without justification or orders from me in attacking your envoys this morning. I can assure you that the two men responsible for this atrocious bloodbath will be brought to justice in Rome.'

'They will submit to the High-King's word!' Cathach bellowed. 'You are under his jurisdiction now. Surrender them to us immediately.'

Patricius paused a moment, unsure if the High-King would be likely to put the centurion to death. 'What assurance can you give that they will not be harmed?'

'Their punishment will be decided once they are properly adjudged!' Cathach stormed.

Leoghaire cut in over the chief Druid. 'The only assurance I am willing to give is that you will suffer if they are not surrendered immediately.'

'I will not order any of my followers to surrender themselves up to certain death,' the bishop stated.

'I will not waste my time squabbling with law-breakers,' Leoghaire stormed. 'I have an argument that I am sure you will listen to.' He turned his horse to face his bowmen. 'Make your arrows ready to fly!' he called.

Tatheus did not waste another second. With two of his soldiers he rushed out to drag the bishop, Tullia and Secondinus back behind his troops. Once they were safely behind the Romans, Tatheus ordered the men to form a shield wall. The soldiers were still linking shields when Leoghaire gave the order for his warriors to loose their arrows.

The shafts flew high into the air to fall almost directly down on top of the enemy, striking many Romans on the shoulders or the head and clattering loudly against body armour. However, despite the deadly flight of arrows, not one Roman fell to a Gaelic bowman. When the arrow storm passed Tatheus looked about him confused. Such an attack at such close range should have been devastating.

He snatched one of the shafts from the soldier who stood beside him to examine it closely.

'This is the only assurance that I will give,' Leoghaire called out. 'The next flight of arrows that crosses between us will not be deliberately blunted so that they bounce off your soldiers harmlessly.'

Patricius pushed his way through the soldiers to stand out in front once more. He was shaken from the show of force. Two of the blunted shafts had struck him, one knocking his mitre from his head the other hitting him in the back to bruise his shoulder blade. 'I have no wish to fight you,' he called out. 'I have come as an emissary of peace!'

'Then show your good faith,' the High-King answered. 'Surrender the wrongdoers.'

Patricius signalled for Tatheus to step forward. 'This is the centurion of my guard. He commanded the fight this morning. His co-accused is a priest and a member of my personal entourage. I have not been able to locate the man. Since he has obviously decided to avoid having to answer for his actions I will stand to receive punishment in his place.'

'You need not go that far,' Enda Censelach called out. 'Even the most slippery of eels are easily caught in a strong Gaelic net.' The King of Laigin spurred his horse on to a gallop, dragging Seginus off his feet and through the middle of the now lifeless fire pit. Enda slit the rope that tied the man to the back of his mount to leave his prisoner lying face down in the ashes.

'Take your soldiers and your holy men and leave this land. You are not welcome here,' Cathach commanded. 'You have broken the sacred bond of hospitality. You have tainted the Beltinne festival with spilled blood. Go now and do not return or I will call on the four elements to pursue you and the gods of my people to destroy you.'

Patricius calmly placed the censer that he still held on the ground at his feet. Then he walked towards the High-King's horse. 'Have you nothing to say in this matter, Leoghaire? Or does this magician always speak for you?'

'Do not interfere in matters that you do not understand,' the High-King answered solemnly.

'I bring you the gift of the word of God,' the bishop continued. 'Will you not even hear what I have to say before you send me back to the Pope?'

'I know the story of Christ well enough. Origen the wise, of the city of Alexandria, has lived among us since before I was first enthroned. He has told me of the ways of the Christians.'

'He is a false believer, a disciple of Satan. His words are tainted with foul lies.'

'He is a great healer,' Leoghaire insisted, 'and an honest man.'

'The Devil has granted him a little power in order that he may attempt to enchant you. He is a heretic and a blasphemer as are all of his kind. Satan has sent him here to bring about your downfall and prevent the spread of the true Word of Christ.'

'He has always been a steadfast friend of the High-King,' Cathach cut in. 'You are not endearing yourself to anyone in these kingdoms by insulting him.'

Patricius turned to the Druid, obviously tiring of his interjections. 'You are no better than that false priest from Alexandria. There is nothing godly about your words and actions. You and your wicked fellowship have kept the people of this island in the dark shadow of ignorance for far too long. But I can see clearly how you have managed to achieve it since the High-King seems afraid to contradict you. Leoghaire is not the real ruler of Eirinn. This country is controlled by the Druid sorcerers who bend him to their will while they let him think he rules them.'

'You are a foreigner here and so may be forgiven for not understanding our ways.' Cathach barked with contempt.

'I understand your ways well enough,' Patricius laughed. 'You are a member of a privileged class who feed off the sweat of the poor and skim the cream off the milk of the nobility. Your gods have no more substance than steam rising from a cooking pot. They are concocted out of hot air bubbling up from a dull bronze container. In the lands where Christ is venerated, kings are assured that their office is not encroached upon by meddlers and conjurors. Superstitious charlatans such as yourself are no match for the Christian God in his majesty.'

'If your God is so great,' Cathach observed, 'why do you need twenty warriors standing behind you when you undertake his work?'

Patricius smiled, seeing the challenge clearly. 'Tatheus, withdraw your troops inside the hall until I summon you forth again.' The centurion reluctantly did as he was ordered, holding his tongue despite his misgivings. As the soldiers smartly filed off to enter the door, the bishop looked directly at Cathach. 'There you are. I will not ask you to remove your warriors for I have no fear of them.'

'It is not your place to request the withdrawal of our warriors,' the Druid reminded him. 'You are a guest in this kingdom.'

'You are afraid of me,' Patricius stated confidently. 'Your monstrous redcapped servants could not stand against the word of the Gospel. Neither can you.'

Cathach did not flinch when the bishop mentioned the redcaps, though he was intrigued that Patricius had somehow encountered some of the Faery folk. 'You are displaying your ignorance, Roman. Your folk seem to delight in carrying your arrogance proudly sewn on your tunics for everyone to see. You seem to think that just because your armies long ago trampled all across the earth in conquest you are the only inheritors of truth in this world. You have never looked beyond the end of your own long nose, Roman. You wear the insignia of a dead empire, you worship the effigy of a tortured man and you bring death to any who do not submit to your King of Peace.' Cathach slipped nimbly off the back of his horse, grabbing his staff from one of his Druid attendants as he did so. 'It was Roman soldiers like those cowering in that hall that nailed your God to a tree.'

Cathach raised the long wooden staff above his head, charging at the bishop in an attempt to bring the instrument down hard on the Christian's head. Patricius was taken aback by this sudden attack but held his own staff out firmly to deflect the blow. The Druid struck and the bishop easily knocked Cathach's weapon aside. For a moment the two men stood facing each other eye to eye, then Patricius noticed something very strange about his opponent. The old man was sweating profusely; his skin was grey and clammy and his eyes yellow where they should have been white.

'Your God may be powerful but it would be better if he lent you a breastplate to wear like you issue to your soldiers,' Cathach jeered. 'Now let him assail me. Let me see if your Roman God is skilled enough to knock the life out of a Gael.' The Druid shut his eyes, lifting his face to the sky. Waiting.

'God has chosen the Romans to make retribution for the crimes of their empire,' Patricius stated. 'Do not challenge him, I beg you, or he will surely strike you dead.'

Nothing happened.

'Your spells have no power,' Cathach mocked. 'Your all-powerful God on high does not have the strength or the will to harm even an old man.'

Patricius knew that he had to do something, though he did not want to see Cathach harmed. That could cause insurmountable problems. He realised, however, that if he did not at least try to challenge the Druid it could be interpreted as weakness on his part. The bishop summoned up all his courage, recalling a Gaelic invocation that he had heard during his captivity. Suddenly he thought that this would be the best way to present any resistance; by using the very methods that the poets practised. Patricius turned the heathen theme of the poem over in his mind until it became a prayer that took on a life of its own.

'I stand this day,
Supported by the strength of Heaven,
Light of the Sun,
Radiance of the Moon,
Warmth of Fire,
Depth of the Sea,
Firmness of the Earth,
Purity of the Breeze,
May Christ shield me today,
From poison, from burning,
From drowning, from wounding,
From the invocations of the false prophets,
From the lying words of heretics.
I stand today,
Strengthened by the prayers of the Patriarchs,

The words of the Apostles,
The actions of the Righteous,
The deaths of the Holy Martyrs.
Christ with me, Christ before me, Christ
    behind me.
In acknowledgment of the one true God,
Who created all things.'

When he had finished speaking, Patricius turned his attention back to Cathach, detecting that the muscles on the old man's face had drooped slightly on the left side.

'That is the only breastplate that I need,' the bishop announced. 'Faith in God and humility in my actions.'

Cathach still did not make the slightest move. It was almost as if the Druid had been struck dumb. The bishop recalled that a priest at Lerins had suffered a seizure which had effectively paralysed the left-hand side of his body. It was well-known that these attacks could kill their victims outright. Cathach's stance reminded Patricius of that priest who had survived the seizure. Nevertheless, he suspected that the Druid had chosen to enter a trance-like state for some reason.

Not wishing to take the chance that the old man was summoning demons the bishop made the sign of the Cross before the Druid in the hope that he would awaken from his trance. Almost as if the old man were reacting to the blessing, the life began visibly to drain out of Cathach. The Druid clasped hold of his staff in an attempt to stay on his feet but it was plain to Patricius that the old man's heart had stopped beating. Cathach smiled incongruously at his opponent before his lips turned a dark blue. They parted slightly as the chief Druid of Eirinn teetered forward to land face first in the dirt at the Christian bishop's feet.

Leoghaire and Enda were off their horses in a flash, but by the time they reached his side Cathach's two attendant Druids were already intoning solemn verses over the still body. It was almost as though they had expected that Cathach would pass away when he confronted Patricius.

Leoghaire was not as distressed by the sudden catastrophe as Enda was. The High-King had known in the back of his mind that Cathach was preparing to die. Censelach collapsed on the ground beside the chief Druid's body in an act of deep respect, averting his eyes from the corpse.

The High-King stood tall facing Patricius. If the bishop had made the slightest move then Leoghaire would probably not have hesitated to strike him down. It took him a few minutes to calm down enough so that he could tell himself that Patricius had not been responsible for Cathach's death. The old man had been ill for some time, he told himself over and over. Leoghaire was sure that Cathach had more than an inkling about the nature, time and manner of his own passing. That was why he had made certain that the High-King had understood what course of action should follow after this meeting was concluded.

Caitlin left Murrough when the news passed down the troops to where they were. She approached the body to join with the two other Druids in singing their master's soul away. The assembled warriors dismounted from their horses or lay their spears on the ground beside them. Every Gael touched his forehead to the ground in respect for Cathach's passing from the world.

'He was my dear friend,' Leoghaire called out. 'The second counsellor to depart during my kingship. No other affairs of state will be discussed until the rites of passage are performed for him. There is nothing so pressing that it can draw me away from the side of Cathach.'

The High-King ordered Enda to prepare a bier for the Druid's body so that he could be carried back to Teamhair with ceremony befitting his rank. While that was being done Leoghaire spoke to Patricius. 'He was a greater man than you could ever aspire to be. He knew of your coming long before you were even aware of him. I know that it was not your God that killed him. It was merely old age.'

The bishop was about to protest this point but the High-King carried on speaking, not letting the Christian interrupt. 'You will pay him the honour he is due if you wish to remain in the land of Eirinn one more night. It may be that your faith has come here to supplant the old ways but it is my wish that for now you show respect for our traditions.'

'I will always respect your ancient laws where they are just,' Patricius agreed.

'In submission to me and in humble repentance for the deaths that have taken place here since the beginning of Beltinne, you will return with me to Teamhair. Your soldiers will bear the funeral cortege of the chief Druid on their shoulders from here to the citadel as an act of repentance. At the gates they will surrender all their weapons. Once that is done they will be confined to the fifth circle as my guests until I have accepted their contrition. The priest called Seginus Gallus will remain my prisoner until I have decided on a fitting punishment for him.'

'And myself?' Patricius asked. 'Am I to be your prisoner also?'

'I have a much more trying destiny in mind for you, bishop,' Leoghaire flashed. 'If you are to stay in this land you will have to win over the chieftains and kings. No matter what I want I must follow their bidding. It will not be easy for you to convince them of your worth. A great gap has been left by one of the wisest men who ever lived in Eirinn. You are going to have to help fill it.'

TWENTY-SEVEN

 awn grabbed Sianan by the hand before they got too close to Teamhair. 'Stop! There is something terribly wrong!' he cried desperately.

Sianan looked about her but she could not discern what had upset him. The hills and plains were the same as they had ever been. The ocean in the east and the woodlands to the west were unchanged. It was only when she turned her attention to the citadel itself that Sianan got a jolt. The ramparts had become low grass-covered earthen walls. The gates were gone altogether as were the wooden stakes that filled the ditches. The mound of testing had become a rocky hill with a whitethorn tree growing on top of it.

The dwelling places, the stables, the heroes halls, the Star of Poetry, the Grianan, the High-King's hall, they were all gone, reduced into the earth as though they had never existed. Sianan was so upset by this that she would not look on it any more. She willed herself away from this place. Mawn reluctantly followed her for he was secretly fascinated by what had happened at Teamhair.

When they were far away from the citadel Sianan let herself drop towards earth again near a river crossing. Mawn sat by the stream looking into the dark pool that was created by the man-made ford. A narrow track led off over a slight rise. Sianan set off to follow it. It led her quite soon to a ruined village, empty and devoid of any signs of life. The houses had no roofing, they were just burned-out shells.

She moved on to the end of the row of houses hoping to find someone about but it was not until she had just about given up hope that she noticed an old man leaning over to drink from a stone trough. Without hesitating she approached him, certain that he could not see her while she was in the spirit form.

To her surprise he lifted his head as she got near to him and greeted her by name. 'Sianan! How glad I am to see you.'

'Do I know you?' she replied cautiously.

'Have I changed so much?' he asked.

Sianan concentrated all her attention on the old man's facial features striving with all her might to remember where she had met him. He was definitely familiar to her but that could have been because he was dressed in the robes of a Druid. 'Are you a friend of my grandfather's?' she asked.

'You could say that,' he laughed and added with genuine sadness in his voice, 'I am sorry that you cannot see more clearly.'

'What do you want of me?'

'I just wanted to wish you well, my child, that's all. And apologise for not being able to wait around for you. You may call on me in your need,' he said and then he faded swiftly from view.

Mawn appeared as if from nowhere at that moment quite annoyed. 'Why didn't Cathach wait to speak with me?' he remarked.

It was not until then that Sianan realised that it had been her grandfather she had seen. 'I did not recognise him. There must be something wrong

with him. I must get back to Teamhair. Cathach
may be very ill.'

Mawn led the way as they rose up once more
high into the air to cast their gaze out over the
eastern ocean. They were high enough after a few
moments to be able to see Inis Mannan in the
distance out on the silvery sea. A large number of
dark shapes floating on the water between Eirinn
and the other island caught Mawn's attention.

'Let us get a closer look before we return. There
may be something important for us to learn here,'
he suggested.

They let the wind take them gently out over the
eastern ocean until they were directly above the
dark shapes. There was little doubt now that the
forms were those of Saxon longboats. 'I want to see
what their ships are like,' Sianan sighed, trying to
put her grandfather out of her mind. 'Let's go to
them for a while.'

When they landed on the deck of one vessel
Mawn curled up in disgust at what was presented
to them. On either side of the ship twenty wretched
prisoners were chained in two banks to heavy
wooden oars which they were forced to pull to
propel the boat through the calm sea. They had all
been severely treated, that much was plain, and
one or two of them were obviously near to death
from their ordeal. Sianan tried to reach out to one
woman but the poor soul was as oblivious to her
presence as she was to anything else around her.

Mawn began to pester his companion to leave.
'I do not like this place. There is death everywhere.'

Sianan could only agree. 'I would like to go
home now,' she admitted. 'I could sleep for a hundred winters after this journey.' She was just rising
up on the breeze again when something caught her

attention; a flash of coppery hair on a figure huddled at the end of the boat.

Sianan could not be sure but there was something familiar about the green cloth that was wrapped about the woman's body. But Sianan was already drifting skyward when a name finally popped into her head.

'Feena!' she screamed.

Instantly the girl with the bright red hair stood up to look around her. 'Sianan!' she answered. 'I knew you would come.'

A large warrior easily three times the girl's size moved across the boat, slapping her unceremoniously to the deck before cursing her in his own tongue. Within seconds Sianan was far out of reach and sight of the ship. She could not come to her friend's aid but now at least she was certain that Feena was alive.

Nine Roman legionnaires with weapons sheathed carried the body of Cathach back to Teamhair at a brisk military pace. Before them rode Leoghaire, Patricius and Caitlin with all the mounted Gaelic warriors set around them. The foot soldiers brought up the rear carrying the wounded Murrough. Enda rode behind them, once more dragging Seginus Gallus.

Along the way remnants of Enda's original force rejoined the column so that by the time they came to the gates of the citadel there were nearly one hundred and fifty warriors in the procession. A rider had travelled on ahead of the column so that the Druid Council was ready to receive the body of their chieftain when they reached the citadel

453

gate. So it was that the lighting of the bone-fire was postponed until Cathach's body could be brought to the plain of testing.

Gobann was waiting with twenty other Druids at the outer gates when the army finally came into view just before sunset. The poet went out briefly to greet the High-King then he went immediately to check the corpse of the chief Druid. The entourage had only now to wait for the sun to sink below the horizon. It did not matter that they were carrying the body of an important dignitary, they still had to abide by the strict rule that no-one enter the citadel before dusk on this festival day.

Leoghaire was a little surprised at first that Gobann seemed so well-prepared for Cathach's passing. The High-King started to think that everyone else but he knew of the Druid's illness and that Cathach's impending death may have been deliberately kept secret from him. The poet did not acknowledge Patricius as he walked by him but the bishop seemed very interested in Gobann.

'Who is that man?' he asked Leoghaire.

'He is the chief druid of Munster and a poet of the Silver Branch. He is the next highest ranked Druid in the land after Cathach. He will take the chief Druid's place on the council for the time being.'

'And what of me? Will I not represent your Christian subjects?'

'The woman who is about to become my queen is a Christian. She will represent the followers of the Cross.'

Patricius was content to let the matter drop for the moment. 'Does this lady have a priest who resides in her household and performs the sacrament?'

'She does not.' Leoghaire clenched his teeth, reminding himself that this foreigner was not deliberately being disrespectful to Cathach by mentioning these things. 'I would be grateful if you would take up that post for the time being.'

'I beg your pardon?' exclaimed the bishop, surprised that the High-King would request him to perform such a task after all that had just happened.

'I do not interfere in her beliefs or those of my people. If she approves of you then the appointment will be confirmed.'

'For the moment I will not approach your queen. Instead I would beg that one of my company be allowed to visit her,' Patricius suggested, 'to minister to her faith and assure her that a bishop has been appointed to this land.'

'And to discover if Christians are really treated without prejudice in Eirinn,' Leoghaire added. 'You have my permission to send one of your people.'

Patricius called for Tullia, informing her of her mission while the company waited for the sun to set. When the bishop was sure that she understood what would be expected of her he thanked his God that she had been directed into his party. Patricius knew that she could prove more valuable to him now than a wagonload of evangelists.

The gates opened as the sky darkened. Cathach was laid on the back of a chariot drawn by two horses. This honour was accorded to him by the Hall of Warriors because he had started his life among their number only later taking to the Druid path.

The Roman soldiers surrendered their weapons to the gatekeeper, piling their swords, spears and armour inside one of the sentry towers. The doors to the tower were sealed after everything

455

was collected then Leoghaire inspected the locks. When that was done the High-King had the captain of the gate lead the foreigners to their lodging as guests in the fifth circle, making sure that they understood the nature of their confinement. 'Tell them, Bishop Patricius, that they are not at liberty for the time being to leave the fifth circle of the citadel. Any who attempt to depart will be dealt with swiftly.'

Patricius passed on the message, translating it into the secular Latin for Tatheus and his men. The bishop also added that he would expect them to follow the High-King's wishes to the letter and that any attempt at escape would likely risk the lives of everyone in the party.

Caitlin went with Murrough to the Star of Poetry where she hoped that the hospitality of the hall would be opened to him. She need not have been concerned whether the Druids would allow a warrior king to rest in their hall. Gobann had made all the arrangements as soon as he had been apprised of the situation. The poet was aware that both Caitlin and Murrough were going to have to be watched very carefully over the next few days. For that reason alone it would be better if they were lodged in the same place during their recovery.

Seginus Gallus and his two servants were locked in the other tower that overlooked the gates of the citadel. This was a place reserved for outlaws who could not be trusted with any degree of freedom within the seven circles of Teamhair. Leoghaire placed a permanent guard, supplied by the King of Laigin, on the tower. The sentry party consisted of nine warriors working in three watches so that there was never a moment when Seginus or his servants would be alone.

Enda Censelach retired to his hall where his daughter Mona was awaiting his return. When he told her all that had happened she left the hall of Laigin and went straight to see the High-King. As it turned out she never stayed in her father's hall in the citadel after that. Aware that she would have to be seen to have some independence from Enda now that her betrothal was announced, she took up lodgings in the Grianan of the womenfolk. This also meant that Tullia could visit with her or stay without her father's interference.

The preparations for Cathach's departure were already under way but Gobann insisted that it would be some time before all the rituals over the body were completed. Usually quite some space of time elapsed between the death of a counsellor and the burial rites. Every detail of the ceremony had to be checked and double-checked to ensure the chief Druid's smooth passage into the spirit world.

While they were waiting, Leoghaire made Patricius and Secondinus his guests at the hall of the High-King. The bishop had not even entered the hall before he started asking about the relevance of the Beltinne festival. Once it was explained to him he remarked that it was fitting for a people to celebrate their first meal in a new land. Patricius drew an analogy with the last supper that Christ presided over with his disciples. 'This was originally a feast time of similar importance to Christ's tribespeople. Nowadays, though, we mourn the death and celebrate the return of our Lord at the feast of the resurrection. It is a sad thing that Cathach was not baptised,' he added.

'Do you think so?' Leoghaire replied as they made their way past the door wardens.

'For he passed away having rejected the word of God. His spirit will be sent to Hell and tortured

457

for the rest of eternity. If he had not been so set against me, I am sure that he could have been sitting among the hosts of the righteous.'

'It is our belief that he is still present until his body is turned to ashes or the rites are completed and that after a period of time spent in rest his soul will return to this Earth in another form.'

'That sounds like something that an Arian from Alexandria might propose,' Patricius noted with suspicion.

'Nevertheless, our people held this belief many generations before the Christians first made contact with us. Arian or Catholic or Pelagian or Manichean; all your different sects seem to differ on exactly what takes place after death. Our customs tell us plainly and simply what becomes our souls.' Leoghaire took the cuaich from one of his attendants, handing the vessel directly to Patricius. 'The spirit does not die with the body,' he finished.

The bishop played out the protocol in full, taking a mouthful of mead from the cup. When he had swallowed the sweet honey wine he paused to examine the vessel. 'It is a source of constant wonder to me that a people with a rich vibrant culture, capable of creating such beautiful artifacts, could still be ignorant of so many things which the rest of the world takes for granted as truth.'

'We may not possess the greatest philosophers in the world, Patricius, but we have a rich land full of excellent craftspeople, musicians, poets and warriors. It is not our custom that men should be coerced into becoming soldiers when they are young as they still do in the old Roman province of Britain. Young men and women are free to choose their vocation here without hindrance from anyone. In this way they are in charge of their own destinies.'

'Does one such as Cathach make a decision early in life to take to the ways of the Druids?'

'The chief Druid was a famous warrior who fought alongside my grandfather, Niall of the Nine Hostages. The Druid Council considered him very worthy so that when he took to their ways he passed through the initiations quickly.'

'I am sorry that I was responsible for his death,' Patricius admitted.

Leoghaire sputtered, trying to stop himself laughing. Then he realised that the bishop was serious. 'He was an old man, already frail when he made the journey to Slané. How is it you think that you were responsible for his passing?'

'It was my prayer that brought the wrath of God down upon him, clearing him out of the way so that I could perform my tasks in this country unhindered.'

'You are fortunate to be on such good terms with your God,' Leoghaire replied, still unsure whether the Christian was totally serious. The High-King took the mead cup and sipped at the brew.

'I would like to put the unfortunate business of last night behind us,' Patricius remarked uncomfortably.

'I wish that we could. For the time being the Druid Council is unable to convene until they elect the chief Druid's replacement. It would not be fitting for me to make any pronouncements without consulting them.'

'The Holy Father Celestine has commissioned me to perform several tasks. How can I undertake them if the High-King of the land will not give me leave to do so?'

'Have you forgotten that your soldiers killed many of my subjects? The mere fact that you brought armed men into this country in the first place without my leave is enough for you to be subjected to the harshest of penalties.'

'But if you banish me from this kingdom,' Patricius noted confidently, 'then you will also banish any hopes that you might have of gaining Roman support in your struggle against the Saxons.'

'What makes you think that I would want Roman aid?' replied the High-King quickly.

'Come now, Leoghaire. With all due respect I did not travel halfway across the civilised world to bandy pretty words with you. I will speak plain with you if you are willing to do the same.' The bishop waited until the High-King had lifted his eyes to meet his before he continued. 'You have been concerned about the Saxon threat since they first turned up in Britain. So would I be. I have heard reliable reports that the heathen Saxons have raided your coastline from time to time and that their raids are becoming more common. You must have asked yourself what will happen if they come to this land in force? What if they decide to take Eirinn for their very own?'

'Of course I have thought about them,' Leoghaire admitted tersely. 'Palladius had Saxon mercenaries among his troops. That was the first experience I had of the savages. I wish it had been the last.'

'I am not saying that if you accept the sacraments of the Roman church that you will be immune from any attacks but I can assure you that if you eject me and my mission, Rome will certainly not be sympathetic to your cause when the first Saxons make landfall.'

'Were the same assurances given to the British kings?' Leoghaire cut in.

'Britain has been a Christian land for two hundred years. Of late, however, they have adopted a particularly evil heresy devised by one of their own people, a man called Pelagius. The Pelagians have spread the false doctrine of the humanity of Christ. They have set about denying the Lord's divinity up to the point of making open threats toward the Pope. They also cling to many old heathen beliefs, the chief of which you have already mentioned; that the soul does not pass to paradise after death but lingers to take a new form. The Emperor was naturally less than enthusiastic to undertake an expedition to aid a nation of heretics.'

'How can I be sure that the Emperor will be keen to help my folk?'

'You have seen what twenty well-trained Roman soldiers can do. As unfortunate as that incident may have been, it illustrates an important point. The Empire would not have to expend many resources in order to help protect your land. Unlike the British kings your nobility still have warriors aplenty at their disposal who could be trained in modern methods of warfare. That is another reason why I brought the soldiers with me, to show you that Rome is willing to dispatch its fighting men to the far-flung reaches of the Earth to protect and train fellow Christians.'

'I have heard what you have to say, bishop. Now I must consult with my advisors before I can give an answer to your request to remain in Eirinn.' The High-King leaned forward on his seat to impress Patricius with his next point. 'You must understand three things. First, that the man called Seginus Gallus was already considered an outlaw before he joined your mission. If you are to have any hope of being allowed to stay you must guarantee that he will submit fully to the High-King's justice and be punished for his crimes.'

'That goes without saying,' Patricius agreed.

461

'Second, that no Roman soldiers either currently enlisted or freed from their service are to remain anywhere in the five kingdoms of Eirinn. Their weapons will be returned to them when they are ready to board a ship for other lands.'

Patricius did not respond straightaway. 'You are right,' he finally answered cautiously. 'If I am to remain here in Hibernia I will have no need of any guards. My protection is guaranteed by my host.'

'There is not a warrior in the whole of Eirinn who would dare strike down a Druid. You may rest assured that your status will be similar to our own holy ones. Third, that you will publicly denounce violence and apologise for your part in the skirmish at Slané. Also that you will never interfere, as Palladius once did, in the established traditions of kingship in Eirinn.'

'I give my word that I will only concern myself with the spiritual wellbeing of your subjects.'

Leoghaire was not immediately certain that Patricius was agreeing to his demand and was about to ensure the Christian promised not to persecute anyone for their religion when he was interrupted with word that the lighting of the bonefire would soon be taking place.

'I must attend to the memorial of my old friend,' Leoghaire informed the bishop. 'I will not invite you to attend only because it is closed to all folk who are not of the Druid kind. Your presence could offend some of the Council. I will speak with you tomorrow after the midday meal at the ceremony of the calling of petitions. Then if all has gone well I would like to bring Seginus Gallus to trial.'

'Very well. I will be going to my devotions now, lord,' Patricius replied, 'for today was the feast of the resurrection of Our Lord. In all the excitement and aftermath of the fighting I have not had an opportunity to say the Mass. Would it be too much to ask your permission for your queen to attend the service?'

'You need not ask my permission. She is free to do as she wishes. But we are not yet wed, so be careful what you say. I would not like her to be offended by anything you say.'

'I will treat her with the utmost respect, lord,' Patricius assured the High-King.

Gobann was joined by Síla at the Star of the Poets but they had little chance for greeting. Their first priority was the washing of Cathach's body and saying the prayers of passing over him. Síla, Gobann and Caitlin were to be his guides at this important ceremony. After the spirit had broken free from a body the period of time until the earthly remains were interred or cremated was crucial to the wellbeing of the soul that was newly released. If the chief Druid was not carefully eased into his new existence he might well be enticed by the Sidhe-Dubh into becoming one of their slaves.

When Gobann had finished explaining to the disembodied soul of Cathach that he had passed on beyond the world, he sang an invocation to the ancestors begging them to come and guide the chief Druid. When that was done mourners were permitted to say their farewells. Many of the common folk from the citadel filed past the body, each with a word of thanks for some help the Druid had given them in life.

Among the many who came was Origen, leaning heavily on the arm of Declan of Saint Ninian's. The Alexandrian lit some incense as a gift for his friend, leaving it to burn at the feet and head of the body. Declan also said a prayer, not out loud because he did not want to offend anyone. The two Christians stayed afterwards at Gobann's invitation to see out the rest of the ceremony.

After everyone else had paid their respects three other visitors arrived. Hooded and robed in dark green cloth though the night was a little warm, they entered the Star of Poetry together. One carried a beautifully decorated harp made from an unfamiliar timber etched with signs that would not have been out of place adorning the interior walls of an ancient mound. He wafted around the room taking a while to observe Origen and Declan very closely, though they were both oblivious to the attention. Then he sat in a corner to tune his instrument. Another of them stood at Cathach's head breathing in the sweet eastern incense while the third moved to stand close to Caitlin so that his robes brushed against her.

None gave any indication of who they really were so that the two Christians naturally assumed that they were Druids who had come to perform some vital part of the ceremony. Caitlin, Gobann and Síla knew otherwise. They had each sensed in their own way that the Danaans would come to pay homage to Cathach. After all, the chief Druid had done more in his lifetime to renew contact with the Old Ones than any other Gael in all the generations since they had come to Eirinn.

As the Danaan stood at Cathach's head he began to sing a slow song, not mournful, just paced so that the words were drawn out and embellished and the harper began to strike on appropriate chords. The accompaniment was low but it lent a depth to the singer's voice that made it sound as though another voice had joined in singing in a lower pitch. The other Druids were as awestruck as Origen and Declan. No-one had ever heard music as sweet and sad before.

Caitlin closed her eyes to concentrate on the melody, attempting in her Druid way to commit it to memory. Instead she found that clear pictures of events that had happened long ago were popping into her head. She recalled standing in the tent of healing after the Battle of Rathowen as Fintan her friend and lover had passed away. Gobann had struck the harp then and Caitlin had joined him on her poor instrument. She realised that she had hardly touched the harp again in all the intervening seasons.

'Why do you not strike the wires?' a strange voice echoed in her head. She was so startled that her eyes popped open.

The Danaan standing beside her took her hand as if he were comforting her in her grief. 'Do not fear. No-one else can hear what passes between us. Why have you put music out of your life?'

Caitlin took her time answering. 'I was very hurt,' she finally replied.

'Music is the language of healing,' the Danaan stated.

'I do not play well enough,' she insisted. Caitlin sensed that the stranger was laughing at her.

'Not good enough?' he finally managed to say. 'Who are you to judge? Or is this just what the Cailleach has been telling you to keep you under her influence?'

'You know about the Cailleach?'

'Of course. She is one of my kindred. You are not the first Gael to fall victim to her attention.'

'Can you rid me of her?'

'Only you have the power to do that. When Cathach visited me last night before he set out for

465

Slané he asked me to do all I could to help you. Perhaps I can suggest a few devices to aid you in your struggle; that is if you really want to banish her from your life.'

Caitlin squeezed the Danaan's hand tightly.

'Very well,' the stranger began. 'When the Quicken Tree was cut down by the savages you managed to save nine berries that were lying near the body of a dead foreigner.'

'You even know about the black bag with the berries in it?'

'There were many eyes watching you and Murrough after the Quicken was murdered. I heard about the little bag soon after you picked it up. We allowed you to keep the rowan fruit because we felt that you would be a good guardian for them. This is what you must do now if you really want my help. Three of those berries must be nurtured into life. You may plant them wherever you will, but remember, they will be the only living representatives of their kind on this Earth. You will be the custodian of these new trees. If even one of them survives the coming conflicts that are to strike this land then the Quicken Tree will not have been lost for the future generations of the Gael.'

'I have thought about planting the berries many times before,' Caitlin admitted, 'but I was not sure if it would be the right thing to do.'

'It is the right thing to do,' the Danaan assured her. 'When you have successfully raised the seedlings you will have proved to me that your intentions are good and that you are a friend of my people. Then we can begin to work together on ridding you of this Cailleach.'

'I will do as you ask.'

'There is one other matter that you need to address,' the Danaan added. 'The Roman.'

'Seginus Gallus. The Quicken killer,' Caitlin grunted with disgust.

'Though this may sound strange to you, it is absolutely necessary that you find it in your heart to forgive him.'

Caitlin stopped breathing for a moment, shocked that one of the Old People would suggest such a thing. It was one thing to ask her to plant the sacred berries and raise three sapling rowans, but this request was incredible. 'Gallus brutally murdered Fintan. This savage cut down the holy tree. Who knows what other atrocities he committed in the name of his God and at the orders of Palladius?'

'I know some of the other crimes he was involved in,' the Danaan whispered, 'but Seginus Gallus knows a fuller account. The reckoning for his wrongdoings is not your responsibility. That is Leoghaire's task in consultation with his advisors. Nine icy winters have passed since your paths crossed last. Until you heal the wounds that you carry you will be bound to him like a saddle to a pony. If you do not reconcile your bitterness, your anger and your desire for revenge, he will return to haunt you for the rest of your life.'

Caitlin remained perfectly quiet while the Danaan spoke, refusing to make any movement that might betray her distress at what he had suggested.

Like a big brother the Danaan gripped her hand tightly and spoke to her reassuringly. 'The laws of Eirinn say that he must be punished. That is undeniable. But the best punishment is not always the first that comes to mind nor the simplest. There are greater laws at work in the world than the Brehon laws of the Gaels. In this lifetime or the next he will pay for what he has done. Let him go. Free yourself so that the Cailleach cannot feed on your anger.'

'The Cailleach has haunted me since Fintan's death because I was a storehouse for the energy that nourishes her,' acknowledged Caitlin, hunched forward.

'She was somewhat weakened in her fight with Síla and Murrough,' the Danaan noted, 'that is why the hag took a band of her redcaps to Slané hoping to stir up a fight. Fortunately Murrough was only wounded as a result of her actions or else she could have gained an even stronger hold over you.'

'The hag was at Slané?' Caitlin gasped. 'She might have killed Murrough.' The Queen of Munster stood up straight and tall once more. 'I will not let her hurt me or those dear to me again,' she vowed. 'Never again.'

Gobann and Síla stepped forward as the other two Danaans finished their homage to Cathach. Lifting his head slightly they placed the milk and the barley in his mouth saying the farewell blessing. Then the covers were drawn up over his face. Nine Druids filed into the chamber to lift the body. It was dark by the time the bearers departed the Star of Poetry making directly for the field of testing. As they passed through the gathered crowds many people stepped forward to pour a little mead on the corpse, sharing a last symbolic drink with the old Druid. Gobann, Síla and Caitlin followed behind bearing Cathach's ceremonial clothing and staff, all of which would be laid beside him on the funeral pyre. Gobann also carried his harp for he would be playing his old friend into the next world.

Near to the mound where Sianan and Mawn still lay, Leoghaire and Enda Censelach were waiting along with every Druid who was lodged in the Star of Poetry. Even the novices were allowed to witness the passing of their master, though they were expected to keep a respectable distance from the mound of testing.

The various remains of seven other old Druids who had passed away during the winter, tightly wrapped in white linen, were neatly positioned all around the bone-fire. One place had been left empty in the centre of the timber stack. Here the nine bearers laid their chief. The trumpets sounded, the chorus hummed lowly and as the torches were touched to the dry fuel Gobann struck the harp to play the lament for the passing. All were silent absorbing the solemnity of the occasion. Those few who guessed that Cathach may have been the last chief Druid of Eirinn to sit by the side of the High-King wept a little for the passing of a long tradition.

Enda Censelach, however, burned only with hatred for what had been done. 'You cannot let the bishop remain in Eirinn,' he whispered to the High-King. 'Now there will be a tidal wave of feeling against the Christians. Every time they come here they bring some disaster.'

'The Christians do not cause the disasters,' Leoghaire mumbled. 'Wars are created by men of no integrity. Patricius is an honourable man. He is not like Palladius. If the people are so set against the Christians then it is because they have been misinformed or because they have misjudged the worth of individuals.'

'For the sake of his own personal safety it would be best if the bishop left Teamhair immediately,' Enda stated. 'I will arrange that he accompany me to Britain when I leave on my embassy to the court of Uther.'

'He will remain in the citadel,' Leoghaire insisted. 'I have not heard all that he has to say. You, however, will be leaving on your mission as soon as the wind and tides allow. You should go to your hall after this funeral and make the necessary preparations to journey.'

Enda silently fumed at the High-King's dismissive tone. The very moment that the ceremony had concluded he stormed off to his own hall to meet with some of his most loyal warriors. Long into the night the feasting hall of Enda Censelach was still buzzing with many men and women gathered around their lord, drinking, boasting and squabbling. There was little preparation made to leave Eirinn, however.

As the night wore on Leoghaire returned to his own rooms to sit alone. Whatever happened from this day on, he felt certain that he alone would be left to carry the burden of the future. Neither Gobann nor Murrough nor all the most wise members of the Druid Council would be able to aid him. This was his duty and none other. He began to consider how much of it he might be able to share with his new queen, Mona.

In the Star of the Poets Caitlin sat beside Murrough, watching over him throughout the night, dressing his wound and bathing his fevered brow. Síla remained for a while to help but the queen would not have her stay all night.

'You should rest now, healer. You have done all that you can.'

When Síla left Caitlin was nursing her child and her king.

Outside in the cool air Síla found Gobann waiting for her. 'Don't worry about that one,' he assured her when he heard the healer's footfall behind him. 'Caitlin could fight off a host of redcaps and then ride home on an empty stomach. She is a strong determined woman.'

Síla stood behind the poet with her arms around his waist. She held him tightly as she spoke. 'The changes that Cathach spoke of have begun. My work here is almost done.'

Gobann nodded in agreement. He had known that this day was coming as surely as he had known that Patricius would one day sit in Teamhair. 'How long?' he asked, trying unsuccessfully to conceal any trace of emotion.

Síla noticed the slight tremble in his voice and turned to face the poet. 'When Caitlín and Murrough are fit enough to ride home I will set off for my tribal land in the north of Britain, 'she said softly. 'There are also changes about to take place there and I must be with my people.'

'Very well,' the poet breathed. 'I am glad that you will be here for a little while longer at least. Mawn and Sianan will be in need of good counsel.'

'Let's sleep,' she whispered.

Gobann did not need to be coaxed. He turned her round and led her back into the Star of the Poets, picking up his harp case near the door before entering. He was just about to close the outer door to the hall when he thought he heard the noise of many feet running in the darkness.

He froze where he stood.

'What's the matter?' Síla asked.

'Shh! I thought I could hear some commotion down near the High-King's hall.' He had not even finished the sentence when they both perceived several forms moving swiftly in the darkness. 'Look there!' the poet hissed, trying to keep his voice low. 'Are they warriors moving about?'

Síla did not wait to find out. 'Go and see to Leoghaire's guards,' she flashed. 'I'll fetch some of

471

Murrough's warriors. The High-King may be in danger.'

Gobann rushed off in one direction while Síla fled in the other, both desperately afraid that Enda had finally decided to strike at Leoghaire now that Cathach was dead. By the time the poet reached the High-King's hall there were many Laigin warriors assembled outside blocking the entrance hall. The poet tried to get to the door but they would not let him approach.

'I am a poet of the Silver Branch!' Gobann stormed indignantly. 'You cannot refuse me entry to any hall in this citadel.'

'Calm yourself, Druid,' one of the warriors grunted disrespectfully. 'The King of Laigin commands me to keep all intruders out. If you have any complaints make them to him.'

'What is happening here?' the poet demanded.

'Leoghaire has been stabbed in his bed by an assassin. A Christian,' the warrior answered as though it were obvious.

'I am a healer! Let me see to the High-King!'

The warrior stepped up to Gobann and put a hand on his shoulder. 'Leoghaire no longer has any need of a healer. Go back to bed, Druid. You are too late.' The soldier pushed Gobann so that he fell on his back in the dirt. Just as he landed twenty warriors of Munster appeared, running down the embankment with drawn swords. Caitlin and Síla were at their head.

'What is going on here?' the queen demanded while the healer helped Gobann to his feet. 'How dare you assault a Druid counsellor!'

'This is none of your affair,' the warrior answered. 'Go back to your beds, all of you, you are wasting your time here. I will not let any of you pass.'

'Who has issued you these orders?' Caitlin snapped.

'The King of Laigin.'

The queen swiftly sized up the situation, quickly deciding to try her luck and the Laigin man's resolve. 'By the order of the royal house of Munster you will stand aside. If you do not I will have my warriors move you by force!'

As soon as the Laigin warrior realised who this woman was he suddenly changed his tone. 'It's more than my life's worth, lady, to let you enter.'

'Believe me, your life will not be worth much if my soldiers have to grapple with you in order for me to visit the High-King.'

'The High-King is dead, lady. The King of Laigin was too late to prevent the murderer slitting Leoghaire's throat.'

Caitlin looked about her in horror trying to get some confirmation of this terrible news. 'Who told you this?'

'King Enda Censelach told us himself. Along with three of his chieftains he was the first to arrive at the hall. The High-King's sentries were all slaughtered where they stood.'

Caitlin was immediately suspicious. 'Stand aside!' she roared. 'Or you will lie beside Leoghaire's guardsmen in pools of your own blood!'

'I cannot do what my king and master has ordered me not to do,' he replied, levelling his sword in preparation for a fight. 'You may not pass by.'

Caitlin turned her head slightly to speak to her troops without taking her eyes off the Laigin guard for a second. 'Strike any warrior who prevents my passage into the hall of the High-King,' she ordered.

The Laigin warrior raised his blade to strike but Caitlin had parried the blow before it fell and punched the hilt of her sword into the guard's unprotected stomach. 'This is not the first time I have been called on to teach the soldiers of Laigin how to handle themselves in a fight,' she declared.

The warriors around the door responded to this insult, raising their weapons to rush forward at the queen and her troops. In seconds steel was clashing heavily against steel as the two sides began to contest the ground around the entrance hall.

Before anyone had a chance to deal a deadly blow, however, the Laigin men threw down their weapons begging for Caitlin's soldiers to stay their hands also. The queen laughed loudly at them, remembering well how so many of their kindred had deserted the battlefield at Rathowen. 'The men and women of Laigin don't have much fight in them,' she chided.

'Not when their king orders them to lay down their arms,' Enda called out from the back of the crowd. His warriors parted to either side of him, letting him pass through the door to stand before Caitlin.

'Where is Leoghaire?' the queen demanded. 'What have you done with him?'

Enda raised a dark eyebrow in mock astonishment, 'I have done what I could,' the king answered enigmatically. 'I came here to rescue Leoghaire not to harm him. Alas I was too late to save the lives of his guardsmen.'

'You may have murdered the High-King of Eirinn,' she spat, 'but the Druid Council will never allow a coward like you to sit in Leoghaire's place!'

'A coward, am I?' Censelach sneered. 'Under the circumstances you should be careful what you say, Queen of Munster.'

'Murrough told me what he saw at Slané,' she yelled, not caring for the consequences of her wrath. 'When he was lying on his back felled by a Roman arrow, he watched helpless as you crawled away to hide in the bushes. Your own warriors were falling all around you while you deserted them.'

'Murrough is an inexperienced boy. He is not a warrior. I would not expect anything more than such a story from one who manages to be struck from his horse in the first few minutes of a battle.'

'Better to be struck honourably than to jump down in order to shelter from the enemy. Do the people of Laigin prefer the rule of contemptible kings? Dichu was a man such as you,' Caitlin added. 'Without honour or integrity.'

'Enough!' Enda cried. 'The person with least knowledge talks most!'

'Stand aside, traitor, so that we may see to Leoghaire's corpse.'

'I'll stand aside but I think you'll find that the High-King still has a need of his body,' Censelach quipped. 'He was only slightly wounded on the hand by his assailant.'

Gobann pushed through the warriors to face the king of Laigin. 'Your warriors told us he was dead!'

'They lied,' Enda retorted, shrugging his shoulders casually and looking about at his soldiers. 'I must apologise for them. It would be a good idea if your troops remained outside, Queen; however, I think that Leoghaire would be reassured if the poet and the healer were to accompany you.' With a sweep of his arm the King of Laigin mockingly cleared the way for Caitlin. As she passed by him Censelach remarked loudly, 'Do not think that I will let you forget your contemptible accusations. I can see now why the King of Munster chose you for his queen. You are both quick to judge and equally slow of wit.'

The Laigin warriors burst out laughing at their lord's joke.

Ignoring their jeers Caitlin pushed past to enter the hall.

Gobann was the first to reach Leoghaire, who was seated at his hearth fire with the cuaich cup in his hand. The High-King stood slowly to offer the welcome draught to the poet. Caitlin and Síla followed soon after and all waited patiently until the cup of mead had been passed around before they asked the questions that they were bursting with.

'Are you hurt?' Caitlin asked, touching Leoghaire's forehead to soothe him.

'My arm was scratched in the struggle. Apart from that I am not injured,' he assured them. 'But it was a near thing. I was just dozing when I heard a shuffle in the outer hall, then the sound of someone falling hard onto the floor. I roused myself enough to go to the chamber door but I was knocked down as the killer thrust it open. The next thing I knew he was pressing a knife at my throat and I was struggling with all my will to push him away.' The High-King was visibly shaken.

'But you managed to overpower him,' Gobann observed, pointing to a corpse that lay by the wall.

'No,' answered Leoghaire, 'that was all thanks to the swift work of Enda. If it had not been for him arriving with his warriors when they did I would most likely be dead now.'

Gobann and Síla exchanged concerned glances.

'What was Enda Censelach doing here with so many of his troops? The Hall of Laigin is on the other side of the citadel,' Caitlin cut in.

Leoghaire looked stunned, as though he had not considered that anything suspicious might have taken place. 'I cannot say. All I know is that he was just here all of a sudden with his soldiers. Enda dispatched the fellow himself,' Leoghaire said.

Gobann went over to look at the body. 'Enda's soldiers told us that the assailant was a Christian. Did you get a good look at him?'

'A Christian,' Leoghaire gasped. 'I did not notice that he was one of the Romans. I seem to remember that he was dressed in white.'

'And so he is,' the poet agreed. 'Not the black or brown of the Romans, but the white of the Alexandrians.'

'He is one of Origen's people?' the High-King exclaimed, getting to his feet to look at the dead man's face.

In that instant Enda entered the room. 'They are all Christians,' he grunted. 'They are all the same as far as I can see, be they white, black or brown.' Then he touched Leoghaire on the shoulder. 'I have taken the liberty of posting a guardsman at every ten paces from this hall to the citadel gates. The entire fortress has been alerted. Now I just need your permission to arrest the Christians and expel them from Teamhair.'

Leoghaire went back to the fire to sit down. 'Whatever you think is best, Enda. Thank you for saving my life.'

The King of Laigin smile a tight uneasy grimace that was the most acknowledgment he ever gave. 'I will see to it then.'

Enda was about to leave when Gobann turned from his study of the attacker's corpse. 'Strange isn't it, Censelach?'

'What is that, Druid?'

'That a Christian in the tutelage of Origen should be wearing a Roman cross.'

'Perhaps he is a Roman Christian,' Enda offered blankly.

'Strange then that a Roman Christian would be wearing the robes of the eastern church.'

'Is it? They are all war-mongers and plotters. The sooner the five kingdoms are rid of every one of them the better I will like it.'

Leoghaire recovered from his shock a little when he realised what Gobann was saying. 'Enda,' he stuttered, 'leave the Christians for tonight. I will deal with them tomorrow when I sit in judgment.'

'But my lord . . .'

'Leave it! They are not going anywhere. You yourself have sealed the citadel. No-one can get to me. There is no good waking up the whole of Teamhair for something that can wait till morning.'

'Very well. I will send two men to clear away the body. If you need anything I will be outside the hall handing out duties to my warriors. Good night.' Without acknowledging anyone else in the chamber Enda Censelach stormed out.

'Be careful of him,' the High-King warned Gobann, 'he is a powerful enemy.'

'And a careless intriguer,' the poet added. 'This man has battle scars on his arms and a tattoo on his lower leg. I think it is fairly certain that he spent his life as a warrior in Censelach's royal guard not as a monk studying under Origen.'

'Would Enda dare try to murder the High-King?' Caitlin cried.

'No,' Gobann conceded. 'Though I do not doubt that this poor fellow believed that was what the King of Laigin wanted him to do. Enda caught the assassin before he had the chance to carry the deed through to the end. No. Censelach did not intend for Leoghaire to die. He wanted to discredit the Christians and add to his own prestige in one stroke.'

Two Laigin warriors came to the door at that moment. After excusing themselves they lifted the dead man dragging him out by the feet. They were almost out of the chamber when the assassin's sword fell from his hand. Gobann reached down to pick it up but one of the warriors beat him to it.

'I will take that,' the poet insisted. 'I am sure that Leoghaire would like it as a souvenir of this attempt on his life.'

The warrior shrugged his shoulders handing over the blade and then the two soldiers left with the body.

'This is a Roman sword. See,' Gobann said stabbing at the air with it. 'Short and narrow for piercing; not made for slashing. It must have come from the arsenal that was surrendered by the Roman soldiers at the gate to the citadel.'

'The Romans were not behind this attempt,' Caitlin observed.

'Of course not,' Gobann laughed. 'This was done by someone who had access to the arsenal.'

'Enda,' Leoghaire said. 'He insisted that extra guards be placed around the Roman weapons. I allowed him to station his own warriors at the door to the tower.'

'We must appease Censelach as much as possible without stirring him into further action,' Gobann suggested. 'If he could get a killer past nine of your crack guardsmen and into your personal chamber, then he could certainly make a challenge for the high-kingship as soon as he wishes. What would Cathach do in this situation?'

'He would pacify Censelach. I must make Enda believe that sufficient action is being taken with regard to the Christians,' Leoghaire replied. 'I think I know what needs to be done.' The High-King looked at Síla, Caitlin and Gobann one at a time and then said, 'Go to your beds now. I will be safe tonight. Tomorrow morning I will receive petitioners and judge outlaws. We should all get some rest before then.'

Then Leoghaire stood up to usher them out of his chamber, all except Gobann who stayed for a long while discussing strategies to deal with Enda. As soon as the poet had gone the High-King bolted the door to his chamber and drew his sword. For what remained of that night he slept beside his blade as he had done in the days of his warrior youth.

TWENTY-EIGHT

he tradition of allowing petitioners to come before the High-King was a very ancient one indeed, going back to the times before the Gaels had arrived in Eirinn. If a landholder felt that their chieftain or provincial king had not done them justice in a settlement they could go to Teamhair on the day after the Beltinne festival to request the High-King's judgment. Usually each Beltinne, a large number of petitioners arrived at the citadel seeking Leoghaire's word.

By custom the hearings began just after dawn, carrying on until midday with Leoghaire and his counsellors taking food at intervals throughout the morning. After a short break at the middle of the day the hearings continued, sometimes until well into the night.

On this occasion Leoghaire's council was made up of three others: Gobann, Caitlin and Mona, daughter of Enda Censelach, who sat to the right of the High-King. Leoghaire considered this was a perfect opportunity to let the people see his betrothed, for she was not expected to take any active duties as yet. She was dressed in a long dark green tunic that was edged in honey-yellow embroidery. The sleeves were fringed in deep red. Over the top of this she wore a rust-brown cloak. Her hair was tied up at the back to expose the fine features of her face.

Caitlin sat on Leoghaire's left dressed in clothes borrowed from Mona since none of her own gowns had been packed for the journey to Teamhair. The Queen of Munster wore the blackest shawl over a long red ochre tunic, tied at the waist with a black band. Flanked by these two women, one a red-haired warrior, the other a dark and delicate woman obviously unused to drawing as much attention as this, Leoghaire was all the more impressive to his subjects when they entered the great feasting hall to beg his help.

The morning was spent settling the trivial disputes of neighbours over whose cow had the right to certain pastures or which brother would inherit the father's right to harvest the seaweed on a certain stretch of coast. One woman had come from Dal Araidhe to request that her husband's sword to be returned to her. He had fallen at Rathowen. Now that her son was old enough to wield a blade she hoped that would be able to carry his father's sword. Of course there was little chance that the actual blade would be found so under the circumstances Leoghaire provided the next best thing. He called for his own sword. The woman was overcome with emotion as he offered it to her with a blessing, 'May it protect your son from all harm in battle as it has done me these twenty winters.' Touching gestures like that one explained why, though he was aging, Leoghaire was still a popular king.

In the afternoon the chieftains and kings came before their overlord to make decisions on boundaries and fines. A chieftain from Connaught brought a charge against Enda Censelach whose warriors, he claimed, had killed his entire family during a raid. Leoghaire had no hesitation in finding the King of Laigin liable, though the offence was committed early in Enda's reign. The chieftain claimed that he had been afraid to come forward until that day. No-one, not even Enda Censelach himself, doubted the man's word. The King of Laigin promised to pay a fine in recompense for everyone who had died.

It was late in the day when two men dressed in black robes came before the high table. Both had the tonsure of Roman monks though one wore a white cowl and carried a staff. Isernus was careful to stay at a discreet distance behind his abbot as they walked toward the High-King. Leoghaire did not immediately recognise Declan for they had met only twice, once before the Battle of Rathowen and once after Dichu and Palladius were captured. However, the abbot of Saint Ninian's had only to open his mouth for the High-King to bring the incident clearly to mind.

'You have changed, Declan,' Leoghaire noted, 'but I could never forget your strange accent when you use the Gaelic. That at least has not improved with time.'

'Lord,' Declan began, not wanting to waste too much of the council's time with pleasantries, 'my monastery lies in the kingdom of Dal Araidhe just across the water in Britain so I think that I can be accounted as one of your subjects. The kings of the Dal Araidhe have not been able to help me with my problem nor has the local chieftain. In fact he and his people suffer more from the predicament than my monks and nuns.'

'What exactly is the problem we are discussing?' Leoghaire interrupted.

Declan took a deep breath. 'Saxons,' he said loudly so that everyone in the hall could hear. 'Two winters ago a warlord called Eorl Aldor built a stronghold some twenty Roman miles down the coast at a place that can only be reached by sea. His men live by extracting heavy payments from us in return for periods of relative peace. The problem is that the intervals between their visits have become shorter and shorter and their demands for tribute more and more impossible to meet. I hardly have enough grain to feed all my flock let alone the starving tribespeople at Dun Righ. The Saxons know what our position is. Now they have begun taking our folk hostage. If ransoms are not paid they murder their prisoners. Sometimes they kill them anyway. I live in fear of the day that the savages discover that we have thirty nuns in residence at the abbey. Up until now I have managed to keep that a secret.'

Leoghaire leaned forward to take a cup from the low table in front of him. 'What would you like me to do?' he asked as he sipped the mead.

'If you could send some warriors to reinforce the folk at Dun Righ and train my monks to fight, it would save many innocent lives. You once told me that if ever there was anything you could do to help me, I had only to ask.'

'That I did!' Leoghaire exclaimed. 'For you were a friend to the people of the five kingdoms when others of your kind brought war to this land. I think that I may have a solution in mind for you, Declan, but for the moment it all depends on the outcome of several other matters that are pending before me today. Sit here in the hall if you like until I can give you a full reply. I trust that I can perform a service befitting the debt of gratitude that I owe you for helping rid us of Palladius. Several of your brothers are here from Rome. I would appreciate your honest appraisal of them.'

Declan bowed very low taking a seat on a bench with Isernus at the side of the hall. From here he judged that they would be able to observe the proceedings without being too conspicuous.

Leoghaire had already signalled to his chamberlain to move on to the next petitioner. Enda Censelach, who had been sitting with the other chieftains to one side of the hall, now stood up, crossed the floor and stood directly before the High-King.

Leoghaire acknowledged his subject king politely giving no sign that he expected any trouble, though it was obvious to everyone that something had upset the King of Laigin. Enda had his best dark grey cloak wrapped over his right shoulder and tucked under his left arm. This was the classic warrior pose adopted by champions when they issued a challenge.

The High-King pretended not to notice this mild breach of hospitality. 'Welcome, King of Laigin,' he intoned formally. 'What petition have you to present?'

Enda coughed in a very formal manner to clear his throat, reminding Leoghaire of the rituals that are performed before the playing of the Brandubh.

'Last night,' Censelach began, making sure that everyone in the hall could hear what he was saying, 'an attempt was made on the High-King's life.'

Up until this moment only those closest to Leoghaire and the guards who had been at the High-King's hall had been aware of the attack. So Enda's announcement drew muffled exclamations and fervent whispers from every corner of the feasting chamber. The High-King smiled a little to himself. Enda had presented his news as if it were the opening gambit in a match of Brandubh.

'It was only through good fortune,' the King of Laigin insisted, 'that I happened to be paying a visit to the High-King's chamber just as the attacker got close enough to strike. For that reason alone the murderer was foiled in his attempt to slaughter Leoghaire. We can now be certain that the man was an agent of the Christians.'

The hall immediately broke out into calls for justice to be done.

Leoghaire held his hand up to still the feasting chamber. 'Let the King of Laigin finish his speech.' Instantly the assembly fell silent.

'Yes,' cried Enda, throwing back his cloak and getting into the spirit of his oratory, 'we must punish the persons who broke the High-King's peace and who within days of receiving our hospitality have made an attempt on the life of our High-King. The King of Munster lies in a bed having been pierced by the shaft of a Roman arrow. These fiends must not be allowed to get away with such outrages!' The hall erupted into cheers for Enda Censelach mingled with one or two exhortations that he would make a better High-King than Leoghaire.

Censelach raised his hand copying the High-King's gesture and bringing his audience to heel again. 'If all that has happened since the Christians arrived were not bad enough,' he continued, 'among our own people there are those who would tear apart the fabric of our society and the sanctity of our customs. I know the pain of this only too well,' he informed his listeners as if he were confiding in them. 'My own daughter has taken on the mantle of the Cross in direct defiance of me and of our ancient traditions.'

The crowd erupted into sneers and hisses. Mumbled predictions of where this would all lead swept through the chamber like a snowdrift. Mona sat at the high table blushing deeply.

Once again Enda held up his hand. The assembled chieftains and commoners responded immediately. 'But this treachery extends to the highest in the land. Last night after I had saved the life of Leoghaire I was openly challenged by one who has trained as a Druid. I was accused of murder and of cowardice on the field of battle. My kingdom was derided and my honour called into question.'

The crowd began to stir, each asking the person next to them who could have done such a thing to the man who saved the High-King's life.

'Today,' Enda went on, 'I come to the feasting hall of Leoghaire and I find that he has my daughter, a Christian, seated beside him. That is understandable since they intend to wed even though it is the Christians who pose the greatest threat to our land. On his other side sits the woman who slurred my name last night, the one who called me a timid untrustworthy king without integrity. Is this the wise counsel that Leoghaire surrounds himself with?'

The whole chamber exploded into shouts and cries as people called out insults at Caitlin and Mona and a few even at the High-King. Leoghaire remained perfectly silent with pursed lips and did not move a muscle.

Enda let his audience vent their anger for a long while, actually returning to his seat at one stage to confer with one of his chieftains. While he was seated Leoghaire took the opportunity to stand, raising his palm to the assembly. It took several moments for them all to acknowledge his sign. When they were relatively quiet the High-King sat down again before he spoke. Now it was his turn to make a move against his opponent, just as if he were moving the white pieces on the Brandubh board.

'What is it that you require in recompense for this insult if the charges be proved true?' Leoghaire asked.

Enda got up to stride across the floor again. 'Such words coming from the mouth of one who did not have all the facts at her disposal and who through her husband holds some animosity for me have no real impact on me. My clan and people know that I am honourable. It was inexcusable, however, that the accusations were made in front of my own warriors. When you insult me you insult my subjects. I have been embarrassed by the lies of Munster for a long time but I have kept my peace knowing that it is better to ignore the ignorant. But now matters have gone too far. I demand the payment of a blush fine equal to my worth as king of the tribes of Laigin.'

His audience were ecstatic, cheering Censelach on and deriding the Queen of Munster. Once more Leoghaire raised his hand but this time he did not wait for silence so that the crowd quickly settled again once they realised that he was speaking. 'Queen Caitlin of Munster should be allowed to answer these charges before you all.'

There was general agreement in the hall and slowly Caitlin stood to face her accuser.

'The King of Laigin has told the truth,' she admitted quickly, hoping to minimise the damage that this could do to her and the High-King at court. She knew Censelach was using her to discredit Leoghaire. If she denied the charges Enda would have an opportunity to chastise the High-King for his weakness. She was about to say so but thought better of it and sat straight back down again. This was very much like a game of

Brandubh where the tactical victories ebbed and flowed between two opponents until one let his guard down enough that the other could sweep in to victory. Leoghaire knew that he could ensnare Enda in the Laigin king's own overconfidence.

The assembly was stunned and disappointed at Caitlin's admission of guilt. It had been far too easy for some of the Laigin chieftains; they wanted a fight.

Enda Censelach replied as soon as Caitlin had returned to her seat. 'I am satisfied with her admission,' he announced even though he did not sound satisfied. 'Now I leave it to the High-King to set the fine for my embarrassment.'

'This will need careful consideration,' Leoghaire answered, fending off the question for the moment. 'There is no doubt that the Queen of Munster has a case to answer but I will have to consider what price to put on the King of Laigin's honour. If you can be patient with me I promise that before I rise today I will give my verdict.'

The crowd hummed approval. Enda suddenly seemed extremely pleased with this result as if he had tricked Leoghaire into an admission of responsibility. 'Thank you, lord. Once again you have exhibited your boundless wisdom. And now to the question of the Christians. How will they be punished for their attempt on your life?'

'I have instituted an investigation,' Leoghaire began, 'into the matter of last night's attack. Gobann of the Silver Branch has been trying to ascertain who exactly was responsible. Perhaps this would be the best time for him to present his findings.'

Leoghaire was sure that if the poet had done his work during the night, his speech would soon disarm Enda. Gobann rose from his seat beside

Caitlin. 'The man who Enda killed during an attempt to murder the High-King,' the poet reported, 'was as far as I can tell a member of a Christian sect.'

The assembly snarled in outrage as if they had rehearsed the reaction. This was what they wanted to hear.

'From the manner of his dress,' Gobann continued when they had calmed down, 'it is almost certain that he was a member of the sect who are known to us as the White Brothers. Since the assassin's body was cremated this morning by Enda Censelach's warriors I was not able to examine his corpse closely for any other signs. It is my opinion therefore that Origen of Alexandria should be held accountable for this crime.'

Censelach realised that Leoghaire was trying to play down the issue of the attempt on his life. Origen was a friend of the High-King who he felt would not be punished severely. 'The man was carrying a Roman blade,' Enda called out. 'He was a Roman!'

'Unfortunately,' the poet countered, pausing as if say that he had considered this evidence carefully, 'the blade is no proof of the assassin's identity as a Roman. Indeed the Romans all surrendered their weapons at the gate tower of Teamhair and were searched in case they carried any smaller blades. The Alexandrians, however, have never been required to hand over their weapons since none of their number has ever been known to break with tradition or the law. Their blades are very similar to the Roman style and could easily be mistaken as such. Alexandria was once a Roman outpost after all.'

'Thank you, poet,' Leoghaire rejoined. 'Call Origen of Alexandria to the justice of the High-King!'

The chamberlain fled the hall to carry out the summons. Within a very short space of time he had returned leading the blind monk towards the High-King's table. It was obvious that he had been waiting in the entrance hall in expectation of his summons.

When Origen was positioned directly in front of Leoghaire the High-King spoke to him. 'Last night it seems that one of your brothers made an attempt on my life. It is not for you to plead in this case for the man is dead and so is already answering before his God. The evidence, however, points overwhelmingly to a member your order. Do you understand the implications of this act?'

'I do, lord,' the monk answered quickly. 'You believe that the murderer was one of my students or brothers.'

'Yes.' Leoghaire knew that Origen would not object to anything he said, even though they were both sure that none of the White Brothers had committed this crime. Gobann had convinced the Alexandrian that it would be in everyone's best interest if the white brothers took some small part of the responsibility.

Leoghaire raised his voice a little to hide his own sadness in having to sacrifice Origen. 'Cormac mac Airt, when he was High-King, gave your folk the freedom of this land and the right to reside in the citadel. But there were conditions placed on that hospitality. You are not responsible for the actions of one of your flock but if you cannot keep a tight rein on your followers then you leave me with little choice but to act according to law and custom. I find that I must banish you and your community from Teamhair forever. Tomorrow you will set out for Ballinskelligs. This is the furthest point away from the citadel still within the five kingdoms of

Eirinn. A place has been prepared for you there where you can worship in your own manner without interference. None of your followers need ever return to Teamhair again except on my summons.' Having finished his judgment Leoghaire looked down at the monk as sternly as he could.

'It grieves me that one of my flock has caused such offence,' Origen answered, playing his part to perfection, 'but I can see the wisdom of your judgment and I thank you for your mercy. When I took the vows of a hermit monk it was always my intention to seek out places where I would not be disturbed from my meditations by the din of everyday life. That is why I came to Eirinn in the first place. I ended up living here in the citadel as your guest for many years, working as a healer. During that time I forgot the real reason that I took to the cowl. Since this blindness came upon me I have been forced to live a somewhat reclusive life and now that I have a taste for it again I would welcome the chance to return to my old ways.'

'You may go to make the preparations for your departure. We thank you for all your work and teachings. I trust that you will find the peace that you seek.' Leoghaire signalled for the chamberlain to lead the white-robed monk out of the chamber.

Enda stood up in shock. The King of Laigin had not expected that events would take such a turn. He had planned that all the Christians would be on board boats bound for Britain within the next few days. And here was Leoghaire trampling all over those designs. 'And what of the Roman Christians?' Censelach stormed. 'Are they too to be rewarded with lands for their part in the attack on our High-King?'

'Did you not hear the poet's report?' the High-King asked in surprise. 'There is no evidence that they were ever involved. I am not giving Origen the title to some vast tract of territory. I am banishing him to an uninhabited and inhospitable part of the southwest. The King of Munster owns Ballinskelligs. Origen's people will pay him rent.'

'Very well,' Enda conceded quickly, seeing that there was no point in pursuing this line of attack any further, 'but the Romans must at least be brought to account for the skirmish at Slané. Need I remind you that twenty of our finest warriors fell there in an ambush?'

'Of course you are right. Patricius and his two stewards will face this court to answer for their behaviour. Fetch the Christians into my hall,' he ordered but the chamberlain was already on his way out of the door.

Within minutes Patricius was standing before Leoghaire. He wore his long white robes and tall hat and he leaned on an ornately carved staff. Declan and Isernus stood in their places to pay silent respect to the bishop they had heard so much about. Enda Censelach positioned himself so that he was a little behind the bishop and facing the High-King.

Tatheus was brought in a few minutes later dressed in his polished military breastplate, red cloak, leggings and stout boots. His scabbard was empty and he carried his shining steel helm under his arm. As he stepped up to stand beside Patricius he bowed his head. Then, unexpectedly, he snapped a Roman military salute towards Leoghaire, punching his right fist to his left breast and then throwing his arm out in front of him with his fingers extended.

Leoghaire did not wait for the third prisoner to be brought forward before he commenced speaking. 'Patricius Sucatus, are you the leader of this warrior band?'

'I am, lord.'

'Do you admit responsibility for the fight which took place on Beltinne on the road to Slané?'

'As commander of the soldiers lent to me by the Pope I alone am responsible, lord. I caused the fight at Slané.'

'It is not true,' Tatheus cut in, speaking broken Gaelic. 'He had nothing to do with what happened.'

The two Romans had carefully rehearsed this little interjection knowing that Tatheus and his soldiers would certainly be expelled from the kingdom no matter what else happened.

'The bishop ordered that we were not to engage any of your people,' the centurion continued. 'I made the decision to attack after Seginus Gallus had deceived me about the bishop's true intentions. I present myself for punishment, but I beg humbly that the bishop be exonerated from all blame.'

'You have impressed me with your honesty, centurion,' Leoghaire answered before Enda had a chance to interject. 'It takes a brave man to admit that he was at fault when the rest of the world points the finger at another. What you did was against our law and custom. Innocent men and women died as a result of your actions.'

'I am ready for the High-King's just—,' Tatheus announced.

Not waiting for the centurion to finish the last word of his sentence, Leoghaire made his pronouncement. 'I find you guilty. That is, half guilty. If you had checked with your bishop, this terrible slaughter might never have happened. Your compatriot Seginus Gallus must share the blame with you. There is no question but that you must be banished from Eirinn with all of your soldiers but what of the Gaelic warriors who died needlessly? How are their families to be compensated? Where am I to find replacements for them in these troubled times?'

'Is there no work that these soldiers could do to make recompense?' Patricius interrupted.

Leoghaire stood up. 'As a matter of fact there may be. Declan, Abbot of Saint Ninian's, step forward.'

The monk got up and hurried toward the bishop, greeting him briefly before facing the High-King.

'I have considered your petition, Declan, and I find that I have a solution to two riddles in the one verse. I place Tatheus and his remaining soldiers in your charge. They will accompany you to Dal Araidhe to do your bidding until such time as I consider they have repaid their debt to me and to the clans of the warriors who fell at Slané. Would the Pope object to my judgment, do you think?' Leoghaire asked Patricius.

'Since they obviously cannot remain here, I think the Holy Father would be pleased with the penance that you have set.'

'You are letting them go?' Enda screamed. 'Off to Dal Araidhe with all their weapons? How do you know that they will not strike again, performing the same treachery as they attempted here?'

The assembly began to stir again, mumbling about the dangers of trusting foreigners.

'You may be right, Censelach,' Leoghaire agreed, talking over the mutterings. 'In which case I shall appoint one of my own trusted servants to be their garrison commander; to watch over them while they work their way out of my debt.'

Leoghaire rubbed his fingers though his beard as if he were searching very hard for a solution. In fact this had all been carefully planned by Gobann and himself during their impromptu meeting the night before.

'I have it!' he announced finally. 'You will be happy with this, Enda, for it solves the payment of your blush fine. If it were not for the fact that you are commissioned as my ambassador to the warchiefs of Britain I would send you to watch over these foreigners, Censelach, but since you will be otherwise engaged in more important matters I will send Caitlin Queen of Munster in your place.'

'What?' sputtered Enda unable to keep up with this turn of events.

'Don't you see? This is a perfect arrangement. Caitlin Queen of Munster, in payment for your embarrassment of Enda Censelach, you will go with all your household to Dal Araidhe in place of the King of Laigin. It will be your duty to enforce my ruling on Tatheus and his men. Any Saxon treasure that may come your way as a result of this expedition will, of course, belong entirely to Enda Censelach, King of Laigin.' Leoghaire sat back, pleased with himself.

'May I wait until Murrough is healed of his wounds?' Caitlin asked.

'I would imagine that you will need to take him with you,' the High-King pointed out. 'This will not be an easy campaign. You may wait in Eirinn therefore until he is in better health but make sure that you are ready to set sail as soon as the King of Munster is well enough to travel.'

'This is an outrageous judgment,' Enda protested. 'It will not nearly compensate me for the insult she brought upon me.' The King of Laigin could feel all his strategies for ridding Eirinn of the Christians turning quickly to dust.

'How many Saxons are there in that raiding party, Declan?' Leoghaire asked.

'Between seventy and one hundred, lord,' the monk answered.

'That is more than I expected,' Leoghaire turned back to Caitlin. 'Very likely you will need to take some of your kingdom's warriors, perhaps Murrough's guardsmen. Without unduly compromising the defence of Munster you are not to return, Caitlin, until these savages are cleared out of the kingdom of Dal Araidhe and sufficient measures have been devised to prevent their return.'

The High-King motioned for Enda to step forward. As he approached, Leoghaire stood up. 'Caitlin, you must also apologise publicly to Enda for the words that so embarrassed him.'

The queen stood and, keeping her gaze directed at the floor, said softly, 'I beg your pardon for my behaviour last night, Enda Censelach. I will strive to beat these Saxons off quickly so that I may return to pay my fine to you.'

'In addition,' Leoghaire added, 'Caitlin will put her warriors at your disposal should you need them at any time during your stay in Britain. She will provide your reserves and be subordinate to you in any situation where the mutual safety of your forces are at stake.'

Censelach looked at the queen, his jaw slack from shock. He was about to protest but he took one look at Leoghaire's expression and changed his mind. No-one among the chieftains of Laigin would think that this judgment was insufficient. The King of Laigin could clearly see that he had no choice but to once again accept Leoghaire's words. Through clenched teeth he answered the Queen of Munster. 'Very well. I accept your word, lady.'

'Good!' cried Leoghaire, relieved. 'Now there is only one more matter that needs to be settled. Bring in the prisoner called Seginus Gallus!'

TWENTY-NINE

long while passed before two of Enda's men returned, dragging the badly beaten priest into the hall. The soldiers threw him down before Leoghaire and the priest landed heavily on his knees, tearing his trousers. Seginus struggled to his feet. Though his hands were tied behind his back, his guards offered him no assistance. As he got up, the Roman glanced around the chamber at the gathered assembly. He immediately caught sight of Declan and Isernus sitting on a bench to one side of the hall and strained to get a better look, unwilling to believe that they were there. He could get no closer, though. Strong hands grabbed his shoulders, turning him forcibly to face the High-King. The next thing he knew he was standing beside Patricius.

Seginus coughed and a little blood trickled from the corner of his mouth. Both Declan and Patricius were visibly shocked by the state the priest was in. His face had been brutally bashed and was blue with bruises. His vestments had been ripped to shreds and hung off his body in tatters. There was blood in his matted black hair and his feet were bare and cut. But Seginus had not been stripped of his pride. He looked straight ahead at Leoghaire, ignoring the gaze of everyone else, especially that of Patricius. Enda's guardsmen stood close behind their prisoner in case he made any move to escape.

The bishop closely inspected the priest's injuries while Leoghaire listed the charges against him.

'Seginus Gallus, sometime follower of Palladius of evil fame, you have eluded my justice more than once before today. You are charged now with being an assistant to the said Palladius in his crimes against the five kingdoms. In his name there was no foul deed that you were not willing to commit. Specifically I charge you with the hideous murder of Fintan MacMuir, whom you had nailed to a cross along with an unnamed lad whom you tortured in similar fashion. That is the worst crime that I can prove that you perpetrated. But doubtless there were many others that you indulged in.'

Seginus coughed again, spitting some blood onto the floor in front of him in defiance. One of the guards slapped the back of the priest's head. Seginus let his chin fall forward to his chest and in that instant he heard a wild blood-curdling laugh.

He did not raise his eyes, for the sound chilled him to the bone and he did not want to believe that the demon that he had encountered at Nantes was somehow present here in the High-King's hall. He tried to convince himself that he was hearing Tullia's mocking giggles and nothing more but no sooner had the thought entered his head than a harsh voice called out, grating and bitter, 'It is not young Tullia. It is your beloved brother the Blessed Martyr Linus who mocks you!'

Seginus jerked his head up to look at Leoghaire, and there standing behind the High-King, with a hand on Leoghaire's shoulder was the hideous creature that had presented itself to him in the bishop's prison.

'Shut up, you foul fiend!' Seginus screamed. 'Damn you to Hell! You are not my brother!' The creature laughed all the more.

Patricius and Declan exchanged worried glances. 'Be still, my son, or it will be all the worse for you,' the bishop soothed, placing a hand on the priest's forearm. Seginus pulled his arm away and when he looked back toward Leoghaire, the spectre had disappeared.

Leoghaire did not understand very much of the Roman tongue so he found it easy to ignore what seemed to be a futile gesture of defiance. 'You and your former master made an unjust war against me, inciting hundreds of my subjects to rebel against their elected chieftains. Then when you recognised that all was lost for Palladius you joined a band of renegade Saxons rather than submit to justice. Your evil knows no bounds, Seginus Gallus, for not content with the destruction that you had wrought warring with Palladius, you inspired those savage foreigners who were your allies to desecrate a holy tree in the Kingdom of Munster. For this last crime alone I could easily persuade the Council of Chieftains to ratify a sentence of death, though that is rarely done in this land.'

Leoghaire paused, looking around the room to see every Gaelic face filled with hate for this Roman. The High-King was satisfied that he had turned all their attention away from the other Christians and onto Seginus. The priest made no sound or sign but Patricius could see that the High-King had struck a nerve when he mentioned the possibility of the death penalty.

'If that were not enough,' the High-King continued, 'you returned to Eirinn despite an order of banishment. No sooner had you set foot on the shore than you went back to your old tricks. You gave false instructions to the centurion named Tatheus, making him believe that your new master Patricius wished him to attack the approaching

Gaels. When you were finally captured you were in the act of personally attacking Queen Caitlin of Munster with intent to murder her and to steal her horse. When you were searched upon capture, the royal seal of Munster was found on your person, though how you came by it is a mystery. If Murrough were not laid low by your handiwork perhaps he might be able to help us with that question. So I am afraid that I have to add thieving to the long list of your crimes.'

'If that were not enough—' another voice began, mimicking Leoghaire's formal tones. Seginus recognised it immediately. The ghost was standing behind Leoghaire again pointing an accusing finger directly at the priest. 'You gave me your word that you would avenge my murder, brother. You lied to me!' it bellowed. Then the demon began to laugh hysterically. 'It is reassuring to see that we share some family traits.'

Seginus struggled to speak. 'I did my best. Surely it is not too late!' Patricius looked at the priest in dismay, certain now that he was not in full command of his faculties.

'You are a worthless piece of dung,' the ghost answered. 'I should have known better than to think you would be able to help me.'

Seginus sensed the anger rising in the creature. The evil presence began to filter through the chamber, filling the air with malice. The priest began to tremble, certain that he was about to be struck down by this demon. Seginus suddenly heard Tullia's high-pitched giggle coming from somewhere behind him but when he turned to look for her a guard struck him hard in the face with an armoured fist and he fell forward.

Seginus spat once more at the floor and noticed that the ghost had disappeared again. Then he

sensed Patricius standing close beside him. The
Roman looked at the bishop. Though the churchman's eyes were full of compassion, Seginus knew
in his heart that Patricius had used him as a scapegoat to ensure that the Roman mission would be
able to remain in Eirinn. If the Gaels vented all
their anger on him, they would not have any left
over for Patricius and his party.

Patricius laid a hand on the priest's shoulder.
'Are you able to speak, my son?' he asked sympa-
thetically.

'You bastard!' Seginus shrieked in his native Latin.
'That's why you wanted me to come to Eirinn, to
draw attention away from you. What sort of a deal
did you strike with the High-King? Was it my life in
exchange for the freedom to walk this land wherever
you will?' Seginus lunged at the bishop in an attempt
to kick him but before he had moved more than a
pace the guards began to rain blows upon him. In
seconds the Roman was curled on the floor in agony.

'What did he say?' Leoghaire asked.

'I would rather not repeat his words, my lord,'
Patricius declared. 'He is full of anger at the
moment. I assure you that he would not react in
this manner if he had full command of his senses.'

'You bastard!' Seginus cried. 'You're no different
from Palladius. You and your kind don't care about
anything but your bloody missions to the heathens.
You give savages more respect than you do your
own people. Damn you and all who are like you!'
Seginus did not get a chance to say anything more.
A guard's boot landed in his stomach, making him
gag as he tried to retrieve the breath that it knocked
out of him. The Roman lay on the floor a few more
seconds before struggling up onto one elbow. For
a moment everyone thought that Seginus had
something else to say but he simply emptied the

blood and saliva that had filled his mouth at the bishop's feet.

Leoghaire allowed the assembly to quieten after the priest's disgusting gesture then he signalled the guards to lift the prisoner to his feet. Seginus stood between the two warriors supported under the arms with his knees slightly bent, refusing to stand without their help.

The High-King regarded the foreigner, searching for words to express his feelings, and it seemed that Seginus was staring back at him with equal intensity. 'I have never met the like of you, Gallus. Even after all that you have done you remain unrepentant. It is not easy for me to decide on a punishment that fits your crimes but I can assure you that by your behaviour today you have out-stripped your former master Palladius. I will take submissions from my subjects on your fate.'

Patricius stepped forward. 'Lord, this man has been beaten with heavy clubs. You assured me that he would be unharmed whilst he was imprisoned.'

'I was responsible for his safekeeping,' Censelach piped up. 'I was not aware that there was a ban on restraining him. Unfortunately my guards found him difficult to handle and so had to use some degree of force to bring him to court.'

Seginus could hear the ghost of his brother Linus laughing again.

'Nevertheless, he has been beaten severely! These are not injuries consistent with mere restraint. The scourging has obviously been pro-longed and aggravated.'

'It would seem that you are right, Patricius,' Leoghaire admitted. 'I am sorry that my word was not honoured but it does seem that the man is incorrigible. He continually sets out to break the

504

law. I am afraid that he will probably never recover from that ailment.'

'You will not have me, you bastard!' Seginus screamed suddenly. 'I will not let you have me!'

Leoghaire gestured to the guards to restrain the prisoner and they held the priest still though he squirmed about wildly, trying to break their hold.

'You cannot destroy me as long as I have Christ and the Holy Church on my side,' Seginus cried defiantly.

'You swore an oath to me, brother,' the ghost answered, and suddenly it was standing before Seginus, just out of reach. The priest redoubled his efforts to break free of his captors, lunging toward the demon, but the warriors held him firmly. 'Oaths are not things that can be taken lightly. You would have died in the Bishop of Nantes' cell if it had not been for me,' Linus said quietly. 'In return you promised to avenge my death.'

Thoroughly exhausted, Seginus ceased his struggling and fell forward in the arms of the guards. 'I promise that I will make amends to you,' Seginus declared.

Patricius heard those words and translated them immediately for Leoghaire. Aside from Seginus, no-one was aware of the demon's presence so they all assumed that he was addressing the High-King.

'Your word is not worth the breath you expend on it,' the ghost noted. 'You gave your word that the man who murdered me would pay with his life for the crime. And yet I see him sitting in this hall and he is very much alive.' Linus leaned forward. 'How would you explain that, big brother?'

'I did not even know that he was in Eirinn,' Seginus pleaded. 'How could I have done anything about him?'

'You have failed me, Seginus. And so as we agreed, you will accompany me to realms of darkness; to Hell.'

'No!' screamed the priest. 'Give me another chance. I will do anything that you say. I am yours to command.'

'Prepare your soul for death,' Linus hissed.

Patricius had continued to translate all of the priest's words, though he felt compelled to comment whenever he felt that Seginus was talking nonsense.

'One more chance!' Seginus begged and then collapsed in the arms of his guards.

Seeing that the priest had suddenly calmed himself, Enda coughed, raising his voice so that the whole hall would hear him. 'On behalf of all who have suffered at the hands of this villain, I demand that he forfeit his life for his crimes.'

The chieftains mumbled general approval. This Roman was old news, not as exciting as the assassin who had been killed the night before. They simply wanted to get rid of him now and move on to more interesting business.

Leoghaire ran his hand through his beard, tugging at the strands of hair as was his habit, but he had already made a decision. He waited now to see if there would be any further submissions.

When no-one else spoke Censelach finally let his impatience get the better of him. 'It will be a lesson to all Christians that there were laws in Eirinn long before the birth of their God,' Enda cried. Once more he seemed to have the ears of his audience. 'Do as was done to murderers in the times before Cormac mac Airt. Strangle him slowly then dump his body in a bog to rot.' This suggestion struck a chord with the chieftains, some of whom stood up to let their agreement be heard.

Patricius made an attempt to protest but the jeering assembly drowned out his plea. Seginus stood still, not showing any emotion and sweating profusely. His brother's ghost now stood in front of the High-King's table, hands on hips and an evil smile on its face.

In a whisper barely audible to Seginus, the creature hissed in a childish taunt, 'You're coming with me to Hell.'

The priest felt that he was no longer able to contain his fear and loathing. He knew that he had done many wrongs and that he would be required to pay for them, but he did not want to be punished like this. 'I will do anything, brother, to make amends!'

In that instant, a high-pitched voice cut through the cacophony of angry chieftains, calling them to silence. Mona, the daughter of Censelach, was standing in her place beside Leoghaire, thumping the high table with her fist. 'He should be judged by one of his own kind!' she yelled. 'By a Christian!'

Enda could hardly believe his eyes and ears. Here was his soft-spoken child who rarely said a word unless he gave her leave to do so and she was fearlessly addressing the whole assembly in the High-King's feast hall.

'He is a Christian priest and was a monk when many of these crimes were committed. He should have been able to set an example to the people. Instead he fell victim to temptation.' She had everyone's attention now, for like her father she had a gift of being able to bend an audience. 'If we execute him we will prove ourselves to be little better than him and Palladius. Besides which, Seginus will have been dispatched quickly and relatively painlessly to his maker. Some of his vic-

507

tims would have given anything to be strangled quickly rather than suffer the tortures he had in store for them.'

The crowd voiced its approval. Generally the chieftains agreed. Strangling was being too easy on this man and it would add some spice to the proceedings if they could devise a more interesting way of dealing with him.

'I believe,' Mona continued, 'that he should suffer great pain for what he has done. Yet he should also have the chance to redeem himself.'

'How would you punish him, my dear?' Enda cut in mockingly. 'Let him go under another banishment only to return again some day when your sons are grown and he can have the chance of murdering them?'

'No. But I would place him under bonds that even one such as he would be afraid to break.'

'Make him suffer!' some chieftain called out from the back of the hall and there was a loud chorus of agreement.

Caitlin stood up and called out, 'I was unfortunate enough to witness many of his worst crimes.' The chamber stilled again. Everyone knew that Caitlin had suffered at the priest's hands. 'Give him to me,' she cried, 'and rest assured I will make him regret what he has done. I will keep him alive just long enough for him to pay the harshest penalty for his deeds.' The crowd roared. That suggestion appealed to a great many of them.

The ghost repeated his taunt. 'You're coming with me to Hell!' Its words were full of contempt and Seginus felt sure that his brother had made up his mind to see him in the Devil's kingdom.

'Nothing can save me now!' Seginus cried. 'I am condemned to the fires of Hell for breaking my word to my brother.'

'Be quiet, my son,' Patricius begged him, 'if you want to sway the High-King's mercy to your benefit.'

Leoghaire knew enough Latin to catch a few of the bishop's words. The High-King stood up quickly, kicking his seat behind him as he did so. In a stern voice that brought silence to the assembly he declared, 'I am not going to be merciful to you, Seginus Gallus. So do not get your hopes up that there will be anything but harsh punishment awaiting.'

Patricius broke in, 'I beg you to reconsider, my lord. Do as the lady Mona asks and spare him long enough to face death only after he has had an opportunity to make amends.'

'Death!' the ghost repeated echoing the bishop's plea. 'Death to Seginus Gallus, the protector of his brother's assassin.'

Seginus feebly struggled with his guards again but was easily restrained. He hung his head so that his chin rested once more on his chest, and waited for the pronouncement of his punishment.

'I have heard all that has been said,' Leoghaire announced. 'By custom I cannot allow him to be judged by his own kind, for they are mostly foreigners. By law he must face the verdict of the High-King.' The chieftains applauded, glad that Leoghaire was standing firm on this matter and eager to hear what he had decided. This story would be repeated before a hundred firesides when they all returned to their homes.

'Roman,' the High-King bellowed, 'prepare yourself for my decision.' Leoghaire paused until everyone was quiet once again. As soon as the room was still he spoke in a moderate tone so that the chieftains had to strain a little to hear what he said.

'Death . . .' he hissed, as the chamber remained perfectly silent and awe-struck, 'would be too easy on you, Seginus Gallus.'

The ghost rushed forward to wrench the priest's head up, forcing Seginus to face Leoghaire directly. 'Listen to him, brother. Your fate is in his hands. I will have my revenge.'

'I am sure that certain of the chieftains in this assembly could devise something suitably horrendous for you,' the High-King continued. 'I tend to agree with Mona and Caitlin. I will grant you your life for the time being but be sure of this, you will suffer for all that you have done.'

Seginus straightened his legs to stand tall but he found that he could not make a show of pride any longer. His brother's spectre hissed in his ear, 'Swear that you will kill him.'

Seginus could hear Leoghaire's judgment over the evil words of the ghost. 'You will be taken from Eirinn in the charge of the Queen of Munster who will be responsible for ensuring that you serve out your sentence to the very end.' The High-King emphasised the words for Caitlin. 'There you will work under the direction of Declan, the Abbot of Saint Ninian's. He will take you on in exchange for the favour that I have granted him.' This was for Declan. 'You will wear chains around your feet and wrists all day long until Caitlin herself decides that they are no longer necessary. In addition you will perform religious penances which Bishop Patricius Sucatus will name.'

The demon beside Seginus still whispered in his ear, 'Swear to me that if I give you this chance at life that you will punish Isernus for what he did to me.'

The bishop cleared his throat to speak and in that instant more than one person in the hall suspected that his speech had been carefully prepared in foreknowledge of Leoghaire's judgment. 'Father Seginus, you will be banned from performing the sacraments for one year. You will work in the fields from sun up to sun down under the direction of Declan, except on Sunday when you will help treat the sick and the infirm who are housed in the monastery of Saint Ninian's. Every day from this day forth for the next three years you will spend at least four hours praying to God for forgiveness of your sins. You will rise at two o'clock in the morning and you will not rest until nine in the evening. You will fast from now until the next feast of the resurrection one year from today taking only uncooked vegetables, water and some oats, except on Sundays. You may have a boiled cabbage on the Sabbath. You will have to earn my trust again, Father Seginus. When you have done so I will welcome you back into the fold and consider your future. You will then perform one last penance that I will name when all your other penalties are paid.'

'A just punishment,' Mona nodded.

'You will make a fine queen,' the High-King whispered to his new consort. Then he turned to the assembly once more. 'Have you anything to say, Seginus Gallus?'

With an intense urgency the ghost insisted, 'Swear that you will avenge my death!'

'I will do anything you say!' Seginus yelled, in the hope that he would banish the demonic taunts from his ears.

Patricius smiled, relieved that it seemed Seginus had accepted his fate. He translated the prisoner's words to the assembly.

Leoghaire raised an eyebrow, doubting the sincerity of what he heard. 'Very well,' he continued. 'You will be locked in the gate tower until Caitlin and her entourage are ready to depart. Before the changing moon you will set off to serve your imprisonment. Take him away! Enda, see that no more harm comes to him. He won't be able to till the fields with broken bones.'

'Yes, lord.'

Seginus was lifted up off the floor so that his feet barely scraped the ground. The ghost floated alongside him, no longer threatening but speaking in a soothing voice. 'You have made the right decision, brother,' it said. 'God honours those who devote their lives to rescuing the souls of the damned.'

Seginus strained to look at the spectre, still amazed that no-one else in the hall had any hint of its presence. He focused on the creature's face and saw that the skin was no longer gray and wasted. The flesh was now pink and healthy and the lips were red and full. Linus returned his brother's gaze with bright eyes that spoke of gratitude. This was how Seginus remembered the boy. This was not the monster that had haunted him since Nantes.

'It is you, after all!' Seginus gasped.

'Did you ever doubt it? 'Linus answered now seeming very much alive and well. 'There is the man,' he whispered, pointing to the monk seated beside Abbot Declan.

Isernus immediately noticed the way Seginus turned to glare straight at him. The monk reacted nervously to the priest's attention, averting his own gaze until he felt Seginus was no longer looking at him.

The ghost floated beside Seginus until they were almost at the door to the hall, then it leaned in close to kiss the priest lightly on the cheek, the way Linus had so often done in life.

'Goodbye, brother. You will not endure too harsh a punishment. I will see to that. But never forget your vow to me,' the spirit soothed, but before the guards had dragged Seginus through the door the priest heard the shrill mocking laughter once more in his head. This set him struggling wildly with his captors again, and the guards manhandled him out of the hall. Once outside they took the opportunity to beat some sense into him. Like a good many of the chieftains they felt Seginus had got off too lightly, and being Enda's men they were not too worried about what their lord would do if he caught them embellishing the High-King's justice.

Within the hall Leoghaire could sense a change of mood in his subject chieftains. Many had expected a swifter and more violent retribution to be delivered to the foreigner. Leoghaire knew that there were some who would be dissatisfied with his judgment. He decided that it would be best to adjourn the assembly as quickly as possible.

'If there are no other matters then we will rise to attend the ceremony of the Serpents and then go to the feast that has been prepared.'

'There is one last thing, lord,' Enda Censelach interjected. 'What is to become of the bishop? Is he going to be permitted to remain in Eirinn?'

'Ah yes. Patricius Sucatus,' Leoghaire breathed. 'What shall I do with him?'

'I would like him to stay. I have a need of a priest,' Mona spoke up. 'Since I left my schooling in Britain I have seldom had the opportunity to speak with an educated Christian woman like his follower Tullia. They are honourable people who are no threat to the peace of this land.'

'No threat?' Enda exclaimed. 'You stupid girl. What do you call twenty or so foreign soldiers trudging through the countryside near the chief citadel of the five kingdoms? If that is not a threat to Eirinn then tell me what is.'

'Warriors are a threat,' she agreed, deliberately keeping her voice calm. 'But the soldiers are leaving. Churchmen, real churchmen and women who are servants of God and not of their own ambition, may have much to teach our people.' Caitlin looked at Mona with admiration: here she was, standing up to her father in public.

'What can they teach us that is of any use?' Censelach replied. 'What do they bring but fear and loathing and war?'

'They bring new ideas. They bring a new age to Eirinn, the promise of a great future when the Christ returns to the world.'

Enda looked at his daughter as if she were quite mad. Then he began to laugh, loud and long. 'I prefer not to spend my days waiting for Christ to pay me a visit. There are more important things in life than sitting around all day praying to the deities. If we all did that the Saxons would have taken this land a generation ago.'

'Still, I would like the Christians to stay here at Teamhair for a while to minister to those followers who live in the five kingdoms,' she said firmly. 'There is also the matter of my wedding.'

'Of course!' Leoghaire exclaimed. 'Mona and I intend to be married by the rites of the Roman church as well as those of our own tradition. With Origen banished to Ballinskelligs and Declan off to Saint Ninian's once more there is no-one who can perform the ceremony except Patricius. If you would do us that honour, bishop?'

'I would be the one who would be honoured, my lord,' Patricius answered quickly.

514

'Good! That's settled then. Patricius Sucatus, you and your fellow clerics have my leave to remain in Eirinn until Mona and I are wed.'

'And after that?' Censelach demanded.

'After that we will review the situation as the need arises,' Leoghaire replied.

Enda Censelach fixed his eyebrows in a deep frown, clenched his fists tightly and a bitter scowl came over his face. 'We will see what the Druid Council has to say about that. And the Council of Chieftains.'

Then without giving Leoghaire the opportunity to answer him, the King of Laigin turned on his heel and stormed out of the High-King's chambers, headed for his own hearth. As he passed through the door to the great hall he slammed it hard behind him, as if to emphasise his opinion of Leoghaire's judgments.

THIRTY

he air was alive with spiralling serpent-like shapes that danced between the midnight stars leaving silver snail-trails in the heavens. High above the orb of the Earth, Mawn and Sianan drifted aimlessly taking in the fantastic sights presented to them. Neither could tell how they came to be here at this time. Looking down on the world they clearly saw the masses of swirling clouds that covered vast expanses of the lands and oceans. The view reminded Sianan of the motifs that had covered the walls of the broch and of the designs all over the inner walls of the mound of testing.

It was Mawn who brought the ringing hum to her attention. Rising up from the land like a magnificent chorus of voices the gentle vibrations enclosed them both, encasing them in sound. Mawn could dimly remember the Druids who had gathered at the hut where he and Sianan had been painted in preparation for their journey. This choir sang a similar melody but the ranks of these new singers were swelled a thousand-fold compared to the one at Teamhair. At times lilting and tender, the melody occasionally grew to a deafening crescendo only to fall away again afterwards so that it was so subdued it was almost lost in the noise of the wind.

The gentle humming drones gradually began to build in intensity for a final stirring climax. Mawn and Sianan allowed their spirit forms to drift closer to one another as many unrecognisable instruments joined in the awesome symphony. The clouds beneath them moved in graceful arcs through the sky like enormous whirlpools of white water drawing the two companions down toward them. The music surged with renewed energy, gathering momentum for the last moments of its performance.

Mawn clung to his companion in trepidation. But Sianan was not afraid. She was willingly losing herself to the lulling bass notes of the song allowing the wonder of the whole encounter to wash over her. She could have stayed there forever in that place, soaking up the music that spoke not just to her ears or to her senses but reached also to the most secluded recesses of her soul.

Mawn experienced the overwhelming sensation that he was being tossed around at the whim of this inexplicable force like a piece of driftwood carried on the tides until it was dumped unceremoniously on a beach. Gobann's warning that it was easy to become bewildered by the many paths that open up before a traveller on this Road rang in his head. With sharp urgency Mawn decided that it was time for them to find their way home. 'If we do not leave now we may never reach the mound of testing.'

The clouds were hauling the two of them down toward the epicentre of their spiralling white masses. Sianan resisted the pull of the earthward current for a few moments but Mawn called out in the most powerful voice he could muster and Sianan woke from her stupor agreeing that they should depart. Even so, she left reluctantly, looking back over her shoulder with longing glances, soaking up the sensual feast of music and light before she was forced to walk in the mundane world once more and this time perhaps forever.

Together they floated momentarily far above the Earth; then, grasping each other tightly, they allowed the force of the cloud whirlpool to draw them down into the place where all the spiral gases converged. As they reached this central spot the sky filled suddenly with bright warm sunlight and all the clouds swiftly evaporated. Sianan looked down at the ground below and saw that they were directly over the mound of testing. The sparks of the dying bone-fire flew up into the blue black night, passing by them like bright fish swimming in a dark sea. The orange points of light danced around them as though they were spun by the force of the clouds.

Sianan reached out to touch one of the sparks, connecting with it so that it exploded in midflight, showering toward the ground again in a last rush of its life-force. She heard her companion gasp, sensing his awe and she turned her attention to what it was that had enthralled him.

All across the countryside as far as they could see there were many little lights appearing as every hearth received an ember from the hill of Teamhair. Then the many lights seemed to join together in procession following the old paths that had been used since the first race of people had come to Eirinn. The lights borne by a hundred invisible torchbearers snaked along the ancient routes, the flames of their lamps reflecting off the standing stones that lined the tracks.

Some of the lights converged on Teamhair, others on the mound known as the house of Aenghus Og, others circled the smaller mounds or ended at the top of some small hill where a fire was lit to celebrate to return of summer. When Sianan looked into the sky it was as if the patterns that the lanterns made on the ground were mirrored in the designs painted by the stars in the heavens.

The Serpents of the Fire these processions were called. The lantern-bearers were tracing out the lines along which the energy of the Earth flowed. These pathways were the veins of the world carrying the force of life just as blood coursed through the body of all living creatures. Here the Earth was being venerated in the solemn acts of many thankful people. Thankful for having lived through another winter, thankful for having enough to eat due to the gifts of the soil, thankful for the return of the warm part of the cycle.

Sianan had seen this ceremony performed eighteen times in her life but she had never realised that the Earth returned the praise of the common folk. Now she understood. She could hear the mighty voice booming out through the ground, shaking the trees and the lakes, turning mist to clear air with its resonance, enfolding her like her warmest cloak on a bitter cold morning. It was reminiscent of the thundering roar that she had witnessed in the broch. It was not unlike the symphony she had heard when she and Mawn had been above the clouds. But instead of a choir comprised of hundreds of disembodied souls singing to the accompaniment of companies of hidden musicians, this was one clear all-powerful voice.

Suddenly Sianan was lying on her side in the dark. She could still hear the echoing chorus as the Earth sang its low enchanting hymn. All around her on every surface there were the spirals, zigzags and twisting shapes that the ancient ones had carved many generations before the Gaels came to Eirinn. But she was not within the mound. She was lying on the ground outside the man-made hill.

Mawn was nowhere to be seen. She could not even sense his whereabouts. She began to panic. Then she heard a movement behind a stone nearby and instantly knew that one of the Danaans was trying to conceal itself there.

'Who are you?' Sianan called. 'Why won't you let me enter the mound?'

The figure moved from behind the stone to stand uncomfortably in the moonlight. 'Tell the queen that I will repay her for her treachery,' an old woman's voice muttered. 'She may keep her children but I promise they will betray her so that her life and everything she values will be left in ruins.'

'Who are you?' Sianan insisted.

'I saw you in the hall of Aenghus Og. Do you not remember me?'

Sianan thought back to the one-armed hag that had grabbed Mawn's hair at the Danaan festival. 'Yes,' she answered.

'Tell the queen,' the hag repeated and then Sianan sensed that the creature was gone. The rumbling of the Earth song still coursed through the ground and even the massive standing stones shook as it passed through them. Sianan concentrated on finding Mawn.

In a few moments she found herself floating above her own body. She was bathed in a gorgeous blue light the like of which she had never experienced. The whole inner chamber was illuminated by this strange glow which made the painted designs on her body stand out in sharp contrast to her skin colour. It was at that moment that Sianan noticed that Mawn's body was missing.

She searched the chamber but the blue light would not permit her to leave the central room. Then she heard a shuffle in a corner of the entrance niche and a familiar voice spoke, echoing weirdly in the chamber. 'Is that you? Sianan, have you returned?'

There was a sudden rush like the feeling of falling from a galloping horse and then Sianan lost her vision and her hearing. She was conscious of this impediment to her senses for long enough so that she became a little frightened but then she lost her concentration and drifted away into dreams.

When Sianan woke her limbs felt as heavy the stones that stood sentinel outside the mound. She tried to rise but the effort required was so great that she soon gave up trying. She could hear the noise of the seals being broken to allow access to the chamber.

'They will be here soon,' Mawn said. 'We will be back in the land of the living in a short while.'

'Back in the land of the living,' Sianan echoed and there she waited until the Druids came to rescue them from their ordeal of the Imbas Forosnai.

EPILOGUE

fter the festival of Beltinne Enda Censelach prepared to leave for Britain on
the next tide. The King of Laigin had
gathered two hundred warriors to
accompany him, raised hastily in his
kingdom with a promise from his chieftains of
another two hundred to follow soon after. Leoghaire
requested that Enda journey to the eastern coast of
Britain and there make his way to the old Roman
garrison town of Eboracum. It was here that Uther
was rumoured to hold court, though no-one knew
for certain whether the Saxons had razed the town
in their furious attacks on the coast.

Gobann was entrusted by Murrough with raising
as many troops as possible from the countryside in
Munster without depleting the coastal defences.
The King of Munster realised that he would need
a good size force if they were going to have any
hope of driving the Saxons out of the area around
the monastery of Saint Ninian's.

Oileel Molt the King of Ulaid, who was
Leoghaire's cousin, returned from the Dal Araidhe
before Gobann's party set out for Cashel to report
that every day more of the savages crossed into
lands that the Gaelic kings claimed. He had come
back to raise more troops for himself but Leoghaire
convinced him to take charge of the coastal
defences in Murrough's place. Oileel agreed and
set about the task with enthusiasm.

Gobann the poet had one other task to complete on his journey to the south and it was a less pleasant one than raising troops. In the entourage that left Teamhair bound for the kingdom of the south was Origen the Christian from Alexandria and his entire monastic community of twelve monks. Gobann and Origen had met when the poet was still a novice. The two had travelled around Eirinn together in the seasons after Leoghaire had been elected High-King and they had grown to respect each other's philosophies and rituals.

This, however, was sure to be the last time they would journey together for Leoghaire had forbidden any Gael to approach the new monastic community at Ballinskelligs without his express permission. Gobann would be in Dal Araidhe over the sea by the end of the summer and Origen was not well. Long nights spent praying out in the open air in all weathers had robbed him of his health, aging him so dramatically that the poet often forgot that the Alexandrian was only a few winters older than him.

Gobann guessed that it was unlikely that the monk would survive the next winter.

The party left the citadel early one morning at the beginning of spring. For much of their first day on the road from Teamhair Gobann and Origen did not speak to each other, content to ride side by side, aware of each other's presence. Mawn and Sianan were never far away, sensing also that Origen was in need of their companionship. Síla rode ahead of the others, often leaving the road to gather herbs that were known to grow only on certain hillsides or in certain glens.

They had only travelled two-thirds of the day and there was still several hours of light left when Síla reported that she had found a suitable place to rest for the night. In the ruins of an old abandoned hill-fort they unsaddled their horses and lay down under the darkening sky around a blazing fire. The evening was mild and the heavens above were clear so it was no great discomfort for them to be outdoors. Síla brewed a tea for Origen which helped him to sleep soundly but despite the calming herbal infusion he woke coughing in the early morning.

Gobann rose soon after to find Origen at prayer with his brothers outside the ruined embankments of the hill-fort. Sianan and Mawn had joined the monks at their morning devotions. The poet noticed them kneeling before Origen's makeshift altar and reminded himself that it did not matter how one expressed respect for the forces that created the Earth. The most important thing one could do was to show thanks.

Síla returned soon after with a skin full of water from the spring at the other side of the fortification. She had washed her hair and clothes in the pool at the spring so they were still quite damp. Gobann could see clearly, from her walk, from the air of joy about her, that she was glad fate had lent a hand in sending him to Britain with her.

'Alba,' she would correct him whenever he used the common name for her land, 'is the true title for the place that the Romans call Britain. They named it after the Pretani people who they first encountered there. The Gaels call the Pretani by the name, Cruitne, and I am a daughter of those folk. We call the land Alba, which means the country of strong women.'

Gobann had never argued that the title was not appropriate. Compared to the Gaelic women of Eirinn the Cruitne were wild and headstrong. They tattooed their faces and bodies with intricate designs that the Gaels reserved only for shields and harp bags. Their hair was invariably dark and tied into long tight strands that were never cut. With her forehead shaved in the Druid fashion from ear to ear and her clothes made of the softened skin of a deer, Síla resembled one of the heroes of the old stories.

No wonder that a Roman army in the time of the Caesars once fled when they were faced with two thousand of these Cruitne women. Legend had it that some of the Roman soldiers were so frightened that they ran until they reached the sea on the far side of Alba and then decided to swim for it.

The poet was still watching Síla when Origen and his monks ended their prayers and returned to the fireside. Everyone in the party ate some food and let their horses drink a little before preparing to set off again for Cashel. Síla preferred this slower pace and there was no real hurry since neither Murrough nor Caitlin would be well enough to travel to Alba for some weeks. Mawn and Sianan spent most of the morning collecting herbs with the healer as the others stayed close to the road. Gobann and Origen rode beside each other, once more passing the time telling stories of their youth.

'There is a great tower in Alexandria,' Origen recalled, 'that is as tall as ten oak trees stacked on top of one another. On the very top of this tower, which stands at the harbour entrance, is set a great fire which burns every night to direct ships toward the port. The light is so bright that it can be seen far out to sea and makes a safe passage for all shipping even in the dark of the moon.'

'There are many wonders in your country,' Gobann exclaimed.

'And many here in Eirinn,' Origen cut in quickly. 'For example, you never explained to me how you knew beforehand that Patricius was coming to this land.'

'It was set down in prophecy.'

'There are many prophets in the land of Egypt,' the Alexandrian commented, 'but none like the poets of Eirinn. From early days they are tutored in the art of future-telling and the wisdom of not revealing what they have seen.'

Gobann laughed at his friend's astute observation.

'Mawn and Sianan are two likely candidates as future-seers, are they not?' Origen asked, but he did not wait for Gobann to answer. 'Of course they are. The lad is very talented but I must say that he sometimes lacks subtlety. As his teacher you may need to help him redress that deficiency. Mawn has decided that he wants to learn to read. I gave him a book that deals with the brewing of liquors for healing. He told me that he would never forget my kindness, but I clearly heard his voice quaver. I may not have my eyes but I still have my senses. He looked at me knowing that I will have passed away before the end of next winter.'

'Surely he didn't say that!' the poet exclaimed.

'No, not in as many words, so don't chastise him for it. I know the truth of it as well as you do. My blood is thinning. My breath is weak. I will never fulfil my dream to cross the western sea in search of the lands that must lie there.'

'We believe that when a soul passes from its body it voyages westward to the lands of peace,' Gobann explained. 'There the spirit takes rest preparing to return in another form when the time is right. So even if your dream of an earthly voyage does not come to pass, you will walk one day in the lands of the blessed as everyone must do at some time.'

'Even your young students?' the monk asked.

Gobann was uncomfortable that this subject had been broached. 'Yes, perhaps. I am sorry, old friend, but I am not permitted to speak of Sianan and Mawn, not even with you.'

'I have known for a long time,' Origen admitted. 'Well I should say that I guessed anyway. But the prophets of Alexandria are not as well-trained as those of your country.' The monk laughed and the poet joined him but Gobann did not say anything more about Mawn and Sianan.

Origen took the hint and launched into the telling of many stories of life in his homeland in the full knowledge that he would never return there. 'I will tell the Wanderers all my tales of the great desert and the holy river that gives life to my country,' Origen promised. 'For one day they may go there in their travels and it would help them to know what to expect.'

Gobann was glad that his friend seemed to have brightened up. His skin suddenly had colour again and he was full of energy.

'I must thank you for helping my brothers find a safe haven,' the monk continued. 'Without your influence they would have had to remain in Teamhair and we both know that the Romans would have stirred up trouble for them eventually.'

'You aided me in protecting Patricius from Enda Censelach,' the poet replied. 'If we had handled that problem by confronting the King of Laigin over his involvement with the attempt on Leoghaire's life, Enda might have turned very nasty. Your agreement to move to Ballinskelligs was very helpful in putting Censelach's plans to rest. When you admitted some degree of responsibility it meant that he no longer had a case against the Romans.'

'It baffles me that you should want to foster a relationship with the Roman Christians,' Origen admitted. 'Or strive to keep Enda and Patricius apart. They were made for each other. The unrepentant heathen and the self-appointed evangelist. Those are the sorts of people that keep the world turning.' Again both men laughed.

As the day drew on Origen began to tire of talking. When Mawn, Sianan and Síla rejoined the party they found the monk nodding to sleep in his seat. Origen had slumped forward slightly in the saddle so that his head rested against the neck of his horse but his hands still gripped the reins tightly as though he were ready at any moment to set off at a gallop.

In the late afternoon the party stopped to water their horses at a clear stream that fed a small lake. Gobann dismounted but noticed that Origen was still asleep on his mount so he went to wake him and get him down from the saddle. The Alexandrian was slow to stir but when he did wake up properly he was still very drowsy. The monk was looking very pale and ill so Gobann made a decision to go no further that day.

Mawn and Sianan helped Origen to lie down by a fire and Gobann covered him with his Raven feather cloak to keep him warm. Síla prepared some food and infused herbs for Origen to take before he slept and he seemed to recover a little after eating. Gobann overheard the monk's prayer before sleeping and knew that his friend would be parting.

'Helper of those who turn to You,' droned
    Origen,
'Light to those who wander in the dark
Creator of all that grows
Now is the time of harvest.

528

Do not examine my sins too closely
For if You notice too many of my mistakes
I will be fraid to appear before You.

Helper of those who turn to You
In Your mercy
And boundless compassion
Guide me westward toward Your home'

Not long after nightfall Origen of Alexandria succumbed to age and illness passing away in his sleep. Gobann, Síla, Mawn and Sianan were with him when he died and they whispered their traditional blessings as his soul fled. Síla prepared a sheet, made out of the blue cloak the Druid Council had awarded him, to wrap the monk's body. The poet played the sleep music, the sorrow music and the love music on his harp. The monks respectfully waited for Origen's closest friends to finish their homages before they said their prayers and sang their hymns.

Next morning, after the monks had sat a night-long vigil beside their chief brother's body, they buried him near the stream where he had died. Gobann helped lay the clods of earth upon his body and poured a little mead into the dead mouth in parting before taking a large gulp himself.

'May he always have music with him wherever he goes,' the poet declared, 'and strong drink like the liquor he brewed. I am sorry that his dream of sailing westwards did not come true.'

'His spirit has already set foot on the soul ship and he is voyaging over the ocean bound for the western isles,' Mawn assured his teacher. 'And soon we too must all begin our own separate journeys in earnest.'

Gobann nodded, remembering that if his own premonitions about the future had any truth in them, his days with Síla, Sianan and Mawn were also running out. One day, in the not too distant future, he would be leaving his native land to sail for Dal Araidhe. In his heart the poet was certain that once he had departed beyond the nine waves of Eirinn he would never set eyes on this land again.

NOTES ON PRONUNCIATION

Words of Irish Origin

Aileesh	aylish
Ardmór	ard-more
Ardrígh	ard-ree
Banba	banva
Beltinne	bell-cheena
Boann	bo-an
Bodhran	bow-ron
Brandubh	bran-doov
Brehon	bre-on
Broch	broh
Caitlin	kaytlin/cotchlin
Cailleach	kal-yuk
Cathach	cat-ack
Censelach	ken-shel-ak
Cieran	keer-an
Conaire	kon-a-ree
Connachta	kon-oh-ta
Cruitne	krit-nee
Cuaich	kwatch
Cúnla	koon-la
Curragh	koo-rah
Dagda	dag-da
Dal Araidhe	dal ree-ah-dah
Desi	dee-siy
Dichu	dee-koo
Éber	ay-ber
Eirinn	air-in

Enda	enda
Eoghan	yo-an
Eoghanacht	yo-an-aakt
Eothain	yo-tin
Feni	fee-niy
Fergal	far-gal
Fidach	fee-da
Filidh	feel-ee
Fintan	fin-tan
Fionn	fin
Flidais	flid-aysh
Gallaighe	gall-a-hee
Gobann	go-bahn
Goibniu	giv-nee
Gorm	gor-um
Inis	inish
Inis Trá	inish traw
Laigin	lah-een
Leoghaire	leer-ree
Macha	ma-ha
Mannan	manan
Miach	mee-ak
Midhe	meeth
Míl	meel
Molt	malt
Morrigán	mor-ri-gan
Murrough	morr-uh
Niall	nee-al
Niamh	nee-av
Nighe	nee
Oghma	ohg-ma
Oilleel	ill-eel
Rathowen	raath-oh-wen
Ruari	roo-ri
Scathach	sh-ka-ta
Sciathan-cog	skee-an-tan koge
Scian-Dubh	skee-an-doov

Senchai	shen-hai
Sianan	shee-an-an
Sidhe	shee
Sidhe-Dubh	shee-doov
Síla	shee-la
Slané	slayne
Teamhair	tar-ah
Tuatha-De-Danaan	too-ah-ha-day-dahn-nan
Torc	tork
Tuan	too-an
Uisnech	ish-nuk
Ulaid	oo-lay

Words of Non-Irish Origin

Belgae	bel-ga
Chi Rho	kee-ro
Cumri	koom-ri
Eboracum	ebb-or-ahh-coom
Hengist	heng-gest
Manichee	man-ee-kee
Nantes	nan-tay
Origen	oh-ri-gen
Palladius	pall-ahh-dee-oos
Patricius Sucatus	pat-rish-oos soo-kaat-oos
Pretani	bret-ah-nee
Ravenna	rah-ven-ah
Secondinus	sec-on-dee-oos
Seginus Gallus	seg-een-oos gal-oos
Tatheus Nonus	tat-ay-oos non-oos
Theodora	tay-ah-dora
Tullia	tool-ee-ah
Tullius Piscis	tool-ee-oos pis-cus
Uther Pendragon	oot-er pen-dragon
Vortigern	fort-ee-gern

aiseal Mór and the band Aisling
have worked closely together to
compose a collection of music
which complements both *the circle
and the cross* and *the song of
the earth*. The band has blended the haunting
melodies that are so much a part of traditional Irish music with the exotic tones of
Indian instruments and the pulse of African
rhythms. The result is two compact discs which
add a unique dimension to both novels.

The compact discs of music from both *the
song of the earth* and *the circle and the cross*
are available on the Earthworks label (email:
ceg@s054.aone.net.au).